Praise for Emily Hourican's Guinness Girls novels

'An utterly captivating insight into these fascinating women and the times they lived in . . . it's an absolute page-turner'

Irish Independent

'Masterfully and glamorously told . . . essential reading for history and gossip lovers alike'   *Sunday Business Post*

'Fans of *Downton Abbey* will adore this'   *Sunday Times*

'A captivating and page-turning novel about a fascinating family. Fantastic'·   Sinéad Moriarty

'Gripping . . . this dramatic novel takes us into the heart of their privileged, beautiful and often painful hidden world'

Irish Country Magazine

'A gloriously good read'   *Sunday Independent*

'An enthralling tale that will dazzle and delight'

Swirl and Thread

'Engrossing and page-turning . . . I loved it'   Louise O'Neill

Emily Hourican is a journalist and author. She has written features for the *Sunday Independent* for fifteen years, as well as *Image* magazine, *Condé Nast Traveller* and *Woman & Home*. She was also editor of *The Dubliner* magazine.

Emily's first book, a memoir titled *How to (Really) Be a Mother* was published in 2013. She is the author of seven works of fiction, including three bestselling novels about the Guinness sisters.

Emily lives in Dublin with her family.

Also by Emily Hourican

The Glorious Guinness Girls
The Guinness Girls: A Hint of Scandal
The Other Guinness Girl: A Question of Honor
The Privileged
White Villa
The Blamed
The Outsider

How to (Really) Be a Mother

EMILY HOURICAN

An

INVITATION
TO THE
KENNEDYS

HACHETTE
BOOKS
IRELAND

First published in Ireland in 2023 by
HACHETTE BOOKS IRELAND

1

Cataloguing in Publication Data is available from the British Library

ISBN 9781399708029

Typeset in Sabon LT Std by
Palimpsest Book Production Limited, Falkirk, Stirlingshire

Printed and bound in Great Britain by
Clays Ltd, Elcograf S.p.A.

Hachette Books Ireland policy is to use papers that are natural, renewable
and recyclable products and made from wood grown in sustainable forests.
The logging and manufacturing processes are expected to conform
to the environmental regulations of the country of origin.

Hachette Books Ireland
8 Castlecourt Centre
Castleknock
Dublin 15, Ireland

A division of Hachette UK Ltd
Carmelite House, 50 Victoria Embankment, London EC4Y 0DZ

www.hachettebooksireland.ie

For Francis and Myles. About time, right?

Cast of Characters

Kathleen 'Kick' Kennedy

Joe Kennedy, United States Ambassador to the United Kingdom – Kick's father

Rose Kennedy – Kick's mother

Kick's siblings: Joe, Jack, Rosemary ('Rosie'), Pat, Jean, Eunice, Teddy and Bobby

Lady Brigid Guinness

Honor Channon, née Guinness – Brigid's older sister

Henry Channon, 'Chips' – American diarist and politician, Honor's husband

Doris Coates – Honor's best friend

Lady Patricia Guinness, 'Patsy' – Brigid and Honor's sister

Maureen Hamilton-Temple-Blackwood (née Guinness), Marchioness of Dufferin and Ava – Brigid and Honor's cousin

Basil Hamilton-Temple-Blackwood, 'Duff', 4th Marquess of Dufferin and Ava – Maureen's husband

Elizabeth Ponsonby – socialite, friend of Honor and Maureen's

Lady Diana Mosley (née Mitford)

Debo and Unity Mitford – Diana's sisters

Sir Oswald Mosley – British politician and founder of the British Union of Fascists (BUF), Diana's husband

Prince Frederick George William Christopher of Prussia, 'Fritzi'

William 'Billy' Cavendish, eldest son of Edward Cavendish, Duke of Devonshire

Minnie – Brigid's maid

Hannah – Doris' Berlin neighbour

Beatrice – Hannah's mother

Chapter One

March 1938
Kick

'It's a ship like a city,' Kick said, tucking Eunice's arm tighter into hers as they walked towards the end of the SS *Washington*'s deck.

It was calm where they were but she knew they would round the corner into a heavy wind that would buffet them like blows from the palm of an open hand. The kind of wind she knew from family summers at Hyannis Port; that her brother Jack had described, with a grin, as 'like being slapped by Kikoo. It can reach out and hit you in places you never expected.' Kick had laughed. They all had. Much as they loved Kikoo, their nanny, for the solid comfort of her presence that was so unlike the brittle distant affection of their mother, Rose, they also knew the feel of her calloused hands and the point at which, when they were younger and, sick of yelling at the nine of them, she would lash out with slaps that stung.

'More like a small town for me,' Eunice complained. 'You get to stay up and go to dinner every night, and then whatever it is you all do afterwards – dance, I suppose – while I have to stay in my cabin with Pat and Jean, and Kikoo looking in on us every ten minutes to make sure we stay put.'

'It's only because Mother isn't here,' Kick said. 'Pa needs someone to entertain with him. And to watch Rosemary.'

'Watch her for what?'

'You know, in case she says the kind of thing Rosie says sometimes, that we don't mind because we know and love her, but that strangers might find mighty odd?'

Eunice laughed. 'Remember the time she told Fr Palfrey that she had a spot, and he said he couldn't see it, trying to be all reassuring, and Rosie said, "No, on my backside," and Mother looked daggers right at her?' Kick, remembering, smiled a little. But along with what Rosemary had said, and the look on Fr Palfrey's face, she recalled how that had been another step in their mother starting to leave Rosie out. Not letting her go to parties or stay up when they had guests even though Kick, two years younger, was allowed. How bewildered Rosie had been at first, and then how she had got used to being left behind and sweetly tried to make the best of it. Kick didn't know which was worse.

'Ready?' Eunice asked now, bracing beside Kick for the wind. Behind them, rows of passengers sat in deck chairs, rugs pulled up over their knees, watching the vast emptiness of sea and sky that wrapped around this ship that was so huge, and yet so tiny on the surface of the ocean. Nowhere among them was the girls' father. He would be at the solid desk he had had installed in his stateroom, insisting that the flimsy dressing table be removed to make space for it, reading and responding to the telegrams that arrived each morning. Later, he would take a turn about deck and watch the little boys at their tennis lesson. Later still he would send for Kick and ask for a report on everyone's day. He would have had a report, already, from Kikoo. But it wasn't enough.

'She indulges those boys,' he would say. 'I can't be sure she's telling me everything I need to know.'

'How do you know I will?' Kick had asked, sitting on the edge of his desk, bare legs swinging.

'I know you won't,' he had responded, 'but I can tell a great deal from what you don't say.'

They rounded the corner that brought them from calm quiet into the hectoring roar. This deck was deserted and smelled of salt and wet wood, and whatever was cooking in the kitchens. Why, Kick wondered, was it never a nice smell, like baking, the way the kitchen in Hyannis Port smelt? Always, it was boiling vegetables. Or worse, boiling meat. Her stomach tightened. They were two days into their crossing, with two more to go, and she still could barely believe she was there. When her father's appointment had been announced – Ambassador to the Court of King James – she had been sure their mother would decide she wasn't to come. Must stay behind even though she had finished at the convent. Rose knew exactly how much Kick wanted to see England. But that had not meant she would permit it. Even as their things were packed for the sailing from New York, Kick had worried that her mother would change her mind. But she hadn't, and the seven of them, eight with Pa, had set sail, leaving Rose behind for an operation, a 'small procedure' as she called it, 'nothing you need to know about'.

What would England smell like? she wondered. Would it have the crisp, leafy air of New York State? The fresh blast that was Hyannis Port? Probably it would be like New York City, she decided. Cars and buses and people and everyone trying so hard.

'Look,' Eunice said, tugging her arm out of Kick's. Someone had chalked a hopscotch grid onto the deck, white lines wobbling over uneven wood, washed away by salt water in places. Eunice balanced herself on one foot, holding Kick's arm momentarily for support, then launched into a series of hops and skips. 'Your turn,' she called once she had finished.

Kick started after her, hopping into the wind that pushed at her, hoping she wouldn't fall. Almost at the end, she looked up. Coming towards them from the far end of the deck, wrapped in scarves, was a man and his wife, both Italian, who had been at dinner the evening before, seated opposite her at the round table where the captain entertained. Kick, in her jersey and skirt, balanced on one leg over her hopscotch square, blushed. She dashed a hand at her hair, whipped into wild curls no doubt, and thought of what she might say to cover what felt like an awkward moment. But they passed her by without so much as a look. They hadn't recognised her. Kick started to laugh.

'What's so funny?' Eunice demanded.

'This.' Kick flung her arms wide, leaning right into the wind and letting it almost support her. 'All of this.' The pale green silk scarf around her neck tore loose then and was whipped right away and over the side of the ship and down towards the water.

'What will we do in England?' Eunice asked, leaning close again when they had watched it go.

'As we always do.' Kick reached out a hand and ran it along the side of the ship. The red paint was blistered so that her fingertips rose and fell over fat bumps and into ragged spots where it had peeled right off. 'Lessons and tennis and riding. The house Pa has found is right in front of a big park, Hyde Park, that has a place called Rotten Row where we can ride.'

'Rotten Row,' Eunice echoed, laughing again. Above them one of the ship's funnels rose up into the blue sky, black and smooth like a porpoise breaching.

'Parties and lunches, that sort of thing. And then, when Pa's time is up, we'll come home again. The boys will visit when they can . . .' 'The boys' were Joe Jnr and Jack, not boys at all but men now, Joe in Baltimore and Jack at Harvard, but still called 'the boys', and distinguished from 'the little boys', who were Bobby and Teddy. 'And the time will fly past. His appointment is for four years, but I don't suppose we'll be there that long . . .' Her mother had hinted as much, but Kick didn't know why.

'Oh, I don't want it to fly,' Eunice assured her. 'I want it to go ever so slow. You've been away before. Italy and France. I never ever have. I plan to make the very most of it.'

'Good for you!' Kick said with a laugh. 'Me too.' She tugged gently at the little gold crucifix around her neck, fidgeting with the chain. 'And then when we go home, we can settle into being ourselves again, only knowing that we've seen other places and met different people.'

After lunch, Kick went to find her father. He liked her to join him while he had coffee. 'Will I come in?' She tapped at the door and put her head around it.

'Shall, not will,' he corrected her. 'You're going to need to get that right in England.'

'*Shall*,' she repeated. 'Though who really cares?'

'Oh, they care alright,' the ambassador said.

'Stuffy,' Kick said, coming and sitting on the edge of the bed, feeling the slip of the satin counterpane under her bare legs. She filled him in on their morning, answering all his questions carefully – how many laps of the deck the little boys had done; the books they were all reading; what Pat, fourteen, had had for lunch. 'No potatoes,' she reassured him. 'I made sure.' Pat was inclined to 'get fat', as Rose said, and that was something to be managed by careful watching of what she ate, especially bread and potatoes. No one said it, but they all knew that when Rose arrived, as she would in a few weeks, the thing she would least forgive would be the extra pounds on her daughters. 'Or for me,' Kick added. 'I'm getting fat too. All those late dinners with the captain.'

She thought of telling him about the Italian man this morning and the way his eyes had slid over her, not for a moment matching her with the girl who had been at dinner in pearls and black chiffon the night before. But she didn't. It was hard to know how her father might take this. Would he think it funny, as she did, that she could still slip between being a young lady and almost a child; invisible, ignored? Or would he be annoyed by some failure on her part that he saw and she didn't? A failure to be attractive enough? Distinct enough? Kennedy enough?

It was too lovely, she thought, being without her mother or her older brothers, to risk it. This was the first time she had had so much of her father's attention – the thing that was as precious as sunlight, made to spread among them all, with the lion's share always going to Joe Jnr and Jack. Shared too with her mother; with the many men who admired and wanted to be close to him; and the women who wanted something else from him, though Kick wasn't exactly sure what. To be noticed, she supposed. Same as she did.

'Eunice asked me what we would do in England,' she said, getting up and pouring a cup of coffee from the silver pot that stood on a tray and adding a splash of cream. 'I told her, pretty much the same as we do at home. But what will you do?' She was genuinely curious. His appointment sounded so grand. Had been greeted by so much excitement – and relief, she thought – at home; a thing long wanted that had come to pass. But what was it, exactly, apart from a 'great honour', as everyone assured one another?

'I will keep America out of another war,' he said, putting aside the pages he had been reading and looking up at her so that the light from his desk lamp glared on the round glass of his spectacles. He looked like a man with shiny silver dollars for eyes. 'I will steer us clear of the quagmire England is sinking herself into. And if I can, I'll help to pull her out. Europe stands on the edge of another war. One false step and she will fall into that abyss. And it is an abyss, make no mistake.' He held up a finger. 'Even though not everyone can see that. There are men who would push for those last critical steps. Who would force their way to war. They refuse to see that compromise with Germany, even at this stage, is possible and desirable. Some are moved by idiotic thoughts of glory, or by shame at what they call England's appeasement. But to say that peace is "shameful" is something I'll never understand . . .' He paused a moment, honestly baffled. 'Some are moved by confusion over what's right. But others again are more cynical – they see the personal opportunities in war. I'm here to stop all of that.'

'But can you?'

'I can. Not even the most belligerent want England to enter a war without America at her back.' He sounded amused. 'As long as I can keep Roosevelt from committing troops or money, even the ardent advocates for war with Hitler will think twice.'

How magnificent he sounded, Kick thought. There with the ship rolling beneath them and his sense of purpose like the engines that propelled them forward, it was like he spoke straight out of one of the Hollywood films he used to produce. He would succeed, she knew it. He succeeded at everything.

'Will you help me?' he said then, putting out a hand for hers and pulling her forward so that she put down her coffee cup on the green leather of his desk, spilling a little into the saucer, and leaned against the side of his high-backed chair.

'By being careful to say "shall" and not "will"?' she joked. She was shy of him, and didn't know what else to say.

'By being yourself.' He ignored her joke and spoke seriously.

'Will they like me, do you think?' It was what she had been secretly thinking ever since she first heard of the trip.

'Yes. I'm sure of it.' She felt his approval warm upon her; light and heat and dazzle. But he hadn't finished. 'But just remember, you are American. Not English. There could be no finer example of what it is to be American than you and your sisters and brothers.' His approval, as ever, came with conditions.

'OK.' She didn't know exactly what he meant, but it was safer to pretend she did. 'You tell me what to do and I'll do it. Where are we now?' she asked then, watching the square of clear blue that was the cabin window behind him moving in a way that was steady and slow. Until you looked down at the rapid roll and curl of the waves.

'About halfway between America and England; more than a thousand miles of ocean on either side.'

Chapter Two

It was her own fault, Honor thought, when her husband
Chips came upon her in the library. She should have gone
up as soon as she came home. Should have been safe in her
room, behind the pretence of sleep, by the time he came back.
But she had found the sandwiches Andrews had left in the
library, and a decanter of wine, and then a novel she had
borrowed from the lending library, *Rebecca*; brand new and
'simply thrilling' according to cousin Oonagh.

It had been such a dull evening. A ball, quite in the old manner,
with ancient royals in dusty knee breeches and tiresome formalities around supper, so that Honor had eaten almost nothing,
so determined was she to avoid the sycophantic line of nodding
and smiling ball-goers. Even among them, her husband had

stood out for the depth of his nod, the broadness of his smile. All around she had seen gnarled hands, cold and stiff, winking harsh diamonds and precious stones under swollen knuckles. When had they all got so old?

She had left early, coming home alone. And then she had sat beside the fire in the library, planning to read only a few pages while she ate the sandwiches. But she had drunk a glass of wine, and kept reading, and now it was after four in the morning according to the dusty bong of the library clock, and here was Chips, swaying slightly in the doorway.

'Darling! What a pleasant surprise.'

'I was just going up,' Honor said hastily, marking her place and putting the book down.

'Don't. Stay. I will ring for more sandwiches and we can have a lovely talk.'

'It's too late, Chips. The servants are all in bed.'

'Well then I will wake them,' he said peevishly. She could hear the brandy in his voice, thickening the vowels. 'They are my servants.' He rang the bell and asked a sleepy footman to 'bring another plate of sandwiches. Bring some of that fruit cake too.' Then, 'Wasn't it a delightful evening?' he asked, crossing to the high-winged armchair opposite her and sinking into it.

'No,' Honor said. 'Deathly, I thought.'

Nevertheless he began to dissect the night, just as he always did. 'Lady Furness can't think much of our hostess if she only wore her *second* necklaces,' he said, 'she has far better pieces than that.' He was, she had discovered, particularly clever at deciphering jewellery – finding meaning in the stones their friends chose to wear; the when and how of a brooch or a set of earrings.

The sleepy footman brought sandwiches. Honor thought how much she would have loved a cup of tea, but decided it would be unfair to ask. 'Do go to bed, Robert,' she said.

The light from the fire fell on Chips' face, burnishing his broad forehead and straight nose. He was still handsome, she thought, but – like all aging beauties – now only in certain lights. Daylight, morning especially, was cruel to him, showing the pouches beneath his eyes, the pallor of his skin and lines about his mouth that spoke of disappointment. But there, lit by soft flames, with the glow of brandy still in him, and the excitement of a topic close to his heart, he seemed, again, the man she had married five years ago: smooth with the confidence of his own good looks, lit by purpose and certainty.

'Did you see how the Duchess of Gloucester has already the royal trick of never sitting down?' he asked eagerly. He loved these after-sessions almost as much as the parties themselves. Once she had been happy to turn it all over with him, cut the deck a thousand different ways to see how the cards would fall. But not anymore.

'Must we?' she asked after a while. 'Wasn't it bad enough to live through it once, but I must now do it all again, in memory?'

'I simply thought you might be interested,' Chip said stiffly.

'In what? Parsing every detail and finding what bits of it all might benefit you?' she responded rudely. 'I am going up.'

'May I come with you?' he asked, reaching forward to put a damp hand on her arm. Sometimes, she noticed, he seemed to almost enjoy her displays of contempt. Finding in them an excitement that repelled her. That was another reason she was careful to keep them under control.

'Not tonight.' She shook his hand off and stood up.

'Not tonight. Not any night. How long has it been?'

'Please, Chips, not now.'

'I know exactly,' he responded. 'As do you. Certainly not since Paul was born.'

What could she say? *It has been a great deal longer. Not since the day you knew I was expecting.* Once he knew she was pregnant, he had turned to mist and vapour, as she had thought of it then; as though his duties were discharged. Had left her entirely alone. It was only when Paul had reached his first birthday that he had begun to try to come to her at night again. And by then it was too late. She no longer wanted him.

'You know I have had a long and confidential natter with Dr Low,' he said, pouring a dash of brandy into a cut-glass tumbler.

'Have you indeed?'

'Yes. And we are agreed, he and I, about the cause of your nerves and difficulties with sleep.' He turned the glass this way and that so the deep slashes in its crystal sides caught the firelight.

'Are you?'

'We are.' And, when she said nothing, 'Aren't you going to ask what it is we agree on?'

'No, because I do not at all want to know.' She stood with one hand on the high back of the armchair, ready to leave, but not quite able yet to go.

'It is a delicate matter, granted,' he said, 'but one we must talk about.'

'I feel certain that we must not.'

'I know it is difficult to resume marital relations once they have been allowed to lapse, but Dr Low is certain this can only be of benefit to you.'

'To me?'

'And to me, of course,' he added hurriedly, politely, 'my dear.'

'I don't wish to discuss this. Not now.'

'But Honor, darling, Paul is nearly three. It is time there were more children.'

More children. How much, a year or so ago, she had wanted to hear those words. How she had clung to the idea of them, when the world of Nanny and the nursery, where she felt always a visitor – like a cat that has snuck into the kitchen and found a warm spot, but knows it will be ejected – closed around her baby son. Taking him from her, briskly, efficiently, cruelly; always in a way that meant she didn't know how to resist: *'It is time for his nap.' 'He must have his bath.' 'It is better for him if he is not spoiled.'*

Perhaps Chips took her silence for contemplation, because he put the glass down and came to stand close beside her, putting a hot hand on her arm. 'It's time,' he said again. He stood so close that he breathed into her ear and, with his thumb, began to stroke the inside of her elbow. Already his breath was fast and jagged. Honor's stomach lurched. She imagined capitulating. Allowing him to move his hand further up her arm, to her shoulder. Imagined him pulling her forward and pressing his mouth on hers. Imagined the wet brandy taste of him. Imagined going upstairs to her bedroom and the way his body would feel against hers after all this time.

'I don't wish to discuss it,' she said again. 'I'm going up. Please do not fall asleep here. It makes things so difficult for the maids if they must dust and set fires around you.' He shot her a nasty look. It was the first time she had acknowledged that she knew this was how he had ended too many nights recently: sprawled across the sofa, decanter empty beside him.

Upstairs, she barely had energy to unhook her dress and wished she had told the maid to wait up. She didn't bother brushing her hair but fell straight into bed. Molly would have to wash it in the morning anyway. Wash away the smell of cigars and hairspray. The memory of another dull night. She must try to be kinder to him, Honor thought as she fell asleep. Only it had become so hard.

Chapter Three

Honor

The next morning he came to her room while she still drank her tea in bed. Though he had barely slept, had been noticeably drunk and had suffered rejection by his own wife, he was now buoyant again with energy and good humour. 'We are lunching with the Duff-Coopers,' he said. 'And I have brought you *The Times*. There is an account of that play we saw. Not a very fond one.' Then, when she was settled with the newspaper and another cup of tea, 'I think I will get another dog. A companion for Bundi. He must be lonely, poor chap, the only canine in this big house. Everyone should have a companion and playmate, should they not?' By which she understood that he had not given up his plan for another child. Only he had decided to approach it by another way – through the guilt she felt that Paul was growing up with only Nanny and a tutor.

'Get another dog if you must,' she said, 'but I will love only Bundi.'

'I feel certain you will come around eventually,' he responded, so that Honor thought she would scream at the endless mannered duplicity of their conversations, the way everything they said meant something else.

'I can't stay long at lunch,' she said. 'I have Brigid coming to tea.'

'How is my sweetest and most adorable sister-in-law? The best of the bunnies, is she not?'

'If by "the bunnies" you mean me and Patsy, then how can I say yes?' Honor said. And how can I not, she thought, when it was so obvious. At least as the world must judge them. Where she and Patsy had their father's shape of face – 'potato-shaped', as Patsy said wryly – Brigid with her far-apart eyes and elegantly straight nose – a neat, triangular face like a cat – had the effort-less glamour of their Ernest Guinness cousins, particularly Oonagh. Which was funny, because, like Oonagh, she really cared very little for appearances, or society, or 'any kind of fuss, really', as she said. And, Honor thought, like Oonagh, Brigid didn't have the same firmness of personality that she and Patsy shared. She was far more vague and suggestible, and far less proof against the influence of others, including Chips.

'I will leave early with you,' he said then. 'I must say, since her coming-out, Brigid has passed even my expectations.'

'I hate the way you talk about her,' Honor snapped. 'As though she were a clutch of eggs and you are waiting to see what will hatch.'

'May I not take pleasure in the success of my sister-in-law? Surely any success of hers belongs also to her family? To you. To Lady Iveagh. To your excellent father.'

'Not everything is yours,' she said. He pretended not to understand, looked blankly at her. 'You think it's all yours,' she continued, 'to do with what you wish. But it's not.'

'Perhaps I will see if Fritzi can join us.' He ignored her. 'We could have tea in the larger drawing room.'

'We'll have tea where I always have tea,' Honor said reprovingly. 'And please do not go to the bother of inviting Fritzi.'

'Oh but it's no bother,' Chips assured her, opening his eyes very round and wide. 'He is a dear boy, and may one day be emperor of Germany. His grandfather, Kaiser Wilhelm, has every hope of it, you know. Inviting him is no bother at all.'

'Germany doesn't have an emperor,' Honor said as though to a child, 'hasn't since they got rid of all that twenty years ago. And even if they were to go back, Fritzi is a fourth son. Handsome, I grant you, but he has never struck me as particularly bright.'

'He is King George's godson.' As though that answered everything. 'And has been quite a favourite ever since he moved here last year. He and Brigid danced at her coming-out ball. I watched them.'

'Made them, more like. Chips, do not plot.'

'Why should I not, just a little, for everyone's sakes? I know you Guinnesses; so magnificently unworldly' – he sounded torn between admiration and irritation – 'you will never do it yourselves. But a girl such as Brigid, so vivacious, such beauty and charm, so quaint and unspoiled . . .' Honor rolled her eyes. 'Why should she not have the highest success? Why should she not be empress of Germany?'

Honor started to laugh. 'And you, therefore, brother to an emperor?'

'And why not?'

'Except there is no empire. Germany has a Führer, Herr Hitler, a man you clearly admire although half the country hates him. How can you square that with a return of the emperors? No, the scheme is absurd, even for you.'

'Nothing is impossible,' he said cosily. 'Hitler is a realist who understands the value of tradition, particularly *royal* tradition. And the kaiser—'

'Former kaiser.'

'—is an expedient man who knows that compromise is the way to survive.'

'An emperor *and* a Führer?'

'Maybe. And if not both, as well to have a horse in each race, is it not?'

'You're more foolish – or maybe just more greedy – than I thought.'

'I can see all around a problem.'

'You look for an awful lot from Fritzi, and poor Brigid.'

'Nothing that wouldn't be of benefit to either, or both, of them.'

Almost, she wanted to laugh. Only Chips could imagine that Germany could be peacefully arranged in a way that particularly suited him, even while all around was talk of war. 'Do go away, Chips, I cannot take your plotting at this hour.'

Even after he was gone, Honor didn't get up. She was afraid that if he heard her moving about he would track her, and pick up again with his talking and planning. She lay in bed until she was certain he had left the house.

His words from last night came back to choke her: *I know it is difficult to resume marital relations once they have been allowed to lapse, but Dr Low is certain this can only be of benefit to you . . .* Worse, even, was the way he had spoken them. She pulled the covers higher about her shoulders, as though to shield herself from the idea that her husband and this doctor she barely knew had discussed her so intimately. So openly. That neither had thought anything wrong with this. And that her husband had laid her out for discussion as though she were a new toy he had acquired and now wished to seek opinion on. And that they had come to a conclusion that was humiliating to her. These things made her feel there was something small and hollow inside her, an empty space the size of her fist, that might open and expand. She turned over in bed, hunching her shoulder to the door, and stared at the window beyond which lay the outside world she was too weary for.

She wished she had someone to talk to. She missed Doris, more even than she had expected to. The letters that arrived from Germany were never enough – never nearly enough. Doris wrote so little of what she did, only asked questions about what Honor did. And Chips. Emerald. All of their friends. She was, Honor thought, far more interested in them all now than she ever had been while living in London and going to their parties.

Her articles, which Honor made sure to read in the *Express*, the weekly paper in which they appeared, told her even less. Fond but bland accounts of the kinds of entertainments she would have thought Doris hated – large communal picnics and days out in the woods. The Germans seemed so, so . . . *bucolic*, Honor thought with a smile. And so very unlike Doris who was all city, all sophistication. How she wished Doris were here, so she could ask her what exactly she was doing, writing such things.

Without her greatest friend, Honor's life had shrunk. Doris was the only person who had ever been fully hers, from the time they had met, aged fourteen, at Miss Potts' school for girls, where Honor had been grand and slow, and Doris had been lowly and whip-smart, so that somehow they had met in the middle. Or maybe not shrunk, so much as stalled. The funny things were so much less funny without Doris to share them. And the sad things, the dreary and frightening things, were so much more terrible without Doris to shake them out. Patsy and Brigid had filled the gap for a little while. The sweet busyness of their comings-out, their artless chatter and charming excitement at their own success had brought much-needed noise and fun. But now Patsy was married to Alan Lennox-Boyd and Brigid – missing the sister closest to her in age – was more subdued, so that the eleven-year gap between her and Honor appeared suddenly greater, not less, than it had first seemed when Brigid had begun to go to grown-up parties.

Then, Honor had imagined her sister as her confidant, a friend to replace Doris, someone with whom she could share the bits of her life that caused her joy, and the many that caused her pain. It hadn't happened like that. And anyway, how could she tell Brigid, just eighteen, things that were tawdry, even shaming? Especially at this stage in Brigid's life? Things that had roots so far back it was hard to understand or trace any of it, and that showed marriage – even love – in a bad light.

She rang for the maid. 'Molly, will you run my bath? And lay out the navy Dior for lunch.'

Chapter Four

Berlin, Summer 1938
Doris

The sound soaked through the walls of her apartment, in through the bricks and plaster in a way that was, Doris thought, determined. As determined as the heavy hand of the person who held the violin bow. Whoever it was, was picking their way through a piece by Dvořák that Doris half-remembered. She followed it in her mind, let it lead her from one sleepy, long-gone image to another; half-remembered, isolated pictures: the dim light of the music room at Miss Potts', Honor on the piano, diligent and stiff, the sound of the girls in the rec room next door, the smell of chalk and beeswax and the unwashed hair of the music tutor. Things she had thought forgotten, and that added up not to a recollection so much as fragments.

She stretched her arms above her head and flexed her shoulders. The practiser was early this morning, she thought. She reached for the tiny gold clock beside her bed. No, it was later than she had expected. They were right on time. Outside, she heard a tram rumble past on Leipziger Strasse. She was four floors up, only one side of her corner flat looked onto the busy road, yet the regular rising-falling-rising whirr of the tram, the soft metallic squeal of wheels, was the sound that accompanied all her days, marking them and ticking them off.

The tram passed and she listened again to the scrape, scrape, scrape of the bow against string. Whoever it was had clearly learnt the order of things, the sequence of the piece they practised, but goodness, how badly they played. She had studied violin at Miss Potts' – had shown the same aptitude for that as for so much else – and she had learned to make her hands quick and light, so that the bow almost flew across the strings. She had understood that her hands must be 'almost not-there', as she had explained it once to Honor. 'They are the medium the music must flow through, but they must not get in the way.'

This person played, she thought with a sudden laugh, like someone running to catch a bus: grimly certain that it must not escape them.

She tried to go back to sleep – how late she had been the night before! – but it was useless. Once awake, she never could drift off again. In any case, she had lunch at Horcher's. She was lunching with von Arent, film director and designer, the man who brought Hitler's vision to life in street decorations and monumental stage tableaux that were drearily realist. A boring man, but a vain one, who liked a great show of attention. She sighed.

The sound of heavy scraping had stopped. Dvořák and the violin were put away.

She decided she would get up and go out early. She could walk about, and try to enjoy knowing that she did not for a while have to turn her feet in any particular direction. Did not, that day, have to encounter a particular person, be somewhere at a particular time, so that she might say a few words under her breath while pretending to stare in a shop window, or listen while a few words were spoken to her by a stranger who seemed to admire the same statue in the Tiergarten but in fact looked at nothing except who was around them to overhear. A day she did not need to look over her shoulder as she crossed roads and changed direction, to see did anyone behind her do the same. And wonder, if someone did, were they following her, or simply going the same way as her.

It was better to go out early, she had learned. To swap her apartment – where she felt safe – for the city's streets and hotels and restaurants, where she did not. Because if she left it too long, the fear that edged forward constantly, stalking her from some unseen place, might grow too much. She needed to stay in motion, to keep playing the part that was set for her so as to hold the fear at bay. Keep moving, she had learned. Keep doing and being what she was here to be: the English girl with such excellent German – thanks to her mother who had come from Berlin to Dorset to marry Doris' father all those years ago, but insisted on speaking to her children in the language of her childhood – the journalist who wrote amusing pieces about daily life in Germany for newspapers in England: gay reports of sports days and festivals and race meetings, so that the wholesome leisure of the Reich was conveyed back to be admired. Who said yes to every party, was always charming and beautifully dressed. A dear friend of Herr Channon and his wife, the best kinds of English people, who had visited Germany for the

Olympics two years ago and been so delighted with everything they saw.

It still gave her a small thrill – that Chips, whom she disliked, should have all unwittingly provided her cover and her camouflage. Because of him, she could be Doris-the-frivolous-girl-about-town, so that no one saw beyond that creature in her elegant silks and smart heels to Doris the anxious listener. Doris the careful memoriser of names and snippets of news. Doris the spy. Although really, she thought as she waited for the bath to fill, that was a silly and dramatic word. She did far more listening than looking.

She pulled open the windows, throwing them wide. This too was part of the preparing. Let the city in, with its smells of baking and coffee lying lightly over the traffic and the dusty smell of trees that reach for water. The outside noises submerged the scraping of the violin. In any case, she knew, the scraping would not resume. Whoever it was who practised so diligently left off at the same time every day. Perhaps they went to work, she thought.

It was her second summer here. She knew by now the way the heat built, sending those who could afford it to the lakes every Friday afternoon, to swim and sail boats for a few days.

She dressed carefully and pulled the heavy wooden door with its square and shiny brass knob closed behind her, forcing herself not to imagine what it would be like to stay there, inside, safe and cool and quiet. She walked briskly down the dark corridor and got into the lift, then made space for the people who came after her. A woman and a girl of maybe eleven with soft brown hair and a round face. When Doris had closed the grille, then pulled the hinged door across, she pushed the last-but-one of the big white buttons. 'Ground floor?' she asked politely.

'Yes, thank you,' the woman said.

The mother nudged her daughter, who studied the grille in front of her. The mother nudged again. At that, the girl looked up at Doris and said clearly, 'I am to apologise.'

'Apologise for what?' Doris asked.

The girl looked at her mother, a little bit uncertain. 'I think my violin practice . . .' she said, with another look at her mother.

'My daughter wishes to apologise for the noise,' the mother said then, leaning over a little so she was almost touching Doris in the cramped space. 'She tries to improve, and so she practises every morning, but I'm afraid the noise must be an inconvenience.'

'Not at all,' Doris said. 'Hard to improve without practice,' she continued sympathetically, looking at the girl. 'And you seem very determined.' She said it with a grin, but the girl nodded seriously at her.

'I am,' she said, nodding her head up and down as she stared at Doris.

'Well, you mustn't mind about me.' She smiled at the girl and reached out to gently touch her shoulder, where the brown hair met the pale blue of her button-down shirt and turned up in a wave. 'I shan't be in the least disturbed. I am a champion sleeper, you know.'

The girl looked back at her, then held out a hand to shake. 'Hannah.'

'Doris.' She shook the hand solemnly, then did the same with Hannah's mother.

'Beatrice,' the woman said.

'You know, I studied violin for a time. When I was a little older than you. There is a particular trick for holding the bow that I learned. Perhaps I could show it to you?' She said it idly, thinking of this only as a puzzle – could Hannah's technique be improved? Would the trick Doris had taught herself be something she could teach? – but the eagerness with which Hannah said 'Yes please' made her glad.

'Are you sure . . .?' her mother began.

'Absolutely,' Doris said. Perhaps, she thought with a grin as she stood politely back to let them out of the lift, she could teach her something that would make the early-morning sounds more bearable.

Chapter Five

Berlin
Doris

Horcher's was filled with cigarette smoke and noise. Loud voices vied with music from the piano in the back and white tablecloths floated like so many conjuring tricks. Doris was welcomed effusively and led to the table beneath the photograph of Wallis Simpson and the Prince of Wales. The waiter bowed graciously in recognition of this elegant touch. Doris nodded and stifled a laugh.

Von Arent was there already, and with him a girl with brittle blonde hair that shimmered pale and melancholy like the underbelly of a chub. There was always a girl with him. Rarely the same girl.

'Doris!' He rose to greet her.

'Benno, darling.' Doris allowed him to kiss her hand and begin the elaborate, inevitable rearranging of table, cutlery and chairs. He never could forget that he was a set designer, she thought, watching as he moved a vase of white flowers an inch or so.

'Off you go,' he said to the girl, who yawned and stood up. She looked vaguely behind her, for a bag or coat, Doris thought. Von Arent snapped his fingers. A young waiter appeared, a heavy white fur draped over his arm. The girl shrugged herself into it despite the heat of the day. That too was part of the conjuring trick of Horcher's. Waiters appearing and disappearing, food in clouds of smoke and the occasional noisy flambé. She really wasn't in the mood, Doris thought, then shook her head slightly. She had to be in the mood.

'You must tell me about your new production,' she said, sitting down in the seat the girl had vacated. She looked to see who was at the tables surrounding them. These were fewer than they had been a month ago – she had heard that Göring, Chips' favourite of Hitler's cronies, had ordered them thinned out to prevent being overheard. 'Although,' the man who had told her had added spitefully in a low voice, 'after a few bottles, the whole street can hear him.'

'Yes, at the Schiller Theatre,' von Arent said, and he was off.

'And you, what are you writing?' he asked when their starters arrived. He had ordered for both of them. Doris' stomach turned when she saw the dumplings – liver, she was sure, steaming greasily – but smiled and picked up her silver fork and knife.

'An account of a most delightful day out,' she said. 'Young people from the cities brought to hike the Müggelberge. Many hours outside, in nature, walking and climbing. So wholesome.'

His lip curled. 'How charming.' He barely tried to cover the sarcasm.

'Charming!' she agreed, carefully enthusiastic.

The wine arrived in a bell-shaped decanter; French, Doris assumed. For all that Berlin society sneered at the degeneracy of the French, they were slow to switch to the coarse German wine. But slower still to be caught drinking French. Gustav Horcher, of course, was quick with a solution, sending out 'house wines' in unmarked decanters that he charged grand cru prices for, even when – as now – they were far inferior. She took a small sip. 'Delicious.'

Von Arent talked about his projects – the design of street decorations for a series of marches – and how he hoped to make a film of *Brave New World*. 'Do you know Mr Huxley?' he asked, so that Doris understood why she was there.

'I imagine I do,' she said lightly. She needed to be thought to know everybody in England. Everybody important. She cast her mind quickly through her London address book. Someone, she felt certain, must know Mr Huxley. 'Would you like to meet him?' she asked sweetly. She took the last of the smoked eel von Arent had ordered for them on her fork and swallowed against a rush of nausea.

She said no to dessert – that was allowed; and indeed von Arent made some heavy pleasantry about watching her figure, then went to pay his respects at a table of high-ranking Nazis by the windows. Doris sighed, lit a cigarette and sat back. It could have been anywhere, she thought, looking around the room. Any restaurant in any city. The same starched white tablecloths and smoothly choreographed waiters gliding between them. Every bit of it as staged as any of von Arent's theatricals. And maybe that was the point? These men – and women, she thought, nodding at the wife of a party official she knew – were so very ordinary. They wanted what all people wanted. Nothing grand or terrible at all. A little more wealth than their neighbours, a sense of security, to see their children flourish. A pity they had chosen to find these things in ways that destroyed them for others, she thought, watching the woman send back a dish, small mouth pursed in disapproval.

They were her enemies, if only they knew, these men and women so seriously studying menus and wine lists. But she didn't hate them. There was so little to hate in most of them. Greed, selfishness, cowardice, dullness . . . common failings, seen as much in London as Berlin. Just as well, she thought. It would be hard to do her job clouded by hate. Or love, she reflected. By personal feelings of any kind. And so she squashed down the anger that came upon her as she watched gangs of young men in uniform swagger about the streets, taking for respect the fear that sent those in their path to huddle in doorways as they passed. She looked away from broken windows and mangled shutters, choked back distress at the crude daubings on building fronts: of '*Juden Raus*' (*Jews Out*), and the ugly twisted Nazi cross. She pushed it all away from her so that she could continue to attend parties and receptions, to laugh and chatter. And listen.

The table in front of her was bare except for her coffee cup and a heavy black ashtray with 'Horcher' written across it in thick gold letters. Her own place was spotless but where von Arent had sat there was a smattering of mustard-coloured stains on the snowy white of the tablecloth. Doris nudged her napkin across to cover them.

The young waiter who had brought the blonde girl's coat arrived silently by her side and leaned forward to pick up her empty coffee cup. 'Perhaps Madame thinks of a walk in Tiergarten on such a day?' he said quietly, face turned so that no one could have seen his lips move.

Doris was careful not to look up at him. 'Perhaps she does,' she murmured.

'The Tritonbrunnen fountain is particularly pleasant,' he said, then straightened up and, with a tiny bow, left her.

Von Arent returned, giddy at having been retained so long at the other table where important men discussed important things. 'Fräulein Coates,' he said gallantly, 'to lunch with you is always a delight. Will you accompany me to the Café Kranzler?'

'Alas I must go and do some writing,' she said, with a show of regret. 'Us poor working girls have so little time to call our own.' This, naturally, led him to more gallantries that saw them along Augsburger Strasse to where he hailed a taxicab and left her.

Was there anything useful in the lunch? Doris wondered as she walked quickly away. Anything he had let slip that could be passed on? Anything unexpected she could file away for later? No, she decided. There was nothing. More and more, this seemed to her the case. The people she met, the parties she went to, the names and news she passed on – they were things anyone could know. Could read in a newspaper or discover by listening to the radio. What she did was pointless. She did not pan for nuggets of gold, sieving sand and stone from precious metal. She didn't know enough to do that. She simply filled the pan and handed it on, in the hopes that buried in all that scree there was something someone else would recognise as gold.

She quickened her pace, shoes tapping smartly on the hot paving stones, but still she felt she was wading through air that was heavy and lifeless. Where was the energy of her first year? When everything she did was made electric by the feeling that she was useful, and that any danger was worth it to be so alive? Now, it was harder to see the value in what she did. Harder to believe that whatever bits she learned and intuited, the scant information she gathered, had any impact on the mushrooming clouds of war. She felt only the danger, no longer the worth. No longer so alive.

And yet, for all the gangs of uniformed youths and the sticky, excitable ambition of the men she met, how she loved this city with its summers that smelt of dusty leaves and car exhaust and the powdered sugar that was sprinkled across fat, round *krapfen*. She loved the wide tree-lined avenues and tall houses that seemed to lean up and back, for a better look at whatever was happening on the street. Loved the way stone was carved and shaped and bent into elegant curls, or placed in large blocks, one upon the other, to create buildings that were monuments; the cafés that were always full, the people who danced in the squares.

She remembered the summer she had spent there with her mother, five years ago now. How they had eaten every pastry her mother remembered from her own childhood, and how she had heard all her mother's stories again, except now Doris knew what the places she spoke of looked like so that they were suddenly real. Sometimes she heard the same story, but from Tante Hannah, her mother's sister, so that it was subtly different, a near-image with tiny distortions that made it fizz. She remembered setting off every day from her aunt's house, returning to it every evening. The solemn cousins and their talk of medical school that had impressed Doris even while she found them a little dull; not gay and quick like her London friends, but serious.

The house was someone else's now. The cousins had moved to England where they no longer thought of being doctors, but were grateful to work in Doris' father's factory, while her aunt tried to take upon herself the duties of housekeeper, despite the fact that Doris' mother was mortified.

The people she passed now, who walked the streets and drank in cafés, those who had lunched at Horcher's – did they know what had happened to Doris' family and all the others like them? Yes. They knew. Enough, anyway. They knew, and approved, because that was one way for them to get what they wanted – a little more than others. By taking it. Or at least by allowing others to take it. And that's why she was still here. That's why she met von Arent for lunch and went to parties with people she despised, and laughed and flirted with them. That's why she put a heavy blanket over the fear, ignored the feeling that what she did was useless and forced herself out, smartly dressed, hair shining and carefully set, every single day.

She reached the Tiergarten and felt the relief that came with shade and grass, even though this was coarse and tufty and more yellow than green. At the Tritonbrunnen fountain she sat on the low stone rim, legs pushed straight out in front of her. The centre of the fountain was a muscular marble youth grappling a large fish that spat water up out of its excessive mouth. The sound, as it splashed back into the basin, was cool. There was no one around and she wondered had the waiter meant no more than he said – 'The Tritonbrunnen fountain is particularly pleasant.' She laughed, feeling more energetic. Perhaps she had the bad habit of reading too much into everything. Of living constantly as if in a melodrama. She would go home, she decided, by the bakery that sold lemonade in glass bottles stoppered by a marble, and lie on her bed with the shutters pulled across so that her room was cool and dim, and write to Honor.

A man approached led by a small dog on a leash and Doris thought of Mimi, her dachshund, with a pang. How she missed the little darling. And how she missed affection, she realised. A gentle, familiar hand on her arm or her hair; a hand that wanted only her comfort, nothing more. A voice to speak kindly to her. At this hour, Berliners were with their families, in the happy after-lunch slump, and wouldn't emerge until evening. There was no one here except the solitary, the purposeless. How lonely she was, she thought, looking around the almost-deserted park. Everyone Doris met wanted something from her, as she did from them; no one ever saying it, but always edging forward to try and gain it.

No wonder she had liked talking to Hannah so much, she realised. The little girl's self-contained solemnity, the gentle curiosity with which she had looked at Doris and the eager way she had thrown herself into the conversation were different to the tone of other interactions.

The dog ran forward, pulling on the lead, so that the man walked more quickly. When it reached the fountain, it put its paws on the fat round rim right beside where Doris sat, straining forward towards the water. She reached a hand to stroke its soft head. The man bent down then, gathered the dog in his arms and leaned forward with it. As the dog drank, the man looked sideways at Doris.

'A hot day,' he said politely. He wore a straw boater with a black band and a light grey suit.

'Very,' Doris agreed. 'No wonder your little friend is thirsty,' she added with a laugh.

The man looked around. There was no one close by. 'There's starting to be trouble about your articles,' he said, switching to English.

Doris, schooled not to betray surprise at these encounters, looked idly away from him, up towards the blue sky. 'In what way?'

'They're rather too good.'

'I thought the point was that they be good?' She thought of last week's – an account of a festival in a town on the outskirts of Berlin, her descriptions of girls and boys singing folk songs and running races. She had certainly laid it on thick, she thought.

'Yes, but not so good. Mosley and his crew of fascists have begun to use them as propaganda. To show what Germany has achieved: prosperity, peace, employment for all.'

She thought of her aunt and cousins. 'Not all.'

'No. But no one reading your articles would know that.'

'They're my cover. We agreed.' She spoke quickly. There was never much time in these exchanges.

'I know.' The dog had finished drinking and the man began to dab at its muzzle with a handkerchief he took from his top pocket, his face mostly obscured by the movement. 'But in Mosley's hands there are unexpected consequences. It may be time for you to go back.'

This was her chance, she thought. A chance to leave. To go back to London, to Honor, her family in Dorset, anywhere but here. She felt a surge of relief. It was exactly what she had longed for, only realising how very much now that it was before her. But could she?

'There's still work to do,' she said, looking away from him, down along the straight avenue of linden trees that led back to the busy city streets.

'There may be new work to do.' He stood up. 'Back home.'

'Why?'

'Things change. We need to change. We are anticipating.' He drew the word out.

She always wondered who 'we' was. Was she 'we', or were others 'we' and she was just herself? 'When?'

'Soon.'

Chapter Six

London
Brigid

'Come with me, do,' Brigid begged Patsy.

But Patsy – still new to being a married lady – said she couldn't, she must be home when Alan came back from the House of Lords. 'Anyway,' she added, her voice tinny down the telephone. 'It's only tea with Honor. You don't need company.'

'Even tea with Honor is less fun without you,' Brigid said sadly. She sat on the bottom stair facing the front door of Number Five Grosvenor Place. She knew she was in the way of the servants who moved through the house at their many tasks, but Lady Iveagh didn't allow her to use the telephone in her sitting room, and Lord Iveagh had forbidden her the library after she had knocked a jug of water over the desk. 'How clumsy you are,' he had said. But he said it fondly. After all, if she was clumsy – and she was – where else did she get it but from him?

'Why did you have to go and marry?' she asked, wedging the chunky ivory-coloured receiver between shoulder and ear so that she could wrap her arms around her bent knees and rest her chin on them.

Patsy was too pleased, and proud, to let that pass. 'Because we all marry,' she said piously. 'And,' with a gush of laughter, 'because I am so very happy. My very own house, Biddy. My own car. You can't imagine.'

'Don't gloat, for I cannot bear it.' Brigid pulled the sleeves of her cardigan down over her hands. The house was cold. Lady Iveagh was clear that there were to be no fires after March, no matter the weather.

'Well, you'll be next. As soon as ever you want, I hear. Rumour has it that men are simply queuing up to ask you.' Now that she was married, and safe, Patsy could afford to be generous.

'Not I!' Brigid said. 'Not yet, anyhow. I know you say it's jolly good fun, but I don't know . . .' She paused. 'It doesn't always look like so much fun,' she said in a rush. 'I mean, not you and Alan. Or Mamma and Papa,' she added loyally. 'You seem very fond, but Honor and Chips . . . Maureen and Duff. The rows.' She shuddered. 'Oonagh and . . .'

'Philip? Or now Oonagh and Dominic?' Patsy supplied with a laugh. Cousin Oonagh was on her second husband, a man her father called The Stallion in a way that Lady Iveagh said 'wasn't quite nice . . .' Neither Brigid nor Patsy knew what was meant, but they knew it was something to giggle at.

'Quite! So you see, I am not so very quick to leap into it. I should like to do other things first.'

'What other things?' Patsy was curious.

'I don't know yet, but more than parties and nightclubs. And those interminable dinners where the entire time one is talking to the man on one's right, one simply dreads the moment one has to turn and start all over again talking to the man on the left.'

'Those!' Patsy laughed. 'But you are so good at them. A steady stream of charming patter . . .'

'I have learned from the best,' Brigid said.

'The best?'

'Chips, of course.' She laughed, then winced as the receiver jerked against her chin.

'Of course. I must say, you are quite a project for him.' Did Patsy sound a little wistful? 'I have heard him say there is nothing you cannot do.'

'All but rubbing his hands in glee . . . He is like Mr Ainsley the grocer at the Elveden summer fete when he knows he has the largest marrow.'

Patsy started to laugh at that. 'How funny you are. Well, don't let him take you over entirely. In any case, I'm sure Honor will not allow it.'

'I'm not at all sure,' Brigid responded. 'Lately it seems to me that she will allow anything that keeps him away from her.'

'Brigid! Do not say so!' Patsy sounded shocked.

Brigid sighed. Was there something that *happened* to girls when they got married? she wondered. Some way in which they changed – became a tiny bit pompous or stuffy, or something? It seemed to happen to them all. As if, on their wedding day, someone took them aside and let them into a solemn secret that only married ladies could know. She hadn't expected it of Patsy – always first to laugh during their nursery days. She never used to say '*Do not say so!*' in that scandalised tone.

'I must get on,' she said. 'Already Minnie is eyeing me most beadily because I am blocking the dusting of the stairs.'

'Liar!' Patsy said cheerfully. 'Do not tell me Minnie is anything but your devoted slave.'

'Minnie is no one's slave. I am positively terrified of her,' Brigid said, then hung up and grinned at Minnie, who stood at the bottom of the stairs, neat in her black-and-white uniform, with a metal pail in one hand and duster in the other.

'If that were true it would be useful, Lady Brigid,' Minnie said. She didn't smile – she never smiled much – but her eyes were merry.

'Oh but it is. Only I don't show it. By some heroic effort, I don't show it. And I wish you would stop calling me "Lady Brigid". You only do it since that ridiculous coming-out, and I hate it. Call me Biddy, like you used to.'

'It's the proper thing now,' Minnie said. 'So you'll have to lump it.'

'That's what I love about you, Minnie darling. Always so accommodating.' Brigid laughed. 'Will you come and help me dress? I have tea at Belgrave Square.'

'When I'm done my other duties,' Minnie said. 'I'm not your lady's maid yet, as you well know.'

'No,' Brigid agreed. 'Mamma says I have no need of a proper maid yet. And so I must share you with the stairs and the dusting.'

'Don't make me choose,' Minnie said. 'Now, get on with you. I will come and do your hair in a bit. You can look out your own clothes.'

Arriving at Number Five Belgrave Square that afternoon, Brigid gave her coat to Andrews and started across the vast hall. Her heels clipped smartly on the marble tiles and as always she had to stifle a laugh at the opulence around her. The hall reached up and around, disappearing into the dim, echoey depths of the house. Everywhere was warm brown marble, softly shining wood and polished mirrors in gilt frames, so that she caught glimpses of her reflection trying to draw her on, this way and that, among the many urns and objects.

'It's as if he has created a zoo for things,' Patsy had whispered to her, the first time they came to the house, nearly two years ago.

'Perhaps they will mate with one another,' Brigid had whispered back, causing Patsy to snigger.

She waited now, looking at the paintings that stared down upon her from gilt frames; some simpering, some stern. Ladies and gentlemen of other times, brought together by Chips as witness to his triumph. Somewhere, she knew, there was a Boucher, a voluptuous nude, that had caused her father consternation when Honor had shyly asked for money to buy it. 'Six thousand pounds,' her father had said, scandalised. 'For a painting of someone else's dead relative. What can he possibly want with such a thing?'

Chips came bustling into the hallway then to greet her, kissing her on both cheeks in a way that she found excessive and taking both her hands in his. 'Let me look at you. Exquisite, as ever.' His eyes ran over her as though they poured something hot and wet across her face, and Brigid felt – as Chips often made her feel – like she was something for sale in a window that had caught his eye.

'I hear you were at the Café de Paris last night,' he almost whispered as he leaned in. 'Oh, don't worry, I won't tell.' He twinkled at her. 'I believe you were in very jolly company. Young Billy Cavendish. Hugh Fraser.'

'Tell if you like,' Brigid said. 'I mean, there is nothing to tell.' She shrugged. 'We danced. Then we danced some more. Hugh ran me home. Everyone was perfectly pleasant and proper and terribly dull. And that's it, all there, in a nutshell. Nothing to tell. Nothing to *not* tell.' If she had hoped to irritate Chips, she failed.

'You say "pleasant and proper" as though they are bad things.' He twinkled at her, all approval and conspiracy, until Brigid laughed and said, 'Where is my sister?'

'Upstairs. Come.'

In the first-floor drawing room, Honor sat beside the fire with a book. She looked, Brigid thought, tired and heavy but her face brightened when she saw Brigid.

'Darling! How lovely. I have a postcard here for you, from Doris. Came this morning.' She handed Brigid a card. On the front was a cartoon of a jolly-looking pig wearing a top hat and tails. On the back, Doris had written '*Darling Biddy – you don't mind that I still call you that, do you? – I saw this dear fellow and thought, is he not fine? And yet a pig still, beneath it all.*'

Brigid laughed. She knew well that Doris was teasing her. She must have seen some of the society pages that went on about '*Lady Brigid Guinness, splendid in tulle, with a tiara of emeralds on her head, attends Lady Astor's ball*' and was gently mocking her, reminding her that she was still her same self beneath all the fuss. Long ago, when Brigid was still in the schoolroom, they had both agreed that pigs were 'quite the cleverest animals, though horses are the dearest'.

'Did she write to you too?' she asked Honor, tucking the card away in the pocket of her cardigan.

'She did.' Honor made a face. 'It's never enough. But better than nothing.' Then, 'I'll ring for tea. Chips, you needn't stay.'

Secretly, Brigid hoped he would. She didn't trust Chips – not at all – but the truth was, he was better company than her sister.

'But I do need. We have other guests.' Chips wagged his finger at Honor in a way that could only have been annoying, Brigid thought. Sure enough, a look of irritation flashed across Honor's face. She wore no lipstick, Brigid saw, and whatever powder she had applied earlier had settled into the deepening crease between her eyebrows and the grooves on either side of her mouth so that her face seemed clogged and weary.

'Chips, I thought we agreed not . . .'

'It's only Fritzi,' he said. 'Company for Lady Brigid. You remember him, Brigid; you danced with him at your coming-out ball?'

'I danced with everyone at my coming-out ball,' Brigid replied.

'Why does she need company?' Honor interjected. 'I am company for her.'

'I have asked Ambassador Kennedy to join us too,' Chips said smoothly. 'He is still quite newly arrived from America, and given my position in parliament—'

'Secretary to an under-secretary,' Honor said scathingly.

Chips ignored her. '—I must make an effort. After all, it is vital he meet the right sort of English person.'

'And what sort might that be?'

'The sort who will steer him away from belligerents like Churchill. Who will show him the side of the angels, led by Chamberlain, those dedicated to finding common ground with Germany, which I believe is exactly what he wants. I have asked Emerald too,' he added.

'He must meet "the right sort of English person",' Honor said, 'and so you bring him together with two Americans – oh, you may be lapsed, and Emerald may be married to Lord Cunard, but you and she are still Americans – and a Prussian.' She started to laugh. 'Chips, you are the limit.' Her laughter was thin wire, Brigid thought, but he smiled benignly at her.

'If you say so, my dear. But we understand the ambassador's mission more clearly than most. The importance of it.'

'Which is?'

'Which is simple.' He looked triumphant. 'Roosevelt must be persuaded to follow his heart and keep America out of international affairs. And Ambassador Kennedy is the key to that. If we can let him see there is no appetite here for a fight with Germany, that on the contrary, we are a country keen to stay friends, to foster better understanding with the Reich, then all the dreadful talk of war will disperse, simply melt away.' He fluttered his fingertips at her. 'And we can all *get on* with things again.'

'You mean things like buying *objets*, filling the house with silly bits and pieces, and scheming to advance yourself ever further?'

He sat back in his chair, right away from Honor. 'I mean men and women going about their daily lives as they wish without fear that those lives will be plucked from them by a row they do not want over far-away territories they do not care about.'

He succeeded, Brigid thought, in sounding grand and stiff and also sorrowful.

'So much to accomplish in one afternoon,' Honor said, indifferent to his grand sorrowfulness.

'Indeed. You see now why I have invited that dear boy Fritzi? So that he might be company for our young guest while we elders talk politics.'

Brigid rolled her eyes. 'Such a fun time as I am to have.'

'And I,' Honor added.

When Fritzi was shown in some moments later by Andrews – who announced 'Prince Frederick George William Christopher of Prussia' in a way that caused Chips to smile approvingly, and Honor to mutter 'good God' under her breath – he stood in the doorway and clicked his heels smartly together, bowing slightly from the waist. Now that she saw him, Brigid did indeed remember him from her party. Even amidst that whirl of dazzling creatures, the boys and girls equally beautiful, and beautifully dressed, so that they had seemed like the shiny floating ribbons on a maypole, Fritzi had stood out for his unruffled beauty. He was like the surface of a lake, Brigid had thought then, as he whirled her into a waltz that had seemed to perfectly fit his solemn grace. His was not a charming beauty nor a lively beauty. He might have been a marble statue from classical times, except for the rosy glow that lit him to the tips of his perfect ears. But it was a beauty as un-deniable as the blue of her own eyes or the fact that she was left-handed.

When he finished bowing, he crossed towards the fireplace and bent over Honor's hand. Only that Honor snatched her hand back, he would have kissed it, Brigid thought with an inward laugh.

'Fritzi, darling boy.' Chips clasped his hand warmly. 'You know my sister-in-law, Lady Brigid Guinness.'

'Of course.' Fritzi bent over Brigid's hand. 'How could I possibly forget?' His English was faultless, in a way that said immediately that he wasn't English. She caught Honor's eye over the top of his head and thought she was about to laugh outright. Luckily, behind her, Andrews announced, 'Ambassador Kennedy.'

The ambassador did not pause in the doorway. He came straight in with a smile that lifted his top lip high above big white teeth but didn't reach his eyes, shrewd and veiled behind spectacles. He walked like a man swimming, Brigid thought. Or at least a man smoothly moving a weightless force out of his way. 'Good to see you again,' he said to Chips, shaking his hand vigorously. He did the same with Honor and with Fritzi, although he seemed to pause slightly as Chips reeled off the boy's title and give a sharper look from behind the steel-rimmed spectacles. When it came to Brigid's turn, he asked her, 'How old are you?' without any kind of 'How do you do?'

'I am eighteen,' she said.

'Are you indeed? Well.' He paused and contemplated her. Then, 'I have a daughter. Kathleen. Also eighteen.'

'Ambassador Kennedy is here with quite the retinue,' Chips said gayly. 'His wife, Rose, and seven of their nine children.'

'Nine!' Honor said. An expression of distaste crossed her face.

'Indeed. Is he not blessed?' Chips said, and managed to look both approvingly at Ambassador Kennedy and pointedly at Honor, in some way that Brigid didn't understand.

'My daughter Kathleen,' the ambassador showed no sign of allowing himself to be distracted by niceties, 'she'd be mighty pleased to meet you.'

'I'm sure that would be delightful,' Brigid said, turning vague and charming. Any English person would immediately have taken the hint. But Ambassador Kennedy was American.

'That's settled then,' he said. 'You'll like her. Everybody does.'

Brigid stifled a groan. Must she now be responsible for some poor little fish-out-of-water? Anyone who 'everybody' liked could only be impossibly dreary.

Emerald arrived, wearing a hat trimmed with so many feathers that she looked, more than ever, like an ancient exotic bird, all beaky nose, deep wrinkles and bright jewel colours. She and the ambassador greeted one another cordially, and soon they were deep in conversation about something called the Imperial Policy Group. 'Chamberlain understands,' Chips said. 'As long as he keeps far away from that old warmonger, Churchill, it'll be alright . . .'

He might have been talking about horses sharing a stable, Brigid thought; which animals did well together and which ones didn't.

'From what I hear, Churchill wants war and will say anything to get it,' Ambassador Kennedy said bluntly. 'All his talk of England's duty, the need to resist Hitler, is nothing more than the empty words of a man who has made up his mind to brawl. You can see them in any dive bar in Hell's Kitchen on a Friday after payday.'

'We think so too,' Emerald said soothingly. 'Most of the country thinks so. There is no appetite for war among the people.'

Honor, after ringing for tea and passing cups around when it arrived, followed by plates of tiny sandwiches and two kinds of cake, picked up her book again – *Rebecca* the title said in bold black letters – and buried herself in it. Bundi lay at her feet, drowsing happily in the warmth of the fire.

Fritzi turned to Brigid. 'Lady Brigid, how much do you enjoy opera?'

'As much as the average English person,' Brigid said cautiously.

He wagged a finger at her. 'I see what it is you are trying to do. You are trying to dissemble in that charming way you English have. But I can't allow it.' He wagged the finger again. 'Because, you see, I intend to invite you to the opera, and so I must know how much you care for it. That way I will know whether to get tickets for Puccini, say – something easy, *comfortable* – or if you might be able for our Germans, Wagner or Albert Lortzing.'

Why did men always treat one as though one were a fire made with damp wood? Brigid thought. A feeble flame that must be coaxed and gentled? Fritzi was sort of hearty in his coaxing, but in a way that felt fake.

'But I haven't said I will go to the opera with you,' she said.

No sign that he thought her rude crossed his smooth face. Instead, he smiled, showing such even white teeth that Brigid thought suddenly of Peter Pan, who had the perfect pearly teeth of childhood always. And how strange that was in a grown man.

'No,' he agreed. 'But I hope very much you will.'

Before she could respond, Chips cut in. 'Brigid, you are coming to Kelvedon for some days soon, is that not so?'

'Yes,' she said gratefully. 'The great unveiling. Chips has not allowed any of us to see this new home, even though he bought it nearly a year ago,' she explained to Fritzi.

'It wasn't fit to be seen,' Chips said. 'A party of nuns had had the place. First as a school, then an asylum of some kind.' He shuddered.

'Only a man of your vision could have seen past that,' Emerald said reassuringly.

'Thank you.' He leaned forward and pressed her hand warmly. Honor looked up from her book, from one to the other, and smirked a little. 'I have had Gerald Wellesley – who will be Duke of Wellington,' he explained to Ambassador Kennedy, 'working on the place and finally, it is ready. We go down as a family party in a week or so. Fritzi, why not do us the honour of coming too?'

Fritzi bowed again and said, 'I would be delighted,' so quickly that Brigid knew immediately he had been asked already. Had already agreed, and that this was only pantomime for her benefit.

'I must go,' she said, standing. 'Mamma expects me back.'

'I doubt it,' Honor said, head bending once more to her book. 'She is at the Women's Institute all afternoon. Destitute widows. Or is it orphans?'

'Both. And nevertheless, I must go,' Brigid said, furious that Honor should have contradicted her. She said only the briefest of goodbyes and ran down the stairs calling, 'Andrews, my coat,' as she went.

'Wait, Brigid!' Chips caught her in the hallway.

'Why did you do that?' She rounded on him. 'Invite him. I do not want him there at all. He is like a man made out of cardboard. Like the footmen in Cinderella, except they are made of mice. Or is it rats?' She was getting confused and incoherent in her anger. It always happened to her. Just when she most needed to be calm and aloof, she became flustered and tied herself in knots.

'You're cross,' Chips said. 'I understand. I see it in your face. The way you stick your lower lip out – adorable!' And he reached a hand out and placed it against her cheek. His hand was smooth and cool and rested lightly, for just a moment. But the gesture was possessive. And something else that she didn't understand. His hand may have been cool but his eyes were hot. 'I will make it up to you,' he promised. 'I will ask your cousin Maureen—'

Brigid rolled her eyes. 'Hardly a real cousin. Years older. Honor's cousin, if you will; not mine.'

'Well, for Honor then, I will ask Maureen and Duff. Even though he is not at all sound on Germany. And for you, Kathleen Kennedy, so that you shall have a friend of your own.'

'You can't arrange us as you see fit, Chips,' she said in irritation. 'We are not flowers in a vase. And I am not a child. You do not need to find friends for me.'

'Of course you are not,' he said. 'Not a child at all.'

Chapter Seven

Kick

It was the hour before anyone else was awake that Kick liked best. The hour when the house her father had found for them, Number Fourteen Prince's Gate, was only the slightest bit stirring. If she listened carefully, she could hear the servants, so silent in that way of English servants, moving discreetly about, but nothing more. Even her mother, Rose, wasn't up yet.

Kick was always first awake, it seemed. She'd always been like that, since she was a child, but now, since coming to London, more so than ever. It was as if there wasn't time to do all the things she wanted to, because the things were so many. There was riding in Rotten Row, watching Teddy and Bobby sail their boats on the fountain, lunch at the Ritz, shopping at Harrods or any of the small boutiques that lay around that monumental department store, afternoon tea at home or at Fortum & Mason.

Most of all there were her new friends, these English girls, and boys, who couldn't seem to get enough of her. Debo Mitford, who came to Prince's Gate to listen to jazz on Kick's gramophone, marvelling that she had the latest records. Hugh Fraser, David Ormsby-Gore, both young-seeming and bashful but awfully nice and always asking her out, driving her home, taking her about.

Almost from the moment they had arrived in England three months ago, the telephone at Prince's Gate had rung and rung, and each time it was for her. 'Will you come for tea? For tennis? For a Friday-to-Monday in the country?'

And Kick had said yes to everything, so that by the time her mother arrived, weeks later, she had settled in such a way that even her mother was impressed. Not that Rose said so, but Kick could see it.

Those three weeks that Kick had been ahead of her had been wonderful. Straight off the *Queen Mary*, she had found the English to be so friendly, their press so interested in everything she had to say. Kick had felt instantly among friends – indeed, had spoken to the newsmen and photographers as if they *were* friends. She had been straight and open and funny and had not thought too much about being careful with her words. And everything she said was reported with enthusiasm and affection so that all of England seemed determined to see only the best in her, and her father laughed in approval and she could not seem to 'put a foot wrong'. Then she began to understand, a bit, what he had meant when he told her to be 'American', not English.

When Rose arrived, Kick had assumed that she would be shuffled to the background again. But Rose had taken in the situation with her usual speed, noting the array of invitations on the chimneypiece, stiff pieces of white card with gold lettering.

Her first action had been to order new clothes for Kick. Lots of them. Dresses, ball gowns, skirts, blouses, shoes, even new riding jackets.

Kick had always made friends easily. At the Sacred Heart Convent in Connecticut, she had been one of the popular girls. She also had what her mother called 'the gift of knowing what to say'. Which Kick didn't exactly understand, because she just said what she wanted to say without thinking too much about it. But it 'came out right', according to Rose.

She stretched and yawned. She wished her mother would let her get up and go downstairs this early. But Rose wouldn't: 'You'll annoy the servants.' Not that she'd have allowed her lie in bed either, Kick thought with a grin. There was a 'right' time to be up, same as there was a 'right' way for everything – how to stand, how to run, how to play tennis, how to dance, how to take part in the heated debates about law and politics and society that happened when they were all around the table at dinner together. A 'right' way, that was a Kennedy way.

'You're more a tribe than a family,' Debo Mitford had said the first time she had seen them all together. That was in the weeks after they had met at Queen Charlotte's ball; Kick had stood in a long line of debutantes, dressed in white like a flock of geese, as they stepped forward one by one and curtsied to a giant cake. How Kick had wished she had Eunice with her, that they might laugh together at the absurdity. All around her, girls were solemn and pious. And then, '*Charmed, Your Majesty,*' she heard the girl in front of her murmur, as she swept low and graceful towards the floor. Kick had snorted with laughter, and the girl, turning to cede her place, had winked at her. Debo. They had been friends ever since.

'It's because we are so many,' Kick had said.

'It's not just that,' Debo had mused. 'You're like us. You have your own language and ways of behaving, and you seem terrifying to outsiders but you aren't. Not really. Except –' with a laugh '– your mother. She is terrifying.'

'You do remember that I have met your father?' Kick had said.

Debo had laughed again and said, 'Yes but Farve is a poppet really, underneath all the shouting. Your mother, underneath all the quietness, is steel.'

Kick checked her watch. Still too early. She got up anyway, pulling on a cardigan although it was already warming to what looked like another bright day. She went to the window, pulling herself up onto the high seat where she could look down at Prince's Gate below. A man with a cart and a shabby pony was walking slowly past. In the back of his cart were piled heaps of clothes. Kick could make out old suit jackets, the arms pulled inside out, and flowery dresses of the sort women of her mother's age wore. Not her mother. Rose would never wear something so dowdy. Even for gardening and quiet afternoons at home, she was always crisply dressed in exactly the right outfit. That was a gift she had.

Behind the pony-and-cart came the knife grinder on his bicycle, with his grinding stone strapped to the front where he would work it with the same pedals that he used for cycling. From the house three doors down, a nursemaid came down the front steps with a pram. Must be a difficult baby, Kick decided with the wisdom of an elder sister. It wasn't at all the right time for a walk. The English, she had discovered, were like her mother. They had a right time and a wrong time for everything. Anything that happened outside those times, well, there had to be a reason.

Teddy came in then, tapping once at the door and pushing it

open. He was dressed, but wore his fawn-coloured dressing gown loosely belted over his clothes and his feet were bare. 'Will you come with us to the zoo today?' he said, putting up his arms for Kick to lift him onto the window seat.

'Sure. What are you doing at the zoo?' Kick settled him in beside her, an arm around his shoulders.

'There's a new petting zoo and we're cutting the ribbon. Mother says we may stay and play with the animals. They say there's going to be a baby elephant, and lambs. Bobby's coming too but I'm the one cutting the ribbon,' he said proudly. 'Even though I'm only ten and he's thirteen.'

'Wouldn't miss it, kid,' Kick said.

'We're going to sail our boats on the pond in the park after breakfast. Will you come to that too?'

'Can't. And shouldn't you be preparing a speech or something?'

'No speeches. They promised. Only ribbons.' His hair stuck up in tufts and Kick smoothed it down with one hand. They looked down at the street below, busier now. The milk float had pulled up, empties rattling loudly in their wire crates. The milkman jumped down and began stacking bottles of milk against the black area railings at the top of the steps that led down to the basement.

'He's supposed to go round the back,' Teddy said. 'He never does.'

Another knock at the door, even more ghostly a tap than Teddy's. The maid, with tea.

'At last,' Kick said, jumping down and holding out her arms for Teddy to jump into them.

'Your mother says you're to go to her study when you're dressed,' the maid said.

'Can I go?' Teddy asked.

'She didn't say for you to,' the maid said. Kick could see she was awkward. If Rose hadn't sent for Teddy, it meant she didn't want to see Teddy. But the maid didn't know how to say that.

'You go down and have breakfast, Ted,' she said. 'Cook said there'd be kippers. Come and see Mother after you sail your boat.'

She looked out the window again. The street below had emptied except for the nursemaid with the high pram now on her way back from the park. Kick opened the window a crack and heard the sound of crying. The nursemaid jiggled the pram, rather too hard, and the baby cried all the more. Kick was tempted to run down and show her how Kikoo always did it, but as she watched, she saw her father step out the polished front door of Number Fourteen and start briskly down the steps. She rapped on the glass and called out. He looked up and, seeing her, waved, then set off down the street towards Westminster, as he did every morning. She tried to be there when he left each day, to see him off. At that hour, Rose was at her writing desk, and the small moment of farewell was a way for Kick to feel there was still the link between her and the ambassador that she had felt on the *Queen Mary* and before her mother arrived.

'I'm off to keep the peace,' he would say jauntily. 'Like a traffic light on "red" for stop.' But in the evenings, when he came home, he was far less jaunty. 'There are more of the warmongers than I expected,' he had admitted to her the day before. 'And they are madder than I hoped. But still not so mad that they would go to war without American help, and so I will stop them.'

'Of course you will,' she'd assured him. 'It's the right thing, and so you will.'

It was the right thing, she thought now, watching him disappear around the corner. How could anyone not see that?

Chapter Eight

Maureen

The sound of Duff's feet on the stairs woke Maureen. No one, she thought, trod with such brisk firmness as her husband. She sat up quickly. She had fallen asleep on a sofa in the drawing room – a long time ago, judging by the gloom of the room. It was nearly evening. Beside her, Pugsy was asleep too, snuffling gently, head sunk on his paws. 'In here,' she called, in case Duff should carry on upstairs to his rooms. And then again, louder, for fear he hadn't heard her, 'In here.'

The feet stopped and Duff's head appeared around the door. 'Why so dark?'

'I was busy writing letters. I hadn't realised how late it was,' she said, hiding a yawn. Thank goodness the lamp on the small corner desk was lit. The pool of yellow light was enough, just, to have been writing by. She didn't want Duff to know she had spent the afternoon alone and asleep.

Even though it was only a month since their son, Sheridan, was born, and therefore a nap could surely be forgiven, she didn't want him to think her feeble. Not now. Not when there was, suddenly, such hope in front of them again.

Since Sheridan, they had been different. The hardened layer of mistrust between them that had seemed to strangle any kinder emotions was thawed. At least for now. Melted by the milky eyes of their newborn son.

She knew about Marjorie – everyone, she thought ruefully, knew about Marjorie, but she also knew that Marjorie meant nothing. Or very little anyway. That deep down, under that silent, brooding surface, she was in her husband's heart in a way that was at times angry, even violent, but also tender and true and, most of all, constant. There might be Marjories – any number of them – and still they would never mean anything. She knew, too, that if they could just stop fighting, they would be able to make their way back to one another.

There had been others for her too. Not as many as was whispered, but a few. Enough to know that they were nothing – nothing – to the man she had married. Whom she had loved and desired since she first met him, even through the years after Caroline's birth, and then Perdita's, when the anger between them had seemed so great that nothing could return them to what they had once been. Over those years they had poisoned the water with rows that were first passionate and urgent, and forgotten in a storm of love, but then became bleaker and more cruel; followed not by love but by days, sometimes weeks, of silence. Those rows had put them far from one another, onto two lonely islands.

She remembered the night, some months after Caroline was born, when he had gone to her dressing room and cut her clothes to pieces, snipped and slashed through every dress she had owned, heaping the floor with torn and gashed piles of silk and satin that lay there like so many smears of paint. And how she, surveying the damage the next morning, remembering too the way he had come to her, after his explosive revenge, had felt a shiver of excitement that she was capable of provoking such emotions.

That had been how they were together. But it had been too much. In the seven years between Caroline's birth and the arrival of little Sheridan, it had become harder to dissipate the anger after those rows. As though each explosion left a residue, one that accumulated over time, layering over and over until everything between them was sticky to the touch. Each new row dragged behind it the memory of all the others.

'You cannot smash something again and again and still expect to mend it,' Duff had said once, sadly, when she had been drunk enough, brave enough, to try and ask him what he thought had gone wrong. 'Eventually there is no strength left in it.'

And then, when she had entirely given up hope, when Perdita was four and Caroline nearly seven, came the old dragging weariness and with it a bleakness that lay on everything so that she feared she was in what her mother – who knew such moods better than most – would call 'a melancholy'. Until the sudden realisation that her sickness was one of hope, of life. And then came a boy. A son.

Duff, she recalled now, had cried. Tears had fallen from his large dark eyes onto the delicate hair of his newborn son, and when Maureen had said, 'Is he not the most beautiful of all our babies?' he had agreed, nodding furiously because he could not speak, was busy blowing his nose loudly into a large white handkerchief.

She had been glad, then, that she had tried so hard to keep them married. 'Why not divorce him?' her sister Oonagh had asked, Aileen too, so many times.

'What, and be as déclassé as you?' Maureen had snapped. 'You forget I'm a marchioness.'

'No one could possibly forget, Maureen,' Aileen had murmured.

'Well then, why would I give that up?'

'Because he makes you unhappy, is rude and often drunk,' Aileen had said.

'He is my husband,' Maureen had retorted. But she had remembered the conversation, many times, in the days when it seemed that even she, with a will her father had once described as 'like iron, only stronger', could not keep the marriage from sinking beneath the weight of his rages, his drinking. And, if she was honest, her own cruel tongue – the habit she had of lashing out, and always with the surest blow, instinctively inflicting the deadliest wound.

'At least I know when you are home,' she had hissed at him shortly before the pregnancy, 'like King David or Solomon, whose presence was heralded by divine trumpets. Only in your case, it is the heavy snores brought on by bottles of brandy that ring out across the house. How are we ever to have another child – the son you say you so desire – when you are asleep in your dressing room, knocked cold by drink, night after night?'

'I'd rather lie in the arms of a brandy bottle than in yours,' he had retorted, face dark with the humiliation she had meant to heap on him – meant, that is, until she saw the pain in his face that she had put there.

And then, when it seemed as though they would never find their way back to kindness, a reprieve so unexpected, a second chance, had brought them to this new and tentative place. A place she must mind and nourish and make strong. Strong enough to withstand the dark fury in both their natures that brought them together with such passion, and drove them to such violence against one another.

She passed a hand over her cropped golden hair to smooth it now, and hoped her face was not creased by the cushion she had slept on. 'How was your day?' she asked, sitting up straighter. Pugsy stirred and stood on his short legs, pink tongue hanging out over his black snout.

'Difficult. Chamberlain is still playing at peace, even though he knows – must know – that he cannot placate and appease forever. He feeds scraps to a beast that is insatiable, one that will take everything he offers, then have his arm off when there is no more. There are no more deals to make with Hitler. No more drawing lines, then looking the other way when he marches over them. Chamberlain talks of being reasonable, of diplomacy and compromise. But those words are simply cover for his weakness.' He sounded angry. He always did, now, when talking of Germany and what he called 'the craven response' of Prime Minister Chamberlain.

'I don't know why we wouldn't just let Hitler have his bits of Czechoslovakia, or wherever it is,' Maureen said on a yawn. 'I mean, what is it to us? Who cares?'

'We'll all care when we see that he has gobbled up most of Europe and stands breathing down our necks,' Duff said shortly. 'If he was to be content with his "bits of Czechoslovakia" as you call it, I might agree. But he won't. Nothing will stop him except force. Just ask Germany's Jews.'

'Ask them what?' She lit a cigarette, closing the lighter with a snap.

'What kind of man Hitler is,' Duff said shortly. 'He is ugly and insatiable. That's what Chamberlain can't, or won't, see.' His voice softened. 'How is our son?'

'Enchanting. I am certain he is especially intelligent. His expression is so alert, so curious.' Actually, she couldn't see any difference in Sheridan compared with other babies of that age. They were all rather alarming, she thought. Formless and yet focused, in a way she didn't understand but that frightened her. But Duff liked her to say such things about their son. And so she did.

She rang the bell, and when the butler appeared, she snapped, 'Manning, can't you get some light in here? Must I peer and squint in my own home?' Then, 'And bring the cocktail tray.' That, she thought, would keep Duff by her side.

'Mix me a Martini, darling?' she said when the tray arrived. 'Nanny will bring Sheridan down any moment.' That too would keep him with her.

The butler came in with the telephone. 'Mrs Channon, m'lady.' How Maureen loved that Honor was only a Mrs now, and no longer Lady Honor Guinness, while she, Maureen, was Lady Dufferin. She stretched her arms above her head and arched her back luxuriously before taking the shiny black telephone. 'Hullo?'

'Darling, I hoped you'd be there. I need to borrow you.'

'Why?' Maureen was suspicious. She looked over at Duff, pouring gin into two glasses.

'I need you to come with me to Kelvedon.'

'Why do you need us to come with you to Kelvedon?' Maureen asked loudly, for Duff's benefit. She saw him stop stirring, a silver cocktail stick in his hand.

'Chips insists that we go, because the house is finally ready, and he has invited that young German prince he's so fond of, who will be desperately dull. Brigid, who comes with us, is cross about it, and so Chips – no doubt thinking he was doing something terribly clever – has asked a heap of Americans also. The new ambassador, his no-doubt monstrous wife – did I tell you they have *nine* children? Roman Catholics of course; what can you expect? – and their daughter, for no better reason than that she is the same age as poor Biddy. You can't imagine how I dread it all. So you see, you must come.'

'The American ambassador, his wife and daughter, some German prince – aren't they all done away with now? – and your little sister Brigid?' she recited for Duff. 'Not exactly the most irresistible, now, is it?'

'Please, darling, you owe me.'

'How do I owe you?' But she watched Duff, who stood still for a moment, then nodded his head several times at her. 'Never mind, you can tell me later. You'll invent something, I have no doubt. And don't forget I made you Sheridan's godmother. But very well, we'll come. And now you owe me double.'

'Anything! I promise!'

When she had hung up, Maureen sank back against the sofa and held a hand up for the glass Duff brought over to her. 'I'm surprised you agreed.'

'I want to know what Chips is up to with the American ambassador.'

'Must he be up to something?'

'He usually is. We need the Americans on our side because we need their money and their weapons, but Kennedy is a born appeaser, just like Chamberlain and Chips. My hope is if I can talk to him, point out how shortsighted they are, I can change his mind. Kelvedon might be a chance to do that.'

'Such a bore,' Maureen sighed. But really, the truth was, she was pleased. In London, there were so many claims on Duff's time. There was the House, his duties as under-secretary of state for the colonies, the time he spent with Mr Churchill – 'trying to ready ourselves for what is inevitable, so that we are not caught entirely napping when war is declared' – his club, his many friends. Marjorie.

At Kelvedon, there would be nothing, except whatever shooting Chips arranged, and given how little he cared for blood sports or physical exertion, not much of that. The young people – Brigid, the Kennedy girl – would be of no interest to Duff, and surely there was a limit to how much Chips and an ambassador – even American – could monopolise him. No, he would be all hers. Nearly all hers.

Suddenly, she recalled the ambassador's wife. She ran through the possibility of threat, imagining a chic, cosmopolitan sort of woman, someone with well-informed views and an air of discreet elegance. Maureen pursed her lips. Then remembered – this was the mother of nine. Some kind of an Irish Catholic. Immediately, the image of a svelte, mysterious, well-groomed sophisticate was replaced by a broad, red-cheeked lady with clothes bought to cover and hide rather than flatter.

Maureen smirked. No, this would be the perfect escape. She would have Duff beside her, with her. She knew he would never have agreed to a holiday – not with such trouble in Czechoslovakia; how sick she was of hearing that spikey-sounding word – except to Clandeboye, his estate in the north of Ireland, where Caroline and Perdita were. But Maureen had no intention of that; too draughty, too damp, too full of his mother, Lady Brenda. Such a happy accident after all, this visit to Kelvedon.

She must tell Honor to put them in the same room, she thought. And she must order some new underwear. She smiled.

'Come and sit beside me.' She patted the sofa. Duff first refilled his drink, then sat.

'We could bring Sheridan?' he said, leaning back. 'Though a pity not to have the girls.'

'The girls?' she said quickly. 'They would never get here on time. And besides they are in a routine with the governess. So important. As for Sheridan, too unfair on the little mite to be moved around.' She didn't intend on sharing her husband with anyone, not even their son. 'And simply dreadful for Nanny. Besides, little Paul is a brute. I wouldn't have Sheridan in any nursery with that child. Do you know what he did the other day?' And she launched into a story about Paul – urged by Chips to speak in French, stamping his foot and shouting, 'I am not a *garçon*' – that was intended to distract Duff, but also to show him how unsuitable it would be to expose Sheridan, the new Earl of Ava, to such company. 'It's no wonder Honor never had another, if Paul is such a monster,' she finished.

'Hush, Maureen.' Duff put an arm around her shoulders and leaned his head towards hers so that their foreheads almost touched. 'You don't know why there are no more. It is not right to speak of it.' He was so large and solid that she felt tiny, fragile, beside him. It was so rare that she felt those things. Only with Duff. Everyone else, she overpowered. Almost too easily. Men or women, it made little difference. Only Duff was able to make her feel that she was delicate, gossamer, beside the dense heft of him.

She buried her face in his shoulder, breathing in the smell that was entirely his. That mix of hair oil with its trace of clove, shaving foam, the French cigarettes he smoked, something that spoke of the damp, peaty air of Clandeboye and that never seemed to leave him no matter how long he spent in London. Her stomach lurched.

'Come upstairs with me?' she said huskily, into his neck. 'We have hours before we need to dress for dinner.'

'You go. I'll follow you.' At the doorway, she looked back. Duff had got up and was at the drinks tray. As she watched, he reached for the decanter of brandy at the back. She must tell Manning not to bring brandy with the cocktails.

Chapter Nine

Kick

In the little upstairs study, Kick found her mother at her writing desk, as she had known she would. The desk was placed against the window looking out onto Prince's Gate Gardens at the back of the house – a scrappy patch of grass and trees, nothing like the grandeur of Hyde Park to the front. 'Nothing distracting about that view,' Rose had said when she first decided this was to be her study. Kick, who had known exactly that she would choose it – and why – had nudged Eunice. Both had been careful not to laugh.

Beside Rose, there was a stack of envelopes addressed in her neat, spidery hand. Thank-yous, invitations, letters of congratulation, of commendation, letters to the boys. And her scrapbook. As Kick watched, Rose finished cutting something from a newspaper, dabbed the back with glue from the little pot that had its own special place on the desk, and pasted it onto a page. Underneath the cutting she wrote something – the date, no doubt, a line perhaps with her recollections of the event.

'Why?' Kick had asked once, when she was much younger, watching her mother fill in an index card following a visit by the doctor to Bobby. '*Laryngitis*,' her mother wrote, '*salt water gargle*.'

'Lives need to be ordered,' Rose had replied. 'There are many of you, and if I don't keep careful track, you will run wild. I believe you will all go on to do great things, just as your father has, and my job is to keep account of that.' She never did specify what these 'great things' were to be. At least not for the girls. For the boys – they all knew Joe Jnr was to one day be president of the United States of America. In private, Kick and Jack called him 'Pres', in the same way they now called their father 'Ambassador' – it was a joke, or half a joke; the same as saying Jack would one day walk on the moon, except that when their father talked of such things he wasn't joking.

'There you are, Kathleen,' Rose said now, not looking up. Only her mother called her that. Kick sat in the armchair set beside the window. The morning sun that came slanting in the corner fell onto her lap. She felt she could almost have petted it. She pulled her feet up onto the chair and tucked them in beside her. At that, Rose did look up. Quickly, Kick put her feet down again, crossing them neatly at the ankles.

'The Buckingham Palace Garden Party tomorrow?' Her mother said.

'Yes.' Kick settled herself more comfortably. 'We're to be there for three and Their Majesties arrive at four. Debo says white or cream, and lace or applique, not silk. Oh, and gloves! She says it's a scrum, and the shaking hands is endless. Without gloves, your hands will be filthy. It all sounds boring as anything.' But she spoke affectionately. So much of what had struck her at first as stuffy, or silly, in England – the excessive formalities and implacable bits of tradition – she was now indulgent of, even secretly thrilled by. She had begun to delight in knowing what was expected. Even though she still broke the rules, more and more she did it because she could, and not because she didn't know what the rules were. When she stayed sitting at a dinner table with the men rather than getting up to leave with her hostess, she knew very well what was expected of her. And she also knew that her not leaving would be greeted by a laugh. London society had decided she was to be indulged and petted rather than despised. There was something in the knowledge that she clung to: a freedom, a way to be both inside and out. But more than that. If London society was a game – and clearly it was a game, with very complicated rules – then she planned to win, same as she would win any game. This was a way to do that. To beat all those English girls on their own turf, so that by the time she went home to America, she would know that she had started as the underdog and come out ahead. And, she thought wryly, it was protection too. It meant that if she really did do something terrible – ask the king a direct question or put on lipstick in public – well, they would forgive her.

'I'll need you to watch Rosemary,' Rose said. 'She is invited, and therefore must come, but I don't want her out of our sight.' Kick sighed. It was harder now to keep Rosemary from wandering if she took a mind to. She was stubborn and resisted the way their mother tried more and more to box her in.

'Of course,' she said. Because even more, she disliked the knowledge that her mother would use Rosie's unruliness as an excuse to leave her out.

*

The garden party was even more boring than Debo had hinted.

'Like Fourth of July celebrations but without the fireworks,' Kick said, looking around at the crowds. 'Or a race meeting without a race. Why do they all come?'

'To see who else is here,' Debo said.

'Really? That's it?'

'What else?' Debo opened her lace parasol and held it above her head. 'Can't we find some shade? It's simply too hot.'

'Any bit of shade I can see is full of old people,' Kick said with a laugh. 'That's where they're congregating, like horses in a field.' Her own parents were sitting defiantly in the open at a round table set up almost in the centre of the vast lawn. Rose, face half-hidden under a smart broad-brimmed hat, was slim and elegant in cream. Her father, distinguished in tails. Around them were some of the people Kick had learned were part of what was called the Cliveden Set – Lady Astor, Lord Halifax, others she didn't yet know – whose views her father approved of. But Kick was starting to understand that for all the British were so polite to each other, and invited these people to their balls and houses, they didn't all think like that; like Lady Astor, like her father. Not about Germany. Or anything, really. But then, that's what old people did, she thought. Disagreed with each other and tried to pretend that it mattered what someone said or another thought. Presumably because they had nothing better to do. No more fun to have.

This lot certainly didn't seem to be having much fun, she thought, looking at them huddled together, heads pushed forward into the centre of the table, presumably that they might better hear each other. Only her mother sat back, angled away from the table, watching what went on around her. She would, Kick knew, turn their way any moment. She checked that Rosemary was still beside her, still neat and pretty.

'I'm going to get more lemonade,' Debo said. 'Will you stay or come?'

'I'll stay,' Kick said. 'I can't bring myself to push through that crowd again. My heels sink into the ground and I feel like I'm hobbling. Rosie and I can sit on the grass.' They sat on their lace shawls and Rosie chatted about the dresses she liked. Kick was conscious of the disapproving looks from people standing around them, but it was too hot to care. The weather lay over everything like a damp blanket, as though to make sure nothing caught fire, she thought with a laugh.

She was in the middle of the laugh when Debo came back, with a couple of glasses and a tall young man with a high forehead and a thin smile who carried a jug of lemonade. 'Billy Cavendish, Marquess of Hartington,' Debo said. 'Billy, Kathleen Kennedy, but we call her Kick.'

'How d'you do?' Billy said.

Terrible teeth, was Kick's first thought. Was it always to be her first thought in England? But then he sat easily down beside her and Rosemary, folding up his long arms and legs in a pleasantly shabby set of tails, and poured them lemonade from the jug. 'I hear an awful lot about you these days, you know,' he said to Kick, with a smile that lit up his face and didn't just twitch at his top lip.

'Do you?' she asked. 'Nothing too terrible I hope?' It was silly stuff, but he responded gallantly and soon he was chatting away to them – her and Rosemary both – while Debo watched. Around them, people wandered past, many of them stopping to salute Billy, or put a hand on his shoulder as they went by. The disapproving looks were far less, Kick saw, now that Billy sat with them.

When it was time to go he helped them to their feet, one after another, Kick last. He didn't linger with her hand in his, as Jack or Joe's friends would have, but 'I might see you later,' he said. 'At the Mountbattens'?'

'Oh, you will,' Debo assured him. 'Everyone wants a look at Edwina's new flat. They say it's the biggest flat in London. A *penthouse*, apparently,' she opened her eyes wide, 'whatever that could possibly be.'

'It just means the top floor,' Kick said with a laugh at Debo's affectation. 'Nothing to be too worried about.' She laughed again and Billy laughed too. A real laugh, she thought, not a polite *English* laugh. And he looked at her for longer than English people usually looked. Right at her, rather than slightly over her shoulder. She wondered had Debo noticed. She needed someone to tell her she was right, not imagining things.

'Isn't he wonderful?' she said as they went to find their cars.

But Debo didn't seem to have noticed. She laughed. 'You still haven't met many Englishmen, have you? He's really very ordinary. Simply *thousands* just like him. One day he'll be Duke of Devonshire, but other than that, I doubt there's anything at all to single him out.'

That evening, Kick dressed with more than usual care. She would never be the most beautiful girl in London, she knew that it was her way of being 'jolly fun' that people – men – liked, but she wanted to look as well as she could. Because Debo was wrong, she decided. There weren't thousands like Billy. And neither, she thought, did Billy think there were thousands like her.

The Mountbattens' flat was at the top of a vast new block, with views across all of London. 'It used to be all one house,' Debo said, 'Brook House. Edwina's grandfather bought it. Farve says he was a filthy Hun so he loathed him,' she continued comfortably. 'He tries to loathe Edwina too, but admits it's impossible.'

They went up in a spacious lift, mirrored on every side so that their reflections came back to them over and over. Kick watched her own familiar face from so many angles, then Debo's wide-apart blue eyes and neat mouth. Such a candid face, Kick thought; as unruffled as a child's. That was part of Debo's charm – the extraordinary placidity of her features, and the whirling mind behind them.

Debo nudged her. 'The mirrors are so Edwina can see if any of her lovers is about to jump out at her,' she said. 'You know she is the most scandalous woman in London?'

Kick giggled and was still giggling when the lift opened into a marble hallway and a tall woman in gold silk evening dress, her honey-brown hair dressed in sleek waves, came to greet them. She felt foolish and tried to cover it by being as 'American' as she knew how. This was how she phrased it to herself when she was particularly casual and irreverent. 'You must be able to see all the way into the king's dressing room from here,' she said. Lady Mountbatten just smiled.

'Come and have a drink,' she said vaguely, turning away towards a vast drawing room that was white and gold and filled with flowers.

Debo nudged Kick once again. 'Her husband is the king's cousin,' she hissed, half laughing, but half not. 'He is always in that dressing room.'

Kick tried not to feel idiotic. How was she supposed to know? she thought. Why, if they came to America, there would be a million things they didn't know.

They had drinks called Negronis and a man played the piano

and sang songs. It was a far more grown-up party than the kind Kick was used to. Serious, even muted, in comparison with the usual giddy debutantes and noisy larks. Older people – Lady Mountbatten must have been at least thirty-five, Kick thought – mostly married, moving discreetly about to form groups, then dissolving and reforming in a way that seemed idle but wasn't. And for all that they were old, they had a humming vitality. They didn't shriek, or rag each other, but there was purpose in everything they did. They talked gracefully and intently, not simply piling up jokes the way Kick's friends did.

Debo disappeared and Kick walked through the two large drawing rooms, watching and trying to understand. No one was interested in her. It was a new kind of feeling. At home in America, everyone was interested.

Maybe it's because she was here alone, she thought, watching the sky through the large windows trade shades of blue in an ever-darkening parade. No Jack, no Joe Jnr to sandwich her between them and see that she was included in everything. No one here was impressed with her family, their wealth – Kick wasn't stupid, she knew that was part of it; the whispers about where exactly that wealth had come from – certainly not her opinions. Beyond repeating 'ambassador's daughter?' as though it were a question, when she was introduced to them, no one showed any wish to talk to her.

By a round table in the centre of the second drawing room, she saw Billy. He was part of a group of older men that included Lord Mountbatten, who was thin and watchful with shrewd eyes that never followed his politely smiling mouth. Kick leaned against the back of a spindly sofa and watched. Here too she saw Billy was listened to, regarded. He was someone, and she – clearly – was not.

'Do help yourself to anything . . .' Lady Mountbatten said kindly, passing by but barely pausing.

Kick went to join the group around Billy. He greeted her warmly, taking her hand in his and pressing it, but stayed where he was. A man with a high forehead was talking: '. . . gas masks will be issued next week.'

'Which will start to panic the country,' a thin man with a moustache said. 'Would it not be better to wait?'

'No.' That was Mountbatten. 'We need to get them into every home, and allow time for them to become ordinary, so that people will no more think of going out without them as without a hat or gloves.'

'Give the panic time to subside?' said the thin man.

'Precisely.'

'My father says the opposite,' Kick interjected eagerly. Thanks to Rose's habit of cutting out a newspaper article each day that they were together at Hyannis Port, and insisting they all debate the topic over dinner, she had no fear of giving her opinion. She understood that debate was just a matter of taking opposing views and giving a convincing argument for them; a game, like touch football or tennis. 'He says that issuing gas masks now just means everyone will be sick of them and bored by them in no time. He says that sending them now is like getting down to the last out.'

'What a great deal he says, your father, Ambassador Kennedy,' the thin man said.

Was it the way he emphasised *says* that made the man with the high forehead laugh? she wondered.

'What exactly is "last out?"' Mountbatten asked politely.

'It's from baseball,' Kick said.

'*Baseball*,' he repeated, as though trying out a brand new word. Kick blushed.

'It means you have nowhere left to go, no more chances,' she explained. But her voice sounded thin.

'There's something to that . . .' Billy said. But he said it kindly. And then suggested they look at the view from outside on the balcony, ushering her away. Was it because she was American? she wondered, as they walked out. Or a girl? At the dinner-table discussions at home, she had noticed that her opinions got more attention when she spoke about books or plays, far less when politics were the topic. Or was it something more, even? How was it that they seemed to see the ways in which she was different, when she saw the ways in which they were the same?

'Was it the baseball?' she asked Billy as they leaned over the balcony railings. The sky was darker now, a deep indigo that was the colour of iodine.

'Partly,' he said.

'Only partly?'

'It's more what the baseball represents,' he said cautiously.

'Which is?'

'How far from this you actually are. You see, for us it's all very close to home. So close that baseball metaphors seem a bit . . .'

'A bit off?'

'Exactly.' He sounded awkward.

'In that case, thank you for walking me away.'

'You don't think me frightfully rude?'

'No. I'm glad. I guess I needed it.'

'You know, I'm half sorry I did,' he said then, looking at her in an amused way from the corner of his eye.

'Why?'

'Most people tell Mountbatten exactly what he wants to hear.

So all he ever hears are his own thoughts echoed endlessly back at him.'

'I wouldn't do that even if I knew how. After all, what's the point of a debate if everyone says what other people want to hear?'

'No point at all. But what an unexpected person you are, Kathleen Kennedy.'

'Kick.'

'Kick.' He sounded faintly amused.

'And is that something good, being unexpected?'

'I don't know,' he responded slowly. And he began to show her things out on the skyline – 'See that building . . .' – so that she knew he was uncomfortable. Kick let him, all the while trying to puzzle out which bit was really him? Was it the bit where he was serious and worried, or the bit where he made jokes and laughed? And why was it so strange that she said what she meant?

She thought back to the exchange with Mountbatten and the thin man. How men liked to hear themselves talk, she decided. And war was just another of the things they liked to talk about. No different to sailing or hunting. None of it meant anything. It was no more real than Teddy boasting, 'I will make the biggest sandcastle. I will jump the highest . . .'

Chapter Ten

Kick

'We have been invited to Essex,' Rose said when Kick arrived for the usual morning consultation some days later. 'A place called Kelvedon. Henry Channon – born in Chicago, but now an MP and married to Lady Honor Guinness. The week after next.'

'But I don't have to go, do I?' Kick asked. 'I told Debo I might stay a few days with her.'

'I don't want you staying anywhere Unity is to stay,' Rose said sharply. 'Not since that incident in the park, applesauce though that all was.'

Kick's lips twitched at hearing her mother say 'applesauce'. It was one of her father's expressions, and Kick had always marvelled that a man who didn't curse could get so much vehemence into an innocent little word.

Then she thought about 'the incident'. That had been Debo's sister Unity Mitford – 'defiance itself', as Debo called her, half exasperated, half in admiration – wearing the black-and-red Swastika badge to a Labour Party rally that had been held across the road in Hyde Park, in open delight at the rumours that she was engaged to Herr Hitler. 'She's no more engaged than I am,' Debo had said, 'only she can't resist the trouble and fuss it's causing. Unity is positively addicted to fuss.'

At the rally, the crowd had turned on her after she heckled one of the speakers. They had torn off her badge and trampled on it, then, giddy with their own daring, had made to drag Unity into the Serpentine and dunk her. She had escaped, twisting furiously out of their grasp, and run straight for Prince's Gate, arriving breathless and laughing at the door with her jacket badly torn. Kick had brought her in and tidied her up.

'I wonder you aren't more scared,' she had said, brushing Unity's wiry hair back off her face that had a streak of mud on it.

'Pooh!' Unity had replied, looking at herself in the mirror. 'I wasn't scared a bit.' She reached a hand up to rub at the mud. Underneath was blood. 'I told them I couldn't wait to become a German citizen, just as soon as ever I can. And I meant it.' Her eyes had blazed and her face – so like her beautiful sisters', only larger, with a more pronounced chin and heavy-lidded eyes that turned down at the corners – had glowed with the excitement of being alone in her conviction.

'Unity won't be there,' Kick said now.

'All the same. I don't like that girl. She's troublesome. And in any case, the Channons would like very much to meet you. There will be other young people – Lady Brigid, Honor's sister, who is exactly of an age with you.'

'Must I really go?' Kick asked again, even though she had

come to love these English country-house stays. The ancient houses and great estates varied, places with one name – Cliveden, Blenheim, Hatfield, Belvoir – arrogant in their modesty, or modest in their arrogance, she never could decide; but the rhythms of energy and idleness were almost identical. If they were invited to shoot, there were guns and dogs and men called 'beaters'. If hunting was the thing it was horses, hounds, 'the sound of bugles and beagles', as Debo said. The mornings were early and intense, followed by blissful lazy afternoons of bath and rest and cocktails in the drawing room or on the lawn. One's friends disappearing in their jerseys and skirts, reappearing for dinner draped in satins or silks in fabulous colours. Different creatures. As though with their evening clothes and hair pomade they had put on a new and languid grace.

Most of all, it was finding so much history everywhere – on the walls, in paintings and tapestries, carved into the stone, even in the layout of gardens. And the families, who seemed to be proud and ignorant at once of what lay around them.

'We hardly see it,' Debo had said airily when Kick remarked on this during a stay at Blenheim, invited by the Duke of Marlborough's granddaughter, Sarah.

'Oh, but you sure know it's there,' Kick had responded. 'Especially if anyone else looks like forgetting.'

'Very true,' Debo had said with a smile. 'How quick you are.'

'It's not that I'm quick, especially, only that I say things straight that you English never will.'

'Not just us English,' Debo had insisted. 'You say things "straight", as you put it, that no one else anywhere ever will!'

But there were reasons not to leave London just now. *A reason,* if she was truthful. Billy. The idea of being away for days, even a whole week, well, she thought, it was awful. He might forget about her. Meet someone else. There was that Irene girl he used to go about with, Debo had said. She was the daughter of an earl or something. Since the night of the Mountbattens' party when he had been so careful not to say it, Kick knew that Billy liked her – she was used to men liking her; her brothers' friends always did – but that didn't mean he would remember that he liked her if someone else distracted him. He didn't ring her up the way other men did – proposing a drive, a drink. Not yet. But when they did see one another – once at a lunch given by Lady Spencer, twice at the Café de Paris and, yes, she knew that keeping such careful count was an instant giveaway – he was sure to talk to her, ask her to dance, stay by her side, in a way that was friendly. But something more too.

'It doesn't sound so much fun,' she continued. 'Maybe I could invite the Guinness girl over here one afternoon instead?' That was just the ticket, she thought. Invite her over, ply her with cakes and sodas from the giant fridge in the kitchen Rose had had shipped over specially, play her the latest jazz records from America. And be free that night, every night, to go out, go to parties, and maybe bump into Billy.

But Rose gave a tight smile. 'It's not for fun, Kathleen dear. It's serious. All of this is serious. Now, take a hat when you go out. You really must keep the sun from your face. English girls are never so freckled.'

Dismissed, Kick telephoned to Debo. 'I wish I wasn't going,' she said, 'but once Mother has made up her mind, well, it isn't at all possible to change it. This is what comes of playing hostess all those weeks before she arrived; somehow I'm now part of the package, like Pa has two wives with him.'

Debo laughed. 'How absurd you are. But you'll enjoy it. Honor is terribly dull, but Brigid is a dear.'

'Maybe. But why now?' Kick wailed. 'Just when it feels like . . .'

'Like what?'

'Well, like something interesting might be about to happen . . .'

'*Something interesting . . .*' Debo mocked. 'You may as well say his name, darling; you aren't at all good at hiding it. Well, maybe something can be worked out.'

'What kind of something?'

'I don't know yet. But come for dinner at Diana's tomorrow? Nothing terribly formal, just a tiny supper with friends? She particularly told me to say "*Please be a darling and don't say no because it will be simply too dreary without you to cheer us all up*".'

'In that case how could I possibly say no?' Kick said with a laugh.

Her father put his head around the door then. 'Walk me to my appointment?'

Kick said goodbye and ran to get a hat before he could change his mind, or her mother could interfere.

They walked briskly through Hyde Park where the trees were thick with summer leaves that rustled, green and important, in the breeze. 'How are you finding it?' he asked.

'Oh, I love it,' she assured him.

'You do, don't you?' He considered her. 'And what do you make of them?' He waved his hand to take in the park, the crescent of houses behind them, the people walking sedately by.

'Well,' she said, then paused. 'I think they might not be exactly what I thought.'

'In what way?'

'I thought at first that no one was ever serious,' she explained.

'Everything, always, a joke. But now I'm not so sure. Or at least, if it is a joke, it's not just a joke.'

'Insincerity,' he agreed. 'Damned irritating.'

'I don't think it's exactly insincerity,' she tried to explain. 'Just that they go about things differently.'

'I hear you coming in at all hours,' he said then.

'Mother knows,' she said quickly. And Rose did. At least, she knew Kick was out. Just not where. Or how late she came home. Rose wouldn't approve of nightclubs, not at all. And so Kick didn't tell her. *We went on*, she would say, vaguely, when Rose asked. It was a phrase she'd picked up from Debo. A useful one. 'Someone always sees me home,' she assured him. 'David or Hugh, any of those fellows.' Not Billy. Not yet.

'And what do these young men say about the situation with Germany?' he asked, direct as always.

'Last night Hugh Fraser said that at least if they were called up they wouldn't have to sit through any more of Lady Furness' terrible dinners . . .'

'Idiotic pup!' her father said angrily.

'I don't think he meant it . . .'

But the ambassador wasn't listening. 'They all told me that England was a spent force,' he said, poking hard at the ground with his sturdy ivory-topped cane. 'If anything, it seems worse than that.'

'Is that what you meant when you said they were madder than you'd hoped?'

'Yes. There's a disregard for consequences . . . They'd sleep-walk into trouble, led by that old war horse Churchill, if it wasn't for Chamberlain. Well, they'll get no help from me. No, sir. And without America, even Churchill's enthusiasm is dampened.' He spoke with satisfaction. 'Oh I know what they say about me,' he continued. 'That darned Randolph, Churchill's idiot son –' he put on a sneering English accent '– "*I thought my daffodils were yellow until I met Joe Kennedy . . .*"'

Kick flinched. She hadn't heard that one, although she had begun to hear whispers that her father didn't have 'enough stomach for a fight'.

'But I don't care,' he continued. 'Let 'em say what they like. I know what war is. If I can prevent it, why, I'll take all they can throw at me. And if preventing it means taking tea with Channon, followed by dinner with Lady Cunard, then drinks with von Ribbentrop, I'll do it. I'll talk to anyone who'll talk to me.'

'You're like the girl at the party everyone wants to dance with,' she said with a gurgle of laughter. She preferred that to the idea that he was 'yellow'.

'You could say that. Although from what I hear, that girl is you.'

'Sometimes,' she said modestly. Then, curious, 'So what really is the difference between Churchill and Chamberlain?' She heard the names mentioned so often, but hadn't got them straight in her head.

'They are the two sides of this coin,' the ambassador explained. 'Churchill wants ultimatums, shows of strength. Chamberlain is a diplomat, a man of compromise and peace. Right now, there are more who favour Chamberlain's way, but Churchill is gaining ground.'

'Churchill bad, Chamberlain good, I'll keep that in mind.'

'Keep distance in mind,' he said. 'Don't be drawn in. Don't give your opinions or agree too heartily with others. Be friendly, but don't be friends.'

'Distance. Got it,' Kick said. But she spoke absently, already thinking about dinner with Diana Mitford. What would she wear?

Chapter Eleven

Berlin
Doris

The Tiergarten encounter was still on Doris' mind days later when she woke, again, to the sound of Hannah's bow scraping. And through that day while shopping in the Kaisergalerie and later when she went to pay a call on the daughter of a prominent newspaper editor, a girl her own age who wanted to improve her English, and who talked, Doris thought, about nothing except tennis. Even as she politely corrected Ilse – '*I think*, not *I am thinking*' – she considered what it was she did in Berlin, and how useful it might still be. She had no way of knowing, she realised.

She had heard nothing since the encounter, but that wasn't unusual. She knew to wait. To go about her life until such time as they told her more. Or indeed, didn't tell her more.

Sometimes, the approaches led to nothing. A half-idea begun and then abandoned without consulting her. That was the way of it. She decided nothing, only played her small part in what others decided.

She thought so much about it that she entirely forgot her promise to teach Hannah, and it was several days before she remembered. Or rather, before Hannah reminded her when they again met in the lift. 'You said you'd show me a trick,' she said bluntly. 'For holding the bow.'

'Hannah!' her mother said.

'No, she's perfectly correct,' Doris reassured her. 'I did say that, and then I forgot. But I will, as soon as ever you'll let me.'

'Now?' Hannah said.

'Come for tea, tomorrow afternoon?' Beatrice said with a smile.

The next afternoon, Beatrice greeted her at the door. 'Hannah is brushing her hair,' she said. 'She wants to make a good impression.'

'Of course,' Doris said.

'Whatever is to be done, Hannah will try to do it as best she can,' Beatrice said, rolling her eyes a little. 'She is so very serious in everything.'

'Your only daughter?' Doris asked.

'Yes, an only child. She's probably too much with my husband and me. It makes her older than her years.'

'Your husband is at work?'

'Yes.' Beatrice hesitated a moment. 'He is out.'

It was, Doris thought, a correction rather than an addition. She shook her head slightly. She really must try to stop parsing every word that was said to her, cutting and slicing sentences this way and that to see if there were more meanings, other meanings, than what they seemed. Hannah arrived, in a white frock that was too tight, hair loose around her shoulders.

The apartment was smaller than hers and had no views onto Leipziger Strasse, but only onto the rather narrow street that ran off it. But it was pleasantly furnished with a great many books and paintings, mostly views of Berlin streets, corners of the city's many parks.

'You paint?' she asked.

'My husband,' Beatrice said. 'In his spare time.'

'Papa is an artist,' Hannah said proudly.

'He's not,' Beatrice said with a laugh. 'He's a clerk. But he does like to paint.'

'Only streets and parks, never people?'

'He says Berlin is his inspiration, that he wants to capture the changing light and shade and atmosphere of the city.'

They talked about art then, about Hannah's school – 'I am on summer holidays now,' she clarified – and then Beatrice asked what Doris knew she would eventually: 'Where are you from?' Her German was good enough that she passed as native in brief conversations. But anything more and she could feel the question building.

'England,' she said. 'But my mother is German. I moved here a year ago, a little more.'

'England,' Beatrice repeated.

'We remember when you arrived,' Hannah said.

'You do?'

'We knew you were one person,' Hannah said, 'because the *hausmeister* told us, and we thought we'd never seen so many dress boxes and trunks for just one person before.'

Doris laughed.

'And because you played such wonderful music on your gramophone,' Hannah said wistfully. 'American, I think?'

'Sshhh.' Beatrice nudged Hannah sharply, making an alarmed O with her mouth.

'But you don't play it anymore?' the girl continued. 'Only classical?'

'I prefer that now,' Doris said evasively. She had quickly understood that her records – Cole Porter, Duke Ellington – were a bad idea, viewed with suspicion, even disgust, by the people she needed to get to know. And so she had thrown them away, wrapping them in many layers of newspaper before putting them in the bin, in case the *hausmeister*, whom she mistrusted, dig through and see them. She had replaced the emptiness with Bach, Wagner, Handel.

'Let me show you the trick I learned with the bow.' She and Hannah went to the girl's bedroom and Doris tried to teach her what she remembered. 'You must hold with the very ends of your fingers, and play as if your arm is on a string suspended from the ceiling. The string takes all the weight, so there is no weight in your hand.'

'Yes, I think I see . . .' Hannah said, grasping the bow firmly.

She didn't see. Doris, squashing a laugh, understood immediately that there was no way the girl would be able to learn what she taught, but so solemn was Hannah in her efforts, so honest in her determination, that Doris sat with her anyway and called encouragement. 'Yes, jolly good, I think you are really getting it now . . .'

When she went back to the drawing room, Beatrice was turning a stocking. She smiled at Doris. 'How kind you are. I don't think she will ever trouble the people of the Philharmonie, but she wants so badly to learn.' Then, 'May I ask you something?'

'Of course.' Doris wondered would she ask her to come regularly, to give Hannah lessons. If she did, she would say yes, Doris decided. She hadn't realised how much she missed the company of her own little sisters and brother. To spend her afternoons with Hannah would be a pleasure.

'How do we get to England?' Beatrice asked bluntly.

Doris felt her eyes open wide.

'I'm sorry,' Beatrice said. 'I know that's abrupt. Probably uncomfortable for you. But we don't have time . . . We have been trying to get to England, and we have found no way, except to try and send Hannah on her own and we don't want to do that.'

'Of course you don't,' Doris said automatically, trying to catch up.

'Is there any way that you know of that we can go? I thought maybe, because you are English, you might know things that we do not?'

'I don't . . .' Doris stalled. Then, 'Forgive me . . . you are Jewish?'

'Yes.'

'I didn't realise.'

'It's not a thing one wants anyone to realise these days,' Beatrice said bitterly. 'It's why we want to leave. Hannah doesn't know yet, but after the summer she won't be going back to her school. They don't want her. There is another school she can go to but it is further away . . . But it isn't that. Not just that. My husband has lost his job. He is out, with his paints, but he no longer works. We want to get away, but there is nowhere for us to go. No country we can reach that will take us.'

'You have family?'

'In Poland, where my husband is from. But we cannot go there. Better even to stay here than that. Please. I know this is unexpected, even rude,' she shook her head, 'but the chance of meeting you, of your being English, I couldn't not.'

'I will think,' Doris said. 'I will see if there is anything . . .'

'Maybe you know someone,' Beatrice persisted, so that Doris understood just how far need outstripped manners in this diffident woman. 'Someone who can help us?'

'I will see,' Doris said again.

'Thank you.'

Hannah came back then. 'I really think I have the hang of it now,' she said. 'Will you hear me?' She played the Dvořák piece again, from start to finish, brows creased in concentration above the chin rest. It was no better, Doris thought, not at all, but Hannah was delighted. 'I cannot wait to play for Herr Meinder,' she said, 'when my lessons start again.' She went back to her room to put the violin away.

'Her lessons won't start again,' Beatrice said bitterly. 'Herr Meinder no longer teaches her. He *no longer finds that it is possible.*' She made a tight, twisting movement with her hands, as though scraping something from them, then picked up her darning again. 'So many things, it seems, are no longer possible . . .'

Back in her own apartment that evening, Doris put a record on the gramophone as she dressed to go out, and began to list to herself the people who might help. There were many, she thought joyfully, trying on a dress of cream lace. And yet, as she listed the names to herself, with every one there came to her reasons why she could not ask them. Until she realised that it was only one reason; each time, the same reason. And that she was the reason. To intervene – to try and help – put everything she did at risk. By reaching out a hand to help this family, she rocked a boat that was barely steady. She exposed herself to being understood in a way that she couldn't be understood. All the work she did – the meetings that weren't meetings, the chance encounters that weren't chance, the lunches and parties, the little bits of news and whispered gossip that came her way and were moved by her onwards to where others might find value in them – all that became impossible if she was seen to act in any way for Beatrice, Hannah, her father. To become friends with them or allow her life to tangle with theirs was to threaten everything else she did.

The knowledge was hateful. She resisted it. Until, having tried to bend it in her mind every which way, she realised there was no resisting. To help them was to expose herself. She finished dressing and went to dinner and then a nightclub and was so very charming, so sophisticated and amusing, that a man she had long set her sights on because he was known to be close to Herr Göring drove her home as dawn was breaking and tried to kiss her. She let him, but only for a moment.

'I must go up,' she murmured. 'The *hausmeister* is such a disapproving fellow, you cannot imagine . . .'

He laughed and she rested her head briefly on his shoulder.

'You will visit me,' he said urgently, 'at my lake *schloss*. You must!'

'I would love to.' And she went upstairs and brushed her hair until her head hurt, because that was better than crying.

The next day, crossing the brown marble lobby, Doris saw Beatrice and Hannah come towards her. She waved and stepped briskly past them. 'I'm just on my way out,' she called. Beatrice smiled and nodded. And did the same a few days later when

Doris, seeing them at the lift, said, 'I have forgotten my purse, I must go back for it. Don't stop the lift for me.'

After that, a card was pushed under her door, inviting her to take tea again. She wrote a note of regret, put it under their door and walked quickly away. She heard her name called as she reached her own apartment, but pretended she had not and shut the door smartly behind her.

It didn't take very long, she thought sadly. Not long at all, before Beatrice understood and walked past Doris with no more than a nod when they encountered one another. Hannah took a little longer, but soon she too, guided by her mother's hand pressing into her shoulder, her mother's quickened step and curt greeting, stopped trying to talk to Doris. Soon, they no longer ran into each other, and Doris wondered did they plan their entrances and exits carefully to avoid her, as she now did to avoid them? If so, it was for the best.

And all the while, she waited, every day, for the sounds of Hannah's violin. She found that if she opened the little window in the bathroom that looked onto the dark side street, she could hear better. She would get up in the morning, when the first sounds started, open the window and get back in to bed, and listen as Hannah scraped her way through the Dvořák, bits of Beethoven, some old hymns that Doris half knew. She never got any better, but hearing her, knowing she was still there, was the greatest comfort.

Chapter Twelve

London
Kick

The 'tiny supper with friends' was in Diana's little house in Eaton Square, and turned out to be Diana, Debo, Unity – Kick had deliberately not asked would she be there, in order to be able to answer truthfully when her mother asked, '*I don't know, but I don't expect so*' – and Diana's husband, Sir Oswald Mosley. Kick had found him alarming the few times they had met – although Debo insisted he was 'a perfect lamb really' – and knew her father would be furious to think she had dined with him; 'I don't say he's all wrong,' was the ambassador's view of Mosley, 'but the man's intemperate, and his mob of fascists are a menace.' *Distance, Kick*, she remembered him saying. *Distance . . .*

With Mosley was a man called David Envers who was small

where Mosley was tall, quiet where Mosley was talkative, indifferent where Mosley was charming, and otherwise like him in every way.

'How sweet of you to come,' Diana said, swooping in and kissing her on both cheeks. Kick was tall, but Diana was taller, and seemed taller again because of how she held herself, all drawn upwards. 'I know we have met, but I feel this time we are really to be friends.' She smiled and pressed Kick's hands, which she held in both of hers. To Kick, who had always seen Diana as coldly glamorous – remote as one of the white-bright stars that shone on black winter nights – this sudden rush of approval was intoxicating.

They ate tiny birds – quail, someone said – that had been roasted whole, with a red wine and mushroom sauce. The food was served at a small round table, polished and bare, no tablecloth, just silver cutlery. And Diana herself brought it in – no footmen, no butlers – although she laughed when Kick asked had she done the cooking.

'I dare you to say you did,' Unity said, looking at her sister. 'I dare you, that's all.' Kick wondered how she was brave enough to mock someone as terrifying as Diana.

But Diana just smiled. 'Found out!' she said. 'I didn't. I couldn't. I have tried. Boud will tell you' – Boud, Kick knew, was Unity – 'a chicken, simply cooked, with lashings of cream. Only it was too dreadful. As hard as that old pheasant Maureen Guinness serves night after night at Clandeboye, should one be unwise enough to go there. Like eating actual gunshot. Too mortifying, wasn't it, darling?' she added, turning to Mosley, who looked back at her with eyes that were dark and shiny like coal in an outdoor scuttle where the rain runs off it, leaving it slick but not wet. 'Since then, I leave it to Mrs Taylor.'

'I don't need you to cook,' Mosley said, taking her hand and kissing it. 'That is not what I need in a wife.' He turned her hand over and slowly kissed the soft white underside of her wrist. Kick felt herself blushing and ducked her head. Imagine married people behaving like that? But then, she knew they weren't married very long. Maybe that was it. She looked up and found David Envers watching her, an almost sympathetic look on his impassive face.

'Darling, do stop,' Unity said to Diana, flicking her eyes to Kick, '*pas devant les enfants*.'

'French, Boud?' Diana said. 'How unlike you.'

'Thoroughly,' Unity agreed. 'You know how I hate all things French – almost as much as I love all things German. But *le mot juste* is still *le mot juste*.'

Everyone laughed at that, and Kick saw that here, with these people, Unity wasn't the absurd, half-mad figure she was made out to be by the rest of the world. Here, they had drawn up their own rules and code, and by them, Unity was someone funny, sweet, precious. She wondered what to make of that.

'How is your German coming along?' Diana asked.

'Badly. You know how too frightful it is to learn foreign languages.' Unity shuddered. 'And how simply mortifying to try and speak them. But I am determined, so that by the time my engagement to Hitler is announced for real –' she looked hard at Kick as she said this, a mean little smile at the corners of her mouth '– I will at least be able to manage a few sentences.'

'Boud, don't *stir*.' That was Debo, who gave Kick an apologetic grin as she said it.

Kick was relieved at the grin. She did hope Unity wouldn't start going on about Hitler. Dinner was one thing, but she knew well what her father meant about distance, even when she pretended she didn't. Sometimes conversations had a way of leaping ahead of her, often only half-explained, so that she struggled to understand exactly what was being said, but knew she had somehow ventured beyond 'distance'.

The three sisters were funny together, Kick thought, watching the way they teased each other, finished each other's sentences, made jokes that no one else understood. It was as though they had their own private language – a blur of nursery slang, references to old jokes and half-finished phrases. They were by turns sharp and affectionate, and quite unlike the open competition, the eager engagement, of Kick and her older brothers. And yet, they were like them too. Exactly as Debo had said – a family that was a tribe, with their own customs. She and her brothers and sisters were the same. How many times had someone said, 'You Kennedys, you're too much', with affection, or resentment?

Mosley watched the sisters indulgently in a way that reminded Kick of something but she couldn't recall precisely what, until Unity demanded, 'What did you think of the Führer's speech yesterday? Did you see how it was reported in *The Times*?'

'Better than it was reported elsewhere,' Envers said.

But Mosley put a hand up. 'Hush, Unity,' he said. 'We said no politics tonight.'

Unity looked as though she wouldn't heed him, opened her mouth defiantly, then closed it and shrugged. 'Very well,' she said, 'but it's not politics to me.'

And then Kick understood. He was like her father, at Hyannis Port, conducting discussion around the lunch and dinner table as though his children were a choir attuned to his baton; calling up now this voice, now that, bringing them out then stowing them away again. The base notes that were Joe Jnr and Jack; hers a contralto maybe; the girls, Eunice, Pat and Jean, altos;

and the little boys, sopranos still, but with depth there. She looked at Mosley, who looked back at her.

'Kathleen,' he said, 'why don't you tell us what you think of England – and us English? You've had long enough to consider us all. And I don't imagine you are slow to opinions.'

'Oh, Kick loves everything English,' Debo said. 'Especially anything beginning with B . . .'

'Why B?' Unity demanded. Diana looked from Kick to Debo and raised her thin eyebrows to high arches. 'Why B?' Unity asked again, looking from Kick to Debo to Diana. 'I hate when no one tells me things!'

Kick could see they were making a big fuss of her, but didn't understand why until, after dinner, when, instead of sitting over their port, the men came straight into the drawing room, and Mosley came to sit beside her. Swiftly, Diana crossed the room and sat on Kick's other side. It was, Kick thought nervously, like sitting between two large cats.

Mosley asked her more questions – about England, about America – that were broad and innocent, and yet made Kick feel uncomfortably as though she was telling secrets when she tried to answer them. He listened so closely to everything she said, smoking cigarette after cigarette, blowing smoke from the side of his mouth away from her, that if he hadn't been married, if his wife hadn't been sitting so close to Kick that their arms were touching, if she hadn't reached over and taken Kick's hand at the very moment that Mosley said, 'I do want us all to be friends,' Kick would have thought he was making a pass.

As it was, she didn't know what to think, and so she said something polite, casting for an excuse to remove her hand from Diana's. Diana must have felt the twitch that meant she wanted it released, but she squeezed tighter. Then, letting go of Kick's hand, she ran a finger lightly down her cheek. 'What pretty freckles you have.'

'My mother says I need to wear a hat, that English girls are never so freckled,' she blurted out.

'A pity for English girls,' Diana said lightly.

She couldn't mean it, Kick thought, looking at the smooth creaminess of Diana's face. But she felt a warm glow that she had bothered to say it.

'I hear you have met the pope,' Mosley said.

'I have,' Kick said, eager to tell her story. 'I was in Rome for Holy Week a few years ago, and I met His Holiness and Il Duce on the very same day, can you imagine?'

'I can try,' Mosley said, twinkling warmly at her. 'If I'm right, it was a family friend who made the audience with His Holiness possible?' Did he choke, just a tiny bit, on the word *Holiness*? Kick wondered.

'Cardinal Pacelli,' Kick agreed, remembering the cardinal who had been so kind to her on her trip to the Vatican, and how, when he had come to America a year later, he had stayed with her family in Bronxville.

'The very man.'

'Do you know him?'

'I hope to,' Mosley said.

'Did you know,' Diana interjected with a laugh, her large eyes with their tiny pupils – black dots swimming in a sea of pale blue – open wide, 'that in Leeds, there are so many Catholic members of the British Union of Fascists that Mosley's nickname is "The Pope"?'

Mosley must have seen the shock on Kick's face, because he shook his head – a tiny shake – at Diana, and said smoothly,

'My wife jokes, of course. Although –' thoughtfully '– it's true that our cause appeals to a great number of Catholics, who understand instinctively, as we do, that there is right and wrong in the world, and that sometimes it is a matter of what we feel more even than what we think.' He paused and looked for a long time at Kick. 'Catholics are clever at understanding that there is only so far that logic can take us. That sometimes feelings lead us to know things that mere logic cannot. Don't you agree? It is this same sense of trust, of *faith* – may I call it the discipline of faith? –' Kick nodded, even though she didn't know exactly what she was nodding at '– that Catholics understand.'

He talked fast, but picked his words with care. Kick could feel him doing it – considering one, then another, discarding, choosing. 'The truth is, we feel certain that, just as Rome supported General Franco in his crusade against communism, so Rome will support Germany.' He paused. Was he waiting for her to agree? How strange it was that he talked of *Catholics* as though they were different to simply *people*. 'But I suppose your father knows a great deal more?' Again, that inviting pause. 'Perhaps one day he might make it possible for me to exchange these views with Cardinal Pacelli.'

'I'm sure he'd love to,' she said, thinking of her parents' delight in showing the cardinal around New York, introducing him to their friends and in turn meeting with his acquaintance. Mosley smiled. Which made Kick remember that she was the ambassador's daughter, and that for all her hosts' charm there was no such thing as idle conversation. The wine at dinner must have made her fuzzy. 'I mean,' she temporised, 'someday, if the cardinal ever visits England . . .' How much simpler things had been in America, where she needed only to think about sports and lessons and who to go to the ballgame with.

'Darling, why don't you show Kathleen Mildred's puppies?' Mosely said, as though reading her uncomfortable thoughts. Mildred was Diana's whippet. 'They are in a basket in the bedroom.'

Diana swept Kick, Debo and Unity upstairs to a room upholstered in shades of peony silk that was so voluptuous as to be positively lascivious, with a bed so large it was impossible, looking at it, not to think of the things that might happen there. Remembering Mosley's hot, wet eyes, Kick found herself blushing. When she looked up, Diana was staring at her, an amused smile on her face.

'Would you like to hold one?' she said, of the puppies. 'Mildred is such a perfect angel, she will not mind. They are the softest little creatures you can imagine. Like stroking baby mice.' She deposited a puppy in Kick's lap.

'Like velvet,' Kick said.

'You know,' Diana said as she handed a puppy to Debo, who immediately began kissing its nose, 'we think it's a jolly good thing that your father should have been sent, and that he should have brought so many of his wonderful family. We all admired – so much! – how *well* you managed as hostess in the beginning, before your mother arrived.'

Kick felt a wonderful rush of feeling at the thought that she had been seen – watched and observed and approved of.

'We do hope you will feel at home here,' Diana continued. 'And that you know you can come to us for anything at all you might need, even the tiniest thing. You do feel that, don't you?'

Kick, locked in the beam of those headlamp eyes, nodded; warm and flattered by the interest of this beautiful, glamorous woman whom she heard spoken of in tones of near-reverence. 'We will,' she said solemnly. 'I will.'

'Why,' Diana said, as though such a thing had only occurred to her, 'you might come to one of Mosley's rallies. You have no idea how they worship him. I do think you would enjoy it. The girls could bring you.' She inclined her head towards Debo and Unity.

'They are ever such a rip,' Unity said. 'You'll see.'

Kick stammered something, unwilling to commit, unsure how to avoid – her father would never allow it, or would he? Obviously he and Mosley had similar views on war – and she knew her mother would appreciate his words on the church and the discipline of faith – but did that mean she could attend *rallies*? Oh why must everything be so complicated? She sighed.

Again Diana was quick. 'Let's go out,' she said. 'A nightclub. Café de Paris? I'm sure it's simply filled with lovely things beginning with B.'

Unity looked cross. 'Why is everyone talking in a code I don't understand.'

Mosley saw them to the club in a taxi but didn't come with them. 'Better I don't,' he said, tilting Diana's face up towards him and kissing her. Kick looked away quickly, face prickling with embarrassment, so that she was looking quite the wrong way when he came to say goodbye to her and was flustered as he took her hand. The chill neon of the Café de Paris sign above them flickered and in its ghostly light Mosley looked as though drawn in charcoal, the thin black dividing line of his moustache and his black eyes picked out stark in the white of his face. He bowed gracefully. 'So nice to meet you.' He lingered over *nice*. 'See you again.'

Without him or Envers, Diana was almost cosy. She found them a table – by staring so hard at two young men seated together that they hastily got up and offered their places, at which Debo laughed and said, 'Ever the hunter, aren't you?' – and ordered Champagne.

'Ghastly crowd,' Diana said cheerfully, looking around. 'Last year's debs and a smattering of the demi-monde. I don't know why they call it the Café de Paris, far more like the Café de Croydon.'

Unity went to 'look for pals'.

'Tell me more about your brothers,' Diana asked Kick. 'We have only the one. Curious lot, brothers, aren't they? I think poor Tom was surprised to find he wasn't actually a girl when he was seven or eight.'

Kick threw her head back and laughed. 'I don't think Joe and Jack have ever been in any doubt,' she said. 'In fact, I'm the one who had a hard time understanding that I wasn't the same as them.'

'What do you mean?'

'Able to run as fast, play football, sail, all the things they did that I wanted to do.'

'Kick is a frightful tomboy,' Debo said.

'Everyone's a tomboy compared with you,' Diana said with a smile. 'What about now?' she asked Kick. 'Do you still want to do everything they do?'

'Oh yes. And more. All the freedom they have . . .'

'To do what?'

'Whatever they want,' Kick said simply. 'Go where they want, meet who they want. Do anything, be anything.'

'It is unfair,' Diana agreed.

'Diana is a great believer in equality,' Debo said with a smile. 'She has all sorts of ideas.'

'Mosley has them too,' Diana said.

A man approached them and after reminding Diana that they had met – 'at the Astors" – asked her to dance.

'Lord, no,' she said, turning cold and languid where she had been warm and funny, so that the man blushed – Kick could see his ears turn red even in the dim light – and retreated.

'How mean you are,' Debo said lightly.

'How absurd they are,' Diana retorted.

After that she fell silent, smoking and looking around with eyes so large they seemed to absorb all the light, leaving less for the rest of them. Unity came back with a girl in a tight pink dress and they both laughed immoderately at what seemed like private jokes. 'Whatever happened to Ratular?' the girl in pink asked. Ratular, Kick knew, was Unity's pet rat, often brought to parties and balls where he would sit on Unity's lap or run from one arm to the other along her shoulders.

'He's alright,' Unity said. 'I need to find him a dear little lady rat friend so they can have sweet babies.'

The girl shrieked. 'You wouldn't!'

'Of course I would. Why not? I'd rather more rats in the world than more people. Rats are jolly intelligent and ever so sweet. Most people are simply frightful.'

'You are funny, Unity,' the girl said.

But Kick didn't think Unity was joking. She sounded perfectly serious. Even more so when she said fervently, 'Some people – some *peoples* – are especially frightful, much more like vermin than dear, sweet rats.' What did she mean? Kick wondered.

'Not now, Unity,' Diana said with a frown that creased her thin eyebrows.

Kick was bored and wanted to dance, but no one asked her. She hoped it was because Diana had scared them all away and not because they didn't want to dance with her. She realised that she had been counting on Billy being here. Had been keyed up with the anticipation of running into him. Now that he wasn't, she felt tired and strangely flat.

Just as she was about to say she wanted to go home, Debo nudged her. 'I spy with my tiny eye, something – some*one* – starting with B . . .' She jerked her head up towards the balcony that curved around the room, finishing in two staircases that descended in a double sweep behind the bandstand. Sure enough, there he was, leaning over the balcony rail with a cigarette in his hand. He saw her immediately. Just as she was wondering how to play it – should she pretend she hadn't seen him? Be deep in conversation with Debo? Or better still, a man? – he waved over and began to make his way along the balcony to the stairs. Behind him a girl in a white evening dress – Irene, Kick saw – started after him, then looked down. She too saw Kick, and screwed her face up in irritation.

'I say.' Billy arrived at their table. 'How jolly.'

'Billy, darling,' Debo said. 'Will you have Champagne?'

'No, for I should only have to drink it.'

'Too exhausting,' Diana agreed solemnly, so that Debo laughed and Kick wondered what was funny.

'Will you come and dance?' he asked her.

Kick, conscious of Diana, Debo and Unity all staring at her, got up quickly. 'Sure, I'd love to,' she said.

He took her hand and as they walked to the dancefloor, she heard Unity's piping tones: '*Something beginning with B . . . Oh, I see . . .*'

The dancefloor was full of couples swaying gently, and Teddy Brown's band were playing 'I Get a Kick out of You'.

'How very apt,' Billy murmured, pulling her to him. He held her close, but not close the way the fellows in America did, so that you were almost crushed against their chests. With Billy, they were still separate from one another, just. And somehow it was all the more intoxicating. She breathed deep, the lemon tang of his cologne and French cigarettes.

'Aren't you brave, having dinner with that lot,' he said when she told him how she had spent her evening. The way he said it, she wasn't sure that *brave* didn't mean something else. 'Diana makes one think of a car simply hurtling along a narrow road towards one, with those great eyes and that tremendously fixed purpose. If she weren't so terrifying she'd be a frightful bore.'

She laughed, and tried to think of something to say that would amuse him. 'She says that in Leeds they call Mosley "The Pope".'

He stiffened, drawing back a little from her.

She quickly changed the subject. 'My little brothers, Teddy and Bobby, opened a new petting zoo. Teddy cut the ribbon with a pair of scissors nearly as big as he is.'

'How sweet,' he said. 'Did you go too?'

'I did, and I nearly took one of the penguins home with me in my pocket. They were just the cutest. If Unity can have a pet rat, why should I not have a pet penguin?'

'I cannot think of a single reason,' he said gallantly. 'Certainly if anyone could pull it off, you could.'

They danced some more – the band were in melancholy humour and all the songs were slow – and Kick let herself drift with the feel of him against her. He was so tall that her cheek barely reached his shoulder. Perhaps she should wear higher heels, she thought. When the music speeded up, Billy pulled back slightly to look down at her. 'All the same,' he said seriously, 'I wonder should you go about with Diana and Mosley?'

'But I don't—' she began.

'Especially now,' he continued. 'Now that things are, well, are uncertain . . .'

Kick tried to think what to say: that she barely knew Diana and had only met Mosley a handful of times? Anyway, what was uncertain?

'My father says this will all settle down,' she tried. 'He says it's just a question of getting used to a new player and that Hitler will be perfectly alright once he's proven himself on the pitch.' Somehow she felt safe telling Billy what her father said, in a way she hadn't with Mosley.

'More baseball?' he said, but his smile was stiff. 'The only problem with that is that it rather looks as though Hitler's way to prove himself means war.'

'Oh, but there is no need for England to fight another war,' Kick said eagerly.

'I'm not sure it can be avoided.'

'Don't worry, my father is here to make sure that doesn't happen.' She spoke gaily, but there was a sharp little silence.

'I'm not sure it *should* be avoided.' He spoke with less than his usual languor.

She was almost grateful when Irene came up behind them then and tapped Billy smartly on the shoulder.

'There you are,' she drawled. 'I've been sent to rescue you.' She shot a cross look at Kick. Billy said something polite about not needing to be rescued, but allowed Irene to lead him away and didn't seem at all upset about it.

Damn the talk of war, she thought. It always spoiled everything. She believed her father; if he said a thing, then the thing was true. That's what she had always learned. But for the first time, she felt the pull of another's opinions – Billy's – that were so opposite to her father's. It was an uncomfortable feeling. Because if Billy was right – if war shouldn't be avoided – then her father was wrong. And he had never been wrong.

She went to sit down. Andrew, Billy's brother, had pulled up a chair and was deep in conversation with Debo, leaning towards her and laughing hard at everything she said. He went to get them more drinks and Debo turned to Kick.

'Well?' she asked sympathetically.

'I don't know.' Kick shrugged. 'I really don't. I mean, if I was in America, I'd know. Or if I didn't, I'd just ask him straight out.'

'You wouldn't!'

'I might.'

'How I should like to see that.' Debo grinned. 'But no. It won't do. We shall just have to find out.'

'How? Especially now when Mother is making me go away with these Channon people.'

'Actually, I think I can manage something,' Debo said. 'I've been asked to the Blounts – their place is jolly near – and Billy and his parents have too. He thought he wouldn't go, but perhaps I can persuade him that he should. Something away from London . . .' she mused. 'Everything is different in the country. Especially in the summer.'

'Would you really?'

'Really.'

'It would be the perfect way for Billy to meet Mother.' Kick's mind began racing ahead. 'Like that, at a weekend party—'

'You really must stop saying *weekend* . . .' Debo said faintly. 'So . . .'

'American,' Kick said firmly. 'It will be just the right kind of way to meet,' she continued. 'Not like at a ball or a London party, with everyone stiff in their best clothes and a thousand people all clamouring for her attention . . . No, this will be perfect. An afternoon, even a whole day. Where they can talk and get to know one another, and then how can she fail to see what a dear he is.'

'You are so convinced that your mother is the stumbling block. What about his lot?'

'His parents will like me,' Kick said with certainty. 'Parents always like me.'

'*Parents*, maybe, but Billy's parents . . .?'

'How different can they be?'

'Now that's a question . . .' Debo said, amused. 'Not one to answer now.'

'But how can you be sure they'll come? Maybe the Channons won't invite them?'

'He's the Duke of Devonshire, darling. You may be certain Chips has already invited him.'

'Well then, maybe they won't want to go?'

'I've thought of that. It's a possibility alright. But I have a plan.' She lowered her voice. 'I shall suggest that Diana and Mosley call to visit the Blounts. That will get Billy and his parents out in record time.' She gave a gurgle of laughter. 'They'd go anywhere to avoid meeting Mosley. All I have to do is suggest Kelvedon.'

Chapter Thirteen

Berlin
Doris

Summer reached a height, and Doris was almost glad of the invitation to a party by the Müggelsee lake where she was to stay two nights. It was given by Hans Fritzsche, the man who had driven her home. He was a smooth and genial broadcaster, the 'voice of Germany', who was adored by house-wives for his light and melodious patter. To celebrate his appointment as head of radio at the Propaganda Ministry, he had gathered half-a-dozen couples – mid-ranking Nazis and their wives – and a smattering of more artistic types to his summer house. It was the kind of party Doris was used to; the stuffy couples leavened by her, perhaps a poet who composed verse in honour of the Führer, occasionally an older actress who mostly played idealised maternal roles these days.

'Dear Doris,' Fritzsche greeted her on the first evening, 'always so tranquil.' There was a steady wind blowing from the lake, and he himself was dishevelled and harried-looking. He's taken on too much, she thought, looking around the garden with its glowing lanterns, tables full of food and couples dancing on the lawn.

'So kind of you,' she said. 'There I was, simply sweltering in Berlin, wishing for a miracle, and behold – one arrives!' She swept an arm out to take in the tables, lanterns, the lake beyond and, with a smile, her host.

He looked relieved. 'You think it's alright?'

'I think it's perfect,' she said warmly, tucking her hand into his arm and thinking that in London she had never once been asked anxiously by a host what she thought of their efforts.

'Let me introduce you . . .' He took her to a group of men in uniform and performed a series of practised introductions, making much of her Englishness, her interest in Germany, her friendship with the Mitford sisters and Herr Channon, how sympathetic she had been to Edward VIII before his abdication. These were the things that were always said of her. They were the things that made her safe.

Doris was there to be charming – she had still heard nothing more since the Tiergarten encounter and so she was as always gay and frivolous; alert to their jokes, flattering in her questions. Some of them she had met before; one, a man with a thick head of blond hair that he tried to comb flat on his head and that kept springing up in tufts, was new to her. He broke off what he had been saying to greet her, then resumed.

'We will be rolling out a new system of identification soon,' he said expansively. 'It is an idea of perfect genius. So simple and so effective that a child might understand it.' He looked around, pleased. 'It is a yellow Star of David to be stitched into the clothing of every Jew over the age of six. At a glance, it will be possible to tell who is who and what is what.' He smiled.

'Genius,' one of the other men agreed. Doris knew him vaguely, some kind of administrator. The woman beside him, his wife, nodded eagerly.

'A relief,' she said. 'No more mistakes. No confusion.' Murmurs of assent. 'But why no younger than six? Surely, at three and four, they are still Jews?' She looked brightly around. 'Not that there is ever much confusion,' she continued gayly. 'So easy to spot.'

The man with the tufty hair drew his brows thoughtfully together, nodding at her. 'We will make a note of it,' he said.

'There will need to be communication,' Fritzsche said eagerly. 'People must be instructed how to respond when they meet a neighbour with a yellow star.'

'They will need guidance,' the administrator agreed. 'From a trusted person such as you, Herr Fritzsche.' Fritzsche flapped his hands modestly, animated at the prospect of his own role in this.

'What do you think, Fräulein Coates?' The tufty-haired man turned to her.

'It certainly seems *simple*,' Doris said. 'So very simple.' She tried to keep her voice light, high, unburdened by the wave of horror she suddenly felt. She thought of her cousins, her aunt, even her mother; coarse yellow stars stitched into their smart, sombre clothing. Of Hannah, her pale blue poplin shirt defiled with a symbol rendered crude and ugly by the intent. 'So simple,' she repeated. 'And yet no child would ever have dreamed of it.' Again she kept her voice light.

The administrator's wife gave her a beady look but the man seemed to find nothing amiss. 'Precisely,' he agreed. 'Will you dance?' And Doris smiled and nodded and pressed her painted nails into the palm of her hand as he took hold of the other. She pressed so hard that a nail broke.

She went to bed as early as she dared and the next day, pleading a headache that would not relent, declined a boat trip on the lake. By lunchtime, despite Fritzsche's almost desperate entreaties, she insisted she must go back to Berlin. She knew it was unforgivable to be so indisposed. He knew it too. 'How unfortunate,' he said nastily as she got into her car. 'Most inconvenient indeed.'

Once clear of the *schloss* she rolled down her windows to let in the humid air and drove too quickly to try and whip it into something fresh. It was like stirring treacle, she thought. But she trailed her hand out the window, feeling it bounce off the air, and sang snatches of songs she remembered from last year's London parties. The day was stale but she felt lighter than before. She had no idea what she would do for Beatrice and Hannah, but now, after last night, she knew she would do something. So what if the doing compromised her, she thought, when doing nothing was likely to destroy her?

At her building, the *hausmeister* was mopping the floor of the lobby. He greeted her warmly, and made a joke – always the same joke – about an English policeman and a horse, that Doris had never understood.

She laughed politely and made for the lift. How hot it was in the city, she thought, longing for the dim cool of her apartment. 'You will have new neighbours,' he said as she passed him. 'You'll be glad of it.'

'Really? Where?'

'The apartment beside yours. The Jewish family.' He didn't spit. But he looked as though he might.

'Where have they gone?'

'I don't know.' He looked affronted. 'East? Back to Poland? Wherever the Gestapo sent them.' He laughed and thrust his mop into the pail of water. He took it out and the smell of carbolic was so strong that Doris choked. He swished the mop against the smooth floor, back and forth, and the sound of it was like a roaring in her ears.

'What do you mean? They were here a few days ago.' She had heard them. The sound of Hannah practising that she waited for and ticked off for reassurance in her mind: *Still there.*

'And now they're not.' He shrugged and moved his mop in a swirling circle that came close to Doris' feet. She knew if it touched her, she would scream. She jabbed the lift button again.

'Not so hard,' he said, avuncular, reproving. 'You must be patient.'

The lift cranked upwards too slowly for her agitation so that she rattled the iron grille. She realised that the sound of the violin had been false reassurance. She should not have hoped to hear it. She should have hoped the opposite – that they were gone. Before the Gestapo came to get them.

Chapter Fourteen

Berlin
Doris

Within days the flat next door was emptied. Two men traipsed up and down the stairs, the *hausmeister* scurrying after them, warning them to be careful. Furniture was dragged down and put into the back of a lorry. Doris watched, trying to believe that it was to be driven to join Hannah, her father, Beatrice, but the way everything was thrown in, without care, told her this wasn't so. She saw a leg broken off a sofa, and an old wardrobe, heaved in sideways, land on a heap of cushions that burst, sending feathers everywhere.

She watched from her window as they carried an old bureau with brass-handled drawers out from the building entrance towards the truck.

'Careful!' The man at the front who walked backwards shouted to the man who held the bottom end. On top of the bureau was balanced a pile of books that slid as they moved, and a small black violin case. Doris left her window, changed her shoes for a pair of high black patent heels and went down in the lift, pulling the grille savagely shut behind her. She waited outside on the street that smelled of rubbish, ignoring the men, who saluted her respectfully from the lorry, where they were making space for the bureau by heaving other pieces roughly out of the way. She stood, as though waiting for a taxi, tapping the toe of one shoe impatiently on the greasy cobblestones. When the men had gone back upstairs, she crossed to the lorry. They had left the back open and the bureau was wedged into the corner within easy reach, the violin case still on it. She grabbed the handle and dragged the case out, tucked it under her arm and marched back into the building and up to her flat. Only when she got inside and closed the door did she breathe, or so it felt. She opened the case at the table, lightly touching the worn green velvet that lined it, then lifted out the violin, small and confiding in her hands. She placed it on her shoulder and plucked the second string with her finger. D. At the sound – so round and sweet and thoughtful – something inside her let go and the tears she hadn't known she was holding back came in a wave.

It was only a few days later that new people arrived. A family. Again she watched from her window as they unloaded their effects and had them carried upstairs. She watched a large blonde lady in a flowered dress stand and talk to the *hausmeister* for a long time. He showed, she thought, a great deal of deference. Two sullen boys of maybe twelve and thirteen wearing the uniform of the Hitler-Jugend – khaki shirts tucked neatly into black shorts – carried what they could manage with ill-grace but left most of the work to the removal men.

They met the next day, although Doris had hoped to avoid them for longer. 'We are neighbours.' The woman thrust a hand at her. Doris took it and felt her own squeezed heartily. 'I haven't had a chance to come and say hullo,' the woman continued. 'We didn't get much warning of the move.' She laughed. 'And we've had such a time of it.'

'How did you come by the flat?' Doris asked, smiling politely. She could feel the two boys watching her, the older one with admiration.

'It became available suddenly,' the woman said. 'We would have moved immediately – we were so cramped in our last place – but the previous occupants' furniture was so dowdy.' She gave a little laugh. 'We had to clear it entirely before moving in. Not a thing could we keep!' She laughed again. 'Did you know them?'

'No,' Doris said. She snapped open her crocodile skin handbag and took out a gold cigarette case. She offered the woman a cigarette, which she accepted, and took one herself. 'I didn't.' She realised her hand was shaking so that she would never be able to hold the lighter steady. 'Be a darling,' she said to the older boy, handing him her lighter. He stepped forward eagerly and lit both the cigarettes.

'Here,' he said, blushing as he handed the lighter back.

'What a pretty lighter,' the woman said, admiring the mother-of-pearl handle.

'A gift,' Doris said. 'From Herr Göring.' She angled the lighter so the woman might read the inscription on the underside: *To a dear friend, affectionately*, and the impeccable regularity of the signature *Hermann Göring* with two dots lettered precisely over the 'o'.

'How wonderful!' the woman cried, clasping her hands.

'I must get on,' Doris said, putting the lighter back in her bag.

'Of course.' The woman stood back respectfully to let her pass. It had been a gift, Doris thought as she walked away. But not to her. The 'dear friend' was Chips. The lighter had been given to him after his visit to Germany for the Olympics two years earlier. Doris had pinched it, with Honor's encouragement.

She began to stay out more, and later even than before. She found so little peace now in her flat. Sometimes, if she woke too early, in the moment before she knew where she was, she fancied she could hear the scraping of Hannah's violin so that every time she had to realise she did not. She no longer liked to sit and read by the open windows or play records on the gramophone. So she said yes to every party, every invitation. And maybe that was how she began to realise these were less than they had been. Something had changed. Maybe, she thought, it was simply the mood, which darkened as summer wore on, swelling angrily with the heat. But maybe not.

First it was Hans Fritzsche, whom she met at a party at the Adlon hotel where more than half the men now wore uniform of one kind or another. How few colours went with khaki, she thought, looking at the women in their carefully muted variations of black, white and grey. 'Such a pity you were indisposed,' he said, handing her a glass.

'Champagne? Thank you.'

'Not Champagne.' He looked affronted. 'Sekt.'

'Far superior,' Doris said quickly. She took a tiny sip.

'How is your head now?'

She decided to pretend to take him seriously. 'Perfectly fine, thank you.' She smiled warmly. 'How kind you are.' She put a gloved hand on his arm. 'I was so sorry to leave, but I feared I would make your party terribly dull if I stayed. And I couldn't have borne that.'

He looked mollified. A little. But it wasn't enough.

Later, Ilse, the daughter of the newspaper editor, came over and asked, 'What did you say to offend Frau Becker?' This was the administrator's wife.

'I cannot imagine,' Doris said lightly. 'Perhaps she is one of those women who loves dearly to take offence?'

Ilse laughed. 'I know them!' she said. 'Never happy unless feeling insulted.'

'The very ones,' Doris agreed. But what had she said? she wondered. She cast her mind back. The evening at the lake *schloss* . . . the twinkling garden lights and the rich smell of water. The plan for the stitching of the yellow Star of David . . . '*Simple,*' she heard herself say. '*And yet no child would ever have dreamed of it.*' Frau Becker's beady look.

That.

'Well, whatever it was, you made an impression,' the girl continued. 'Frau Becker says she thinks you *don't have a real understanding of important matters.*'

As well brand her as a subversive, Doris thought in alarm. 'I understand *this* important matter,' she said, holding up her glass of Sekt and making a face.

The girl laughed. 'Isn't it foul?' she agreed. 'Come with me, I know where we can get proper Champagne.'

But Doris, who dared everything, didn't dare. 'Perhaps later,' she said. 'It's not so bad.'

The girl shrugged – 'Suit yourself' – and walked away.

*

A few days later, again lunch at Horcher's. 'What did you say your aunt's name was? The German aunt?' von Arent asked her.

'Anna. Anna Klein.' A perfectly ordinary name. 'She died.' This was what she said. Her mother's only relative, dead some years now. No other family in Berlin. None she knew of. Only her many friends.

'*Anna Klein,*' he repeated. Was there something in the way he said it? 'And I suppose it is from her you get your dark hair and black eyes?'

'No, my colouring is from my English father,' Doris said lightly. 'My grandmother and mother are both as yellow-haired as Rhinemaidens.' She laughed, but something inside her squeezed.

When von Arent went to do his usual table-hopping and Doris sat with her coffee, the same young waiter came to clear. 'Where might one walk today?' she asked him quietly, head bent as she fumbled with the clasp of her handbag.

'May I refill your coffee?'

'Please.' He went away, then returned with a fresh silver pot. 'I believe the Märchenbrunnen fountain will be pleasant later today.'

It was certainly noisy, she thought later as she sat on a low stone wall beneath a statue of Lucky Hans. The shallow tiered basin had nine fountains playing in it, one for each of the fairy tales told by the Brothers Grimm and commemorated here in stone statues that were, she had always thought, heavy and sentimental. Hefty children with knowing faces reaching for pigs or fawns or ducks, entirely unleavened by any delight. And perhaps that's what it was to be a German peasant child, she thought. Everything a deal to be struck, whether with witches, robins or fate.

This time, she saw the man immediately although he had no dog with him, and instead of a neat suit he wore the weekday clothes of a labouring man. He came and sat at a slight distance from her and took out a sandwich made with dark bread. He unscrewed a tin cannister and leaned forward, almost into the froth of water that fell from one of the fountains, to fill it.

'You're to go back,' he said, bent over.

'London?' She took a book from her bag and opened it at random, inclining her head away from the sun, the better to read, and closer to him.

'Yes. And then wherever your friends the Channons are. They have interesting guests. Prince Friedrich Hohenzollern. Ambassador Kennedy.'

'What am I to do?'

'The usual. Listen, watch, understand. There are many possibilities right now. Everything is of interest.' He straightened up, took a swig of water from the tin can and wiped his mouth with his sleeve. 'Go soon.'

'For good?'

'For now.' She left him sitting there, passing a stone girl with blank eyes and a grotesque little man in her lap. At the girl's feet clustered more little men, staring balefully out from behind curling stone beards. Snow White. Beside her, a stone wolf licked the elbow of a different girl, its long grey tongue curling out from sharp stone teeth. Before coming to Germany, Doris had always thought these stories – Snow White, Little Red Riding Hood – were pretty tales for children. Here, in the land of their creation, they seemed different. Darker. Twisted with the creeping roots and impenetrable canopy of the Black Forest.

At her building, the *hausmeister* blocked her. 'Two men came for you.'

'What men?'

'I don't know. Men. No uniform.' He seemed curious at such an absence, now when uniforms were everywhere.

Ordinary Germans, Doris had noted, prided themselves on being able to tell one from another immediately, correctly address the person wearing it – who was a *blockleiter*, an *ortsgruppen-leiter*? – and shade their deference accordingly.

'I told them you would be back,' he said.

Chapter Fifteen

London
Honor

The morning they were due to motor down to Kelvedon, Honor came downstairs to find Andrews hovering in the hallway. Her heart sank.

'Madame, may I have a word?'

'You are having a word, Andrews. What is it?'

'There is a lady in the library, Madame.'

'Well, why have you not shown her in? I will receive her in the small drawing room.'

'The lady is asleep, Madame.'

Hence, she thought, the hovering. 'You'd better tell me.'

'I believe it to be Ms Ponsonby but it is difficult to be certain.'

'I see. Well, I'd better go and have a look. Will you bring coffee? Strong coffee.'

In the library, the heavy green velvet curtains were still partially closed, so that light came through only in one narrow shaft. The whole room looked as though Andrews had been interrupted in his task. A collection of sticky glasses had been herded to one corner of the vast leather-topped desk but not yet removed. Beside them, a near-empty bottle of crème de menthe had the same thick green hue as the light coming through the curtains, so that the room made Honor think of the swimming pool at Elveden after winter – when jade-coloured algae grew dense around the concrete sides and bottom, turning the trapped rainwater to the same greenish hue as the copper-domed roof. Beside the bottle, a dusting of white powder told her that Chips had been at his trickery again; 'dynamite' he called it.

On a sofa in the corner, illuminated by a finger of light, someone lay sprawled, half covered by a fringed shawl. Honor moved closer. The someone's head was tucked in under a bare white arm, and the corner of the fringed shawl had been pulled almost to the top of the head so that only a few dusty brown curls were visible. It was a woman, and indeed there was something about the lanky form, the insolence of that flung-out arm, that said Elizabeth Ponsonby. Momentarily, Honor marvelled at Andrews' discernment.

'Elizabeth.' She shook the arm. Her skin was cold to touch. It was already warm outside but the library never saw sun until lunchtime. Nothing. 'Elizabeth.' She shook the arm again, harder. A slurred murmur from beneath the shawl. 'Elizabeth.' Louder, harder.

'What is it?' A voice raspy with sleep and whatever had been drunk and smoked the night before.

'Elizabeth, get up!' Honor said sharply. The figure stirred and the arm dropped, taking the shawl with it so that a face was visible. It was indeed Elizabeth, her round eyes – like a surprised baby, Honor had always thought – more heavily lidded than usual.

'Oh, it's you,' she said, struggling to sit up. The straps of her evening dress, some kind of deep red silk, slipped down so that Honor saw far more of her bosom than she wanted to.

'Who else would it be? What are you doing asleep in my library?'

'I wasn't entirely sure where I was,' Elizabeth confided. She pushed her hair back from where it hung, tangled, around her face. 'Might you have a cigarette?'

Honor fetched a box from the desk and offered her one. Elizabeth's hands shook so badly she could barely get the cigarette into her mouth, let alone light it. Honor plucked it from between her lips, lit it herself and passed it back, blowing out a cloud of smoke. 'Yeuch. I don't know how you can at this time.'

'Don't be censorious, darling, not so early.' Her voice shook too.

'Now, what are you doing here?'

'Well,' Elizabeth leaned forward, confidingly, 'I don't *quite* know . . . We were at the Café de Paris, and then some darling little dive off Mayfair. One of Ma Merrick's, I expect. Your husband was there. Or was he somewhere else?' She screwed her face up, trying to remember.

'Never mind that. Why here?'

'Well, the police arrived and broke up the Mayfair place. Which makes me think it can't have been Ma, because of how she's so careful to pay the poor fellows so they don't have to waste their time at such silliness . . .'

'Elizabeth!'

'I'm getting there, darling. Be patient.' She took another drag of her cigarette, blowing smoke into Honor's face. 'Your husband – ever so jolly! – suggested we come back here for just *one*. And, well, here I am.' She looked around brightly.

'You came back here, alone, with my husband?' Surely not even Chips, in their own home, with Elizabeth . . .?

'Oh no! You mustn't worry.' She reached out and patted Honor's arm. Her fingers, thin and white with their crimson nails, were stained yellow at the tips.

'I'm not worried,' Honor said, drawing back her arm.

Elizabeth gave her a mischievous look, then opened her eyes very wide. 'Of course not,' she agreed. 'In any case, you need not be. There were quite a number of us here. Billy Cavendish, at least one Mitford – although where there's one, there's usually more, don't you find?' she added, nodding wisely.

Honor found herself nodding too, then stopped. Chips had had a party, here in the library, while she slept oblivious upstairs? There was something she didn't like about the idea. And yet, the truth was that, so big was the house, so great the distances between its rooms – many of which Honor hardly visited – he could have had a dozen parties and she would never have known. There was something a little sinister about that. She shook off the thought and returned to the matter in hand.

'But why are you *still* here?'

'I fell asleep. Must have, else I wouldn't still be here, would I?' As though it were the most logical thing in the world. Beside the sofa Honor noticed for the first time a pair of silver sandals with high spikey heels. They were placed neatly, lined up one beside the other. She wondered had Elizabeth done that, or someone else?

'Well. Here's Andrews.' The butler entered with a tray on which stood a silver coffee pot and two china cups. Honor hoped Elizabeth wouldn't break them. Her hands still shook alarmingly. 'You may have a cup of coffee and then I'm sure you'll want to be getting on. You must have so much to do.'

'Not a thing,' Elizabeth said cheerfully. 'Not 'til lunchtime at least. I say, be a darling, Honor, may I have a bath before I go? You wouldn't send poor tiny me out in last night's fug, now would you?' She stared at Honor, an expression that for all its childish defiance held something else too. Something hopeful.

So that Honor said, 'Very well. I will ask Molly to draw you a bath.'

As she crossed towards the door, she caught sight of one of Elizabeth's bare feet poking out from under the shawl. The sole was entirely black. She shut the door behind her. 'Where is Mr Channon?' she asked Andrews.

'Just returned, Madame. He has been shopping.'

Of course he had. More antiques, she supposed. He never would go to Kelvedon empty-handed. 'Ask him to come up to my sitting room.'

When Molly had drawn a bath for Elizabeth, Honor sent her to pack and, while she waited for Chips, began to compose a letter to Doris: '*You cannot imagine what I found this morning, quite as though some bird had flown in and started a nest in a corner: Elizabeth Ponsonby, rather the worse for wear, fast asleep on the sofa like something from an Aubrey Beardsley sketch – all charcoal smudges and spikey lines . . .*' She tried to make the telling something amusing, a trivial but curious episode. But it was hard. She felt furious. With Elizabeth, with Chips, obscurely with herself, for being the sort of person a thing like that could happen to. No one, she thought, would ever dare fall asleep on a library sofa in her parents' house. And if they did, one look at Lady Iveagh's face in the morning would be enough to send them packing. There would be no cups of coffee and – imagine it! – baths.

'What is the meaning of it?' she demanded when Chips came in, as soon as the door was safely shut behind him.

'What was I to do?' He put his hands out in front of him, palms up, fingers spread wide. 'I tried to find her a taxi but it simply wasn't possible to get her out of the house.'

'Why could not one of the others have taken her?'

'They were gone and she was left and there seemed nothing at all to do only cover her and leave her on the sofa where she was already asleep and snoring. In a way that was surprisingly loud.'

'What about that chap she goes about with, Ford?'

'They seem to have had some sort of a row earlier in the evening. He stormed off and she said she wouldn't go with him because he was "simply beastly" when in that kind of humour. Truth is,' he said, 'I'm not sure she had anywhere much to go. I rather got the impression she didn't. Surely you do not think I wanted her here?'

No, Honor knew him better than that. Poor Elizabeth had none of the things Chips looked for. Neither power nor influence; little beauty, certainly not now. Nothing attached to her name except exasperation, indifference and, among those who had known her a decade ago when she was the very brightest of the Bright Young People, a lingering pity.

'No, I don't suppose you did. Though why you must go giving late-night parties . . .'

'Not a *party*,' he said, 'just one or two friends. Now, Brigid is downstairs.'

'And Maureen and Duff will be here any moment. We must be ready to leave.'

By the time she got down, Maureen had arrived and was standing, tapping her foot impatiently and blowing smoke in exaggerated fashion from a cigarette held in a long ivory holder. She was far too smartly dressed for the country, in a cream jacket and skirt that were too hot for the already-sultry day. Pugsy, her bad-tempered Peke was slumped at her feet, defeated by the heat. Beside her on the hall chair Duff sat and read *The Times*. Maureen looked up. Duff did not.

'I thought we would be gone by now,' Maureen said. Behind her, in one of the smaller rooms, Honor could hear Brigid chattering on the telephone.

'Andrews has ordered the motorcars,' Honor said soothingly. The last thing she wanted was a row before they even set off. 'You and I and Brigid and Duff will go together. Chips will follow with Bundi. Those dogs had better not travel together. The servants will come after with the luggage.'

'I say, where are you going?' It was Elizabeth, leaning over the heavy banister and calling down to them from the first floor.

'Kelvedon. Essex. And we should have left by now,' Maureen said. Then, in an audible hiss, 'What is *she* doing here?' to Honor.

'Essex. What fun,' Elizabeth said, starting down the stairs.

She looked fresher – Molly must have done her hair as well, Honor thought; what were the bets Elizabeth hadn't tipped her – and also familiar. 'I say, is that my dress?'

'Yes, I knew you wouldn't mind. You can't expect me to wear last night's. Red silk. So simply perfect for a nightclub. Not at all the thing for daytime. You must see that, Honor? I told your maid – darling creature, you are lucky! – that you wouldn't mind a bit. I hoped you would have trousers, but of course you don't have the figure for it.'

Beside Honor, Maureen was laughing openly. 'I'd forgotten you could be amusing, sometimes. You should come with us,' she said lightly.

'Now that's a jolly idea.' Elizabeth beamed. 'I think I shall. It's much too hot in London anyway.' She had reached the hall and stood close enough, fanning herself in exaggerated fashion with a limp hand, so that Honor could smell her own geranium soap, a gift from Chips.

'Don't be absurd, Maureen,' she said crossly. 'Elizabeth must have a million things to do. Besides, there simply isn't time for her to gather her things. The motors have been brought round and we mustn't keep Michaels waiting.'

'I'll just borrow some of yours,' Elizabeth said. 'I know we aren't at all the same size,' she smiled kindly at Honor, 'but you do have so many heaps of clothes, I'm sure that clever maid of yours can find a few things. I don't need much. I don't imagine there will be any real fun in Essex.' She said it almost reassuringly. At that, Duff looked up and grinned.

'Excellent plan!' Maureen said with a snigger, so that Honor felt she could have cheerfully murdered her.

'Well, if you must come, at least let us stop and let you pick up some things. It really won't do . . .'

'The truth is,' Elizabeth said with dignity, 'my effects are scattered. I have been staying rather here and there this last while. My own flat has . . . too many people in it.' She opened her eyes very wide, as if daring them to ask more.

So Chips was right, Honor thought. 'But there isn't room in the motorcars,' she tried one last time.

'Oh, little me can squeeze in anywhere.' Then, 'Duff, darling, why don't you fix us a drink before we go, and Honor can send for her adorable maid to do the packing?' Duff stood up and tucked *The Times* under one arm, holding the other out politely for Elizabeth.

'Damn you, Maureen,' Honor said when they had moved away. 'What was that?'

'A joke that may have got rather out of hand,' Maureen said, watching her husband and Elizabeth disappear into the library.

Chapter Sixteen

Kelvedon, Essex
Honor

Bringing Elizabeth meant that Duff had to travel with Chips and Bundi. Which clearly annoyed Maureen because she sat in silence, staring out the window, Pugsy on her lap, ignoring Elizabeth's chatter until eventually Elizabeth fell asleep, head tilted back against the upholstered seat of the car, mouth slightly open. Honor plucked the smoking cigarette from her fingers and flicked it out the window.

'Who is she?' Brigid asked in a fascinated whisper as Elizabeth started to snore.

'Who *was* she, more like,' Maureen said.

'Don't be cruel.'

'When we were all as young as you are now, and doing the season, Elizabeth was the girl of the moment,' Maureen said.

'She knew all the best parties, and planned many of them. She was outrageous and wild and the despair of parents everywhere, not just her own. She was up to everything, neck deep in everything, invited everywhere.' She watched Elizabeth draw a ragged breath in and exhale on a snore. 'And then everything changed, and everyone changed, but Elizabeth stayed exactly the same so that now, she is like finding a faded dance card and seeing the name of a young man you once danced with. You may not remember him at all clearly, but you might feel a moment's sadness because, back then, it was probably terribly important that he danced with you . . .'

Maureen sounded almost wistful, Honor thought. Which was so unlike her that she looked over, a question in her eyes. But Maureen turned her face to the window.

'She seems rather fun,' Brigid said thoughtfully. 'Though not at all like a grown-up.'

'She is like those poems by Mr Hilaire Belloc, so cleverly illustrated by Duff's father: *A Cautionary Tale*,' Honor said.

Brigid began: '*There was a girl, her name was Lizzie,*
Who always seemed so terribly busy
She plotted here, she planted there,
But all she produced was empty air.'

'More like a limerick, but jolly good,' Maureen said.

'I'm sure it is very unsuitable that she should be coming with us,' Honor said. 'Please do not tell Mamma. I am certain she wouldn't like it.'

'You needn't worry,' Brigid said, 'I bet I'll hardly speak to her. Apparently I shall have dear little Kathleen Kennedy to keep me busy.' She sighed. 'Not to mention Prince Fritzi. Of all the . . . I don't know why Chips *does* such things . . . When all I wanted to do was play tennis and walk and swim and ride, and try to forget all about London and parties and who wore what.'

'What a funny child you are,' Maureen said. 'At your age, it was the tennis and riding I wanted to forget, the better to think only of parties and who wore what.'

They were finally clear of the city – even the trailing fingers of small, dirty houses and narrow streets that lingered so long after the city proper was wound up, were gone now. Around them, the landscape grew broad and the air settled to a thick yellow glow.

'It's like driving through custard,' Brigid said.

The car purred along, eating through miles and miles of road, fields of cropped golden stubble stretching out on either side, bordered by trees already leaking copper into the green leaves. The harvest was in early, Honor's father had told her, almost with the pride of a man whose livelihood depended on the safe gathering of a few small fields. No wonder there was an air of dreaming over the countryside, she thought. A feeling of quiet celebration. She imagined the setting right of houses and barns, the mending of fences, all the chores that would have been left undone in the great rush to take in the hay. And the voluptuous sense that there was time, finally, to do these things. She thought of pies baking, fruit pickled safe into jars. She sighed happily.

'Did you bring your gas mask?' Brigid asked. 'I almost forgot, only Minnie ran out after me to remind me. I said she should take it in their car with the luggage, but she insisted that, no, I must carry it with me.' She patted the bulky black case beside her. 'I cannot get used to them. They make me think of poor sweet elephants with their trunks cut off. Too sad.'

'Chips says there will be no need of them,' Honor said. 'But I confess, I had Molly pack mine anyway.'

'Duff says there will be need, but not yet. He wants me to go to Clandeboye if things get worse,' Maureen said.

'Will you?' Honor asked, curious.

'Certainly not. To be buried in the Irish countryside would be even more terrible than anything that could happen in London. In any case, nothing will happen. I know Duff. He likes to "look life in the eye", as he puts it. Prides himself on not taking the easy road. Only it can make him pessimistic. He's so busy not swallowing easy lies that he hunts down difficult ones. All will be well, I'm sure.'

'I should like to join the Women's Voluntary Service if there is a war,' Brigid said vaguely. 'Or drive a truck. But Mamma says I may not.'

There was silence then, all faces turned towards the windows, watching the steady unfolding of fields and hedges, small copses and winding rivers. It was, Honor thought, like a film reel, something that felt both near and distant, real and imagined. She tried to imagine it all torn up, ploughed not by farm machinery but by guns and the tramping feet of soldiers; the gold turned to black, the green scorched to brown. But she couldn't. And there was no need. There would be no war. Chips had said it. She no longer had the habit of believing what he said of himself – where he had been, who he had seen – but in this, how could he be wrong? He spent so much of his time, both in the House and out of it, talking about what would happen. Talking to Chamberlain, whom he adored; to Rab Butler, who after all was deputy foreign minister; to von Ribbentrop, who had the ear of the Führer, and Mussolini's man Dino Grandi. How could he be wrong about this?

'So, did Chips want Kelvedon because of how it sounds so like your own dear Elveden?' Maureen asked after a while, breaking the silence. 'Perhaps he sees himself as another Lord Iveagh?'

Brigid sniggered and Honor gave her a cross look. 'I'm just glad he settled on somewhere at last. You have no idea the pain of these last few years, looking at country house after country house, only for him to find fault with everything.'

'Like the Three Bears,' Brigid piped up. 'Too big, too small, too shabby, too old . . .'

'Not old enough,' Maureen joined in.

Honor stirred irritably. 'Must you?'

'Yes,' Maureen replied. 'I must. When it comes to Chips, everyone must. His bumptiousness can only be kept in check if all who know him tease him mercilessly. And now that his political career is finally taking off . . .' She smirked at Brigid as she said it, but it was Honor who answered.

'Parliamentary private secretary to Rab Butler. Hardly a career taking off.' She spoke dismissively.

'Not by the standards of your family, maybe,' Maureen said, with a curious look at her. 'But all the same, not nothing.'

'And he is terrifically pleased,' Brigid chipped in.

'Of course he is,' Maureen said. 'I've seen Chips receive a passing remark on the size of his dog as though it were the most delicate personal compliment.' She began to laugh. 'He really is able to spin gold out of the drabbest of metals.'

'Dear Bundi . . .' was all Honor said. 'Chips talks of getting a second dog, but I do not know how I could ever love another as I love Bundi.' She fell silent then, remembering the background to this talk of another dog.

'Where is Paul?' Maureen asked, as though reading her mind.

'At Kelvedon already, with Nanny. And Sheridan?'

'At home in London. With the Nanny. Duff wanted to bring him . . .'

'Oh, how sweet,' Brigid cried. 'I wish you had.'

'Don't be silly, Brigid,' Honor said. 'Babies aren't puppies, you know, to be dragged around and played with. They need routine, order, discipline.'

'Exactly,' said Maureen.

It was late into the afternoon by the time they arrived at Kelvedon Hatch, a village of pretty cottages that lay beyond the walls of Kelvedon Hall. The motorcar drew up to the front gates, black and very new, with, in the centre of each, a hefty wreath-shaped crest painted in silver.

'What is it?' Maureen asked, in genuine curiosity. 'The Channon coat of arms?' She started to laugh.

'Don't tease, Maureen. Chips is very pleased with it.'

'Look.' Elizabeth was awake. 'There's a tiny disembodied arm coming out the top, clutching, what is that . . . mistletoe? I suppose that would make sense, given Chips' reputation . . .' Then, catching sight of Honor's face, 'Sorry, darling. Too much?'

'Too much.'

The gates were opened by a small boy in a checked cap, his face burnt and freckled by the sun. On each side of the road stood a shiny new lodge, the two joined by an archway overhead. 'It's like driving through a wedding cake,' Brigid said, looking around at the glossy white plaster of the lodges and up at the castellated arch above them.

They continued in silence up the straight tree-lined avenue until they came within sight of the house at the far end of a long, manicured lawn. No trace here of the blistering sun that had parched the fields and turned London streets fetid. Everything was green and fresh and soft and new, grass mown in stripes like a calico bedspread.

Maureen started to laugh. 'How very like Chips.'

'What do you mean?' Honor asked. Half of her wanted to hear Maureen mock Chips as only Maureen could. The other half felt furious that her cousin should think to sneer at the man she had married.

'After all that – all that looking, all that rejecting, all that talk of somewhere fitting to his place in society – and in the end he settles for something so . . . suburban.'

'Hardly!' Honor said. 'Georgian. Late Georgian.'

'But so very square and red-brick. So neat and tidy and *contained*. Nothing like Elveden at all. Quite the pocket squire, isn't he?'

'Maureen, if you're going to be—'

'I'm not, I promise. I'll be as good as gold. It's only that, in comparison with Clandeboye . . .'

'Must we endlessly have comparisons with Clandeboye? Not everyone wants to live in a vast tumbling-down barracks of a place, you know. Why, there are entire wings that are scarcely habitable. And I believe you still have never seen the kitchens.'

'Why would I want to see the kitchens?' Maureen asked, eyes open wide.

Inside, Brigid ran about exclaiming at everything she saw. Honor hadn't been there since well before the work was complete, and found herself marvelling – again – at the sheer determination of Chips' vision. The last time she'd seen Kelvedon, there had lingered, still, a distinct memory of nuns and institutional living. Dim light and the acrid smell of fatty oil lamps. A kind of sad communality born of sacrifices to economic efficiency – how best to keep the most people, spending the least money. It had been badly heated so there was a general air of damp and even patches of mildew. Hasty sectioning of grand rooms had meant a warren of smaller ones; even – she shuddered at the recollection – a kind of communal lavatory block where a row of stalls stood side by side, seven or eight of them, each with a corresponding small washstand.

Now, not a trace of these bleak efficiencies remained. Nor any hint of what she had then smelled in the air – boiled cabbage and dashed hopes. Now, the hall was painted a celestial blue with plasterwork picked out in white. A plump sofa upholstered in a deeper blue and white, heaped with silk cushions, stood invitingly in an alcove. On the polished floor were thick Persian rugs, overhead swung a chandelier so fat with carved fruit and flowers that, should it crash to the ground, as seemed possible given its weight, she wouldn't have been surprised to see actual pulp and flesh and petals mashed into the marble floor. Through the open front door behind them came the smell of fresh-mown grass, joined from somewhere else by that of newly baked bread.

Chips, although he had left later, had taken a different road and made better time. He came now into the hallway, Bundi padding beside him like a golden lion. 'Welcome,' he cried expansively. 'I have tea ordered for the drawing room, but perhaps you would rather tea in your rooms, then gather by the swimming pool?'

'I'm going straight to the pool,' Brigid said. 'No tea for me!'

'Tea in our rooms,' Honor said firmly. 'Where have you put Elizabeth?'

'Well,' Chips said peevishly, 'it wasn't easy, at such short notice, and you know not all the bedrooms are ready, but I have had them prepare the Yellow Room.'

By which Honor knew he was very cross indeed. The Yellow Room – all rooms were named for colours of wildflowers found on the estate, something Chips thought 'charming, bucolic', and Honor thought childish – was small and looked out to the stables. Really, it was a room for a child. But then, Elizabeth, as Brigid had said, wasn't exactly an adult, for all that she had been married and was now separated, and with an unsuitable lover.

'Maureen, you are in the Fuchsia Room,' Chips continued. 'Duff is in the Green.'

Maureen's face twitched irritably. 'Where is my husband now?' she asked.

'By the swimming pool.'

'I'll go straight out. What time do your Americans arrive?' She was careful, Honor saw, to distance herself from these unknown guests.

'Not 'til this evening. Fritzi too.'

Chips followed Honor to her room – she knew he wanted to complain of Elizabeth, so she leapt in with 'I have a headache. The drive down . . . intolerable. In fact, I may need to find an excuse to go back to town early.' That silenced him. He needed her to play hostess.

'A letter came for you, arrived to Belgrave Square just as we were about to leave.' He fished it out of his pocket. 'From Doris, if I were a betting man.' On the corner of the envelope was a navy stamp with a profile of Adolf Hitler. Doris indeed. The Führer looked better from the side, Honor thought, when you couldn't see the silly way he parted his hair.

'Well, what does she say?' Chips asked a moment later. Honor hadn't noticed he was hovering, so absorbed in Doris' letter was she.

'She's coming back to England!' she said, looking up, eyes shining. 'She doesn't say for how long or why, but says she is leaving soon, and asks can she stay. I must write to her immediately and tell her we are here.'

Chips' face fell. 'Surely she would be more comfortable in town? And we could see her when we are back? I don't know that I care to have her here at the same time as the ambassador, with her no-doubt exaggerated tales of Berlin.'

'Nonsense.' Honor ignored him. 'She must come straight here. I will write at once. And I will telephone to Belgrave Square to leave instructions in case she arrives there first. Her letter says she means to set off from Germany almost at once and it was written a week ago. We must send the motorcar back so it is there when she needs it. Will you ask Mrs Meadows to prepare the Scarlet Room?'

'But I have given that to Fritzi.'

'He can move.'

'Very well.' He gave in so easily that she wasn't surprised when he added, 'I thought we might stay on and spend some time together once everyone has gone?'

'I have matters in town. My mother . . .'

'Lady Iveagh wouldn't mind at all.' He came closer. 'If she knew the reason . . .'

'What reason?'

'I thought, while we were here, if we had time alone, well, we might be more . . . companionable.' He took her hand and traced his thumb in light circles over the back of it. Honor flinched.

'No, Chips.'

He dropped her hand. 'You think I don't know about the baron, don't you?' he said, almost conversationally.

'What are you talking about?' She moved sharply away from him.

'The baron, and your little affair. *Very* little . . . But of course I knew.'

How was he so . . . *glib* was the word that came to her. Why didn't he care more? 'You never said . . .'

'No. I didn't see the point.' He shrugged. 'These things happen.'

'Not to everyone, they don't. My parents—'

'Naturally!' he conceded gracefully. 'But to so many marriages. And really, there is nothing to make a fuss about. Not when two people wish to stay together. When they have so much to stay together for. As we do. But given your lapse, surely you see that an effort is now required?'

'Are you trying to blackmail me?' she asked.

'Hardly! I exert a little pressure, that's all. Who could blame me?'

Who indeed? Most of the world, their world anyway, would think him perfectly correct. Perhaps he took her silence for acceptance.

'We do well together, do we not, darling?' he continued, coming closer again. 'And think of Paul, whom we both love so much . . . You would do anything for him, I know you would. And a brother or sister is what he needs most.'

'No, Chips. I cannot.'

He looked into her face for a long moment, then narrowed his eyes. 'Are you sure it was *you* the baron found so attractive? Men of his type don't usually make a play for you.'

'Why should it not have been me?' she responded wearily.

'No reason. No reason. Only that kind of man, well, often it is *money* they find most irresistible.'

She left the room, even though it was her own bedchamber. Later, when they met before dinner, Chips was at his most charming and attentive, full of concern for her wellbeing – 'You look tired, may I fetch you anything?'

But Honor couldn't forget, as she had allowed herself to forget so much else. Which was worse, she wondered – just in the way she might have pressed on a bruised or swollen ankle to see how much it hurt – that her husband found the idea of another man desiring her so ludicrous, or that he should think first of her money when he thought of losing her? She pressed the sore place again. Both, she decided. Both were worse.

Chapter Seventeen

Maureen

Honor must have forgotten to tell Chips to put them in the same room, Maureen thought crossly. Typical. She really was too vague these days. Barely half-engaged in anything, forever slipping away to read or God knew what. And she couldn't ask that Duff's things be moved into her room. Not now. It would be too mortifying. Servants carrying bags to and fro, guests whispering . . . Damn Honor, she thought.

Chips had said Duff was out by the pool. He liked to lie in the sun far more than Englishmen usually did. His dark, almost swarthy complexion meant he did not freckle and burn the way others did. He would be out there, sprawled on a sun chair, surrounded by books and newspapers, perfectly happy. Or so she hoped. The idea made her hurry, impatient of the butler who was leading the way in that stately fashion butlers always had. Even Manning, at Clandeboye, who was positively a villain, liked to adopt a measured formality when they had visitors.

'I see it,' she said, catching sight of a curved sweep of aquamarine water shimmering in the late afternoon haze. 'No need to come any further.'

Sure enough, there was Duff, already turning brown, lying, book in hand, beside a wrought-iron table on which stood a pitcher of something cool. In the water, Brigid, in a striped red-and-white bathing suit, was splashing up and down. Bundi lay in the shade close to the pool, watching her, head sunk onto his paws.

'Ahoy!' Brigid cried gayly, waving over.

Maureen ignored her. That child was altogether too noisy, she thought.

'Good trip?' Duff asked, stretching a hand out to her. She went and sat on the reclining seat with him.

'Elizabeth slept and snored, and Honor couldn't make up her mind whether to lead the attack against her husband or spring to his defence. Most agitating.'

'Interesting,' he said. Then, 'What do you think of this?' He swept a lazy arm up and around, to take in the pool, a pair of terracotta statues of women with deep bosoms and flouncy robes that stood at either end, the copper-roofed pavilion beside it, stretches of green rolling lawn and the house behind them.

'Like a doll's house,' Maureen said. 'Neat and cosy and altogether a little bit silly. Hardly a real country house. More a pretend. Perfect for Chips.' She smirked.

'Something Germanic about it,' Duff said, glaring at the pool pavilion. 'Chips described it as "neo-Austrian baroque".' He sounded revolted. 'There isn't a patriotic bone in that man's body.'

'Rather blissfully comfy though, isn't it?' Maureen said, wriggling right down so that she lay beside him. He shifted over and put an arm around her. If Brigid hadn't been there, she would have kissed him. As it was, she moved in closer.

'Comfort!' Duff said darkly. 'What man cares for such things?'

'What are you drinking?'

'Gin fizz.'

'Pour me one, then tell me what you are reading.'

She was nearly asleep, drowsing in the last of the sun's rays, when the butler returned, this time leading a young man of such golden beauty that, watching him from under half-closed lids, Maureen found that she wished she had gone to her room following the journey after all; had at least reapplied lipstick and brushed her hair.

'Prince Friedrich of Prussia,' the butler announced.

How butlers loved a title, Maureen thought. As much – more, almost! – as Chips. So this was the young man he raved about. It was no wonder. He really was exquisite. And Chips, well, Chips liked exquisite young men. Was that why he had invited this prince? Surely not.

'Please,' the young man said, coming forward and bowing slightly, 'you must call me Fritzi. All my friends do.'

'Fritzi,' Maureen said obligingly.

'Prince Friedrich,' Duff said.

Brigid pulled herself up and out of the pool in one swift movement, and stood dripping on the stone flags.

'Lady Brigid,' Fritzi said, 'how charming to see you again.'

'Charming,' Brigid said, so that it wasn't at all clear if she meant it was charming to see him, or agreed that it was charming for him to see her. Maureen swallowed a laugh.

'There you are, dear boy.' Chips came hurrying up. 'They told me you were down here. I would have been on hand to meet you if I had known. You are early. It is wonderful' – lest there be any doubt. 'Have they settled you in? And your man, Albert, is it? Have they shown him to the servants' hall?'

'Yes, yes.' Fritzi said something stiff then about what a pleasure it was to be received in such a gracious house. Maureen sank back down beside Duff and sighed. The handsome young man was going to be a bore.

'Maureen,' Chips said, looking beadily at her, 'there are plenty of extra sun chairs, you know.'

'I know,' she said lazily, draping a leg over Duff's and, turning her face in towards his neck, inhaling deeply. The heat of the day had brought out a sheen of sweat; he smelt, she thought, better than ever.

Brigid, drinking from a glass of lemonade the butler had brought, choked, and Chips said, 'Really, Maureen, I hope you will behave better when the ambassador arrives.'

'Why, will I compromise Anglo-American relations?' she drawled.

'You jolly well might,' Chips snapped.

'I think they're compromised already,' Duff said, putting his book down, 'by the mealy-mouthed inclinations of the ambassador himself, and his determination to talk England into retreat.' He glared at Chips, who took a step back.

'I hope you won't be argumentative, dear boy,' Chips said.

'As it happens, I won't,' Duff said shortly. 'In fact, I hope it might be possible to talk sense into the man.'

'Is that why you're here?' Chips asked. 'I did wonder, when you can hardly be brought to leave Churchill's side. Or should I say, let go of his hand? I do hope you're not going to spoil my party.'

'Hardly possible,' Duff said dryly. Maureen's lips twitched, but she kept her face straight. 'No, I simply want him to meet other English people,' he emphasised the word *English*, 'and listen to views that aren't the views of Emerald Cunard or Lady Astor.'

'Darling, you aren't going to talk endless politics, are you?' Maureen said, touching the side of Duff's face with a finger.

'It's not *politics*,' Duff said shortly. 'It's now the stuff of life. When will any of you realise that?'

'We do realise,' Maureen said softly. 'We've all been fitted for gas masks and even practised those dreadful air raid drills. But must one think of nothing else every minute of the day?'

'It will come right,' Chips said reassuringly. 'Mr Chamberlain goes to Munich in just a few weeks, where he will head off all this unpleasant talk of war. You'll see, he will arrange everything. There will be no need of these precautions.'

'It is already not right for Czechoslovakia,' Duff said, sitting up sharply so that Maureen almost fell from the sun chair. 'Hitler will hardly rest until he has taken the Sudetenland. And even then he will not rest. All of Europe may wake to find his army massing at their borders.'

'Not here, dear boy, where our borders are protected by the ocean,' Chips said comfortably.

Duff might have said more – indeed, Maureen knew that the kind of provocation Chips gave could mean long, angry diatribes about 'wilful blindness' and 'cowardice' – but just then Elizabeth, dressed in a white sundress – presumably Honor's, that she had belted tightly with a wide black belt – and a floppy sunhat, came towards them. 'There you all are. Isn't this nice?' The others murmured agreement and Fritzi did his stiff little bow again. Elizabeth, ignoring him, poured herself the rest of the gin fizz and handed the empty jug to Chips. 'Ring for more, darling,' she said, and settled herself on a chair beside Maureen. 'Now, I was thinking – after dinner tonight we could get up a game of some kind.'

'Ooh yes!' Brigid said, coming to sit, dripping, on the stone tiles at Elizabeth's feet.

'No games,' Chips said.

Chapter Eighteen

Brigid

Her room was pretty, Brigid decided, with a view out to the walled garden and beyond that tennis courts, and then a broad river than ran past the end of the formal gardens. By leaning far out of the window, sash pulled up as high as it could go, she could see weeping willows drooping gracefully towards the still water and smell the dank, weedy smell of the banks. She thought how cool and quiet it looked and wished she were there, among the mud and wet rushes, not in this house that suddenly made her think of a baker's oven, all those red bricks laid one over the other in neat hot rows.

Her head ached, and she flopped down on the bed, admiring the brightly coloured cornflowers on the silk canopy around. Really, she thought, Chips was almost a girl, he cared so much for things like fabric, cut, colour, design. But she had to admit, he had a talent for comfort. If Honor had been responsible for the house, it would be drab and spartan in the extreme. She never seemed to feel the cold or understand how important little comforts were.

And if Maureen were in charge, they would all be subjected to endless jokes – some jolly, some cruel, many bawdy. Certainly, she was a better guest than a hostess. Although even then, she did only what she wanted.

'Will you sing for your supper?' she had asked Brigid earlier, by the pool. 'I shan't.' She had moved by then, from the lounging chair she had been squeezed into with Duff, to a seat beside the table where Brigid was. Brigid was glad. There had been something . . . *embarrassing*, she thought, about the way they had been so close together, Maureen's leg, bare under her pretty cream-coloured skirt, pressed so hard against Duff's, and the way she hadn't seemed to mind that he was positively sweating through his white shirt, like a horse at the end of a long gallop, patches of dark wet soaking through the crisp white.

'I suppose I shall have to,' she had said wearily. 'All that chatter and groups of people everywhere and never any time alone. How tiring country stays are.'

'You sound like Oonagh. Really, you are far more like our side of the family. You know I mean that as a compliment?'

'I suppose you do,' Brigid had said, keeping her eyes to herself so that Maureen wouldn't see the laugh in them.

But Maureen must have heard something in her voice – some tremor of mirth that gave her away – because she said snappily, 'Not that you are in any need of compliments. Already I would say you have received more than enough. What do you intend to do with them?'

'Not a thing. What should I do?' She had wished Maureen would stop. Even her mother was nothing like this bad. It gave Brigid a hot, stuffy feeling to be quizzed like this, about who she went about with – worse, might marry – when the whole idea seemed so ridiculous. She could no more imagine being married to one of the pleasant, sometimes foolish, young men who danced with her and asked her to sit out on cool balconies or in darkened gardens than she could imagine going to, say, India or Burma – places Maureen sometimes talked of, where she had been on her honeymoon, and that were as remote as the stars.

'Good girl. There is nothing to be done *yet*.' The way Maureen had stressed the word and looked at Fritzi – trying to throw a stick for Bundi, who showed no interest – had made Brigid feel terribly tired. It was then, she thought, that her headache had begun. 'In a little while, you might decide that you do want to.'

'I won't.'

'How do you know you don't want to marry him? The handsome prince?' That was Elizabeth, coming to join them. She had sat on the ground, legs long and white stretched out in front of her.

'Well, how would I know I do? I barely know him.'

'Why don't you find out?' Elizabeth had said lazily.

'Find what out?'

'How well you do together? There's only one way to know. And really, one must know. Otherwise, all that fuss of a wedding, and then' – she shuddered – 'the disappointment of the wedding night. Too crushing. No, by far the best thing is slip into his room one night and make sure.'

That was when Brigid had announced the headache and said she would go to her room. She was shocked by the casual way

Elizabeth had said what she did – imagine if Lady Iveagh, or even Honor, had heard? – but even more than that, she was simply sick of being the focus of everyone's interest. Was that what it was to be young and a girl? she wondered. To be the draw for so many eyes, the source of so much speculation, simply because one was not yet married? She was sick of having to give an account of herself. Of featuring in other people's plans, as though they all played a game with rules she didn't understand. It was like being a servant, she thought. Others made plans, and she was somehow required to carry them out.

She sighed and turned her face to a cool patch of the pillow. 'This bed is simply heavenly,' she said to Minnie, who came in then with an armful of clothes to put away. 'And look, short-bread!' She pointed to a plate of biscuits by the bed. 'Not just the usual digestives.'

'I've ironed your dress for dinner,' Minnie said. 'And you've had too much sun.'

'I know I have. How I wish I could have supper on a tray and go to bed. What a long day it has been already, and the Americans haven't even arrived yet.' She sighed.

'I saw them, pulling up just now in a car as long as a horsebox.'

'I would get up to look, but my head aches so.'

'Let me fix you something. It tastes nasty, but will do the trick.'

'I wish you would. I am glad Mamma lent you to me for the week.'

'I am not a hat, Lady Brigid. I cannot be lent.' She put the last of the clothes away and laid a cool hand on Brigid's forehead.

'Hat or not, you are jolly kind. And I do wish you would call me Biddy. Doris still does, you know.' She held a wan hand out and Minnie clasped it quickly.

When Minnie had gone, she pulled the pink silk curtain of the bed over, so it blocked the last rays of sun, and closed her eyes. The window was open and she listened gratefully to the jaunty sounds of early evening. A breeze had started up and the trees were set rustling by it. Birds went about their bedtime rituals, singing out a last sleepy chorus to let the world know it was time to fold itself away. Below the birds was a steady rhythmic throaty chirp that said there were frogs by the river. She was almost asleep when another sound joined what was there. Music. Loud music, something *delightful. . . delicious . . .* rang out from nearby. It was jarring, injecting a spikey energy where there had been drowsy harmony.

'What's that?' she asked, sitting up, when Minnie returned.

'The American girl brought a gramophone. Here, drink.' She handed Brigid a glass half full with cloudy liquid. Brigid sniffed at it.

'Lemon juice?'

'With salt. Drink it.' Brigid screwed up her face, but she did as Minnie told her, throwing back the foul-tasting liquid.

'Now, drink some water. I'll draw you a bath and by the time it's ready, you'll feel better.'

'I doubt it,' Brigid muttered, sinking back onto the bed. The sound of the gramophone was irritating, she decided. How dare this American girl clatter in and break the peace of their English country house? 'Boor,' she muttered, pulling the pillow over her head. After a little while, the music stopped and she heard splashes and laughs coming from the swimming pool. The Americans must be having an evening swim. The idea annoyed her somehow.

Chapter Nineteen

Kick

The drive down to Essex had reminded Kick why she disliked being alone with her parents. It was that they so patently disliked being alone with one another. If Jack or Joe Jnr had been there, the conversation would have been assured; their father would have questioned them closely on everything they saw, demanding their opinions on the size of English farms, crop production, cattle. And Joe and Jack would have done what they always did – answered to the best of their ability, while also teasing him gently, but only ever as much as he would take. They all knew the line. And what happened to those who crossed it.

The little boys, Bobby and Teddy, would have distracted everyone with their chatter had they been there. Rosemary too brought distraction – not to their father, who tended to ignore her, but to their mother, who watched her so carefully that she had no attention left. But alone, there was not enough conversation after the first half hour, and they lapsed into silence. Her father read the newspaper. A different newspaper to the one he had read that morning. Rose looked out her window, occasionally touching her hair with a gloved hand when they rattled over a bump or hole in the road. Kick tried to play silent games with herself – she awarded herself a point for every horse (two for a grey) she saw, and took a point away for every field of cows. It had to be a field, she reflected; individual cows were too many.

Even so, she was well into minus numbers when they drove over a particularly deep pothole and the car bounced high, jolting them all out of their silence.

'You will come and say your prayers with me before bed each evening,' Rose said, turning to Kick. 'It won't be possible to attend mass. I imagine there isn't even a church, so that will have to do.'

'Of course, Mother.' Kick spoke eagerly. That was the time she and her mother were most in harmony – at mass or saying prayers together. Kick, of all her brothers and sisters, was the most conscious of her faith. In her trunk, packed into a silk purse stitched in the papal colours of yellow and white, were the rosary beads and holy picture she never went anywhere without. Each night they sat beside her bed and were the last thing she laid eyes on before she turned off the lamp. The times she spent on her knees in silent contemplation, either in church or at the little Prie-dieu in her bedroom, were some of her happiest. The repetition of words known so much by heart – *'Hail Mary, full of grace, the Lord is with thee . . .'* – and the way in which her mind, anchored by the familiarity, was set free to roam by those words, given structure by their rhythm; the sound of her mother's voice alongside hers; the way their two voices, together, became something greater, swelling into a broader chorus – all these things were, not a comfort, as others called them, but to her, a delight.

And then her father surprised her. 'I want you to be nice to the German prince, Kick,' he said, folding the newspaper in that deliberate way of his.

'Why?' Rose demanded, head whipping up like a bird that sees something move on the lawn below.

'Because we need to know about him.'

'Know what about him?'

'What he is about. Who he stands for.'

'Princes usually stand for themselves, I should think,' Kick said. She expected a laugh, from her father at least, but didn't get one. God, this car journey was long, and hot, she thought. She tried to open the window, just a crack. Her mother reached a hand out and stopped her. Rose's hair didn't stand for sharp breezes.

'Know what about him?' Rose persisted.

But the ambassador didn't answer that.

'Anyway, what do you mean by "nice"?' Kick asked.

'I want you to listen to what he has to say.'

'OK, I'll listen,' she said cheerfully.

'And remember.'

She knew what the remembering meant. It meant that he would quiz her later – what had the prince said? What did she think he meant by it? Half, Kick was flattered by these questions – that her father should ask them of her and listen to the answers – but she found herself more and more confused about how to answer.

Through Billy, Andrew, their other friends, she now understood that many saw her father not as she always had – a hero, a peacemaker – but as a coward; as 'yellow', as Randolph Churchill had dubbed him. Someone concerned for his money if stability should be disrupted. Concerned for the safety of his own sons if America should decide to join England and go to war with Germany. Ready to sacrifice dignity, honour, what was right, for safety and prosperity. She didn't believe it of him, but who really knew what her father thought? Or rather, when he clearly thought so many things, who could be sure these weren't among them?

She must ask Jack, she decided. He seemed to understand the many tight compartments of their father's mind, far better than she did. She wasn't used to questioning anything the ambassador thought or said. How uncomfortable it was to feel new thoughts growing in her, pushing up through tightly packed ground and into the light; spikey and insistent. Especially when these thoughts brought her into conflict with what Billy said to her. Recently, he had told her more than he used to of what he felt – his shame that Chamberlain tried always to appease, to placate – 'rolling over like a puppy, to show his stomach' – and how he refused to believe that peace at any price was worth having.

Kick listened and said little, but she thought about what he said. She had tried to ask her father – 'Maybe resisting Hitler is right after all?' – but he dismissed her: 'War is a terrible thing, and must be avoided.' They couldn't both be right. And yet, how could she decide who was wrong?

They swept through a pair of gate lodges that arched above them, as though linking arms, and up a broad driveway far better surfaced than the road they had just left. Kick rolled her window down. Now that they were moving slowly, her mother allowed it. She wanted to hear the sounds of this place. Above the crunching of tyres on gravel, there was the swelling of evening birdsong and the scraping rattle of someone pushing a lawn-mower, along with a throaty clicking noise that made her think of crickets. Did they have crickets here? The house came into view, square and neat and red, like the doll's house back home in the nursery. Beside her, her mother sat up a little straighter and dug an elbow into Kick to do the same.

At the house was the usual receiving line of servants, spreading out in a fan shape from the front door. The first such country-house visit, Kick had said hullo, warmly, to the young man at the end of the line, only to have Debo squeeze her arm tight and whisper, 'No.' Later, Debo had explained that if she must say hullo, 'at least say it to the butler, darling. Not the lowliest footman who's probably just a boot boy in a borrowed uniform, put there to make the family look good.'

'What *would* I do without you?' Kick had responded with a laugh.

The motorcar drew to a gradual halt, stopping exactly oppos-ite the open front door. 'Dear friends!' That was Chips, she assumed, coming down the front steps towards them, arms spread theatrically wide. 'Welcome.'

He was unexpectedly handsome. Blond, well-made. With the skill given her by her drawing teacher, Kick noted the even proportions of his face, all his features held in perfect balance. Looking a little closer, when he took her hand in his and shook it vigorously, she saw the beginnings of pouches under his eyes, a network of tiny red veins across his cheeks, a softening of jawline that hinted at disappointment. He made her think of that curious book she had read the summer before at Hyannis

Port, *The Picture of Dorian Gray*. She had never finished it – her mother had come upon her reading it and immediately taken it away – but she remembered it well enough that now, looking at Chips, she thought immediately of the painting starting to corrupt, leaking signs of dissolution into the perfect beauty of its subject.

'Let me show you to your rooms,' he was saying, leading them in through the door to the hallway. He paused a moment, the better that they might admire, Kick thought, looking dutifully around. It was a hallway thick with things. Why, it would take a whole day to look at everything he had crowded in there – paintings, lamps, vases, china and glass objects, a tiny gold clock – all proudly craning forwards to be admired. Above them was a white marble chandelier with carved fruit and flowers so thick upon it that they looked, she thought, like clusters of insects. Fat beetles or moth chrysalises. She imagined them all hatching at the same moment, swarming out of their cocoons and drying themselves on the light. She shuddered.

'Some of the others are down at the pool,' Chips continued. 'You'll meet them when the bell goes. How well you will all get on, you'll see!' His enthusiasm was either infectious or excessive, she couldn't decide which. She was too tired after the journey.

'There's a pool?' she said. 'May I swim?'

'Now?'

'Yes. Please.' She stood on one leg, eager for him to say yes. 'It is so hot and the drive was so stuffy. Mother didn't want the windows down for fear of flies.'

'The bell is about to go,' Chips said. 'It is nearly time to dress.'

'Really, Kathleen!' Her mother. Then, with a gracious smile, 'My daughter is impatient.'

'Oh, let her swim, Chips. There's time.' That was a tall man with a heavy, dark face, wearing creased linen trousers and a white shirt. He came through the hallway from the back of the house and passed them, going upstairs.

'Well, alright,' Chips said. 'I will have someone show you to your room.'

'Honestly, you need only tell me and I will find it. No need to show me.' Barely waiting for instructions – 'around the bend in the landing, third door on the right, the Mauve Room' – Kick dashed upstairs, hoping that the mysterious alchemy of English country houses would mean her trunk was already there.

It was. And her little portable gramophone. She put the needle on the record, thrilling as always to the loud crackle that seemed to demand quiet and attention. Cole Porter's voice filled the air: '*It's delightful . . .*' She changed quickly into her bathing costume and took a towel that lay folded neatly at the end of the bed. Shoving her feet into sandals, she went back the way she had come and out towards what Chips had proudly called 'the pavilion'. She met no one, but everywhere there was a sense of waiting – of doors about to burst open and send forth beautifully dressed men and women, of plans set in motion that needed only a signal to begin to play themselves out.

The air was so hot it resisted her, and the pool, when she reached it, abandoned. The relief of getting into the water was such that she nearly whooped, stopping herself only because, looking back towards the house, she could see that windows everywhere were open. She imagined the effect of a really loud whoop – figures appearing in each open frame, peering out to see who had done this unseemly thing. Instead she flung herself underwater, kicking right down to the bottom of the pool and touching its smooth tiled floor before rising up again to burst above the surface. Drat, she thought, wiping water from her eyes, now her hair would be a sight. She wondered would Mrs Wilkes, the stern lady who was her mother's maid, have time to set it to rights. Probably not, but what did it matter. She could simply brush it and tie it back.

Through the thickening evening air she heard the sound of a gong. Time to go in. But she couldn't bring herself to leave the cool water just yet. She lay on her back, looking up at a sky the colour of spilled ink. At the far end of the pool, swallows were diving, skimming the smooth surface, then rising abruptly, only to circle about and swoop again. They were like the paper aeroplanes her little brothers and sisters made and flew from the windows of Prince's Gate, light and swift, wings angled to catch the wind. If made well enough, they flew as far as Hyde Park so that sometimes when she was out riding she came across one, stuck in a tree or a bush, and laughed to think of Bobby or Teddy or Eunice, folding the paper this way and that energetically, then flinging it out, borne aloft on eager hope.

The gong went again. Now she would be late. She pulled herself up and out of the pool and, catching a towel, set off barefooted towards the house.

Chapter Twenty

Brigid

Minnie was right, Brigid thought. After the vile drink, the throbbing in her head began to recede and in a while she sat up, pushing the hair out of her eyes, and looked critically at the dress Minnie had laid out. Crisp white linen with a full skirt embroidered with tiny white flowers in silk thread. Would it do? After all, this American had been chosen as Most Important Debutante of the season by the *Tatler*. Not that Brigid cared – she had come out the year before, and anyway, who paid heed to such nonsense? But still, she thought, the girl might be snooty, best not to give her anything to be snooty about.

'Minnie, is there anything more grown-up?'

'It's a country-house dinner, not a London party. White linen is very suitable.'

'Suitable!' Brigid muttered. 'Still, I suppose one doesn't want to look like one has tried too hard . . .' She knew Minnie wouldn't give in, no matter what she said. She had strict ideas about what was 'suitable'. 'What are your rooms like, Minnie?'

'Room, not rooms, and it's just as it should be,' Minnie said. 'Why would you ask such a thing?'

'I want to know.' Then, 'What about Kathleen's maid; has she brought someone?'

'There's a maid has come with Mrs Kennedy – I assume she'll do for both. And a gentleman for the prince.'

'What's he like?' Brigid was curious. 'The prince is German but doesn't sound it. Not that he sounds English either . . . What about his man?'

'German, and sounds it, though he speaks good English, I'll allow. Albert, he's called.'

'What kind of a fellow is he?'

'Young; dark hair.'

'Handsome? Will he do for you?' Brigid laughed, and caught the sparkle in Minnie's eyes that said she did too, but all she responded was, 'That's enough, Lady Brigid, or I'll write to your mother and tell her that Elizabeth Ponsonby is here and you'll be sent for, straight home.'

'Do you know everything, Minnie? How did you even know she was here when she didn't know herself until the very last minute?'

'Molly told me.'

'Of course. The servants' chorus, passing news and snippets by your own mysterious means.'

'By which I suppose you mean that we sit and have our tea and talk, just the same as you do.'

Brigid laughed again. 'Don't disappoint me. I wish to imagine you have secret ways.'

The dinner bell went as Minnie was putting the finishing touches to Brigid's hair, and she turned her head this way and that before the glass, finally nodding and saying, 'Very nice.' Minnie had coiled her hair in a thick roll at the top of her head, allowing strands to fall loose in easy curls on either side. 'I bet the American girl wears lipstick. May I? Just a touch?'

'No. Not in the country. In London, it might be allowed but not here, not at your age.'

'Well, it will be your fault if I am quite eclipsed.'

'No one will eclipse you,' Minnie said fondly.

The pale blue carpet in Brigid's room gave way to highly polished floorboards on the corridor and landing, so that her feet in their pointy white shoes made a pleasingly grown-up sound as she walked. She made her way slowly down the stairs and towards the drawing room, hoping she would meet Honor or Maureen along the way and not have to go in alone. It wasn't just that she disliked Chips speculating about who she might marry – although she did – it was the way that being talked about made her feel breathless and prickly, like she was only half-dressed, had forgotten to put on underclothes or shoes. She hoped there would be others in the drawing room, even the American girl who was new and therefore someone for others to be curious about instead of her. But she was early and only men were gathered.

The drawing room, she saw, was like the concentrated essence of the house. So painted and plastered and upholstered, so set about with things, that there was not an inch of it that did not seem as though it had been dressed. It reminded her of Cook and the way she made a pie: first rolling out pastry, carefully lining a tin, placing the filling, then the top layer; cutting leftover pastry into swirls and curls to decorate the crust, then brushing it all with a beaten egg so it would glaze in the baking. That, she thought, was what Chips had done with this room. The whole house, yes, but this room most of all.

The walls were grey-green, like lichen, and the chairs and sofas set about were piled high with silk cushions in different shades of green. The ceiling was painted with a mural of London city in smoky greys and blues. She could make out St Paul's, Nelson's Pillar, a cluster of buildings in between. The effect of so much colour – no white – was to draw the room in on itself, close it over at the top so that they were in a sealed cauldron. She wondered had Chips done it on purpose. And if so, why?

Although the evening was warm, a fire was laid in the wide grate; a pile of burning logs that cast a glow of light as well as heat. Too much heat. She wondered how the men could stand so close to it.

Chips was there, with Duff and the ambassador, who wore white tails. Chips introduced her – 'Ambassador Kennedy, you remember my sister-in-law Brigid' – and Kennedy said, 'Of course, how do you do?' and gave her hand a firm shake. He looked expectantly at her, lips peeled back over his big white teeth as though waiting for an answer, so Brigid said, 'Jolly well, thank you,' but her voice came out too high and she felt gauche. Kennedy looked disappointed, and as though he might say something else.

'Drink this.' Chips handed her a cocktail and the ambassador turned away.

Brigid took the drink with relief. Duff gave her a sympathetic look but stayed silent. There didn't seem anything more to say so she clicked her fingers for Bundi and walked to one of the large windows, open to the evening air. She stood looking out into the garden that shrank even as she watched, retreating steadily as it veiled itself behind the blackout curtain of night.

'Spencer-Churchill?' she heard Duff say, jerking his head towards the ceiling.

'Yes indeed. How quick you are,' Chips said, pleased. 'I commissioned it specially. He worked on it for many months.'

'What is he to your Winston?' Ambassador Kennedy asked.

'Nephew,' Duff said.

'And an artist, not a politician?' the ambassador said thoughtfully. 'Churchill also paints, I believe? Maybe he too should allow himself to retire and pursue it. More painting, less politicking.' He looked at them, eyes veiled behind his spectacles.

'Churchill is the greatest statesman we have,' Duff said calmly. 'The fact that he won't retire, can't, while all this is going on is proof of that.'

Chips looked panicked, and Brigid nearly laughed out loud. She wanted to remind him how much more blunt Duff could have been, how uncareful.

Honor and Maureen came in together: Honor large and flushed in red, Maureen like an icicle, Brigid thought, cool and elegant in palest blue satin that trailed along the floor after her. Behind them, after a beat, came an older woman, whippet-thin, in yellow, and a tall girl wearing a black dress picked out with white flowers that was almost the mirror image of Brigid's, only hers was of shiny silk, with a tulle underskirt that rustled. Her hair was brushed back off her face and pinned to frame it. And yes, she wore lipstick.

'Mrs Ambassador! Kathleen!' Chips moved smoothly forward, making introductions, handing around drinks, cigarettes, pulling forward a chair for Mrs Kennedy and, finally, bringing Kathleen over to where Brigid still stood by the window, scratching Bundi's heavy golden head.

'How do you do?' she said politely to Kathleen.

'Oh, I do great,' the girl assured her. 'Just great.' She looked around. 'Isn't this room neat? And the weather! I don't know why people say England is a damp country when since I have been here there has been just the most glorious sunshine, day after day.' No wonder Ambassador Kennedy had found Brigid's *Jolly well, thank you* inadequate. 'Anyway,' the girl continued in a rush, 'you must call me Kick. Everyone does.'

'Why do they?' Brigid asked, careful to sound as though finding out were the least important thing in the world to her. It was a trick she'd learned from Maureen.

'I think it's not meant to be a compliment,' the girl said with a laugh, wrinkling her nose. She had blue eyes that flashed in her tanned face. They weren't blue like Guinness blue, Brigid thought; that pale, almost ethereal colour. Kathleen's – Kick's – were deep, almost inky, like flax or cornflowers. She had even white teeth, a big nose and a firm jaw. She wasn't beautiful, Brigid decided, not at all really, but she was sort of *concentrated*. As though, squashed inside one person was enough energy, opinions, lively expectation to do two. 'I have the most terrible habit of kicking off my shoes everywhere I go. Probably I'll do it right here, in a little while. Why, I was at a weekend party at Hatfield only last week and some of the boys took all my left shoes and hid them.'

'I was meant to go to that party,' Brigid said quickly, reflexively. 'But I had another party to go to.' Then she blushed for being so childish.

'Well, I wish you had,' Kick said warmly.

'What did you do?' Brigid asked. 'About the shoes?' It was, she thought, just the kind of mean trick those boys would play.

She knew the ones – Eton-and-Oxford-educated, heirs to estates and ancient titles; the kind of young man who could do no wrong in Chips' eyes, but who could be – where they felt encouraged by a person's timidity or lack of place in the world – thoughtless, even mean.

'Why, I wasn't going to let them see I cared, so I walked around in two right shoes for the whole time, one black and one white.' She burst out laughing. 'I limped a bit, but that was OK.'

Brigid, who had planned on looking pained and polite and walking away, found herself laughing too. 'I'm sure they thought you wonderful,' she said kindly.

'I think one of them asked me to marry him,' Kick said with a grin, 'but the next day I couldn't remember which – don't they look the same, some of those fellows? – so I said nothing about it.'

Brigid burst out laughing again. She had never heard anyone talk like this girl – a mix of audacity and deprecation that meant you had no idea what she might say next, but you waited eagerly all the same.

'Where *is* Elizabeth?' Chips asked then, loudly, fretfully, consulting his watch. The dinner gong had gone a second time and still there was no sign of her. Fritzi had arrived, impeccable in his dinner jacket, and was being made much of by the grown-ups, as Brigid thought of them, over by the fireplace.

'Probably passed out,' Maureen drawled. 'I saw the cocktail tray being brought up to her quite some time ago.'

Chips winced.

'I'll go and knock on the door,' Brigid said. 'Perhaps she can't hear the gong.'

'Everyone can hear the gong,' Chips said. 'I had it designed purposefully that they would.'

'I'll come with you,' Kick said. The girls set off together, Kick chattering happily as they went. She admired everything they saw, the paintings, statues, rugs, even lamps. 'You know, I was scared half to death to come here,' she said as they rounded the top of the stairs and set off towards the Yellow Room.

'I don't believe that for a moment,' Brigid said.

'Oh, but I was, I assure you!' Brigid thought how she, in Kick's place, would never have admitted such a thing. And how disarming it was that this the girl 'fessed up so cheerfully. 'Then I asked myself, what's the very worst that could happen? Maybe I use the wrong knife, or turn up in the wrong gown, or say the wrong thing in that game you English play, where questions like "How do you do?" aren't supposed to get an answer.' She burst out laughing. 'And I decided, I can live with those things.'

'I can't believe you care about any of that.'

'Well, I guess you're right. I don't really. My mother, though – she does. Ever since they went to stay at Windsor Castle with the king and queen, which by the way, don't you know, she describes as "the fifth best weekend of her life" – well, she cares a very great deal that I shouldn't disgrace myself, or the family.'

'Only fifth best?' Brigid couldn't bring herself to say *weekend*. 'What were the others?'

'I don't exactly know, but certainly a visit to the Vatican and an audience with His Holiness must come first.' Kick spoke so unselfconsciously that it took Brigid a moment to realise she wasn't joking. Imagine mentioning something so mortifying as your religion – especially if you were Roman Catholic – so casually like that!

'Here we are,' she said, knocking politely on the door of the Yellow Room.

No answer.

'You need to knock louder than that,' Kick said. She hammered briskly on the door with her knuckles. 'Who is this Elizabeth, anyway?'

'Oh, you'll see,' Brigid said on a gurgle of laughter.

Chapter Twenty-One

Maureen

'**M**rs Kennedy – Maureen, Marchioness of Dufferin and Ava.' Chips, as she knew he would, lingered on her title, playing it out to its full length. How Maureen disliked those hosts who mumbled it, running out of steam somewhere around the end of 'Dufferin', leaving 'Ava' to fend for itself. She held out a hand graciously.

The ambassadress took it politely. 'Please, call me Rose.' She wasn't at all what Maureen had expected – or hoped for. Where was the blousy, red-cheeked woman, the worn-out mother of nine? This woman was cool and chic, tiny in her buttery yellow silk, with an elegantly brittle jawline that spoke of ruthlessness and self-control.

'Nine children,' Maureen found herself saying, and not at all in the way she had meant to say it, with a laugh, as though it were something too absurd to be credible – almost, she thought crossly, she had sounded admiring. 'How do you manage?'

And Rose, instead of throwing off the question as Maureen would have, answered seriously. 'Like every mother, you want them to be morally, mentally and physically as perfect as possible.'

Maureen thought about her own ambitions for her children – that they would survive childhood. That the girls would be pretty. That Sheridan would be good at games. 'Of course,' she said.

'I always thought,' Rose continued, 'that if you bring the oldest one up right, the rest will watch and copy. My son Joe Junior has a great sense of responsibility and a great sense of the family.' She talked about the duty towards their young minds, the importance of early discipline, never being late – 'in our house, anyone who is late for meals goes without' – but then, too, the need for freedom, 'and plenty of fresh air and sports,' she finished. 'All my children play football, and tennis, they swim and dive and sail. You cannot have a healthy mind without a healthy body.'

Maureen made a face. Behind Rose, Honor raised a sympathetic eyebrow at the crassness. Bodies, really; must she?

But Duff, who had been almost silent so far, looked up in interest. 'Tell me more,' he said. 'Do even the girls play football?'

'They do. And each has their own sailboat.'

'How do you keep them from competing with each other?' Duff asked.

'But I don't. That's the point. They are always in competition with each other.'

'Girls and boys?' Duff sounded sceptical.

'Yes indeed. Kathleen' – she said it with a long aaa sound, *Kaaathleen* – 'can hold her own with any of her brothers. Indeed, Young Joe and Jack and are quite in awe of her.'

'There are no differences between my sons and daughters,' the ambassador said complacently. 'They are all Kennedys.'

'You have an elder daughter, do you not, Mrs Ambassador?' Maureen asked.

'Rosemary,' she agreed.

'Are her brothers not in awe of her? She is not here, I think, is she?' Maureen looked around, as though Rosemary might be tucked away behind a chair or table. There was a strange little silence then.

'Rosemary is delicate,' the ambassador said.

'So,' Maureen swooped, 'the extremes of healthy competition are not for all your children?' She looked from the ambassador to his wife but neither would quite meet her gaze. Beside her, Duff put a hand on her arm.

'How much I admire America,' Fritzi said smoothly, 'the energy and freedom of those vast spaces.'

Maureen saw Chips give him a fond look.

'Well, you must come and visit,' the ambassador said, 'we would be delighted to host you. I can think of many who would be very happy to make your acquaintance.'

He looked eager, Maureen thought, like a huntsman who hears a promising rustle.

'It would be a pleasure to show you around,' Rose said.

'You two have met?' Chips asked, smiling broadly.

'Yes indeed, at Kathleen's coming-out ball just a month ago. Prince Friedrich' – Rose placed a light hand on Fritzi's arm – 'was kind enough to dance with my daughter and sit beside her at dinner.'

So, thought Maureen, looking from Rose to her husband to the prince – that was the way the wind blew. Or one of the ways.

'It was entirely my pleasure.' The prince did one of his slight bows.

'How sweet,' Maureen said, 'that *both* these delightful young girls should be so friendly already with our prince. Isn't it, Chips?'

Chips' smile grew less broad.

At dinner, Duff was beside Rose, and at first Maureen was pleased. She had dreaded him being next to Elizabeth, fearing the influence she might have. She was definitely half-cut by the time she arrived into the drawing room, with Kick on one side and Brigid on the other, as though keeping her upright. The girls were giggling. Elizabeth, swaying slightly between them, laughed too, but not, Maureen thought, at the same joke.

'So terrible of me,' she had declared, 'to keep you all waiting.' She sounded delighted, and showed no interest in any of the introductions, nodding cheerfully, then whispering loudly to Duff, 'Fix me a drink, darling,' even though Chips had already begun to organise their progression to the dinner table – 'Mr Ambassador, if you take Lady Dufferin . . .'

But, watching the attention Duff now paid to Rose Kennedy, the graceful, deferential way she inclined her head towards him, and noting again the determined thrust of her jaw, Maureen began to feel cross. Why was he listening so intently to her? What was she saying to him that caused him to lean in so close? Chips, on Maureen's left, talked over her to the ambassador, describing a recent party Emerald Cunard had given – 'Herr von Ribbentrop, Hitler's man in London, a most charming fellow. I must arrange a little soiree for you two to meet . . .' – so she was free to give all her attention to Duff and Rose. As she watched, Duff said something – one of his wry jokes, judging by the slight twitch of his lip – and Rose threw her head back, laughing prettily. Maureen gritted her teeth. Rescue came from an unlikely source.

'I say,' Elizabeth drawled, nudging Rose's arm with her elbow, 'what do you feed that daughter of yours? I saw her in the pool earlier, tearing up and down as though pursued by a shark. Quite ferocious, I must say.' Reluctantly, Rose's attention was dragged away from Duff, and Maureen saw her cast a disapproving glance around the table, no doubt wondering why there weren't even pairs for the *placement*.

On the other side of the ambassador, Honor stared down at her lap and Maureen wondered had she snuck her book in and was now reading it covertly. If so, Maureen thought, well, Chips would never notice. As well as talking to the ambassador, he was keeping an eye on Kick, on his other side, and occasionally interjecting in her conversation with Fritzi. He had no time to spare for his wife.

Fritzi was between Kick and Brigid, and Maureen watched as he turned first one way, then the other, engaging each girl smoothly in correct conversation. If he occasionally looked uncertain, it was the uncertainty of choice, she decided. The difficulty of knowing where to land the bulk of his attentions. And, perhaps, uncertainty at the speed of the back-and-forth between the girls, who chattered to one another across him as often as they spoke to him. That seemed to confuse him. Perhaps he expected them to wait their turn, she thought; silent unless he spoke to them.

'Lady Dufferin,' the ambassador interrupted her thoughts, 'you must know a great deal about Ireland. I understand you grew up there. I thought you might help me to understand what the thinking of that country is about the situation with Germany?'

Maureen was half bored at the thought of 'more war talk', as she thought of it – although quickly she realised that Joe Kennedy was a man determined that there would be no war – but flattered by his certainty that she knew 'a great deal' that was of use to him. Not flattered enough to give in easily, however. 'I thought you were Irish,' she said, raising an eyebrow. 'And therefore must know all there is to know.'

'Irish-American,' he said smoothly. 'Meaning I have a sense of kinship, but I don't pretend to know the country the way you do. But it's strategically important, which means I need to know more. What do you make of this man de Valera?'

Maureen told him what she knew, mainly parroting things she had heard her father, Ernest, or her husband say. That de Valera was cunning, a realist, pragmatic but only ever had one view in mind – the successful independence of his own country. As she spoke, she realised it might be time to know more. She resolved to ask Chips to order an extra copy of *The Times* while she was at Kelvedon, and to pay more attention to what was said – by Chips, Duff, even this American. She would, she decided, be as well-informed as Rose seemed to be.

As they talked, she saw that Duff was watching them, even while he conversed with Rose and, as much as he could, with Honor on his other side. Good, thought Maureen. If she could be jealous of the attention he paid his dinner companion, so could he. She leaned in closer to Joe Kennedy, letting it be seen that she considered his questions thoughtfully.

After dinner, the men didn't linger over port but came straight to the drawing room. Duff caught up with her where she stood looking at a display of tiny animals in fantastically coloured glass that Chips had positioned on a small table. A seal, a swan, a fawn, a lizard, all in colours like boiled sweets. 'Pretty, or hopelessly vulgar?' she asked. He ignored the question.

'What were you and the ambassador talking about?'

'What were you and his wife talking about?'

'War. Peace. What America might do – what else? You?'

'The same.' She smiled and fluttered her eyelashes at him, hoping he would think she dissembled.

'Good. Later, you must tell me exactly what he said.'

And she realised with fury that he wasn't jealous. He really did hope she had been quizzing the ambassador on America's intentions, storing up nuggets, like a squirrel putting away nuts, that would be useful to him in his understanding of what was to come. She picked up one of the glass animals – a stork with orange beak and long spindly blue legs. Her hand closed hard around it and one of the legs snapped. Quickly, she shoved the pieces into the evening bag that hung by a slender chain from her wrist. She would tell someone later. Honor, not Chips.

Chapter Twenty-Two

Kick

'Might I ask something?' Kick said to Brigid after dinner.

Without any discussion, they had set themselves a little apart from the rest, in a corner of the drawing room. Now that the sun had finally set, and the lamps been lit, the grey walls and painted ceiling seemed to have drawn in and down, making it more intimate. The pools of light cast by the many lamps that stood on every surface – lamps with fringed tassels, with glass shades in gaudy colours, angled to cast their glow now up, now down – deepened the colours and parcelled up the room into fascinating pockets, like a series of lighted tableaux or small stages. Between each of them was the unknowable dark of an auditorium. On one such stage was Brigid's cousin, Maureen, looking cold and glamorous; on another

Honor, pretending not to read although Kick could clearly see the book held in her left hand; her own mother, turning the pages of a big heavy book of photographs and watching Elizabeth flick ash from the end of her cigarette into the fireplace, missing so often that the hearth was littered with flecks of ash and even a few cigarette butts. Elizabeth stood with one foot up on the fender and Kick wondered that she didn't burn the sole of her shoe.

'You might,' Brigid said.

'It's about the prince.'

'Fritzi? What about him?'

Kick paused. How to put into words what she wanted to know. 'He was at my coming-out ball,' she began.

'Mine too,' Brigid said. 'I danced with him. Twice, if I recall.'

'Me too. And he was seated beside me at dinner.'

'And?'

'Well, don't you wonder? I mean, it's like every time I turn around, there he is. But now it seems like every time you turn around, there he is too . . .'

'I see what you mean.' Brigid's lip twitched. 'You think they are setting us up?'

'I do.'

'I knew they were setting me up. Chips is shameless. He tells me all his plans because he thinks I'm a willing co-conspirator. But what is one to do?' She shrugged. 'I mean, that's what they do, isn't it? Set us up? Wonder and speculate and plot. Who we might marry, who we must not marry, how high we may aim. It's hateful, but it's what they do.'

'Is it? It isn't in America.'

'Well, now you are in England.' She shrugged again. 'Anyway, Chips may do what he likes. And I' – she tilted her chin a little – 'I shall do what I like.' Then, with a giggle, 'I say, do you think they know they're in competition?'

'As long as *we* know we aren't in competition.'

'Are we not?' Brigid asked, giving Kick a level look.

'Not. Leastways, I'm not. Not a bit of it.'

'You seem awfully sure. He *is* a prince. And, if Chips has his way, will one day be an emperor.' She burst out laughing.

'Terribly cute,' Kick agreed solemnly. Then, 'But I am oh-so-sure. You see . . .'

'Oh.' Brigid smiled slyly. 'There's someone you like, isn't there? Who is it?'

'You can't tell.'

'Who would I tell?'

'Anyone. You can't tell anyone.'

'Not a soul. Cross my heart and hope to die.' She blessed herself quickly and sketchily, a loosely drawn sign of the cross, then saw the shocked look on Kick's face. 'I say, sorry! It's what we used to say in the nursery at Elveden. It only means I promise I won't.'

'Well, OK then,' Kick said after a moment. 'He's called Billy.' Her voice snagged on the name.

'Billy Cavendish?'

'You know him? Well, of course you do. All you English know each other.' *But how well?* she wondered in a sudden panic.

'Everyone knows him,' Brigid said. 'He sat on my other side at my coming-out.' She began to laugh. 'Chips was *quite* persuaded he'd do. Until he thought of Fritzi.' She laughed again, then saw Kick's face. 'No one thinks he'd do now. Least of all me. I mean, he's a dear, sweet fellow. In fact, they say he might do for the princess Elizabeth . . .'

'She's – what? – twelve!' Kick said.

'Yes.'

'Awful!' Kick made a face.

'A princess,' Brigid said, shrugging. 'It's what they do,' she repeated. 'Match names, families, houses, fortunes, consider all possibilities. And then move on to consider someone else. Like a game of chess, only with people. Anyway, never mind that, what do your parents think of Billy?'

'Oh, they don't think anything of him. They haven't met.'

'And have you met his parents? The duke and duchess?'

'No. Debo thinks they won't approve.'

'Debo may be right.'

'Oh, I'm pretty certain I can show them Americans aren't so very different,' Kick said comfortably. 'After all, I've met other Americans here – Lady Astor, Emerald Cunard – and they do alright.'

'It's not being American . . .' Brigid began awkwardly. 'Not anymore. We're used to Americans. It's . . .'

'It's what?'

'Well, you're Roman Catholic, aren't you?' She squirmed a little, Kick saw.

'What of it?'

'They do say the duke has rather strong views. Why, I read a pamphlet he wrote only a few weeks ago. Chips gave it to me. He thought it would be a good conversation starter with Billy.' She giggled, then broke off when she saw Kick's face. 'Sorry!'

'What pamphlet?'

'About Catholic girls marrying into the aristocracy, and what a threat it is. Terribly silly stuff,' she added hastily. 'Only it does rather seem he believes all that papist conspiracy rot.'

'What papist conspiracy rot?' Kick was confused.

'Well, you know . . . That Catholics aren't to be trusted.'

'Why not?'

'I'm not really sure. I mean, I don't pay attention to that sort of thing. But I think it's the incense . . .' Brigid said thoughtfully.

'Incense?' Kick was baffled.

'Yes. It chokes people, makes them think of, I don't know, rich spices and hidden things and complicated intrigues, you know.' She made a vague motion with her hand, sketching something in the air. 'It makes Catholics *exotic*. And that's never good.'

'But we're just . . .' Kick trailed off.

'Of *course* you are,' Brigid reassured her briskly. 'Only the burning and chanting makes it seem like you aren't.'

Kick paused for a moment. 'I don't pay any attention to that sort of stuff,' she said decidedly. 'It can't be one bit relevant.' She changed the subject. 'He's a bit like King Midas' son, isn't he?' she said, nodding her head in Fritzi's direction.

'After he gets turned to gold?' Brigid asked thoughtfully.

'Maybe midway? Sort of statue-like and composed and not terribly human but not actually solid gold yet.'

'I wonder which way he'll go?' Brigid mused. Then, 'Tell me more about all your brothers.'

So Kick began to describe the summers at home, at Hyannis Port, and the way the days were entirely given over to being outdoors – to sailing and tennis and games of football. Of the blue sky and sea that seemed to swap shades between them. Of the rivalry between Joe Jnr and Jack that meant that everything one did, the other had to do too, no matter how dangerous, so that even in a gathering storm when Joe boasted that he would sail around the farthest marker and back, Jack had instantly run for his own boat, and how they had only been persuaded not to when Bobby, then barely ten, had said he too would go.

Of the holiday mood when their father came to stay for a few days when he wasn't working – 'Before he was the ambassador he produced motion pictures, you know?' – and how everything changed in his presence. 'Like turning on an electric light switch,' she said, glancing over at her father fondly, then describing how he took them out, to the theatre, the ballgame; how he sought their thoughts and opinions on everything, allowed them to say whatever they wanted – never complaining that something wasn't 'suitable' or was 'mean' as long as it was clever and the arguments were sound and, crucially, not boring. To be boring was unforgivable. 'It matters more what the boys say,' she said frankly, 'because of what they will do in the world, but he makes sure that Eunice and Pat and me can hold our own too.'

'Not Rosemary?'

'Rosie is different,' Kick said. 'The dearest girl alive, and the one we all go to when we are unhappy or in trouble, but she doesn't take part in the discussions so much. She dislikes arguments and cannot be made to see that a disagreement is just that, not personal. She cries if the boys are too hard on her, and tears always make Mother angry, so we have learned to leave Rosie out of it.'

It was more – far more – than she usually said about Rosemary, and still not enough to fully explain how much she worried. There was a part of her that knew her mother wouldn't wish her to reveal even that much. More, even, there was another part of her that felt the sharp sting of disloyalty at putting into words the things about Rosie that made her different – as though to say such things made her seem less a Kennedy.

But Brigid's face was so sympathetic, her expression so warm, that Kick had been borne along. And Brigid seemed to understand that she had said enough. 'What about the younger ones?' she asked, skilfully changing the subject. 'Surely they don't debate too?'

'Oh yes. Even the little boys – Teddy and Bobby – give as good as they get.'

'I worry you will find Kelvedon very dull,' Brigid said. 'For we are not at all like that.'

Kick shook her head, smiling. 'Maybe not, but with you it's all hidden,' she said. 'We are all out in the open and even quite blunt, and no one needs to wonder for very long what it is that someone thinks or wants. Here, everything is a mystery. How can that be dull?'

Chapter Twenty-Three

Maureen

Maureen looked over to where Brigid and the Kennedy girl were sitting a little apart – the Kennedy girl was barefoot and had her feet curled up under her. Brigid sat on a footstool beside her. Both were laughing at something, oblivious to everyone else. Maureen could see how much Fritzi wanted to approach them, and how he cast around for some excuse that would allow him.

'May I offer you a cigarette?' he tried. But that was no good.

'My mother doesn't allow it. She says I am too young,' Kick answered, with a quick look at Rose.

'I don't.' That was Brigid. 'I find I cannot bear the taste.' And they went back to their private laughter.

Maureen remembered what it was like to be that age. How interesting one was, to everyone, as they strove to understand who one might marry. How interesting one was to young men, who strove to understand if one might marry them. Or, in the case of a different kind of young man, how much fun one might be, without there being any talk of marriage.

She missed it, Maureen realised. Missed the hot spotlight of being centre stage. Once you were married, well, that was you settled. Unless you were to go about bolting in the way Oonagh had. The way Elizabeth had. Even then – no one cared very much for one's second marriage. And if you chose to behave well, to stay married, then something of dullness clung to you. You no longer had the capacity to surprise.

It was that, more than anything – the feeling of being, no longer, a main player in the performance of her life, but rather a supporting part – that preoccupied her. No wonder she filled her parties with bowls of fake vomit, disguises and other practical jokes, she thought gloomily – so much of the natural excitement had receded, slipping away like the tide. It was that, too, that made her call out to Fritzi, 'Come and sit by me,' patting the sofa. And when he did, 'They tell me you have been at Cambridge? You must tell me all about it.'

She bent the full force of her charm upon him and watched, gratified, as it began to have an effect. Soon he was leaning closer, talking more, sharing his impressions of England and how it differed from the Germany he had grown up in. Like that – animated by memories and the effort of comparison – he was, she decided, less of a bore. Rather sweet really. He squinted and frowned and wrinkled his perfect features trying to remember, looking human rather than divine, and was the better for it.

The prince was embarked on a story about hunting wild boar that seemed complicated – like all hunting stories, except that really, they were simple – and Maureen pretended to follow it so as to flatter him. She looked up and found Duff was watching her. He caught her eye and gave a quick smile. A sympathetic smile. Sympathy for what? she wondered. For her? She wanted to fling her glass into the fireplace and watch as the broken shards flew about the room, cutting and slashing where they landed.

Duff went back to talking intently to the ambassador, and she knew that was how he would be: talking, talking, as though he alone could persuade Joe Kennedy to act against all the shrewd instincts of his selfish heart – there was no hiding that from Maureen, who recognised self-interest where she saw it – and throw his lot in with Duff and Churchill, with the few who believed that England must stand up to Germany at any cost. Her husband was a romantic, a patriot. How she loved him for it, and despised him.

'Yes, and in the end you killed it,' she said, moving irritably in her seat. Fritzi looked surprised, then hurt. 'All hunting stories end the same,' she added, standing up.

'Actually, the boar got away,' Fritzi said with dignity.

But Maureen didn't stay to listen to him. She went to poke the fire, shivering exaggeratedly until she was certain Chips was paying full attention to her.

'Why do you invite these people?' she hissed. 'I would never have come if I had known who would be here.'

'But you knew,' he said. 'You knew exactly. In any case,' slyly, 'I see your husband is having a rather jolly time.'

They both looked to where Duff sat with the ambassador. Both had large glasses of brandy and were seemingly wrapped in a pocket of space all their own, talking in low voices, heads inclined towards one another. They looked, she thought, separate to the rest of the room. Different to it in substance and density. Maureen felt the silliness, the emptiness of everything even more keenly.

'I can't believe you don't smoke, Biddy,' Elizabeth said loudly then. She was a little behind everyone, like a train running late, puffing to catch up. 'I don't know what I'd do sometimes without a gasper.'

'Have another drink?' Maureen said nastily.

'Don't mind if I do,' Elizabeth said cheerfully. 'Chips, ring the bell, darling. Don't be mean.'

Chapter Twenty-Four

Honor

Dinner, Honor reflected as she finished her morning tea, had been frightful. Ambassador Kennedy on one side, Duff on the other, both more interested in the person to the other side of them than in her. When the ambassador had turned his attention to her, it was to ask questions – so many of them, so detailed: how her parents occupied their time, who they read and admired, the size of Elveden, how many employed there – that she had felt as though she were back at the London School of Economics, before one of her professors. Then he had wanted to know what lessons Paul was doing, what musical instruments he learned, did he keep a pony in town? 'He is not yet three,' she protested, but her answer didn't please him. None of her answers did. And the more he asked, the more she took refuge in the kind of vagueness she had learned from her cousin Oonagh – a veiled obliqueness that was charming in Oonagh, accompanied by those large blue eyes and perfect-shaped face, and rather less so in herself, she suspected, so that she felt it had been a test, and she had failed.

Afterwards, she had excused herself as early as she could, but even so she felt tired. Even after coming to bed, she had lain awake for hours, as she so often did these nights. Ears attuned to every sound, heart set racing by any sudden thud – a door closing, loud footsteps on the stairs, a window thrown open in a nearby room. The house had its own sounds, and she was not used to them.

Here there were the unexpected sounds of nature, too, rather than the steady hum of traffic outside their London home. A fox screaming had set her bolt upright in bed, eyes wide, until she realised what it was – a vixen, she had decided, calling for her cubs; it was too late in the year for a mating call.

Only after the sounds had all died down, when she had heard dawn stirring outside and seen the sun straining through the dark like milk through muslin, only then did she sleep.

This was the first night she had spent at the house since they had bought it, when they had almost camped, she and Chips, companionably together in one bedroom, because everywhere was so uncomfortable. Then, Chips had talked and talked of his plans for modernisation, improvements he must make, ways to make the place splendid and comfortable. 'It will be a paradise,' he had said, arms sweeping wide. 'An oasis, an escape from the demands of society and the House and London.'

But it wasn't an escape, she thought now; he had brought society, the House, London, with him.

Back then, Honor had listened to him, or, at least, half-listened to him in a way that was indulgent. Now, when he spoke, the

effort of not allowing herself to hear him was so great that it
sapped her energy for other things. More than anything, she
wanted not to hear him.

Now, she lay in her bath, knowing that next door Molly was
waiting, having laid out her clothes for the day, to brush her
hair. But she couldn't seem to hurry. She stared out the window
above the wash-hand basin at the blue of the sky. Another hot
day. Reaching to the bottom of the window were the branches
of a chestnut tree, splayed leaves stretching up towards the glass.
Their edges were trimmed crisp and brown by the weeks of
sunshine, and they moved hardly at all, she saw. Another day
with almost no wind. Lucky it wasn't a sailing party. That made
her remember Rose Kennedy, and her strange exultation in the
physical achievements of her children. Such a tiny woman, Honor
thought, to be mother to so many.

She allowed herself to imagine it. Or try to, anyway: Paul at
the head of a procession of little ones, his brothers and sisters.
What would they all be like? Would they be like Paul, only
younger, and girls as well as a boy? She thought about him in
the nursery yesterday when she had gone to say hullo after they
arrived. He had kissed her politely, answered her questions –
'Did you have a good journey down?' 'Has Nanny given you
your tea?' – solemnly. 'Yes; we saw a hare'; 'Yes; we had toast
and crumpets', lisping slightly on his S's still, so that Honor had
wondered was almost-three too old for that, and should she
talk to the tutor about exercises to correct it? They had run out
of things to say, as they so easily did, and Honor had found
herself wishing that Chips was with them. It was, she thought
now, squeezing water from a sponge onto her arm and watching
it trickle back into the tub, the only place she missed Chips. In

her interactions with her son. With Chips, Paul was lively, talk-ative. Somehow, he and his father knew one another, in a way that she and her son did not. They understood one another, even through the net of nanny, nursemaid, tutor, nursery hours – all the ways in which Paul had been separated from her, almost since the very moment of his birth, when Nanny had said, 'I will take him, Madame. You need your rest.'

Honor, not understanding that this was to be the way, had agreed, thinking it was only for a short time – an hour, a day – while she recovered the strength she needed to care for him.

But it had not been an hour or a day. It had been a pattern. One that set hard so quickly that she could find no way around it. She had lost sight of the child she had given birth to, whom she had known so completely in the moment of his birth but who had become a stranger to her. A small, not terribly polite stranger.

And yet, with Chips, he was not strange. 'Papa!' he would cry, 'I did it, just like you told me . . .' and would spill the story of his triumph – a cricket ball smartly hit, a pony disciplined – confident that his father knew exactly what he meant.

But Chips was not with them, and so after the first questions there were no others and then the tutor had come to say it was time for Paul's walk. Whereupon the boy had stamped his foot and said, 'I won't.' The tutor, clearly embarrassed in front of Honor, had insisted in a jocular kind of way that even Honor could tell was awkward. But Paul only stamped his foot again and insisted, louder, that he wouldn't. Honor, feeling she was making everything worse by being there, had quickly said, 'I must get on. Paul, be a good boy now,' and she had left the nursery. Behind her, the sound of Paul's screams: 'I won't, I tell you, I won't!'

Should she send for Chips, she had asked herself. He could get Paul to do anything, cajole him into any activity, using the same mix of charm and energy he brought to everything he set his mind to. But no. That would be unfair on the tutor, who must learn to manage these moments for himself. And so she had gone away, blocking her ears with shaking hands until she was out of range.

There in her bath, she imagined nine children, all stamping and screaming. And her, Honor, unable to make herself heard or noticed above the noise. Did any of Rose Kennedy's children behave like that? She felt they did not.

Honor wondered if they were all as athletic as Kick. Or were there some among the nine for whom the regular competitions and the proofs demanded of their excellence were hard, even humiliating? Who was the daughter, Rosemary, Maureen had seemed to know about, who was not in competition with the others? And why the strange little silence around her name?

'Madame?' Molly tapped at the bathroom door. 'Can I get you anything?' By which, Honor knew, she meant, *You are very late, what are you doing in there?*

'I'll be out directly.'

She could hear Chips, next door, moving about his dressing room. It had been dawn before she heard him come up. Heard his feet along the corridor, the way he paused at her door so she had almost stopped breathing, then Elizabeth Ponsonby in a loud whisper: 'I'm not sure which you resemble more, lurking before your wife's door – a secret lover, or a suspicious husband. Which is it, Chips?' Followed by a snigger. It had been infuriating, but enough to send Chips to his own room, where he shut the door with a bang that was too loud for that hour.

She could hear him now, whistling 'September in the Rain', and marvelled at his energy. As soon as dinner had finished, he had begun to plan a tennis tournament – 'If we play singles, then mixed doubles, we should manage three matches each . . .' – ignoring equally Maureen who said, 'Well, I won't play,' and Kick who had said, 'I'll play twice.'

Chapter Twenty-Five

Kick

Kick sat over the end of a slice of toast, breaking the
crust into pieces and crumbling them idly, and half-
watched her reflection in the many shiny surfaces – the
curved domes that covered dishes, the flat trays and slanted
sides of teapots that were everywhere she looked; morning sun
on polished silver. The toast crusts had traces of marmalade on
them and she had just realised her fingertips were sticky, when
Chips came in.

'Eddie Cavendish,' he said loudly.

Kick looked up in a sudden panic. Here?

'Just telephoned,' Chips clarified, looking around at them all.
'They are staying nearby, with the Blounts, and have said they
will motor over later for a swim. On such a day, what could
be more perfect?' He threw his arms wide and Kick guessed it

was not the thought of the weather that thrilled him, but the company. 'Their sons, Billy and Andrew, come with them. A friend of Billy's called Hugo. And Deborah Mitford. Brigid, you must think of amusing games for the young people.'

Kick felt her face grow hot and plump and knew it must be like fresh-risen bread, damp and swollen. She looked up and found Brigid watching her, eyes dancing as she said, 'I'm sure we can think of something.' She spoke to Chips, but it was Kick she looked at. Kick didn't know whether to laugh at her or frown her into discretion. What if her mother saw? She shook her head the slightest bit.

'I must plan lunch,' Chips said, all energy. 'We will eat outdoors, I think.'

'That will be charming,' said Rose. 'May I help? At Hyannis Port, where we spend our summers, I ask Cook to prepare a great many salads and cold dishes. It is very pleasant to simply eat when we are hungry and nothing spoils.'

'What a good idea,' Chips said. Kick got the feeling that he would have thought anything at all a good idea just then. 'Why not come with me and we can talk to Mrs Bath together?'

'Are you going up to change?' Brigid whispered, falling into step beside her as she left the morning room through the double doors that led straight to the garden. Outside was sunny and bright and somehow smooth; like a well-poached egg, Kick thought with a lurch of elation.

She looked down at her cream shorts, pale-green-and-white gingham shirt and white plimsolls. 'Why? Should I?'

'No, only I thought for sure you would. That always seems to be what the girls I know do, when meeting a chap they like. *I must change*, they squeal, and they run off and reappear in something frightful.' Brigid laughed.

'Do they really?' Kick asked, stopping at a lavender bush. 'I wonder do they know the change is a frightful one?' She sounded amused.

'Of course they do not!' Brigid said. 'They imagine they look simply wonderful.'

'Well, I won't change. I mean, what's the point? We will only be outside anyway.'

'I should have known you would not.'

'So, what "amusing games" shall we arrange?' Kick asked. 'We can't play the tennis tournament, darn it, because the court will not be ready. They are still painting lines. In any case, it is too hot.' She pinched off a piece of lavender and sniffed at it.

'Swim?'

'Yes, but that will not keep us occupied for an entire day.'

'Certainly it won't keep *you* occupied for an entire day. Croquet?'

'Boring!' Kick made a face. 'But if we make teams and put up a prize for the winners, it'll be more interesting.'

'What kind of prize?'

'Doesn't really matter. Anything, as long as it's clear what it's for.'

'A tooth mug?' Brigid asked with a laugh.

'Perfectly daisy!' Then, 'What to do with Fritzi, though? He isn't really the tooth mug type.'

'Oh he'll be alright.'

'Isn't Debo a pal?' Kick asked then.

'Certainly seems like it. But I don't know how you have made her so. Those Mitford girls are terrifying. Diana,' Brigid shuddered. 'The way she looks at one, with those great big eyes of hers. And Nancy, so cutting she's like a giant pair of dressmaking scissors.'

'And yet Diana can be oh-so-nice too, you know? I went to supper there, and she was just darling. Unity too. Although she's a funny one alright.'

'Funny is not what most people call Unity. You should hear what Duff says about her. Calls her a traitor to the country, and would say worse except respect for Lord Redesdale holds him back a little.'

'You should have seen her, that day of the Hyde Park riots . . . She came racing into the embassy for all the world like a fox with the hunt after it. Except the most brazen fox you ever saw. "*I don't care a bit*," she said, tossing her head. And I could see she meant it . . . We had to persuade her not to go out and address them all from the steps of the embassy, and then only by saying Pa would be furious.'

'Imagine being that sure of anything,' Brigid said, wondering. 'I mean, so sure that you would stand up and defy anyone who didn't agree with you. It's like half the fun, for Unity, is that everyone is against her. Can you imagine? I can't bear if people are cross with me even for the slightest thing. And there's Unity, delighted that the whole world is furious with her.'

'I say,' Debo's rather high voice came to them from the house, 'there you are. Chips said we'd find you out here. He said you were plotting.'

'And here we are. But only plotting for fun,' Brigid called, waving her over. 'Hullo, Billy. Hullo, Andrew.'

'Jolly nice of you to invite us,' Billy said as they crossed the lawn. The boys wore white flannels and Billy had already taken his jacket off and rolled up his sleeves. Debo wore wide navy trousers with a white-and-blue striped top and was fanning herself exaggeratedly with the brim of a straw hat.

'I rather think you invited yourselves,' Kick said. 'But who can blame you, on a hot day, with rumours of a swimming pool.'

Andrew turned pink at the ears, but Billy laughed and said, 'That's it alright,' then introduced the young man with them: 'This is Hugo. I promised him tremendous fun, so you see, you mustn't let me down.'

'You make wild promises, and we must honour them?' Kick asked with a laugh. 'Well, alright then. Shall we start with a swim?'

'Yes, please,' Debo said, fanning her hat harder. 'I feel like an ice cream that has begun to flop down the side of the cone. Isn't it simply too hot?'

'Not a bit,' Kick insisted. 'It's perfect.'

'You always say that,' Billy said affectionately. 'Even that day at Goodwood when it rained in a steady drip for hour after hour.'

'Just perfect,' Kick said with a grin. 'Now, let's swim. You can change in the pavilion.'

'I wondered what it was,' Hugo said. 'Thought it might be a museum.' By which Kick knew he thought it excessive, silly, even vulgar. That he was mocking it while pretending not to. The knowledge made her feel suddenly protective of Chips.

'It's very useful,' she said firmly.

They changed – Debo into a pink-and-white bathing suit of such extraordinary modesty that Kick laughed out loud. 'Don't,' Debo said, face screwed up in mock-pain, 'it's too awful. But Farve insists. I may be the same age as you and Brigid but that counts for nothing with him. And if it's that or not be allowed go anywhere, then, well, it's that . . .'

'You look darling,' Kick assured her. 'You always do.'

They didn't swim so much as splash about, she thought, throwing water at each other and floating lazily in the shallow end, watched by the simpering terracotta ladies in their flouncy petticoats. She swam lengths and Billy kept pace with her for a few, then dropped away, saying, 'You are far more energetic than I.' He pulled himself out of the water and went to lie on a reclining chair, water dripping off his bare chest and legs and down the sides of the chair onto the warm grey stone, where it quickly dried. Kick did another couple of lengths, speeding up and down, turning gracefully in one fluid movement at either end, then climbed out and went to the chair beside him.

She stretched out, admiring the pearly polish on her toes and ruefully lamenting the freckles that dotted her calves. But she realised she was conscious of her bare legs and arms in a way she never had been when swimming or sailing with the boys back home – Jack and Joe's friends who came to Hyannis Port for the summers. Invariably, these young men arrived half in love with whichever brother was their friend – especially Jack's friends all adored him – and left almost more in love with Kick. She tried not to mind that their highest expression of praise was 'You're like a female version of Jack . . .'

She had gone out with one or two, but never paid them much attention. Never been conscious of them beyond that they were friendly, easy-going, sporty, like her brothers. Certainly not the way she now was conscious of Billy beside her.

He was pale, with a smattering of cinnamon-coloured freckles on his shoulders. Thinner than her brothers, but wiry and stronger-looking than she had expected. His height and the slight stoop all Englishmen seemed to affect had made him seem weedier. Stripped of his beautifully tailored suits and shirts, he was muscled, with the arms and shoulders of a horseman. She remembered hearing that he had rowed for Cambridge and thought she could see that in the flat stomach and lean legs.

Then she looked up and caught his eye and realised that he had seen her staring at him, and blushed horribly, turning quickly away. The only consolation, she thought as she picked up a copy of the *Tatler*, was that he had blushed too.

The blushing was new, the self-consciousness, and so too was the pang she felt when Brigid came and sat on the edge of his chair in her bathing suit – a neat blue number that showed off her elegant legs. 'What have you been doing at the Blounts?' she asked Billy. 'Fun party?'

'Some shooting,' he said, shifting up to make space for her. 'Snipe mostly. A great deal of badminton, some strenuous walking. It's a larger party, rather older. The Mosleys were arriving as we left this morning. Less jolly than this, I should think.'

'Hard to tell what this is just yet,' Brigid said. 'We've just arrived. Yesterday.' She yawned. 'But I should think we'll be alright, isn't that so, Kick?'

Kick nodded, unsure what to add. Still bent over her magazine, she observed Brigid and Billy as they chattered, about people they knew – a girl called June who was staying with the Blounts, a party they had both been to in London before coming away – and tried to understand what might be between them, even while she pretended to read the *Tatler*. She found herself trying to understand the angle of Brigid's body and what was meant by the way it was turned towards Billy's; the tone of his voice as he said, 'I say, don't you worry that you will burn? You're awfully white,' and she hated herself for doing it. Brigid had said there was nothing between them. Billy was just being friendly. So why was she cutting and splitting and analysing, when she had never done anything like that before?

Maureen arrived, trailing a rose pink silk peignoir and a broad hat with a rose silk scarf tied around it, Pugsy wheezing along beside her. She looked impossibly sophisticated, and Kick wondered how she managed to be so much more herself than the other women. Like a diamond, dense, compacted, rather hard, but sparkling. She largely ignored them, beyond saying, 'Oh, hullo, Billy,' in tones of surprise, then sat in the shade with a copy of *The Times* and a tall glass of what looked like lemonade but probably wasn't. She lit a cigarette and the smell of the smoke blanketing the hot air made Kick feel sick.

Andrews appeared at the head of a group of footmen with sun umbrellas, which they placed at intervals, carrying chairs into the shade and drawing small tables towards them. 'Crumblies approaching,' Brigid said with a laugh, getting up from Billy's chair. Kick forced herself not to watch the way she patted Billy's bare arm as she went to greet his parents. She clearly knew them well.

While Brigid chattered and Debo answered questions put by Billy's father – 'Have you been having fun?' 'Shall you swim again?' – Kick was able to get a good look at the duke and duchess. He was tall and thin and looked a lot like Billy – the same angularity, the same apologetic stoop. He wore a shirt with a collar so frayed that she, who hated sewing, itched to take a needle to it, and a pair of trousers worn almost completely through at the knees. The duchess – 'Moucher' was apparently what everyone called her – had a face that was lined and careworn and kind. She looked clever and thoughtful, Kick thought, and terribly harassed, as though in her mind was a constant turning-over of duties and responsibilities. Was that what the mistress of a place like Chatsworth, like Lismore Castle – places Kick had never seen but which she had read about – looked like? she wondered.

She had only been a duchess for five months, since the duke's father died – Kick knew all about it because of Debo – and already Moucher looked like a horse that has been boxed into a stall too small. As though forever worrying about roof slates and rising damp. Neither of them looked anything – anything at all – as she had imagined a duke and duchess to look. She wondered what her mother made of them. Especially the duke, with his tattered collar and Turkish cigarettes. The thought caused her to bite the inside of her lower lip, to stop herself laughing aloud. She could have explained to Rose that nothing could be more English than this – the biggest landowner in the country, one of them anyway, dressed as though he were a rag-and-bone man. But she knew her mother wouldn't get it. Wouldn't want to get it. It would be another chance for her to warn Kick not to get too involved: 'We don't live here, Kathleen; for all that we are here now, this is not our life. It is your father's job.' How many times already had Rose said this, or a variation on it? Kick had stopped listening, because she had begun to understand that, in fact, England didn't feel to her as it felt to Rose – like a transitory place, somewhere quaint to pause and amuse oneself for a while. It felt, more and more, as though the strange instant familiarity she had discovered when the *Queen Mary* berthed at Southampton and she stepped ashore meant something serious. That, she knew, meant trouble too. Her parents still talked of 'home' meaning Bronxville, and of 'after' as something to look forward to.

Honor came out next, followed by Elizabeth, then Chips in close conversation with Rose about lunch. She heard the words 'potato salad . . .' and watched Chips frown with the effort of decision.

'I might walk to the village this afternoon,' Elizabeth said to no one in particular. 'See the world beyond the four walls.'

'There's nothing there,' Chips said impatiently. 'A village hall, a church.' He shrugged. 'And it's further than you think. If you want an excursion, at least let me plan something. There are Roman remains worth a visit. I can arrange it.'

'But what if I don't want you to arrange it?' Elizabeth asked. 'What if I want a tiny bit of a break from your arranging?'

'How long *are* you staying?' Chips asked. 'I don't think you were ever terribly clear about that.'

'Oh jolly good, Chips,' Elizabeth said warmly, so that Brigid laughed. Chips shot her a nasty look and she turned the rest of the laugh into a cough.

'We thought we'd walk to the river later,' Brigid said hurriedly. 'Billy wanted to see it.' Kick couldn't remember Billy saying anything of the sort, but he nodded now, and immediately Chips began to explain the best way to go – 'Past the stables, but be careful when you reach the banks, they are less robust than they look. You don't want a wetting.'

The duchess looked alarmed and he reassured her that the water was low and slow-moving. 'Hasn't rained in weeks. The first big downpour will churn it, but for now it's more of a trickle.'

Fritzi didn't seem to know where he belonged, with the older or younger, and Kick felt sorry for him. 'Come and sit here,' she said. 'We can be strangers together.' He smiled at her with, she thought, something of relief and sat in the chair she had indicated. Almost immediately he began to pay her compli-ments – how well she swam, how smooth and fast were her turns – that were tedious and laboured so that she regretted the kind impulse that had called to him. She remembered her father, '*I want you to listen to what he has to say* . . .' But it seemed he had nothing to say.

'No need to talk,' she said firmly after a while. 'It's nice to just sit here and hear the birds and the trees.'

'It is,' Fritzi agreed immediately. He closed his eyes, which had the effect of making Kick realise how tired he looked, dark purple circles and the pallor of late nights. But his silence left her free to listen to Billy, who was telling Hugo something about a car race he'd watched. His voice, she decided, might even be what she liked best about him. It was low and seemed to come from deeper in his chest than other people's voices. He spoke slowly, as if half-inclined not to speak at all. And yet, there was nothing half-intentioned about what he said. So unlike Fritzi and his vague, almost rehearsed compliments.

Their not-talking seemed to strike others as odd. Her mother sent volleys of significant looks in Kick's direction, that slight drawing together of her finely pencilled eyebrows that wasn't a frown, but was close, and that told Kick she didn't like something she was doing or wearing. When Kick failed to respond, her mother was reduced to holding her gaze and shaking her head slightly. Kick looked back at her, eyes wide in innocent enquiry. Chips, meanwhile, seemed determined to find a job for Fritzi – 'Darling boy, perhaps you would help me with this umbrella?' 'Could I ask you to go to the house for another cushion? Brigid will show you where.' Except that Brigid said, 'Not I,' lazily, and Fritzi, each time, did what Chips asked then returned to his seat beside Kick, so that Chips ended by looking cross and announced, 'We might as well eat,' quite sharply.

Lunch was almost like being back at Hyannis Port, Kick thought. Her mother's influence was everywhere – in the food, the many salads and cold dishes, but also in the energy of conversation. Rather than the usual idle round of gossip and desultory tearing-apart of plays seen and books read, broad topics appeared and were debated vigorously. The table had been set up in the shade, and the chairs drawn close together that they might all fit, so that there was an energy to the kind of remarks that might have fallen flat if they were delivered at the long tables that were usual for meals in England – lost somewhere between the first and second salt cellars, abandoned between the decanters and flower arrangements.

Even so, when her father steered the conversation around to politics, Kick could see how hard he had to work at it. None of the others wanted that talk. They wriggled away from even his direct questions – 'What do you make of the Sudetenland now?' – with polite dissemblings: 'Seems a frightful mess,' Billy's father said soothingly.

'Jolly complicated, I should think.' That was Billy. She knew they thought a great deal more than that, but didn't want to discuss with the ambassador.

Kick squirmed at the transparency of her father's efforts, and how much this was at odds with the English way of doing things. But he seemed not to care. Thwarted in one direction, he simply shifted to another. It was, she supposed, his great strength – he was neither tactful nor even particularly polite. Unembarrassed by their evasions, he simply asked the question again, in a different way. 'It's a question of co-existence,' he said at one point. Kick could almost hear Billy's mother groan aloud. 'That's the way of it now. Democracies and dictatorships, side by side, finding ways to live together. The idea of making the world over in an ideal image – well, that's simply not the point any longer.'

'So you would have us step back and let Germany do as she wishes? Grab with both hands land and territory and homes and farms that do not belong to them, then demand that we pretend they do?' Duff asked.

'Co-existence,' the ambassador insisted. 'It's the only way.'

'We must continue to seek peace,' Chips said sonorously. He looked around. Only her father met his eye, nodding enthusiastically.

'That's so,' he agreed. 'I suppose, even in the sorry event of a war, you won't actually fight, Lord Devonshire?' he asked, laying his knife and fork neatly across an empty plate.

'Of course we will fight,' Lord Devonshire said wearily. 'I want war no more than you do. But if it comes to it, I will enlist, and my sons too.'

'You can't be serious?' Her father looked from the duke to Billy, then Andrew.

'Naturally,' Billy said.

'Of course.' That was Andrew. 'I turned eighteen in January,' he added proudly.

Kick saw the sudden alarmed twitch of his mother's mouth, but she said nothing.

'Some of us have joined up already,' said Billy's friend Hugo, eagerly, turning this way and that in his chair to look at them all. 'So as to be ready.'

'Who is "us"?' her father asked.

'A lot of the chaps who are at Cambridge with me,' Hugo said. 'One wouldn't want to wait for conscription. Wouldn't look right.'

'And so you rush to join, pledging yourselves to go and fight a war you cannot possibly win, in order to *look right*?' Her father was incredulous, and with the bullying tone Kick knew from dinners at home.

'I say, of course we'll win,' Hugo said, looking around again. Neither the duke nor Chips would meet his gaze, Kick saw.

'What fools young men are,' her father said. He said it angrily, the way he might have spoken to Joe Jnr or Jack if they had done something to annoy him.

Looking at her father's angry face, the way all the other men at the table had drawn a little away from him and closer together, she thought again about what Jack had said when he first heard of the posting, and the laugh with which he had said it – '*The least diplomatic person I ever met is to be America's senior diplomat. Well I never,*' adding, '*Roosevelt must know something we don't. Or want something we don't understand.*' At the time, Kick had wondered what he meant and if he was just being clever. But it was true that her father was blunt and straight-talking, likely to antagonise and offend more than he was to placate. Why had he been sent here to deal with people so skilled at artfulness that they rarely said what they meant unless forced, yet understood each other perfectly?

'It makes little difference if they enlist early or not,' Billy's father said stiffly. 'If it's war, there will be conscription and they will go anyway. Might as well do the decent thing.'

'*The decent thing,*' the ambassador repeated scornfully.

'At least we know Chips won't be rushing to enlist,' Elizabeth said, head to one side, eyes bright and round like a greedy bird, as she turned to her host. 'Such a relief,' she added sweetly.

'I will be far more useful where I am, in government,' Chips said, leaning back in his chair with his arms folded behind his head, elbows resting complacently wide on either side of him.

'So, Duff, that means you won't go either?' Honor turned to him.

'No,' Maureen said swiftly. 'He is *certainly* more useful where he is.' She shot Chips a sarcastic look.

'I wonder if Mr Chamberlain agrees,' Chips murmured.

He looked as if he might say more, but Debo interrupted. 'Don't,' she said hurriedly. 'Don't let's. Not today. It's so lovely, and feels so far away from awful things like enlisting and gas masks and blackouts. Talking only makes it worse.' She looked at Andrew as she spoke.

'Indeed,' Billy's father said stiffly. 'Hardly the time.'

Kick knew that her father didn't believe in such things as a right time to pursue whatever it was he had set his sights on, or to have hard conversations, and was unsurprised when he leaned forward, his elbows heavy on the table, and said, 'What I can't understand is how you all behave as though war is a sure thing, a definite, when it is nothing of the sort. Nor need it be.' He glared around at them, neck sunk into his shoulders as though he would physically push his convictions onto them. 'Britain isn't ready for another war. Fight one, and she will lose.'

'*She?*' Duff asked with heavy irony. 'You mean us?'

'Who will walk with me? I want to explore the gardens.' It was Rose, standing hastily and looking around. She had eaten, Kick saw, almost nothing. The sight of her barely touched plate – food moved into discrete piles, entirely distinct one from another, asparagus spears lined up neatly alongside a small heap of garden peas, beside the scarlet O of a radish – made Kick want to hide her own enthusiastically cleared one. But it was too late. Her mother had seen it. Again, the eyebrow lifted a fraction of an inch and Kick felt suddenly ungainly. Large and sprawling alongside the doll-like neatness of her mother in her crisp linen dress.

'I will,' Billy's mother said. The lines that etched her face were more evident. 'Andrew, come with us.' As though she would keep him close. 'And Kathleen, perhaps you might join us?'

'I thought I might change . . .' Kick began.

'I shouldn't bother,' the duchess said. 'I thought you were walking by the river later?'

'We'll wait for you,' Debo said.

'No rush,' Elizabeth agreed, lighting a cigarette and pushing her plate away.

Billy's mother asked her questions that began with the garden and moved quickly on to other things. 'Billy tells me you were in Italy. What did you see?'

'I saw the pope,' Kick said, eager to talk about her travels, her impressions. She looked up and saw the expression on Moucher's face. 'We saw the Raphaels,' she amended hurriedly. 'And a splendid Caravaggio.'

'I believe Chatsworth is especially fine at this time of year,' Rose said then.

The duchess look startled. As though Rose had said, 'I believe birds nest in springtime' or 'I believe cows give milk.'

'Yes,' she agreed politely.

'And that Mary Queen of Scots lived there for a time,' Rose persisted. 'How very interesting it must be.'

'More like rotted away there,' Andrew said cheerfully. 'She was imprisoned. On Elizabeth I's orders. On and off for fifteen years. I'll show you over her apartments if you come and stay,' he said to Kick. The duchess looked momentarily alarmed. Kick wondered was it at the idea of her coming to stay.

'Why imprisoned?' Rose asked.

'Catholic,' Andrew said, still cheerful. 'Not to be trusted, you see.' A sharp little silence fell then, broken quickly by the duchess asking, 'I believe you have older boys, Mrs Ambassador. Do they ever visit?'

In all, it was an awkward walk; one in which Kick felt she was held up for comparison with something she didn't understand. Something that might have been a version of her own self, one that must be confirmed or denied, only she didn't know which. It felt as though there was a purpose to everything Billy's mother asked, and that Kick's answers were either too close or too far from what was expected. And even though she was willing to mute her answers, to be whatever this woman wanted, she couldn't, because she didn't understand what that was.

The walk to the river took them through a meadow of tall grass and Kick, walking slightly behind, thought how soft it looked until you were standing in it, and then how much it scratched.

'Jolly lunch?' she heard Hugo say in an undertone to Billy.

'I do think it's hard luck on the old pair. They leave the Blounts to get away from Diana and that sewer Mosley, and come here only to be button-holed by His Excellency.'

Hugo sniggered and repeated, '*Excellency.*'

Billy turned a little then, and saw Kick. His face flushed, the freckles standing out dark against the red, and dropped back to her. 'I say, that was rude. I'm sorry.'

'No, it's alright.' Kick struggled with the Kennedy part of herself that wanted to punch this young man for insulting her family, and the ever-growing part that wanted to listen to him, understand him. 'I mean, I know he's different, the way he does things. I guess we all are. He means no harm. Or at least, he means only to do what he thinks he's here to do, but I understand how strange his way must seem to you. Can you see that he thinks another war is a truly terrible thing and wishes to prevent it?'

'I try to believe he means well.'

It would have to do.

Chapter Twenty-Six

Brigid

Brigid watched Kick play a masterful game of croquet.
She didn't win; Billy – who seemed almost not to play,
so languidly did he make his way around the hoops –
did, but she competed fiercely. Brigid was glad of it. She would
have hated to see Kick hold herself back in order to be more
appealing to the man she liked.

At first, she had thought Kick's confessions – that she liked
Billy, that her shoes had been taken and hidden and that she
had understood she was being mocked and had decided to play
along with that – merely showed that she was unsophisticated,
naive. But over the last day she had come to realise that it wasn't
that. Instead, it was a kind of determination to be straight, as
Brigid called it to herself. A deliberate choosing of the direct
way, so that she was like someone approaching across a wide

open lawn – nothing at all on either side to hide her or distract attention from her – rather than taking a stealthier route through shrubbery. There was something pretty brave about that, Brigid thought. She herself, she knew, could not do it. She was too conscious of who watched her – her mother, Chips, Honor, Maureen, everyone – to do anything so out in the open.

But there was something reckless about it too. How *could* Kick have told Billy's mother about meeting the pope in that way? As though saying she had tried pear tart or seen a seal. Brigid, tucked away in a shady swing-seat Chips had placed at a clever angle so that it was easy to see the house, the gardens, but not so easy to be seen, felt herself smiling.

Kick had no idea – none at all, Brigid thought, watching her stroll around with Billy – of how deep the feeling against her ran. She thought people like Billy's father 'didn't much like' Catholics, as though that was the same as 'not much liking' Americans – something a bit silly that could be got over easily simply by knowing a few nice Americans. She couldn't see – even Brigid could only barely see – how deep it ran; the almost violent disgust they felt.

American Catholics were different to Irish ones, she decided, thinking back to summers at Glenmaroon, Maureen's parents' estate outside Dublin. Or maybe just rich Catholics; Kennedy Catholics, with their exquisite rosary beads – yes, she had seen Kick's gold-and-pearl beads beside her bed – their private audiences with the pope and friendships with cardinals. There was less obvious blessing and muttering every time a church was passed or a saint's name invoked. Smarter, more restrained. But they were still Catholic. As alien as if they had been African.

Leaning back in her chair and pushing off from the ground with one foot so that the swing moved farther back, higher up, she wondered at the sympathy that seemed to exist between Duff and Rose. If they had been younger, Brigid would have said that Rose found him attractive. Obviously that was silly – she was too old; why, she must be nearly fifty! – but she was keen for his good opinion, that much was obvious. She liked talking to him, sitting near him. Lucky she *was* old, Brigid thought with a grin. Too old for Maureen to bother with.

But all the same, liking Duff seemed an interesting thing for Rose, because otherwise, from what Brigid could see, she mostly talked about how she managed things, organised things.

She saw Honor coming out of the walled garden then with Paul. His mouth was stained with some dark fruit he had been eating, and he was crying.

'I told you not to eat so many,' Honor said. 'No wonder you have the stomach ache.' She looked around rather desperately, and Brigid wondered whether to go to her, but she was too lazy.

'Give me your hand, Paul, and we will go back to Nanny.' Honor reached for the boy's hand but he snatched it away from her.

'No Nanny,' he said. He sat down on the gravel path and cried more loudly.

'Paul!' Honor sounded shocked. 'You cannot sit here crying. Get up at once. If you have a pain, we must go and find Nanny.'

'No Nanny,' the child said again. 'Not Nanny!'

Honor grabbed at his hand and tried to pull him to standing but he resisted her, hauling himself the other way so that he was heavy and unwieldy. Each time she pulled him up enough to set him on his feet, he simply collapsed his body onto the ground again.

'Stand straight, Paul,' Honor snapped at him. 'You are behaving most awfully badly.'

'Papa!' the boy called. 'Papa!'

'Papa isn't here, and I cannot allow you to behave like this. I am positively ashamed of you,' Honor said. 'Get up, now.'

But the boy only cried more and then, as Honor stood dithering beside him, began to shout, 'Go away, Mamma. Go away.' The croquet players were watching now. Brigid saw Honor's hand twitch as though she would slap him, and she got up quickly.

'Paul, darling, what is it?' she asked, moving quickly to where they were.

'Oh, Brigid, thank goodness,' Honor said. 'He is being simply impossible.' She sounded as though she might cry too.

'Let me,' Brigid said and she bent down and scooped the boy into her arms. 'Shall we go and see if Cook has anything to make your tummy better?' she said, kissing Paul's hot little face. 'I think a cup of milky tea with sugar, don't you?'

He nodded and Honor looked gratefully at her over Paul's shoulder. 'Thank you, darling,' she said. She turned then and walked towards the front of the house, in a hurry to get away from her crying son.

Brigid sighed and hoisted the boy higher on her hip. 'Poor little poppet,' she said, 'is your tummy terribly sore?' She kissed him again.

She was still carrying him when she rounded the side of the house and came upon Chips, Bundi loping along by his side. 'Is that my darling boy?' Chips called when he saw them.

Paul took his head from Brigid's shoulder. 'Papa!'

'Yes, it is Papa, come here my dearest lamb,' and Chips held his arms out.

Brigid passed Paul to him. 'He has the stomach ache,' she said, 'too many berries. We were going to see would Cook give him a cup of milky tea.'

'Poor little mite,' Chips said. 'I shall take him. Sweet milky tea is just the thing. Brigid, would you go and tell the Devonshires that I will be with them directly, just as soon as this little fellow is on his feet again?'

Brigid watched him carry Paul the last bit to the house, chatting to him, telling him something funny Bundi had done. Paul laughed, stomach ache clearly forgotten.

Her feeling of charity for Chips lasted all the way to tea time and beyond, until she walked out with him to say goodbye to Billy's parents, who insisted they 'must get back'.

'What do you make of our American friends?' Chips asked as they waited for the motorcar to be brought around.

'Interesting,' Moucher said politely.

'And young Kathleen; shall we be seeing much more of her, do you think?'

'A dear girl,' Billy's father said doubtfully, 'but I don't imagine she'd be any sort of a match for any of our young men. Even if one did get her out from under the papal shadow.'

'She must have so much to get back to, in America,' Moucher said.

And Chips nodded and smiled and glowed with approval and pleasure. And Brigid, who could see what Kick wouldn't quite admit – just how very much she liked Billy – thought how mean he was after all, to try to wreck her hopes so casually.

Chapter Twenty-Seven

Kick

Billy, Andrew, Hugo and Debo were easily persuaded to stay for dinner, especially when Chips said, 'Ambassador Kennedy has sent to London for a projector and a screen, and plans to show us a film later.'

'How splendid,' Debo said. 'I wonder what it will be. Something new from Hollywood? Kick's Papa gets all the very latest films. He used to be a producer, you know.' This to Billy, who looked startled. 'Perhaps something with Hedy Lamarr?' She looked wistful. 'Farve won't allow us to see her films.'

Dinner was merry, as though the departure of the Devonshires had set them all a little freer. Kick watched how easily Billy conversed with everyone, whether it was talking about Cambridge with Duff, answering the many questions put to him by her mother, or making jokes with Elizabeth. She saw, too, how he looked over, often, to where she sat beside Fritzi. And stayed looking when she looked back. Their eyes met and tangled in a way that felt to her as though everything else at the table – the chatter and laughter, the food – was distant and background.

Her father was quiet but perhaps that was because he was thinking about the film. She hoped it would be a comedy.

Once dinner was over, they went immediately through to the library, where chairs had been placed in two rows before a screen that had been hung in the space between the windows. To Kick, it looked entirely familiar – they had a movie room in the basement of the house in Bronxville – but the others ooh-ed and ah-ed as though this were something special, arranging themselves in seats, dragging them this way and that, that they might have a better view.

She noticed that Billy was quick to take the chair beside hers, and even pulled it in a little closer to her. Her father was on her other side, with Brigid behind her. Chips, she saw, made sure to seat Fritzi beside Brigid, who edged her chair slightly away. Kick smiled to herself.

'Lights, please,' her father called, and the room was made dark. The footman operating the projector turned it on and Kick immediately relaxed into the familiar whirling sound that had heralded so many happy hours.

First, an uneven square of light, then the words '*Flashes of Action*' appeared. Another lighted square, and '*Actualities of the World War*', followed by '*Signal Corps of the US Army*'. Beside her, she felt Billy stir, and all around she could feel the disappointment. 'Not the latest Hollywood Funny, then,' someone muttered. She thought it might have been Elizabeth. She half-turned in her seat to make an apologetic face at Brigid, and turned back to find the screen filled with men, swarms of them, boarding a troop ship. They were pouring up the gangplank and spreading out across the ship in a dense wave. So many that they were like sea birds, gathered thick on a rocky outcrop.

'The Leviathan,' words on the screen read.

'Largest ship in the world,' her father said. 'Over ten thousand troops left New York in her in 1918.' Beside Kick, Billy's leg twitched.

The images on screen were now of men dancing, boxing, passing time as the great ship made her way across the ocean. 'I'd put a few bob on that chap,' Hugo called out as two men squared up to one another and exchanged good-natured blows. Everyone laughed, except her father.

The steady lurching motion of the images made Kick feel sick, and where the camera panned out across the wide expanse of empty ocean, she felt an obscure terror. She was glad when the mighty ship reached France and disembarkation, spilling men like black dots, thousands of them, waving and grinning at the camera as they walked down the gangplank and onto French soil. There was chatter around the library now – Elizabeth was loudly asking was there nothing else to watch, while Hugo had started a story about his last visit to France, frequently interrupted by Brigid, who questioned him on everything he said.

The pictures changed, and one by one, they fell silent. Now, it was the landscape that was vast; empty fields and men spaced out in clusters, running in desperate, speeded-up motion from one paltry clump of trees to another. The silence was the worst of it, Kick thought, as she watched clouds of smoke and grit explode in front of her and watched men fall and struggle to rise, and fall again. Without sound, the film had a nightmare quality at once remote and immediate. She felt as though she was responsible for their fate, could have stopped the painful progress with a gesture, a hand up to say halt. Even though they had run and fought and lived and died twenty years ago.

Behind the lines of soldiers came the stretchers; men in twos with a strip of canvas between them, onto which they frantically tumbled bodies while the ground and air exploded around them. Not all the bodies were taken. Some were left where they had fallen.

Now the pictures were of a hole blown in the ground in which men lay and hunkered down like prairie dogs, one on top of the other. There was bandaging of legs, of knees, of heads, blood black and thick on the thin white screen.

'Those were the lucky ones.' Her father's voice. 'They were Americans.'

More landscape, picked out in fog and smoke. The figures were ghostly now, appearing and disappearing, crouching and running, swallowed up by white clouds then spat out again. Another change. This time a pretty French town with slated roofs. The kind she had visited often during her year at the convent in Paris. She watched – they all watched – as shells landed and roofs blew apart.

'I think that's enough.' Her mother, standing, motioned to the footman to turn on the lights.

As though a spell had been broken, everyone was suddenly on their feet, moving to get out of the room. Kick had expected angry questions – 'Why? What?' – but there weren't any. Even Duff left politely, standing aside for Maureen and saying, 'After you, please.' The room had emptied like sand through a sieve, clean and swift. Kick busied herself taking down the screen the way she had been taught. She needed time. She didn't want to see Billy's face.

Only Elizabeth stayed behind, and her father.

'What on earth was that?' Elizabeth asked, with a directness that was unusual for her.

'That was a much-needed show of real life,' Kick's father said. 'Those young men talk of honour, of glory, with no thought for what war really is. And so I've shown them.'

'You're wrong,' Elizabeth said quietly. 'They know. They talk of honour and glory to distract themselves from what they know very well is the reality. They have known what war means since they were children, when their fathers and older brothers went off to the same conflict you've now shown them pictures of. Billy's father served in Egypt, then in Turkey.'

'He didn't say . . .'

'Of course he didn't.' Elizabeth was scornful. 'Hugo's brother, William, is buried in Normandy. His father came home but left half of himself behind at Verdun. These young men have grown up knowing what war means. They soaked it in with the very air they breathed. They don't talk of it, I grant, but that's different and doesn't mean what you think it means. And now you've rubbed their noses in it.'

'It is to avoid another war that I did it,' her father said. 'After this, they might think twice before they rush to join up.'

'Do you think, for one second, that they will not enlist, should it indeed be war?' Elizabeth asked, almost conversationally. How strange that it should be her, Kick thought. 'They will, you know. Only now, they will do it without ever a shred of illusion to comfort themselves. This was a bad night's work.'

'It was necessary,' her father insisted, but he spoke to a room empty except for Kick. Elizabeth had gone. Kick kept her head down, busying herself with folding the screen away, so that she need not look at him. He stood awhile, she thought he even tried to catch her eye, but she kept her gaze firmly where it could not be intercepted, and after another moment, he too left. He shut the door behind him so that Kick was alone. Why, she thought, had he done this? Yes, there were the reasons he had given Elizabeth – to make clear the reality of war, to cut through the talk of honour and duty to an ugly truth. But there was something else too in what he had done, and it took her some time to understand it.

It was that he didn't see these young men as quite real, she realised when she had tidied the screen away and put back all the chairs against the walls, motioning 'no' with a shake of her head to the footman who came in to do it. He didn't understand that they were as real as his own sons. Maybe it was their Englishness. Their habits of indirectness in conversation, the faintly cartoonish way they behaved according to a code. Maybe it was simply that they weren't American, and therefore no concern of his. But certainly, he hadn't behaved towards them as though he understood that beneath the careful, stiff exteriors they were flesh and blood and bone and fear and hope, the same as any men.

By the time she was able to leave the library, the party had broken up. Billy, Andrew and Hugo stood by the open front door. At the bottom of the steps, the motorcar had been brought around and waited, headlights on so that two beams of light lay across the gravel of the driveway.

'Debo will be down directly,' Andrew said. He spoke to the air behind Kick, not meeting her eyes. 'She has gone to fetch her coat.' Billy stayed quiet and she had no idea what to say to him. What could she possibly say? She couldn't apologise for her father – that would be disloyal, and Kennedys were unfailingly loyal – but neither could she pretend that nothing had happened. She stood there awkwardly and was almost grateful for the English habit of dissembling when Hugo said, 'Yes, it's jolly late, we'd better be getting back. The Blounts will wonder where we are.'

'I'll walk you out,' she said. She stepped through the open door and into the night-time world beyond. The air smelled like a pond, she thought, thick and wet, teeming with mysterious life she couldn't see. At the bottom of the steps, she watched a squadron of pale moths dancing in the beams of the car headlights. 'Will they fly away when the car starts to move?' she wondered aloud.

'No.' Billy had come down the steps with her. He stood close behind. 'They will linger too long, and be crushed against the windscreen as we drive.' His breath on the back of her neck was warm. The feel of him so close behind her made her want to lean back and rest her weight against him. 'The glass will be thick with bits of wing and leg and broken bodies by the time we get back.'

She forced herself to straighten up. 'I didn't know.' It was the most she could say.

'I suppose you didn't,' he agreed. And just when she was about to cry out '*He did not mean it. Or at least, he did, but he did not mean what you think he meant . . .*' he spared her.

'It doesn't matter, you know.'

'How does it not matter?'

'None of it matters. What he says, what my father says, Chamberlain. Any of them. Whatever they think, they don't make any of this, they just respond to it. We all do.'

'My brother Jack thinks the same as you do,' she said. 'He doesn't think like my father. He thinks like you.' It was the closest she could come to disowning her father's views. Would it be enough?

'Does he?' He was, as always, polite, but the politeness now was like glass behind which he hid. She could see him. He looked the same, but she could not reach him. Could not feel him or know him.

After he left she thought about what she had really wanted to say – '*I don't believe him anymore. I believe you.*' But you couldn't blurt a thing like that out. Especially when the feeling of it was so new and strange. All her life she had believed her father. Believed what he said, what he did. And now, she didn't. She didn't know the moment it had started, this change in her. Maybe that evening at the Mountbattens when Billy had gently shown her the absurdity of Americans coming to tell them what they must and must not do? But she knew the moment it had crystalised. There, in the library, against a screen of dying men. The pity of it was that she was too late. Just as she felt herself moving beyond her father, she felt Billy pull away from her. Politely, maybe with regret, but also decisively.

She stood and watched the lights of the motorcar down the long driveway, until they turned a corner at the gate lodge and were lost in the dark.

Chapter Twenty-Eight

London
Doris

One look at the front of Number Five Belgrave Square and Doris knew Honor wasn't there. It was a feeling, she thought, walking up the three steps and in under the portico to ring the bell, rather than anything visible. Something about the vast façade that turned itself away from her. And the door wasn't opened immediately, as it should have been. She felt, suddenly, the full exhaustion of her journey. The hours by train, through Germany and then France, watching the countryside flicker past. The Night Ferry from Paris, leaving the gloomy Gare du Nord and depositing her at Victoria Station that morning at five minutes past nine. Her face felt tight and dirty. Inside her gloves, her hands were sticky.

Behind her, the taxi driver was removing her luggage from

the boot and lining it up on the pavement. She wondered should she tell him to wait. If Honor wasn't here, perhaps she should go to a hotel.

The door opened. Robert, the footman, stood there, not Andrews. Definitely Honor wasn't here.

'Miss Coates.'

'Robert.' The taxi was already gone. Now she would have to call for another one. She sighed.

'Madame said to expect you.' Robert stood aside, ushering her in. 'They are at Kelvedon, where Mrs Channon hopes you will join them, but meanwhile your usual room is ready for you.'

Dear Honor. Doris felt her eyes prickly with grateful tears. How tired she must be. She never cried.

'May I bring you some breakfast?' Robert continued. 'I will have your luggage brought up immediately.'

'Thank you, Robert.'

After breakfast and a bath, she decided not to sleep but to go for a walk. She was impatient to see how the city had changed – if at all – in the year since she had last been here. Would the old woman who sold packets of bread crusts to feed to the pigeons still be at the corner of Green Park? The same display of marbled writing paper in the stationery shop? But first a phonecall. She dialled the number from Chips' library, looking around at the walls of green-and-gold leather-bound books. Anyone else, she would assume they had never been read, but with Chips, one never quite knew.

'I've arrived,' she said into the receiver when the phone was answered.

'We'll see you for tea,' came the response.

Outside, she let herself luxuriate in the relief of walking without thought for who walked behind her. Striding out on streets that knew nothing of her and were content to be that way. She walked about as she wished, never looking over her shoulder, stopping to chat – the old lady with the crusts was indeed there – when she chose to, without a thought beyond what amused her.

Later, back at Number Five, with the man she knew to expect and two others who introduced themselves as 'Mr White', 'Mr Black' – so that she knew these were not their real names – she poured tea for herself, brought by Robert, and whiskey for them.

'When do you leave?' Mr White asked her.

'Tomorrow. I'll take the train and then a taxi. I am expected.'

'Very good.' He lit a cigar and settled back in his armchair. They talked openly then, even bluntly, of what Doris had seen in Berlin – was von Arent still close to Hitler? No, Doris thought not, there was an edge to him, a striving petulance that hadn't been there before. And what of Hans Fritzsche? The coming man, if Doris wasn't mistaken; close with Goebbels.

As they spoke – plainly and without allusion, their voices discreet but not whispers – she became aware that something inside her unknotted and unwound and relaxed, and how that was the first time she had realised the coiled tension was there at all. As though, she thought, it were like the snake in Berlin Zoo that was so perfectly camouflaged among the leaves and branches of its cage that it was only when it moved you saw it.

'If you can do anything with the ambassador, do,' Mr Black said. 'Anything that you can tell him that will incline him to push our cause with Roosevelt would be useful, but that's the least important part of what you're there for. It's the prince you're to concentrate on.'

'What, exactly?'

'What kind of man is he? Where do his sympathies really lie? Can he be trusted? Will he answer the purpose? That sort of thing.'

'That sort of thing,' Doris echoed, nodding. She didn't say anything about Hannah, even though the girl was who she thought of always. She had wondered would she, but knew it would do no good even as she wondered.

Doris did what was asked of her because it was the best way to help the people she wanted to help. People like her aunt and cousins, Hannah and her family. And even though she knew that the men who gave her instruction, this Mr White and Mr Black, cared far less about these people than she did – they cared for big things: England's safety, Europe's stability, the dismantling of the Reich – all the same their intentions and hers meshed at times, overlapped in ways that might help the people she cared about.

She didn't tell them that she cared for their plans only in as much as they assisted hers, and they didn't tell her that her plans – her people – were unimportant, except incidentally, to them.

She supposed that no one told each other the full truth anymore. That was a luxury for more settled times.

'Only telephone if you need to,' Mr Black told her as they left. 'Better to have as little contact as possible.' She closed the library door after them, then opened the window to let out the smell of cigar smoke. Within half an hour there was nothing to show they had been there.

Chapter Twenty-Nine

Kelvedon, Essex
Honor

I f she were to leave, go back to London, go to Elveden and her parents – go to the devil himself – would any of them even notice? Honor wondered. She was like a ghost in her own house, moving from room to room unnoticed and unlooked for. She drifted into conversations and drifted out again. Nothing depended on her, nothing waited or hurried for her. Anything that Chips didn't do, Brigid did. Even Rose Kennedy seemed more knitted into the fabric of Kelvedon than Honor was, familiar already with the kitchens, Mrs Bath the cook, the head gardener. Her sharp-elbowed energy pushing into the house and grounds. Chips should have married someone like that, she thought. Such a person would have been a match for him. Not someone so . . . *reluctant*, she decided, was the word. She thought of Chips then with a different kind of wife. Someone like Rose or Emerald, whom he could consult with, plot with, scheme with. Would he have been proud of such a person? Yes, undoubtedly. Would he have watched them betray him with another man and spoken only of money? Undoubtedly not.

She looked into the library. No sign of the ambassador's screen or projector. The room was still and withdrawn as though ashamed of the part it had played last night. What was the man thinking? What had he hoped, showing those terrible things? And how dared he presume to do so without a word? Again, she couldn't help thinking of her mother. No one would have shown such images in a house where Lady Iveagh was, she thought. No one.

But by the time she got to the morning room, it was as though the day before had been wiped away. As if a maid with a mop had come and simply scrubbed it out. The tennis tournament had become a reality, and Brigid and Kick, cool in shorts and thin button-down shirts, were seated side by side at the break-fast table, empty plates pushed in front of them – china islands on the smooth polished surface – poring over a page on which they had written everyone's names. 'Chips is good, but he cheats, so we need to match him with someone who will keep him honest,' Brigid said as Honor came in.

'Well then you may put him with Kick,' Ambassador Kennedy said. 'She is the straightest person in the world. Wouldn't know how to cheat if her life depended on it.'

Rose, beside him, looked composed in a crisp white cotton sundress. On the chair beside her was a broad-brimmed white hat. She nodded in agreement and said, 'Duff, will you play?' Honor heard the use of his pet name – only Maureen, and her family, called him that – and wondered at it. Did the woman not understand the impertinence? Maureen, she noted, wasn't down yet. Probably wouldn't be for hours. Duff, head bent over *The Times*, only looked up quickly and nodded once, then went back to his reading.

'You can play with me, Duff,' Brigid said. 'We are a good match. You are stronger, but you don't concentrate as well as I.'

'I had hoped *I* might be Lady Brigid's partner,' Fritzi, sitting opposite, said then.

'You can play with Elizabeth,' Brigid said. Kick giggled and Fritzi looked dashed. 'It's because I know you to be good,' Brigid added kindly. 'Chips has told me. And Elizabeth will need that.'

'If she ever gets up,' Chips said petulantly. He was sitting at the head of the table. Seeing Honor come in, he had patted the empty chair beside him. But Honor chose to ignore him, instead taking a cup of tea and going to sit in the armchair by the window. This was open and, beside it, a clematis had been encouraged to grow up and around. The sweet almond scent of the flowers came to her like a reminder that outside, elsewhere, there were other ways to be, other things to do, that had nothing to do with this house and these people.

'What about Maureen?' Rose said then, looking around. She sat so straight it was as though she had stitched fine steel rods into the white cotton of her dress. She held an empty cup out towards her husband, who filled it from the silver coffee pot at the centre of the table.

'My wife won't play,' Duff said with a quick grin at Honor. 'She thinks her energies are better spent elsewhere.'

'She won't play because she knows she won't win,' Brigid said tartly. Then, catching Honor's eye, 'I say, sorry! In any case, there are no more men to partner with.'

'My man would play, if needed,' Fritzi said. 'Albert. He is a stronger player than I am.'

'I don't see Maureen playing with a servant,' Brigid blurted out.

'He isn't exactly a servant, more a companion. My grandfather—'

'The kaiser,' Chips said enthusiastically.

'The kaiser,' Fritzi agreed. 'He didn't want me to come to England entirely alone. Albert's family have been with my family for a jolly long time. And so Albert came with me and has been companion, friend, sometimes valet, but mostly a chum.'

Idly, Honor wondered where exactly he had learned his English. It was faultless, but his expressions were wrong. Too schoolboyish.

Kick giggled again and Honor gave her and Brigid a look. Perhaps this wasn't such a good friendship after all. Rose may have been thinking the same, because she said, 'Kathleen, if you are done with breakfast, perhaps you would take a little walk with me. Prince Friedrich, would you join us?'

The prince stood immediately, while Kick blurted out, 'Must I?' Then, seeing her mother's face, 'Of course!'

Once they were gone, Brigid said she would speak to the gardener to make sure the court was properly marked, and left. Honor felt a moment's irritation at the easy way she assumed the right to take control, then realised that her irritation was more than balanced out by relief that she didn't have to go herself. It was hotter than the days before, with an angry kind of heat that felt ready to boil over.

'Will you play?' Chips asked her.

'Not in this weather. I wish it would thunder. It's been threatening it for days.'

'We could wait 'til later, when it's cooler,' he said eagerly. 'If you would like?'

'Don't bother.' Why, she wondered, was he making such an effort? She refilled her tea cup and sat again by the window, enjoying the sounds of the day outside whispering to itself about everything that must be and must be done. It was like a hostess, she thought, making plans for the smooth running of a visit. Birds chirped and called, branches rustled lightly, leaves shook themselves and spread out further into the warm air, plants swayed and scraped against their neighbours and, at the far end, the sound of the river moving lazily along. She could see Rose Kennedy, Kick, Fritzi, walking slowly, stopping to admire a flower here, a bush there.

'Hmph.' Chips, at her shoulder now, was watching them too. 'What *does* she mean?' he said quietly.

'What does who mean?'

'Sshhh.' He twitched his head irritably, back towards the dining room where Duff and the ambassador were now sitting side by side, with *The Times* spread open in front of them. Honor could make out the headline: *Hitler Calls Up 750,000 Germans for Military Exercises*. She had a vision of all those men, dressed in their tight-fitting uniforms as she had seen them on their visit to Germany two years before, doing star jumps.

'I wonder what her plans are, that's all,' he murmured, looking back towards the gardens.

'Must everyone have plans?'

'Of course they must.' He sounded honestly astonished. 'Really, Honor. What do you think about all day?'

She considered her responses: *How to live my life contained in such a way that the sides of it touch yours only as much as is absolutely necessary? And even then, how to prevent my flesh from shrinking from that touch?* 'Right now, I am thinking about how to get Elizabeth up so the maids can do her room.'

That, he understood. 'You should have seen the amount of gin she put away,' he said with gleeful maliciousness. 'Duff too. Egged on by her.' Honor looked over at Duff again. He looked, as ever, dark, handsome, rather forbidding, but his eyes were bloodshot and there was a slump to his shoulders.

She went to Maureen's room first, tapping on the door then going in when she heard her voice: 'Come.'

The curtains had been opened and Maureen was sitting up in bed wearing a coffee-coloured silk peignoir. Her hair had been brushed and fell about her shoulders in shining golden curls. Beside her on the table was an array of pots and jars. Some were open and Honor could smell rose oil and beeswax.

'I thought you were Duff,' Maureen said crossly.

'He's downstairs, with the ambassador. Have you breakfasted?'

'Yes. And yes I will get up, you needn't badger me.'

'I'm not. I only wanted to see how you were.'

'You slipped off pretty smartly last night, didn't you?'

'I had the headache. All that sun . . . the ambassador's film.'

'Dreadful, wasn't it?'

'I quite thought Duff would murder him.'

'He has some other plan in mind. And indeed, hard to know what to do after that. But all the same, Honor, disappearing like that with all those guests? Really, I don't know why you invite people if you don't know how to treat them. At Clandeboye, I am always last to bed.'

Goodness, she was cross, Honor thought. 'What's in all those jars and bottles?'

'The only good piece of advice Mummie ever gave me: *Care for your face the way Lapham cares for the silver.*'

'Really? The only piece of good advice?'

'That, and *Give your husband everything he wants*,' Maureen said. Then added, 'Yes, Honor, *everything*,' grinning maliciously.

'I'm going to check on Elizabeth,' Honor said, in order to escape.

'*Now* you play hostess . . .' Maureen got up, jumping from bed to ground in one quick movement. She was still, Honor saw with a mean kind of relief, stout around the waist since Sheridan. And her legs were plumper than they had been. She could imagine the expression of distaste on Aunt Cloé's face if she were to see her daughter like that. But somehow, with Maureen, it didn't much matter. Not when her face glowed with life and mischief the way it did. Not when you saw the energy of her. She went to the window and pulled the sash up, standing in full view so that anyone who looked up could have seen her there in her night clothes.

'Maureen!' Honor said.

Her cousin looked at her, head to one side, and said nothing. Then she untied the belt of her silk dressing gown, letting it fall to the ground so that now she stood in only her slip, short and strappy so her arms and shoulders emerged, white and soft like cream from the coffee-coloured silk.

Honor took a step backwards, away from the brazenness of Maureen's exposure. 'I'm going to check on Elizabeth,' she said again.

'Send Duff up if you see him,' Maureen said. 'And tell the maid not to disturb us.'

Honor, shutting the door behind her, found her heart was thumping as if she had just climbed a long flight of stairs. What was Maureen about? She certainly wouldn't tell Duff anything. She couldn't imagine herself saying the words – knew her face would betray her should she even try to, flushing red and swelling up like a hot cross bun. Was that what she had gone looking for with the baron? she wondered. Or was it proof she looked for that it wasn't ever to be for her? Whatever she sought, she hadn't found it, she thought, remembering the strange, brief, unexceptional nature of the affair.

She followed the hallway down past the bit where it turned at an angle and faded to something more spartan, rich Persian rugs replaced with simple woven affairs, down towards the nursery and the Yellow Room. 'Elizabeth?' She tapped at the door. Nothing. 'Elizabeth?' She knocked, loudly now, and again.

'What is it?' The voice was thick with sleep.

'May I come in?'

'If you must.'

The room was dark, curtains closed, and the air was thick and sweetish-smelling: last night's cocktails, cigarette smoke; sour reminders of the night's exertions. One of her dresses lay in a crumpled heap on the floor. She bent to pick it up, shook it out and draped it over the back of a chair.

'What do you want?' Elizabeth asked.

'To see if you need anything.'

'How insincere you are. But while you're here, pass me a glass of water.'

Honor poured a glass from the jug that stood by the dressing table. It was yesterday's water, but it would do. She held the glass out to Elizabeth, who slowly pushed herself up to a seated position, took it and drank it down in one go, so fast that a trickle spilled from the corners of her mouth and ran down her chin. She appeared to be naked under the sheet, and Honor hoped the hand holding it wouldn't let slip. The heavy linen looked the colour of oatmeal against her skin:

white, traced with blue where her veins showed through, twisting a map of roads and byways down her thin arms. She had a rash on the inside of one elbow, a red patch turned raw at the edges.

'Another.' Elizabeth held the empty glass out. Honor refilled it and Elizabeth drank half before putting the glass on the table beside the bed.

'May I open the curtains?'

'Oh go on.' She winced at the sunlight that poured into the room, and Honor remembered that was another reason why they had decided this would be an unimportant sort of a bedroom – the morning sun was too direct and unkind. Looking back at Elizabeth, tangled up in the sheets and counterpane, she asked, 'How did you sleep?'

'Badly. But I usually do, so don't start to fuss.'

'I do too,' Honor said in a rush. 'I heard you coming up.'

'Did you now?' Elizabeth gave her a look. Her face was blotchy, with smudges of black around the eyes where last night's make-up hadn't been removed. She must have fallen into bed the minute she got her clothes off. Honor's clothes.

'Yes, and even then it was another hour, I would say.' It felt strange to tell Elizabeth anything. She couldn't remember ever having had a real conversation with her.

'Curious, aren't they,' Elizabeth mused, 'those night vigils? I sometimes imagine I am the last person left alive, and that the world will end come dawn and I am simply watching, and waiting, for this end – in order to see it through, you know?'

Honor shuddered. It was much too close to what she herself felt; only Elizabeth seemed to find the fantasy interesting, even amusing. To Honor, it was terrifying; a dark loneliness so complete that she sometimes thought she would never speak again, never feel the touch of another person's hand to hers. 'How dramatic you are,' she said quickly.

'Well, what do you do?'

'I make lists,' Honor said, shrugging. 'Of things I must do.'

Elizabeth laughed. 'Of course.' Then, 'I used to have the most divine doctor, who gave me these little yellow pills that put me out like a light. Sometimes for days at a time. It was so simply heaven, you cannot imagine. If there was something I didn't care for, or someone I was sick of, I simply counted out the pills – a couple more than he said – and swallowed them, and that was me gone, out, away.' She gazed off in silent contemplation. Then, sadly, 'The police found him and got terribly cross and took away his licence. So now I am back just as I was.'

'They have put you with Fritzi, for the tennis,' Honor said, to change the conversation. 'I think they will want to begin soon.'

'The cardboard prince,' Elizabeth said. 'How furious he must be. I amn't in his plans at all.'

'Does he have plans?' Did everyone have plans?

'Oh yes. Only he can't work out how to put his plans in motion.' Elizabeth gave a gurgle of laughter. 'And that indecision may cost him everything.'

Honor was going to ask more – ask Elizabeth to be more definite in what she said – but she had already lost interest in the conversation.

'Pass me a cigarette,' she said, and Honor did, privately wondering how she could possibly sit there in bed and smoke, surrounded by last night's squalor.

'May I open a window?' Honor asked.

'No. And I say, I'm going to need a pair of shoes. I can't play tennis in anything I have.'

'I'll have Molly find you something. But speaking of plans, I think you are getting in the way of Maureen's.'

'Duff?'

'Yes, Duff.'

'Serves her right,' Elizabeth said, suddenly vicious. 'Though it's not my fault that he'd rather stay up with a bottle of brandy than go to bed with her.'

'I'll send Molly to you.' Honor felt how much she needed to get out and away.

'Yes, run away, there's a dear.' Elizabeth stretched out her legs and lay back against the headboard. She took a deep drag of her cigarette and reached an arm to flick ash into the half-full glass of water on the bedside table. The sheet held up under her arms began to slip.

Honor hurried out.

Chapter Thirty

Kick

The walk with her mother and Prince Fritzi was slow and dull. Rose insisted on looking closely at all the plants, asking questions that the prince couldn't answer. To Kick's annoyance, that didn't stop him trying. He ventured weak half-opinions – 'perhaps a member of the dahlia family . . .' – that were of no value. There was nothing to distract her from thinking about Billy, even though she had sworn not to. She must ask Brigid, she decided, what she thought.

The day was hot and really what she wanted was to swim. Better still, float lazily in the cool water and watch the few clouds drift past. But Brigid had her heart set on a tournament, and so that is what they would do. In any case, she thought, this lot weren't the kind to spend a peaceful day by the pool. Or anywhere, for that matter. Landing in amongst them was like being thrown into a bag of horse chestnuts. Spikey and prickly and secretive.

Maureen, with those large light-blue eyes darting everywhere – seeing everything, considering it, weighing it; reflecting a polished surface but with something churning behind it that Kick didn't understand. Chips, doing the exact same watching and assessing, but without the same sort of inner fire that was Maureen's. His was more an inner anxiousness, she thought, remembering the way he plucked at his sleeves, eyes darting from his wife to Kick's mother, from her father to Duff and back again.

Honor, his poor dowdy wife, going about like someone had stuffed her with a bolster – badly, so that there were lumps everywhere – and sent her out to pretend to be a person; walking amongst them, saying things at intervals, but without really being part of any of it. Then there was Fritzi, 'King Midas' son' as she and Brigid now called him. He was so golden, so burnished, so unreal. A statue come to life; a boy become a statue. She compared him in her mind with her brothers, Joe and Jack, her father – all three so full of life that it felt like a strong river inside them would break its banks sooner than be squashed down. She wondered what Fritzi had done with that river to subdue it so. 'He's agitated,' her father had said to her the evening before. 'Something wrong with him.' He didn't say it as though he were sorry for Fritzi, but more as if he were curious.

Elizabeth – worn, a bit tattered, but at least she seemed real in her efforts to enjoy herself. Her own parents, so much older than everyone else, even than Chips who must be next to them in age only he seemed more of an age with Maureen and Duff. If anything, Kick thought, it was Honor who seemed the older of the two in that marriage. Her parents' age felt almost awkward, she thought, watching her mother bent – slim but stiff – over a bush with tiny white flowers that released a cloying scent into the air. It was as if they were everyone's parents, there to watch and judge, not to partake.

She knew her father would hate that. He liked to consider himself a central part of everything – even if it was Kick's friends from school, gathered in the kitchen at Bronxville over ice-cream sodas, he would talk about the teachers and games as though he were one of them. With Joe Jnr and Jack, it was even more pronounced. Kick had heard – only ever by mistake – the way they talked about girls. Not, she had thought, quietly shocked, the way father and sons should talk about girls. More as if they were all three the same age, with the same interest. But surely that couldn't be? Her father was married. Her brothers were not.

The three were alike in many ways: a kind of outward chivalry – holding coats, holding doors, carrying parcels – that had beneath it something else entirely. A mocking assessment that rated features individually and collectively. So a girl might be forgiven for having small eyes if she had 'a good bust'; long legs might offset a thick waist, and so on. Kick tried not to hear these conversations – closing doors or leaving rooms so as to be away from them – but she knew the effect of them worked away at her all the same. When she was younger, she would look at herself in the mirror, trying to see what they – what other men – might see. Was her nose too big? Definitely. But did the generous size of her mouth camouflage that? Maybe. Her eyes were too deep-set, but her teeth were even and her smile, she knew because she had been told so many times, could be 'dazzling'. But was that enough? Her hair was nothing remarkable – not blonde or brown but somewhere in between. Her skin fair but freckled . . . It was only when she realised how unhappy she was making herself that she gave up.

By every comparison she had learned she was not 'first rate'. And so she decided she wouldn't bother so much with the way she looked. Instead, she had decided, aged maybe thirteen, she would try to have fun, as she phrased it to herself. By that, she meant she would play tennis and not worry about how much she perspired. She would swim and boat and not think of what the wind and salt did to her hair. She would never be too tired to dance, too sophisticated to sit out a game of catch. Whatever fun was going, she would grab it.

Because after all, she thought – for all her imperfections, people liked her. Men liked her. Rosemary, who was far more the ideal of beauty, did not have what she had. Other girls, prettier than Kick, didn't have it either.

And yet these men – her men – were her measure, whether she approved of their ways or not. They were 'Man', by whom all other men were instinctively judged, and usually found wanting. Until now. Until Billy. It was their voices, their standards, that made her so uncertain of Billy's regard for her. As though she heard one of them, Joe perhaps, with a snigger, '*Now that she's so keen there's nothing for it but to turn and run a mile*,' followed by the laughter of Jack and her father, all three united in despising any girl who made the mistake of being *keen*. Had she, she wondered? She knew she had. She also knew that it wasn't in her to behave any other way. She knew there were games around this stuff, she'd heard the men in her family often enough to know – well – what the rules were. But she couldn't, she told herself. She wouldn't. And until yesterday, with Billy, she had never felt that she should. He had seemed keen too, and not bothering to hide it. And then that terrible film. How strange, she thought, if he was indeed driven away, it wasn't her keenness – unforgivable to Kennedy men – but rather her father's politics and way of pushing that had done it.

'You must be tired, Kathleen,' Fritzi said, coming over to her then.

'Not a bit,' she said. 'I'm only wondering how quickly the tournament will begin, and if there is time for a quick swim beforehand.'

'How energetic you are,' he said.

She couldn't tell if he were impressed or disapproving. His face was schooled to give very little away. His lapse yesterday by the pool, when he had shut his eyes and looked suddenly tired and defenceless, was uncharacteristic.

'My daughter is never tired,' Rose said fondly. Kick tried to take her mother's arm, but Rose stiffened instantly. 'Let me get you a hair grip,' she said, stepping away and reaching into her bag. 'Your fringe is quite untidy.'

Chapter Thirty-One

Maureen

Maureen knew Honor wouldn't tell Duff to come up to her, but she also knew that he would arrive of his own accord. She had been asleep by the time he came up the night before – had known she would be, seeing the rate at which he was drinking – and still asleep by the time he got up that morning. But she was ready when she heard his tap on the door.

The house had quietened a little by then. Breakfast must be over, and the servants had moved on to the next phase of their days.

She was ready for him. She had bathed, brushed her hair and let it loose around her face. She had half-closed the curtains again, wondering with a laugh if Honor would notice and what she would think, and was sitting up in bed when she heard his knock.

'I've brought you the newspaper. And a cup of tea.'

'You are kind. Come and sit with me?' She patted the side of the bed closest to her.

He came and sat, the bed shifting under his weight. 'Breakfast was a bit like boarding school,' he said, putting a cigarette to his lips. His hand shook slightly and his eyes were rimmed with red. She stretched out a hand and took the cigarette from him before he could light it and dropped it onto the floor. Then, kneeling up in bed, she leaned forward to kiss him. After a moment, he leaned back, pulled away, then reached out and patted her face with his hand.

'I'd better get on,' he said. 'I must go and change. The tennis.'

'Never mind the tennis.'

'Oh, but they do mind. Brigid has done a plan. It wouldn't be fair.'

How often had she done it herself, Maureen thought when he was gone. Pretended something wouldn't be fair – to the servants, the children, even her dogs – in order to get out of what she didn't want to do without direct confrontation. Why did they all pretend so hard?

With Duff gone, she lay back down in the bed, hating the faint damp that had already gathered under the feather bolster, anticipation of the day's heat. She knew she should get up, dress, turn back the bed, but Duff's departure had left her without the energy.

She knew he loved her. Knew he desired her. She could see it in the way he looked at her. It was in his voice, the touch of his hand. Had even been in the rage she could drive him to in those terrible fights of theirs, that were so often followed by love-making almost as intense and violent as the fighting. Was that what was missing? she wondered now. Was it that the rows had been necessary? A prelude? Surely not. Except that when she thought of it, the two things had dwindled at the same time. Her resolution not to allow the furious arguments, not since she had discovered she was pregnant with Sheridan, had held good. There had been no more of those violent exchanges between them, no broken glass, no objects thrown.

But since then, it seemed that he avoided her, so subtly that it was only now she looked for it that she saw a pattern. In public he was courteous, attentive, if anything more so than before. But in private, when it was just the two of them, he sat always at a slight distance, and shifted out of her way if she came too close to him. Almost, she thought, as though something about her smelled bad.

What was she now to him? A companion and hostess? Someone to further his political career and bait traps for men he wished to entice? She would not be those things, she thought furiously. She would not. Better to be the person who drove him to white-hot rage, than one who brought about only a dull shrug.

Chapter Thirty-Two

Honor

Even the light was hot, Honor thought. Yellowy, almost tobacco-coloured, it made the day seem older than it was. She crossed the garden, passing banks of summer flowers in a strict colour code of blue and white, blue and white, alternating like the stripes on a sailor's top. Nowhere did she see the riot of pinks, yellows, oranges that characterised the gardens at Elveden so that there, in high summer, it was as though a series of small fires had broken out and blazed cheerfully in borders and flower beds. Chips thought the profusion inelegant, but Honor missed the pretty chaos of colours.

She was late, the others already gathered at the court, and she hurried the last bit, heels sinking into the tufty grass. The court had been freshly marked and the white lines that ran up and across it were crisp as the tennis dresses Brigid and Kick wore. Elizabeth had on a pair of shorts that were too big for her; Honor's, presumably, although she didn't recognise them.

Fritzi's fellow, Albert, had been drafted as umpire and someone had dragged a high-backed rattan chair out from the house for him to sit in. There at the centre of the court, he looked, Honor thought, not nearly as embarrassed as he should.

Lawn chairs had been arranged in a row, backs to the house, facing the players. The farthest two were occupied already – the ambassador and Mrs Kennedy sat in the only bit of proper shade, afforded by a chestnut tree whose large, wide-spread leaves cast a kindly protection from the hot sun. The remaining chairs were shaded by parasols, but inadequately. Honor sat down beside Maureen, disliking the long drop into the low-slung chair, already wondering how she would get out of it without having to heave herself about awkwardly. She tugged at the parasol to try and shield her face from the heavy sunlight. On the other side of her, Fritzi – impeccable in white flannels – and Elizabeth, who already had a glass of something on the go.

'How d'you like that?' Maureen drawled, watching her and petting Pugsy, who had a blue bow tied around his fat neck. 'We've been left out to fry by the Americans.' She had that slightly squint-eyed look that, with Maureen, meant trouble. Honor edged her chair away and put a slight angle between them.

Brigid was still lamenting the lack of another couple. 'It's uneven,' she kept saying. 'We should have one more pair. Maybe Billy would come over . . .'

'No,' said Kick sharply, adding, when she saw Brigid's face, 'it's too late to ask.'

For the first match, Brigid and Duff faced off against Kick and Chips. Kick was crouched low over her racket, knees bent, shifting her weight from side to side. She looked deeply serious.

And she was. She served hard and quick, returning balls with precision, calling shots, even disputing the umpire's decisions. Brigid was less good a player. Lazier, Honor thought critically. At least until she realised what Kick was like. Then, she began to try harder, chivvying Duff to do the same. Chips played better than usual, possibly spurred on by Kick or, more likely, by the audience and the many loud comments from the Kennedys. Both the ambassador and Rose called their encouragement to Kick. Rose's were general – 'Keep it up!' – whereas the ambassador was more precise and critical. 'You were slow to that,' he said. 'Adjust your weight, you're behind the ball.' Kick didn't respond, but looked, to Honor, to be as finely attuned to her father's voice as a hunting dog, shifting this way and that as he spoke.

Duff, it was immediately clear, was off his game. Not that Honor had seen him play for years, but once upon a time, he had been better than this. He was slow, sluggish even, easily distracted. He missed shots, returned them badly. He had put on weight, she realised. Not the way Chips had – all over, filling out from the slender young man he had been to a more broad-shouldered, solid version. With Duff, the weight was around the middle, and it slowed him and made him less agile.

The day was starting to cloud over, the blue of the sky thickening to a darker grey. But it was as hot as ever. Hotter. And quiet, muffled even, except for the drone of insects, the thwack of the ball and comments from Ambassador Kennedy. Even Chips was silent, squinting into the light as he played, Kick slim and fast beside him. Over, back, over, back, Honor followed the ball with her eyes until they began to hurt. She closed them and allowed her hands, which had been gripping the hard, spindly arms of the lawn chair, to relax. The sounds, now that she no longer followed the action, were soothing. All the heaviness of mind and limbs that she had longed for last night was upon her now. Then, her thoughts had raced here and there in tight loops, as though pursued through a maze by something that frightened them. Now, in the heat of the day, they settled, slumped even, and gave her the rest she had craved.

Perhaps she dozed off, because when she next paid attention, it was to hear Maureen, beside her, say sharply, 'Keep up, Duff, you are letting the side down.' Honor jerked forward, hoping no one had noticed her slide downwards in her chair. The butler had brought a tray of drinks – a jug that had the soapy smell of elderflower mixed with the dull tang of gin, and many glasses. The jug was clouded with condensation and fat beads of water chased each other down the ridged sides. 'Keep up!' Maureen said, sharper again. She tipped Pugsy off her lap, the better to sit forward in the low chair and watch.

From the set of his shoulders and the way his thick eyebrows were close down over his eyes, Honor could see Duff was furious, but he said nothing. He hit the ball back over the net, but without enough force, and was off-balance when Chips returned it, smartly. Duff swung his racket desperately and missed, the ball bounced, then travelled past him and landed at the edge of the court.

'Fault!' Albert the umpire called.

'Never mind,' Brigid said. 'We're still winning.' It was, Honor thought, exactly the wrong thing to say. If they were winning, it was clear that Duff had little to do with that. He served and hit the net, served a second time and hit it again, ball landing with a defeated thump into the thick rope.

'Honestly, darling,' Maureen drawled, 'we might as well go and watch someone throwing rubber balls at a coconut shy.'

The game continued in silence. It really wasn't going well, Honor realised. Brigid was almost as annoyed as Duff. Only Chips and Kick played well, especially the latter. Any other girl, Honor thought, seeing how furious Brigid was, would drop a few shots; send back a couple of soft ones; anything to even up the score. Not Kick.

Duff missed another serve. 'You need more practice,' Maureen called to him, 'and not the kind that comes with lifting a brandy glass up and down, up and down.' She mimed raising her hand to her mouth and returning it, raising and returning it. Fritzi laughed and Honor turned to look at him. He smiled broadly at her. Did he not understand the sullen atmosphere that gathered as surely as the heavy clouds overhead?

'Can't you shut up?' Duff asked, through thin lips. Maureen, Honor saw with horror, smiled at that, peeling her lips back to show small sharp teeth like an animal's.

'If you're going to lose your temper,' she drawled, 'I daresay you'll be even more off your game.'

At that Duff flung his racket to the ground. 'Why don't you play if you're so damn good.'

'I didn't say I was good,' Maureen said, 'although I couldn't be worse than you.'

'Are you conceding?' Chips asked eagerly.

With an effort, Duff pulled himself together. 'Certainly not.' He picked up his racket and they played on but it seemed obvious that no one except Kick really cared for the outcome.

Maureen got up, rising out of her lawn chair in one easy movement that made Honor envious, and poured herself a glass from the jug Andrews had brought and drank it fast. 'Isn't it time someone else had a go?' she asked. 'You are rather hogging the court. Elizabeth, you must be raring to play by now.'

'Don't stir, Maureen,' Elizabeth said. 'Everyone is perfectly peaceful except you.'

'Everyone is perfectly deathly except me,' Maureen muttered. She threw a stick for Pugsy, aiming it, Honor saw, right onto the court. The little dog ran after it, darting towards it just as Duff stepped back. His heel caught the dog a solid blow, and sent it, yelping, several inches into the air. The dog landed hard on its side and yowled more. Duff cursed viciously and Elizabeth giggled; 'Aren't you *eloquent*,' she said admiringly. Maureen had reached the dog and knelt beside it, making great play of stroking and kissing it. 'Poor baby,' she said, catching Pugsy up in her arms and standing up. 'Poor sweet baby; what did that clumsy brute do to you?' She spoke to the dog, but she looked at Duff. He raised his racket and for one awful moment Honor wondered would he fling it at his wife. He didn't. He didn't move at all. No one did. They were like creatures in a fairy story, she thought, held fast in that moment, unable to tear themselves from it.

A fat drop of rain landed on her arm. The afternoon was as thick and grey as nursery porridge. She opened her mouth to suggest they give up and go inside, and then, from behind her, a voice.

'Well, here you all are.'

There was a note of lazy amusement that she recognised. Honor turned awkwardly in the low-slung chair. 'Doris!'

'Me,' Doris agreed. And it was indeed her, more delicate and weary-looking than ever, her face wan and pale and utterly beautiful. The dark smudges under her eyes were pronounced, but her eyes shone with delight and affection. Honor began to struggle out of her chair.

'When?' she asked. 'How? What . . .?'

'Just now. The usual sort of ways,' Doris said, laughing and putting out a hand to help Honor up. 'Train, car. Any more questions?'

'All of them, but they'll have to wait.' Honor threw her arms tight around her friend. The smell of her was, she thought, like walking into one's own house after long days away. Familiar. Reassuring. 'Oh, darling, I've missed you.' She was, she realised, crying. She pulled back to look and saw that Doris' eyes were wet too. Close up, she looked truly tired, not the affected exhaustion that she used to disguise the ardent energy that was her real nature.

'Hullo, Doris. Wonderful timing – you'll play,' Brigid said immediately. 'You're already wearing trousers – divine ones; Schiaparelli? – so all you need are shoes.' They had all come forward to cluster around the newcomer. 'At least, if we had someone for you to play with . . .'

'Doris will hardly want to play the very second she arrives,' Chips said. 'Why, you must be exhausted. Perhaps you'd like to go and lie down.'

Barely was Doris in the house, Honor thought, and Chips wanted rid of her. She started to laugh, and as she did, she realised it was the first time she had laughed – properly laughed – in a long time. 'Doris is never tired,' she said. 'Are you, darling?'

'Exhausted,' Doris insisted. 'I can barely lift a cigarette, let alone a racket.' But her eyes sparkled.

'But who is she to play with?' Chips said irritably.

'Albert,' said Fritzi. 'He will be the very thing.' Doris caught Honor's eye and gave a tiny grin. Because he said it, Chips didn't immediately reject the idea. Fritzi went off to speak to Albert, who had remained in his rattan chair, and Chips took Doris by the hand.

'You'd better come and meet our Americans,' he said.

'Americans? How forgiving you are, Chips!' she murmured. 'I quite thought you had sworn off your fellow countrymen after Wallis Simpson turned out to be such a frightful disappointment.'

'Dear Wallis. Never a disappointment,' Chips said. But he said it mechanically. It was true, Honor thought, that he had largely forgiven Wallis since she had settled into her life as Duchess of Windsor, but somewhere he would always resent the spoiling of his plans that had come with Edward VIII's abdication in order to marry her. Only someone who knew him as well as Doris did would have known to look for that buried chagrin.

She remembered then how it had always been between Doris and Chips, her friend and her husband – the way they circled one another, tested one another; how much Doris loved to tease Chips, how easily goaded he was by her. And she realised that, where once this had made her uncomfortable – split her loyalties so that she didn't know which way to jump, always forced to work at keeping an uneasy truce between them – now she could simply watch them, because there was no division. Not since she had watched Chips' face when he had revealed he knew of her affair. Her loyalties were entirely whole at last.

'Fritzi, I suppose you'd better come and say hullo to Doris,' Chips said then.

'We've met,' Fritzi said, coming forward immediately.

'Have you? Where?' Chips asked, instantly alert.

'In Berlin,' Doris said, holding out her hand. 'A year ago, was it?'

'Nine months,' Fritzi said. Then added, 'I remember because it is the last time I was there. On a visit to my family.'

'It was a party,' Doris said, calling up details. 'At the Steinplatz hotel. You wore your Luftwaffe uniform. In fact, if I'm not mistaken, it was a celebration of you and your brothers joining?'

'My father said it was the right thing to do at that time,' Fritzi said evasively.

'*At that time*,' Doris echoed.

What did that mean? Honor wondered. That it was no longer the right thing? And what did Doris understand by it? Something to puzzle over later. She saw that Duff looked over at them. 'We danced,' Doris continued, head to one side as she looked at Fritzi.

'You remember.' He looked elated.

'I have a good memory.' He looked downcast. 'You were *very* popular that night,' she said, still consulting her memory – as though, Honor thought, she sifted through a well-organised drawer. 'Yes,' she continued, 'you and your brothers, all looking dashing in your new uniforms. As I recall, your joining the Luftwaffe was called "a wonderful example of the unifying of ancient and modern Germany".'

Fritzi looked momentarily terrified. Curious, Honor thought.

By then Chips had brought the Kennedys forward, so Honor had no time to puzzle out what exactly any of this meant. Introduced to them, Doris was at her most charming, and within minutes, Honor saw them smiling and nodding at her. Indeed, the ambassador tried to draw her away with him, to look at a plant with pale spidery leaves. He tucked her hand into the crook of his elbow and made to set off. Doris couldn't possibly have seen the thinning of Rose Kennedy's mouth into a hard line – a line that Honor recognised with weary familiarity – because she had her back to her, but even so, she was far too clever.

'Oh no, I know nothing at all about plants,' Doris said. 'They require far too much effort, besides not being so *terribly* entertaining.' She smiled dazzlingly. 'I'd much rather, Mrs Kennedy, if you would introduce me to your delightful daughter.' Yet she kept her hand in the ambassador's arm, so that they walked, all three, towards the tennis court where Kick was bouncing a ball, hard, and catching it each time. And Honor marvelled, as she always did, at her friend's swift reckoning, the swoop of her understanding and resourcefulness.

'Come on!' Brigid called to them all. 'If Doris and Alfred play Elizabeth and Fritzi, then the winner of that can play Kick and Chips, and we'll have an overall winner.'

'Better hurry up,' Duff said. 'Before rain comes.' He was over beside the drinks tray and Honor watched as he poured a large glass from the jug, drank it down, then poured another, ice cubes tinkling merrily. Beside him, Maureen hissed something that Honor was too far away to hear, but caused Duff to scowl. She leaned forward, took the glass from him, raised it to her lips and drank, then held out the half-empty glass and, just as he reached for it, she let it slip through her fingers and fall onto the stone terrace, where it smashed. Honor, even though she had seen it fall, jumped at the noise.

'Silly me,' Maureen said. The tennis players ignored her. Duff did not. He glared at her, then turned his back to watch the play. This was a faster game than the first one. Pretty quickly, Elizabeth gave in, making only the feeblest effort to keep up. Mostly, she let Fritzi do all the running, calling 'Good shot' encouragingly. Doris, in a pair of borrowed tennis shoes that Andrews had magicked up from somewhere, had dropped all pretence at languor. She was fast and sure, moving with all her usual grace, only speeded up, like one of those reels of film they showed at the cinema. Albert was indeed good, as Fritzi had promised, seeming able to anticipate exactly where the ball would go each time.

He behaved, Honor thought, nothing like a servant on the court. Too energetic, even ebullient when things went well. He had, she saw, broad shoulders and nicely browned forearms. Soon he and Doris were slapping their palms together to celebrate a point scored, or crouching side by side, shoulders touching, as they anticipated what was to come. They fell into the way of one another, seeming to understand by instinct when to leave a ball to the other, when to reach for it. Except once, when he put a hand out and placed it on her arm to restrain her, before answering the shot that came from Fritzi.

'Rather unexpected.' It was Maureen, back beside Honor. They both stood – no way was Honor getting back into that low-slung chair.

'What is? Doris?'

'No. Or rather – yes, but not that. Him.' She jerked her head towards Albert. 'You sort of forget they're human, in uniform all the time. Then you see them in different clothes and you realise . . . well, he's a man.' With shock, Honor realised what she meant. Albert's powerful build, the confidence of his movements, the way he dominated his section of the court. 'Like taking a bridle off a horse and turning it free into the field,' Maureen said thoughtfully. '*Quite* a different creature . . .'

'Good God, Maureen.' Honor was disgusted, as much by the way Maureen spoke as by what she said.

'No, I suppose you wouldn't notice,' Maureen said, looking her over beadily. 'You have no idea about that sort of thing at all, do you?'

It was humiliating – why did everyone assume she was some terrible prude? Honor decided she had had enough. She would go back to the house and they could join her when these silly games were done. It was still hot – too hot – but there was no sun at all anymore, just that bank of damp cloud that lay over everything, making all movement an effort. The yellow-ish tinge to the air was worse now, like looking out through a glass filled with lemon barley water.

She turned but before she had gone two paces, there was a loud clap of thunder and rain began to spill from the sky, hitting the hot ground and sending up an acrid smell. For a moment, big heavy drops chased each other almost singly, one landing before the next arrived, as though an advance party had been sent out, and then, with another loud clap, down it came in a torrent, like the moment a basin overflows.

'Quick, inside!' she called. The group scattered and began to run. Kick and Brigid squealed in excitement and ran laughing, zig-zagging through the rain as though they could avoid it. The ambassador produced a large umbrella he must have taken from the house and snapped it open. Rose stepped under it and the two of them walked away briskly. Albert caught up a jacket and held it over his head – held it out for Doris to duck under too. She did, and the two of them ran together towards the house, close together in that tiny patch of shelter. Honor, not nearly as fast, ran behind them but quickly was out of breath. She was so wet anyway, what was the point, she decided. And so she slowed down, walked, watching the flowers flatten under the weight of the rain. The garden was quickly blotted out around her, hidden by the lowering gloom. The ground couldn't absorb water fast enough and soon there were busy rivulets running alongside her as she walked. Another clap of thunder. She wiped her soaking fringe from her eyes, licking her lips where drops had trickled down and over them. The rain tasted ferrous.

Ahead, she could just about make out a figure in the porch of the side door. Who, she thought, would stand in a porch, even if it was partly sheltered, when they could be inside? Perhaps it was a guest, fussing about wet shoes. She speeded up, ready to call and tell them not to bother, but as she got closer, she saw it wasn't one person but two, standing huddled together. Later, she realised she would never have known it was two, so close were they, except that one of them pulled away and the space between them showed the truth. The one who pulled away was Doris. She slipped in through the door behind her, leaving whoever it was she had been talking to. Albert. Honor watched as he turned and went towards the back of the house.

What, Honor wondered, could Doris possibly have to say so intently to a man she had only just met? A servant, at that.

Chapter Thirty-Three

Kick

Thermore first match had been a bit of a dud, Kick reflected, but she was looking forward to playing that Doris girl. *There* was someone who knew how to swing a racket. Although, she reflected, the speed with which Duff had been drinking whatever was in that jug – gin, mainly, judging by the taste – was unlikely to have improved his serve. She must make sure not to get partnered up with him if they played again. That fellow Albert was more like it. How funny the English were about servants, she reflected. The way they had drawn back from him, as if he had some kind of rash or cold they might catch, until Fritzi went on about how he wasn't exactly a servant . . . Even then, they had been pretty wary. Except for Doris. She, Kick thought, seemed alright.

She dried her hair vigorously with a towel. A tap at the door. Her mother.

'Kathleen! Put that towel down.'

'But my hair . . .'

'Will dry fluffy. Leave it. I will send Wilkes to you.'

'Oh, who cares?'

'Don't be irritating, Kathleen. I am not having this conversation again. What did you make of all that?' she asked, sitting carefully on the edge of Kick's bed and smoothing out the counterpane on either side of her with thin fingers.

'Brigid would play well if she concentrated better. Chips isn't bad either, but he gets excited and misses easy shots . . .'

'I don't mean the tennis. All that with Maureen and Duff' – Kick looked at her mother sharply. Something about the way she said his name – 'and then Fritzi and his manservant. That girl Doris arriving . . .'

'That's the English,' Kick said wisely. 'Always pretending to have everything so perfectly under control, whereas in fact they're just a few steps away from chaos, like the rest of us.'

'How do you mean?'

'It's a thing they do. I've seen it before.' As she spoke, she was magnificently conscious, for the first time, of knowing more than her mother. Knowing this place better than her mother. 'They make such a deal about everything being exactly as they expected it – nothing unplanned, ever. Except it's an illusion. Plenty of unexpected things happen, only they immediately all get together and make believe they are anticipated.'

'But surely if they all do it together, they all know it isn't true?' Rose sounded honestly baffled.

'Maybe, but it's the pretence that matters. They behave as though there is an invisible audience to everything they do, watchers with pens poised, ready to make judgement, who they must deceive.'

Kick expected to be complimented for her clever understanding, but all her mother said was, 'Don't waste too much of your time understanding all this, Kathleen. It is important that you get on well, now, for your father's sake. But after all, we won't be here so very long.' And, when Kick didn't answer, 'Let us say the rosary now because it will be difficult to get away later.'

So Kick took up her beads from the bedside drawer where she had placed them; not exactly hidden, she thought, but out of sight. They knelt together at the side of Kick's bed. Her mother began in low, clear tones, 'Our Father, who art in heaven . . .' Kick listened, then joined her voice to her mother's, her mind free to wander as the familiar words she loved ran their own course. Even though they didn't talk at these times, beyond the saying of prayers, there was a harmony between them that she treasured and that was as much a part of her religion as the mysteries and miracles. When she said, 'Hail Mary,' it was Rose's face she saw – only Rose's face as it so rarely was: gentle and soft. Without criticism or calculation.

Chapter Thirty-Four

Doris

Doris stood in the hallway. Her clothes clung to her, wet and unpleasant, like a skin only half shed, she thought. There was no one in sight and she didn't know where her room might be. If she even had a room yet. She could always go along the corridor upstairs and open every door she found, she thought with a laugh. Or indeed step out of her wet clothes right where she was and wait for someone to appear and tell her where to go.

Honor came in behind her. Doris turned. 'Thank goodness,' she said. 'I thought I might have to improvise.'

'You'd better come to my room, I have no idea where to put you yet. I don't even know how many rooms there are.' Honor half-laughed, but helplessly. 'Some are not ready yet. Only Chips knows what's what.'

'*Only Chips knows*,' Doris teased. 'I see nothing has changed in your marriage.' But even as she spoke, she realised how wrong she was. One proper look at Honor was enough to tell her that. Told Doris so much more than her letters had. It had been little over a year since her last visit, yet in that time Honor had aged. Not yet thirty, she looked older. It wasn't just lines and wrinkles, it was the defeated stoop of her, the thickness around the middle, that spoke of unhappiness that was general and did not lift. Not the specific misery of, say, a love affair gone wrong, Doris thought; that might have expressed itself in agitation, something abrupt and intense. This was the sodden misery of a life only scarcely lived.

Sure enough: 'Except things *have* changed,' Honor said dully. 'A very great deal. I am only really seeing that now.'

'Let's go up and you can tell me.'

Honor allowed herself to be led upstairs, as though she were the guest, Doris thought, pointing out her room and allowing Doris to take her to it, shut the door behind them, and even remind her to get out of her wet things as she stood, shivering, looking out at the buffeted garden.

'Those plants will be destroyed,' Honor said. 'Chips will be furious. They are only just laid down. Everything here is only recently finished. There is almost a smell of fresh paint.' She wrinkled her nose. 'He has no idea how vulgar he is.'

'Nonsense, darling,' Doris said briskly. 'That sort of thing means nothing anymore. This is a mighty comfortable house, and that is what matters.'

'Is it?' Honor asked vaguely.

'Yes. You know that. Now, as for Chips' failings as a man, and a husband, that is something other entirely. Please tell me.'

'I do not know where to begin,' Honor said. She said it

helplessly. As though, Doris thought, not knowing meant that there was no way to begin.

'It doesn't matter where. Begin in the middle. Go backwards from there, or forwards, it will all come out.' She remembered this of Honor from the time they were at school together – how overwhelmed she could be by too much information.

'Ask me questions,' Honor begged. 'It's easier that way.'

'Very well, but first, sit down.' Honor had dragged on a plaid dressing gown, her clothes left in a damp heap on the floor. 'Ring for tea, then come here and I'll brush your hair.'

'As you used to.'

'As I used to.'

Meekly, Honor sat at the dressing table after the maid had been and gone, and Doris began to run the silver-backed brush through her hair that she had once described as 'the colour of milky tea'. There was grey in it now, and it was coarser than it had been. 'So, where shall I begin,' she wondered aloud. 'Because it's Chips, I rather feel I had better begin with the obvious. Are there others?' She spoke briskly, but she was careful to avoid Honor's eyes in the looking-glass in front of them; to offer her some refuge from shame.

'Yes,' Honor said, with a dismissive wave of her hand. 'Always. It wasn't that. Or not exactly that. It was that . . . well, between he and I . . . there has been nothing. For so very long. Since Paul in fact.'

'I see.' As usual, Doris thought, Honor squirmed to discuss anything intimate. She was twisting her hands in her lap so rapidly that they looked like small writhing creatures.

'At first he didn't seem to notice, or much care. But then he did and was agitated. Said we were not "proper husband and wife". That there must be more children and how were there to be if we were never in the same room together. I said we were in the same room a very great deal, only there were always other people in the room with us. I tried, Doris, honestly I did. Only I could not. Could not bear it. Could not bear him.'

'What did he say then?' Doris asked.

'A very great deal.' She made a face. 'On and on, as he does. Then he sent a doctor to me. Dr Low.' Honor was so red now that her face looked painful. 'The doctor was at pains to tell me that everything that is wrong with me – the sleeplessness, the lethargy, the ill-humour – all this is because of that. Or rather, because of not that, if you see what I mean.'

'I see what you mean.' Doris stopped herself from laughing – Honor's inability to be more precise, to say what she meant, using only 'that' and 'not that' to express herself, was typical. But what lay behind it was not funny at all.

'As though I were a farmyard animal,' she continued bitterly. 'One that will not breed right and must have a vet sent, to stare into her mouth and twitch her tail and pronounce her fit, or unfit.'

'Vile,' Doris said with a shudder.

'In any case, if he hoped to reawaken my interest in him through the doctor, he was a fool,' Honor said with spirit. 'If anything could have made me more resolute to keep away from it, that was it.'

'I can imagine.'

'And there was someone else for me, also. For a little while. A very little while.'

'I see. And?'

'Well, no. I mean not really.'

'Not really what? You will have to tell me a little more.' Doris hid her face so Honor wouldn't see her lips twitch.

'Not really anything,' Honor said with sudden spirit. 'I cannot understand why everyone goes on about love and how they will die for it, or kill for it, or whatever it is they say they will do. How they leave their homes and children and risk everything to be with someone they shouldn't. But for what? I tried it, and I found it all perfectly flat. And really rather awkward.'

Doris laughed at that – how could you not, she thought. 'Oh, darling, you are too funny.'

'I am not being funny.'

'Of course. So, what then?'

'Chips found out. Although I didn't know that until a few days ago. He said nothing at the time. Nothing until it suited him to say something.'

'How does it suit him?'

'He hopes to use his forbearance to bargain.'

'For what?'

'To persuade me that, having been a bad wife, and he a forgiving husband, now I must make an extra effort to be a good wife.'

'So he wants to stay married?'

'Oh very much so. He's worried. Afraid of what it will cost him if the marriage ends. And so certain that money – the Guinness fortune – was really at the heart of everything.'

'In what way?'

'That without all that money, I would not be nearly so enticing a prospect. Not enticing at all, really.'

'He said that?' Doris paused, brush in mid-air so that the silver back of it was turned towards her. She saw her own face, distorted and faint in its smooth, polished back. Honor's initials – HC – in looped, spidery writing, were engraved across the reflection.

'He did.' Honor had stopped twisting her hands. They lay, inert now, in her lap, no longer animated creatures but defeated. 'He said it was a plot, a seduction, to get money from me.'

'You know that is not true,' Doris said gently. 'You know that he lies? That you are delightful and a darling in every way. As enticing as ever anyone could be.'

'Am I? I do not feel it. But then, I do not feel very much, if the truth be told. I do not feel humiliation as keenly as I once would have. I do not feel joy or mirth. I do not even feel the pain of my situation as I should. Mostly, I am indifferent even to that.'

'What about Paul?'

'Even Paul . . . I can see he is a darling child, but somehow, I cannot feel it. Days may go by without me seeing him, and I barely notice. Chips says he has my family's obstinacy and contrariness. Maybe he does.' She shrugged. 'He's a stranger. I hardly know him. It's not that I resent him, it's that I resent how little I know him. But even resent is too strong a word. Too staunch a word for what I feel. When I look at my life, there aren't high and low moments. Everything seems to happen in a line that is flat and thin and rather low to the ground.'

'For how long?'

'Oh, a long time. Almost since you left. But that's enough of me. Tell me about you. About what you have been doing.'

'Well, I will, but that does not mean that we are entirely finished with this. May we talk more, another time?' It was the best she could do right then, Doris decided. Everything Honor had told her made her sad. It was so clearly the truth – as conveyed already by her friend's face, her form – and yet Doris had expected to hear only a version of it. A version twisted by Honor's capacity – learned from her mother – to insist that all was well when it was not. 'No reason to cry over milk that is already spilled,' Lady Iveagh would say briskly, no matter the circumstances.

Honor had learned to say the same, to live the same. And yet here she was, without even any prodding, telling just how unhappy her life had become. Yes, Doris thought decidedly, they would return to this. To Chips. But not now.

So she talked of Berlin. Of her apartment with its wooden floors and high ceilings, the walls dressed in dark wood carved into whorls and knots that shone warm in the lamplight. The high brass bed heaped with cool linen and airy feather bolsters. Of how safe she felt there, tucked into the fourth floor of a building so large it covered a whole block of the city, and how exposed when she walked the streets – as though even the wind were suspicious and might blow rumours of her to the wrong people.

She talked of the high-ranking Nazi officers who bowed low over her hand and praised the ivory glow of her skin, who spoke to her of Goethe and the beauty of Wagner, and slipped notes into her evening bag that implored her to meet them alone, while their wives, in stiff fur and diamonds, stood close by. Of how careful she was to never accept, but never offend. To be always – always! – laughing. Charming, encouraging, affectionate, but also aloof. To be remote when they hoped she would be accessible, and accessible when they assumed she would be remote. Of how easy it was; that men, each time, are just men. How little it mattered what language they spoke or uniform they wore; still they were distracted by the curve of a cheekbone, the flutter of eyelashes, the shining whiteness of bare arms in evening dress.

She talked of the late nights wreathed in thick clouds of cigarette smoke and laughter. Of the way the sharp click of their heels as they drew them together and raised their arms in salute, even now, made her jump a little. Of the quiet mornings and lonely afternoons where she wrote letters home, parsing, always, the words she used and how much she told. She told a little of the anger and vicious pride on the streets, the growing fear of some amidst the triumph of others. But not much.

She did not talk of the other meetings. The ones that did not exactly take place. There were so many things she didn't talk of. Not yet. The gap between her recent life and Honor's was too great; could be bridged only gradually if at all.

Honor listened and asked questions; practical ones that Doris answered: *What of your mother's family?*; blunt ones that she deflected: *Are you safe?* And at last, 'What were you talking to that fellow Albert, Fritzi's man, so intently about?'

'I wasn't talking to him.'

'What were you doing then?'

'Kissing him.'

'What? Doris! Why?'

Doris laughed. 'We reached the house and as I was about to go in, he tried to kiss me, and I let him.'

'How could you . . .? A servant . . .'

'A jolly handsome chap!' Doris insisted. 'Call it an instant of madness. The tennis, the rain, the thunder, those absurd flashes of lightning. Who could resist?'

'I could,' Honor said.

'Yes, I suppose you could,' Doris agreed. 'You haven't the habit of letting men kiss you.'

'And you do?'

'I do. Especially if it's worth my while.'

'How could it possibly be worth your while?' Honor sounded baffled. So baffled that Doris laughed again.

'Really, darling, you are like a child sometimes. Or someone who is only half paying attention . . .' And then she remembered all that Honor had told her and she put her hand to her mouth. 'I'm sorry. I didn't mean—'

'It's alright, I know you didn't.' Honor put a hand behind her and took hold of Doris' so that she had to cease her brushing. 'How happy I am that you're back.'

'Me too.'

'How long can you stay?'

'I don't know. It depends. Now, tell me about the Americans.'

'And then you must change. You're soaked too. I'll find out what room you're in.'

She met Duff on the stairs, coming up towards her. 'Doris.'

'Duff.' She moved to one side, to let him past, but he stopped. 'How's Berlin?'

'Interesting.'

'Are you on an unexpected visit home?'

'Not entirely. Perhaps undertaken a little sooner than expected.'

'I see.' She moved to go past him and he put out a hand. 'I imagine the ambassador will want to chat to you. He seems keen to hear happy stories of Berlin and Germany.'

'Just the kinds of stories I write,' Doris said carefully.

'He might also listen to other kinds of stories, if you had those to tell,' Duff said, looking straight at her.

'I see,' Doris responded thoughtfully. Then, 'Thank you.'

By the time she reached the drawing room, Chips was already there. 'It's like being upside down,' she said, gesturing to the painted ceiling. 'Or perhaps like watching the city from below the water of the Thames. A fish-eye view.'

'You always did talk nonsense,' he said peevishly.

'It's only nonsense if you don't understand it,' Doris said, smiling sweetly at him.

'Have you settled in alright?' he asked.

'No, but I will.'

'I suppose you can settle anywhere at this stage.'

'I can,' she agreed. 'Just as you can. What is it now? The last I saw of you, you were picking up the pieces following the abdication. What a blow that was to you.' She smiled again, not bothering to keep the mockery out of it. 'What have you been at since? What new plans and schemes for Chips?'

'I hear you use my name all over Berlin,' he said peevishly. 'Von Ribbentrop congratulated me just the other day on having sent such a charming emissary.'

'Oh, you would be simply thrilled to see the doors it has opened for me. Old Göring himself told me to be sure to remember him to you.'

'Dear fellow,' Chips said warmly. 'So ostentatious, and yet disarming . . . Well, and what if I were to withdraw use of my name? Tell everyone what you really are?' He poked viciously at the fire.

'Indeed. But you can't, can you?' She laughed at him. 'And I know very well that you can't. First, think what it would do to you, in the circles you care about, to have it known – your wife's dearest friend, a Jew.'

'Half a Jew,' he corrected.

'There are no halves,' Doris said. 'Not anymore. Not now.' She felt her voice tremble and took a deep breath. She would not betray herself in front of Chips. Neither would she try to appeal to anything that might be decent in him. She would not tell him her stories of watching men and women hustled off the pavement and into filthy gutters, sometimes by children; the look on a young boy's face as his mother stood in the baker's while everyone around her was served first, until the shop was empty of all but them. These were things she hadn't yet told Honor. She certainly wouldn't tell him.

'And, what's more,' she continued, 'I know very well that you are under instruction that cannot be disobeyed to stay quiet. And so, I may do as I please.'

'Well, I hope you are not making mischief,' he said. 'We' – he laid heavy emphasis on the word – 'are working hard to bring this thing off. To cement the understanding between England and Germany, so that there will not be war.'

'There is already war.'

'War with England. You know that is what I mean.'

'There is already war,' Doris repeated. 'It is now just a question of degrees.'

'You give up far too easily,' he said. 'I' – he paused, to thump a hand against his chest – 'will never give up. I will keep fighting to prevent this.'

How to tell him that he had prevented nothing? Could prevent nothing. No one could. Oh, they might keep war out of England, and indeed England out of war, just as they wished, but the rage and cruelty were already happening where they couldn't see it and didn't wish to look. Someone needed to fight against that, even if men like Chips wouldn't.

'Your energy does you credit, Channon.' It was Ambassador Kennedy, standing in the doorway. 'If only more of your countrymen were of the same mind.'

'There are enough of us,' Chips said. 'Mostly, there is Chamberlain. And that will be enough.' He looked at Doris in a pleased way and she, because she didn't want to impede whatever the ambassador might say next, ignored him.

'I didn't realise you had so recently come from Germany,' Kennedy said to Doris, crossing the room. 'I would so like to hear your thoughts and impressions.'

'Delighted,' she said. 'Shall we sit?' And she deliberately led him to a sofa far from Chips, a small one, with room only for two.

Chapter Thirty-Five

Brigid

Brigid changed out of her wet clothes quickly, pulling on a clean skirt and, because she was chilly after being soaked, a long-sleeved blouse.

'How clever you are,' she called as Minnie came in. 'Always appearing exactly when you are needed. How do you do it?'

'I heard you on the stairs,' Minnie said. 'And it could be no one but you. Galloping along.'

'Gliding,' Brigid insisted. 'Like a swan. Will you button me up? They are so fiddly, and at the back. I cannot reach.'

Minnie pushed her hair away from her shoulders and began buttoning. 'Mrs Kennedy is having a bath drawn,' she said.

'Goodness!' Brigid was shocked. 'Another? And she hasn't even been out hunting.'

'Apparently being wet is reason enough. But I understand that

Americans are like that.' Minnie had finished the buttons and was twitching Brigid's skirt into place, smoothing the tweed over her hips.

'Funny lot, aren't they?' Brigid said thoughtfully. 'Kick is a dear, and jolly amusing. But so ruthless, Minnie, you cannot imagine. Beating me up and down the court until I quite felt I should like to beat her at something. Only I don't know what. It won't be swimming,' she added gloomily, 'not after watching her this morning. Poor Fritzi could barely keep pace.'

'That young man does not know what to keep pace with,' Minnie said wisely.

'What do you mean?'

'He is like a puppy that hears its name called on all sides and doesn't know which way to run. And his man, Albert, is the same.'

'How?'

'Busy about all sorts of things that shouldn't concern him.'

'Such as?'

'Anything. He listens to everything, watches everything.'

'Nosy,' Brigid said, tying up her hair.

She went along the corridor to Kick's room, tapped and went in. 'I say, am I interrupting?' she asked when she saw Rose was there.

'I was just leaving,' Rose said. She looked, Brigid thought, disapproving. But then, she seemed to mostly look like that. 'My bath will be ready.'

'What shall we do with the rest of the day?' Brigid asked, throwing herself down on Kick's bed. 'That rain looks like it won't let up, so there will be no more tennis or swimming, or even getting out of the house.'

'At home on days like this, Cook would let us into the kitchen and we would bake,' Kick said. 'I once made a Key lime pie.'

'How very odd,' Brigid said. 'I cannot see my sister letting us be a nuisance in the kitchens. I cannot see Cook letting her let us. No, it will have to be something else.'

'Charades?' Kick suggested. 'We played at Hatfield when I went on a visit there . . .' She trailed off. 'Brigid, may I ask something?'

'Ask away.'

'Last night, the film my father showed . . .'

'Dreadful,' Brigid said firmly.

'Dreadful,' Kick agreed. 'But afterwards, everyone walked out of the room so quietly and no one had a thing to say about it, except Elizabeth, who gave him a piece of her mind. And then when Billy was going, I tried to find some way to tell him that it wasn't my idea, that I didn't know anything about it, and he wouldn't let me.'

'I imagine not,' Brigid agreed.

'But how am I to tell him if he won't let me?' she said, fidgeting with the things on her dressing table. 'Do you think he'll ever talk to me again?' Kick finished miserably, face screwed up.

'I don't know,' Brigid said slowly. 'It's rather hard for him . . .'

'How much easier it would be to be you,' Kick said. 'Then I would be exactly what he knows and expects and all this would be just simple.'

'But then he wouldn't like you so much,' Brigid said wisely. 'After all, it's not me he likes, or Irene, or any of us. It's you. It's not the girls his parents think are suitable—'

'Princess Elizabeth,' Kick said with a grin.

'Exactly. If it's going to be alright, it will be because you're odd and adorable, and, just as Billy says, "utterly unexpected," not despite it.'

'If,' Kick said morosely. 'If?'

'If, darling. You must know . . . well, how hard it is for someone like Billy, from a family like his, brought up the way he has been . . . It's like those poor horses they still have for pumping water in some of the smaller villages. They go around and around and around all day, turning the pump or grinding grain, and then on Sundays when they put them out into the fields, the poor things go around and around for hours before they remember they don't have to. That's Billy now. Trying to set himself straight so he can reach you.'

'You don't think he'll succeed, do you?'

'I don't know. He has been going around for so very long. Just like all his family before him. Generations, going around the same pump . . .'

Kick went to the gramophone that stood on the window sill. In its neat red leather case it was, Brigid thought, like a vanity case or even a doctor's bag. 'Can you play something?' she asked.

Kick put a record on then and the rhythmic sound of the needle bumping softly over grooves and scratches filled the air. Then the sound of a woman's voice, energetic and languid both at once.

'She's called Billie Holiday,' Kick said. 'Mother hates that I listen to her.'

They were silent, letting the music fill up the space between them. 'I can see why,' Brigid said after a while. 'That voice does rather make one want to do terribly bad things . . . or at least, to be out in a world where it's possible to do such things.' She looked around the cosy, neat bedroom. 'Do you ever want to kick and kick like a horse in a stall it hates? To break it all down?' Then she laughed. 'Of course you do. With a name like yours . . .' She lay back on the bed, against the pillows, and Kick came and sat on the end of it, hands under her thighs, legs swinging in time to the music. 'It's not that I hate it,' Brigid continued. 'Not at all. But I do rather feel that it isn't *life*, if you see what I mean? Just sort of a waiting room for life. As though one were permanently sitting in the ladies' first class at Paddington Station. Lots of things put on for one's entertainment, of course – lunches, and tennis, and visits, but none of it quite real.'

'I feel that more here than I did at home in New York,' Kick said. 'There, everyone did what they did, just like that. Here, there's a very great deal of waiting around alright. At first, I hated it. It made me so impatient. I'm getting better at it. But I don't know if that's good – to be better at waiting around?'

'I shouldn't worry,' Brigid said with a laugh. 'I can't see you ever being very good at it.' Then, 'I say, how untidy you are.' She looked around the room, at the shoes scattered about the floor, the dressing table where an ivory-backed hairbrush lay surrounded by jars of cream, make-up, hair pins, a dusting of spilled powder over it all.

'You sound like my mother,' Kick said idly.

'I'm sure I sound like *everyone's* mother. Mine wouldn't be able to stand for it. She'd tidy it herself rather than look at it.'

'My mother believes I must do things for myself and won't let her maid tidy after me.'

'In case you marry a poor man?' Brigid said sympathetically. Her own mother, Lady Iveagh, had drilled into her and Patsy that they mustn't be wasteful or careless, for that very reason.

'Goodness, no.' Kick laughed. 'Because it's good for my soul. No one expects I'll marry a poor man. I simply never meet any.' Something about the bluntness with which Kick said it made Brigid feel awkward, so she didn't respond.

The record ended and Kick got up to change it, putting on something lighter and quicker. 'Charades is rather a good idea,' Brigid said after a while. 'Especially if Elizabeth will play. No one takes a costume more seriously than she does. I once went to a party where she wore only a bedsheet, twisted into what she claimed was a toga, only it was a single bedsheet and not any bit big enough for a toga.' She began to giggle. 'More like a napkin held over her lap. As though she went to dinner but forgot her clothes. Too funny! The others will be awfully sticky though,' she continued. 'Maureen won't play, she only dresses up for her own games and tricks. And Chips will only do it if there's someone he terribly wants to impress.'

'And is there?'

'No. I mean' – she said hurriedly – 'he wants to impress your parents, naturally, but not the way he would want to impress, well, someone royal.'

'It's OK,' Kick said with a grin. 'I won't take offence.' Then, 'Well, what about Murder in the Dark? We play that a lot in the evenings at Hyannis Port. Although it barely gets properly dark there during the summer.'

'We wouldn't even have to wait,' Brigid said eagerly, looking out at the rain. 'Once we draw the curtains, it'll be plenty dark enough in an hour at this rate. Come on, let's go down.'

They were last to the drawing room. Everyone else was there, and all looking rather bored. Except the ambassador and Doris, who sat apart and talked a lot together. Chips and Fritzi stood at the bookshelves, Chips pointing something out to the boy. Brigid caught the words 'one of your ancestors'. Maureen played a complicated version of Patience, batting off advice from Elizabeth, while Honor sat beside them, engrossed in her book. Rose Kennedy had a book in her hands too, but she scarcely turned the pages, instead looking carefully around the room, giving everyone her attention for a moment, before moving on. Perhaps, Brigid thought, she gave the most attention to Duff, who sat by himself with a newspaper. He turned a page in one sharp movement so the paper crackled.

Outside, the wind cradled the house roughly, rocking it and throwing the occasional handful of rain against the windows.

'You're late,' Maureen snapped, looking up.

'Only a little,' Brigid said soothingly. 'And we have a jolly plan for what to do.'

'Why do we need a plan?' Maureen asked.

'Of course we need a plan, isn't that so, Kick?'

'It'll be fun,' Kick said, as though reassuring a child.

Maureen frowned.

'Murder in the Dark,' Brigid said excitedly. 'If we turned off all the lights and drew the curtains, this room would be dark already. All we need is to make cards, pick and play. There's a murderer, a victim, a detective, and everyone else is an innocent party.'

'Oh yes,' Elizabeth said, getting up and coming over to them. She looked, Brigid thought, decidedly odd – one of Honor's flowered afternoon dresses looped up in handfuls around a belt so that it fell to just below her knees, and a cardigan dragged over her shoulders. Her hair straggled. But her face was alight with excitement. 'We could play in character? I was at a party once where we adopted parts as people from the novels of Miss Christie. I was Monsieur Poirot. It was the jolliest fun imaginable. I had a moustache drawn on with burned cork, and a silk scarf tossed over my shoulder.'

'I suppose it might be amusing,' Maureen said. She looked around the room. 'Honor, you are clearly the sacrificial victim. And Duff, I rather think you are the murderer. You look like you could kill any one of us just now.'

'Only you,' Brigid heard Duff mutter, before snapping the pages of his paper.

Elizabeth must have heard too, because she said, with a sly grin, 'We could play in couples. Only we'd need to work out, are the couples playing *with* one another, or against?' She looked from Duff to Maureen. 'And if against, are they to kill one another, or merely betray?'

'You can't choose,' Kick said patiently. 'That's why we make cards. It's all a secret. That's the point of it.'

It was Chips who Brigid looked to then. She saw him glance over at the ambassador, one eyebrow faintly raised. Whatever he saw in Kennedy's face caused him to turn and say firmly, 'No Murder in the Dark. It's a nursery game.'

'Spoilsport!' Brigid cried. 'Fritzi, say something! Perhaps you have influence with him? It's terrific fun, and otherwise you will all simply sit here and *talk* all afternoon.'

'And what is wrong with that?' Chips asked.

'Everything is wrong with it!'

'I would play, most willingly,' Fritzi said cautiously, looking from Brigid to Chips, 'if that is what is decided upon.'

'No Murder in the Dark,' Chips said again. 'Sorry, dear boy, it simply won't do. But perhaps you and Lady Brigid would like to take a look at the watercolours in the Green Room?' His eyes gleamed so that he looked, Brigid thought, like an owl, tucked into that dim corner.

'Watercolours!' she said irritably. 'The very idea.' She left, and Kick followed her, catching up with her on the stairs. 'What a spoilsport he is,' she said again. 'Unless something is *his* idea, and then he cannot hear no. But I've got an idea.' She grinned. 'One that will be fun, and will jolly well pay him back.'

'Oh yes?'

'A haunting! We're going to create a ghost and scare the life out of them.'

'Yes,' Kick said instantly, 'and let's do it quickly, while they are all gathered there together. It will be much easier.'

They ran upstairs, to Kick's room, and began to plan. They had got little further than agreeing to take the sheets off Brigid's bed when there was a tap on the door. Elizabeth.

'I say, what are you two doing?' she asked, eyes wide and round. 'And can I play too? It is simply no fun downstairs at all.'

'You can,' Brigid said. 'We are planning a haunting. A real live ghost story.'

'The very thing!' Elizabeth agreed. 'How?'

Brigid explained about the sheets, and added that they hoped to borrow a lipstick from Kick's mother, 'to make it look bloody—' when Elizabeth interrupted.

'Wait.' She held up a hand. 'That's all very well, but the real trick is to set the scene. It's all about illusion. If you create the possibility of ghosts in their minds, they will be the quicker to believe that's what it is. Otherwise someone will say, 'Is that the water system acting up?' and they will all go around tapping at pipes. The real trick is to suggest, rather than say, and let them do the rest.'

'She's right!' Kick's eyes gleamed. 'We need to set the scene!'

Chapter Thirty-Six

Doris

Then ambassador asked a great many questions, listening closely to the answers, blue eyes steady in the way they held hers, as though considering not just what she said, but the way she said it. He asked simple questions – how many cars on the roads of Berlin, about the rail network, the price of basic items – and questions that were not simple: what sense of itself had Germany now, and how was that changed in the time since she had been there? Did she believe the German people were united? What were their feelings about the possibility of war? She answered as best she could, even though she could see that some of her answers displeased him.

'What do you make of morale?' he asked. 'The mood of the people?'

'It is hard to say,' she answered truthfully. 'Bullish, mostly, but there are things to make them uneasy. People disappear. Families. Some go because they are afraid. Others simply vanish.' It was more than she'd said to Honor, or Chips.

'These are Jewish families?'

'Yes, but it unsettles others too. You cannot take a family out of a community and not leave a gap, a hole behind. And even if those families are no longer believed to be "German", that is still true.'

'I have heard the stories of disappearances. I believe them to be exaggerated.'

'I do not.'

'What have you seen that suggests they are not?'

'You asked my impressions, and I'm giving them to you, that's all.'

'I don't read much of this in your newspaper articles,' he said, eyes shrewd behind his glasses.

'You read my articles?'

'I read everything.'

'Well, that is not what I have been sent to write about. I am to write about daily life.'

'Race meetings and sports days and village fetes?' He raised an eyebrow ironically.

'Yes, and even that not very much anymore. There isn't much appetite for these kinds of accounts in England now. Not since gas masks were sent out.'

'I've heard there is plenty of appetite in some quarters,' he said shrewdly. 'Mosley is a fan.'

So he'd heard that too.

'I write what I'm asked to write,' Doris said. She didn't say by whom, and he didn't ask.

'And if there is no longer such an appetite for simple stories, what will you write about?' he continued.

'I don't know yet.'

'Perhaps you will not return? Perhaps you are back home to stay?'

'No, I will return.'

'Strange.' His blue eyes, the blue of Prussian army uniforms, rested thoughtfully on her.

'Hardly.' She shrugged. 'It's my home. For now. The truth is,' she smiled at him, 'I do not work so *very* hard, and that is something that suits me very well.'

'Honor tells me you have a great many friends. That you go everywhere and know everyone?'

'I do,' she twinkled. 'Am I not lucky? Mostly it is thanks to Chips, who has himself a great many friends in Berlin and has been most generous in his introductions.'

'Oh, I am sure you have your own charm to thank for it,' he said with heavy gallantry. All the same, she thought, he looked more carefully at her than ever, and she couldn't determine if that was because her dress, a graceful print of blue and white flowers, was exceptionally becoming, or something else. 'And you and the prince are old friends?'

'Hardly.' She smiled politely. 'We have met, that's all.' She remembered the evening more clearly even than she had admitted. How desperately young Prince Friedrich had seemed, in his grey-blue uniform with the silver eagle over his heart, wings spread aggressively over that ugly, twisted cross the Nazis wore. How the correctness of his posture had disguised his apprehension, but only until you looked properly at him. Then, the fear he had buttoned tightly inside with his tunic was so obvious. And small wonder, she had thought. The deal his father had made with the Nazis – the shine of the Hohenzollern family in exchange for the power of the National Socialists – was a fragile, even dangerous one. Greed might motivate both parties, but glamour was never a match for ruthlessness.

But also how, every time she turned around, there he was, close to her, always with an offer of a cigarette, a drink, a lift. How, when he drove her home through a city where day was stirring, the sky around them opening into a brief wash of pale pink and lilac, then almost immediately closed over to a dull grey, she could see that he wanted to kiss her, but didn't dare, and how she had thanked him warmly, then got out of the car quickly, before he could work up the courage.

'You've met,' the ambassador repeated thoughtfully. And again those shrewd blue eyes rested on her. 'What do you make of him? I'd like to be able to report back to Roosevelt, where do Germany's princes stand in all of this?'

'Certainly they do not stand united, that I can tell you. Every great family has their own desire and determination. But *our* prince . . . I wonder does he stand, so much as *lean* . . . I think he is in the centre of a group who all have different ideas about where he should be.'

'You speak in riddles.' He was annoyed. 'All you English do.'

'I'm half-German.'

'Then speak with that half.'

'Fine. If that's what you want.' She looked amused. 'It's not what anyone else wants . . . So, there are people who would use Friedrich, a Hohenzollern prince, for their own ends.'

'Who are they? What ends?'

'How unlike a diplomat you are,' she mused. 'Positively *abrupt*.'

'So I've been told.' He gave her a rare smile. 'Those fellows must think they have double the lifespan of the rest of us, the pace they move at. Now, go on.'

'It varies. Many people. Many ends. Fritzi could be many things: a tame royal for Hitler to dangle on the end of a string or a rallying point for dissent.'

'Why does everyone think he'll do what they want?'

'Because they want to think it. And because they have no reason to think he won't. So far, he has shown himself very pliable.'

'So far?'

'Yes. Now, I wonder . . .'

'Wonder what?'

'If he isn't finding a little steel within himself. Or without.' She laughed.

'More riddles?'

'Oh, quite an easy one this time.' She looked to where Fritzi sat, alone, watching the door Brigid and Kick had gone out of.

Chapter Thirty-Seven

Maureen

It was an hour almost before the girls, and Elizabeth, reappeared in the drawing room. The tea things had been cleared and Chips had made the first round of cocktails. Smoke drifted from cigarettes, and in the background, the gramophone played something melancholy. Maureen wondered was Chips afraid that anything jazzier would offend the ambassador.

The room was quiet, those in it had drifted into small knots together and spoke quietly – or stayed silent. She had tried to go and sit beside Duff, but he had got up and moved away, to a chair beside the fire that stood alone so there was no way she could join him without having to stand awkwardly, at the mercy of whether he spoke to her or not. She couldn't bear that. Not in front of everyone.

Did she regret how cutting she had been during the tennis

tournament? A little, yes. The humiliation of his rejection that morning had stung, so that she had wanted him to feel as hurt as she had. She knew he was sensitive about his drinking, his weight, the high colour that had come to dominate his face so that he looked, now, far older than she did. She had used these things precisely because she knew they wounded. But as soon as she saw that she had succeeded, she had felt his hurt as though it were her own, and been sorry.

But how to go back? She shuffled the cards and dealt another hand of Patience. None of her hands were coming out, which was a surprise, because usually Maureen found it no more difficult to make the cards do what she wanted than she did to make people do what she wanted. She sipped the drink Chips had made for her. Too strong, like all Chips' drinks.

She looked over at Duff again. Anyone could see the anger in his face – it was right there, in the lowered brow and the set of his jaw – but she saw, buried beneath that, the upset too, the humiliation. She watched Rose cross to him and ask him something, the soothing way she listened to the answer, flattery in every receptive line of her body.

Maureen thought how much more she felt the sorrows of her husband than those of her children. When the crying of her babies had made her feel on edge and uncomfortable, she had simply called for Nanny to take the crying child away. No wonder she had seen so little of Caroline, she thought now. Mostly, she had heard her, wailing night after night in the nursery at Clandeboye. Until she had requested that the nursery be moved to a floor above so that they might be spared her plaintive cries.

But Duff's moods were her moods. When he was happy, it infected Maureen with gaiety; when he was tired or gloomy, she too was cast down. And when he was unhappy – even though it were she who had made him so – she could not shake that misery from herself. He looked up and she tried to catch his eye, but he ignored her and turned back to Rose. She looked down at the cards on the table in front of her. They were knotted and snarled. Again she had failed to bring it about.

She walked over to where Duff sat, conscious that she was watched – by Honor, sympathetically, and by Rose, beside him, with an expression that was difficult to read. 'Darling,' she leaned down by his ear, 'are you sure it is not too hot? I can have Chips ring for someone to move the chair further from the fire. After all, it may be dark but it is still summer.'

'I can do that myself,' he snapped, keeping his voice low. 'Do you think I am so infirm that I cannot move a chair? Or is it just that I am too crocked, too much of a sot, to play a decent game of tennis?' His voice was gravel.

She recoiled as though he had slapped her. Standing straight, she met Rose's gaze by chance. To her surprise, there was a look of sympathy in the older woman's eyes. For a moment, standing there beside her angry husband, Maureen didn't know what to do. She felt marooned, unsure whether to step one way or the other – where to go? She didn't even have a cigarette in her hand, she thought. Or anything to cover her confusion. Rose's look of sympathy had unnerved her. She who hated to be pitied.

'Here you all are still.' It was Brigid, returned with Kick, and Elizabeth who made straight for the drinks. 'I say,' Brigid turned to Chips, 'is there something being done in those empty rooms at the end of our hallway?'

'What kind of something?'

'A workman of some kind? Servants? I heard a noise, almost like someone crying, but when I went to look, I couldn't see anyone. The room was mighty cold, however. Far colder than my room which is only next door but one. Perhaps a window has been left open?'

'Not that an open window would make much difference on a day like today,' Elizabeth said, looking around at them all. 'It may be wet and dark, but hardly cold. That fire is really just for show.' She looked disapprovingly at the grate, then raised her glass to catch the light of the flames against the cut crystal.

'Since when have you been such an authority on weather?' Chips said irritably.

'Not *weather*,' Elizabeth said. 'I couldn't give a tinker's curse for weather' – Maureen saw Rose draw her thin eyebrows together in disapproval – 'but I am an authority on strange *goings-on*, even you will admit.' She giggled. 'And that noise – I heard it too – was strange. Perhaps a housemaid has a headache, or has received bad news, and is crying alone in an empty room?'

'Poor thing,' Honor said vaguely.

'That is certainly not happening,' Chips interrupted. 'The household is entirely accounted for. I would know if it were not.'

'Well then, a phantom or poltergeist,' said Brigid enthusiastically.

'Surely no one actually believes in such things?' the ambassador asked.

'Duff's mother does.' Maureen joined the conversation. 'She is a firm believer in the spirit world. She sees fairies everywhere. Hears them. Does what they tell her to.'

'And what do they tell her to do?' Elizabeth asked. 'Is it offerings of sweetmeats and little drops of wine in acorn cups?' She laughed.

'At Sheridan's christening just a month ago, the fairies told Lady Brenda he was a changeling, and she tried to dash his brains out.'

'Goodness!' That was Rose, but the shock was in everyone's face.

'Maureen!' Honor looked alarmed.

Maureen wondered had she been wrong to begin the story. Too late now. She tossed her head. 'You know it's true. You are the godmother; you were there, at the christening,' she insisted. She recalled how Brenda, the Dowager Lady Dufferin, had picked baby Sheridan up and held him close to her thin chest, had seen the moment when her face changed – the way her eyes grew wide in fright, the set of her thin lips, the way she straightened her arms sharply, so that the baby was jerked forward and began to cry, the strange angle she held him at, and how instantly Duff had moved to her side and grabbed the child from her. Lady Brenda had clawed the empty air where the baby had been, saying, 'He's not your babe, let me have him,' then begun to cry when Duff, passing baby Sheridan to Maureen, had led her out of the chapel at Clandeboye.

'I did not imagine anyone would speak of it,' Honor said.

Maureen looked at Duff then. It was true that none of them had spoken of it afterwards, and here she was, telling the story as though it were just another piece of tittle-tattle. Duff's face was thunderous.

'I am only trying to tell the ambassador that people do believe in such things. Maybe not in America, where everything is new and shiny' – she made it sound like an insult – 'but here, and especially in Ireland. The beliefs are old and strange and go very deep indeed.'

'They do say this house is haunted,' Honor said thoughtfully then.

'They say that about anywhere older than last week,' Chips said indignantly.

'Oh, what fun!' That was Elizabeth. 'Do tell – a woman, jilted on her wedding day, waiting through all eternity for her faithless lover? A man murdered by a rival, compelled to return again and again to the bloody scene?'

'Nothing like that,' Honor said, looking around at them all. Even the ambassador and Doris had drawn near, Maureen saw, so that they all sat or stood close. 'Rather sad, really. This was a girls' school, a boarding school run by nuns, after it was the home of the Wrights who built it. But only for about five years. It closed because some of the girls died, not so much mysteriously as just horribly. Someone drowned in the river. Then there was a fire, only a small one, but a couple of girls got trapped in a dormitory.'

There was a silence then. Those who had drawn closer – Doris and the ambassador – stepped back again, but almost without knowing they did it.

'How horrid,' Doris said.

'After that, I imagine not even Catholic parents wanted to leave their daughters there any longer,' Duff said. Maureen felt rather than saw Rose flinch, as though someone had leaned over and pinched her. 'I imagine you'll find a few walled-in nuns too, if you poke around long enough. There are always walled-in nuns. Shut away for disobedience, or impiety, or lasciviousness. Isn't that what they call it?' He grinned around at them all, and Maureen felt Rose turn stiff and hard like stone. Her jawline tightened so it looked like it might shatter, but she said nothing.

'What a grisly tale,' Elizabeth said. Even she sounded subdued. She flashed a quick look at Brigid, who, Maureen saw, seemed equally struck.

'Yes. And the house was in a frightful state when we bought it,' Chips said. 'Actual blackboards in some of the reception rooms.'

'How dreadful for you,' Maureen said tartly.

'Honestly, you have no idea the mischief the nuns made,' he continued. 'The work Wellesley had to restore it. Every nook and cranny had been boxed off into tiny, terrible rooms. Or decked out with altars and those ghastly statues they love so much.'

'That is not Catholicism, that is ignorance,' Rose said. Maureen could hear the creak in her voice, the effort required to sound mild. 'After all, is there any finer artwork than in the Vatican?'

'She's right, you know.' That was Doris, placating. 'I have seen it.'

'Don't talk to Duff about ignorance,' Maureen said with a laugh. 'Darling,' she reached a hand out, 'do tell them about McMahon's wake?'

Duff rolled his eyes. 'One of our tenants at Clandeboye,' he said. 'A Catholic tenant, but a decent chap. Died about a year ago. I was home at the time so I called to the family. He died suddenly and left behind a widow and five small children. I thought I'd stay just a moment but I was shown into the parlour, where the coffin was. An open coffin. There he was, in a suit they couldn't afford to bury, and the children, all except the baby, had their hands in the coffin with him, stroking his face and touching his hands, wailing and saying his name again and again. It was barbaric. The baby played around on the floor, and these children pawed at a dead man's face, tears falling from them to him, as though they thought he was alive and could hear them, while their mother sat there and let them do it. There was no decency,' he said, shuddering. 'No decency at all. It was obscene.'

'What did you do?' Chips asked, curious as always.

'I gave them money and I left,' he said. 'Left as quickly as I could, to get away from that grotesque sight. The whole thing is grotesque – the way they are forever looking towards a paradise after this life, and neglecting to protect those in their charge in this one.'

'They?' Rose asked.

'Yes. Positively relishing misery and privation, and gloating over all the virtue that will accrue to them in the next world.' He looked around in a way that told Maureen he thought himself among friends, friends with the same ideas as he had.

'Ah. Not *they*, then,' Rose said tightly. 'In this case, *we*.'

There was a terrible pause then, and Maureen saw Duff flush red – whether with rage or embarrassment or both, she couldn't tell. Only that he was furious. With her. With himself. For all that his gruff nature led him to be blunt – too blunt at times – he was almost always clever and tactful too. He did not blurt things out if those things would harm a plan of his or his companions. And now here he was, led on by her, insulting the very people he wished to charm. People he needed to charm. Rose walked away.

'Duff, darling, much as I love you, when you say things like that, I'm afraid you do rather remind me of some very dreadful people I know in Berlin,' Doris said lightly.

'What dreadful people?' Almost, Maureen thought, he was glad that someone had broken the silence, even if it was to confront him.

'Chips knows the ones I mean, don't you, Chips?' He ignored her. 'The sort who have all kinds of ugly words and names for Jews. Who think them capable of dark plots and cunning subterfuge and that everything they do is in service of some secret end.' There was nothing light about her voice now.

'I don't see—' Duff began.

'You will if you think about it,' Doris insisted, almost kindly. 'For you are not at all stupid. Everything starts somewhere. Bad deeds begin with vicious thoughts and foolish words.'

'But . . .' Duff was still wrestling with the implications when the ambassador interrupted.

'It is not at all the same thing.' He looked appalled.

'It is exactly the same thing,' Doris said, giving him a level look.

As though released from a binding spell, Chips swept in then, quickly, with something soothing: 'Honor, didn't you say that you didn't think much of *These Foolish Things*, at the Palladium?'

'Indeed,' Honor said quickly. 'For all that the reviews were good, I didn't care for it at all . . .'

'How disappointing,' Maureen said. 'We also heard good things.' Conversation was eagerly joined as everyone threw themselves into discussing shows they'd seen – which had been good, which poor. Even Elizabeth ventured an opinion that was neither confrontational nor inflammatory. The girls, Brigid and Kick, looked upset; both their faces were stiff, even as they tried to join in, keep the conversation moving, all to try and cover the bare spot where Duff's remark and Doris' response still lingered.

We are like cats, carefully kicking dirt over a mess, Maureen thought. Only it is not fastidiousness that makes us, but fear. 'If only this infernal rain would stop,' she said.

But it was worth it, she told herself, watching Rose sit close beside her husband.

Chapter Thirty-Eight

Kick

'How I wish we'd never started that.' Kick was in the hallway. She pulled open the side door and looked out. The garden smelled of earth and wet grass and the scent of flowers dragged down to the ground rather than released upon the air. Heavy and dense.

'It did rather backfire,' Brigid agreed. 'I thought we'd play a trick on them, scare them a little bit . . .'

Kick thought about their feeble efforts to set the scene for a haunting, how eagerly everyone had joined in, and the horrid turn it had taken. 'If ever a plan misfired . . .' she agreed.

'I never imagined there would be anything so awful as actual dead schoolgirls.'

'How quickly it turned nasty. And only Doris was brave enough to speak out.'

'She made it worse,' Brigid said.

'Not for me, she didn't. It is hard to be despised, not for anything you've done, but merely for what you *are*.'

'No one could despise you,' Brigid said. She said it vaguely, the way one might reach out and pet a cat or dog, because it was there.

'Diana Mitford said she admired the way I was so open about my religion,' Kick said.

'Did she? She can't possibly have meant it.'

'Why not?' Kick was inclined to bristle.

'Darling, it's simply impossible, that's all. Diana, of all people . . .' Brigid laughed. 'But you must be very flattered that she bothered to say anything of the sort.'

'Must I?' Kick asked shortly.

'Why do grown-ups dislike and disapprove of so very many things?' Brigid asked thoughtfully. 'I can't think of a thing I dislike – except for tapioca, and it really isn't the same. Do you think you gather hatred as you age, the way a rose grows hard, gnarled thorns so that you can tell how old a bush is by the viciousness of the thorns?'

'Let's never be like that.'

'I should think not!' Brigid said with energy.

'Like what?' It was Fritzi, who had come up behind them in the hallway.

'Like them.' Kick jerked her head back towards the drawing room. 'Like our parents.'

'My parents aren't here.'

Kick looked at him. 'Sometimes, I don't know if you are joking,' she said.

'I think every generation says this,' he said.

'Says what?'

'That they don't want to be like the generation that has gone before them. In German we have a word for it.'

'We don't want to hear it,' Brigid said.

'Well, they can't all mean it,' Kick said. 'But I do.' Then, 'Let's go out, it's hardly raining anymore.'

'Shall we get coats?' That was Brigid.

'Never mind coats. Let's just go.'

'May I come with you?' Fritzi asked.

'Alright,' Brigid said. 'But only if you come now and don't start fussing.'

They set off, the three of them, across the gravel. 'If we stay on the path and keep off the lawns, we won't be seen from the house,' Brigid said. 'They'd only come after us.'

The path led to the front of the house, where they left it before it veered close to the drawing room windows. These were covered, the curtains drawn inside, but as Fritzi said, 'You never know . . .' Instead, they set off towards the stables, on a dirt track that was soggier, where their feet made almost no noise. It wasn't true that the rain had stopped, but it had slowed to what Brigid, after some silent moments, described as 'a wet trickle'.

'Anyway, what brings you with us?' Kick asked Fritzi at last. 'Did you follow us?'

'Not exactly. I wanted to get out of there and thought I might go to my room for an hour. But when I came into the hallway, I saw the two of you. There was something about the way you were, with the open door in front of you and the smell of evening that came through it – you looked like you were about to take flight. And I wanted to go with you.'

It was, Kick thought, the first thing she had heard him say that wasn't dull to a fault, correct and lifeless. Brigid, too, must have noticed, because she smiled at him. 'How romantic.' And she wasn't as mocking as she might have been.

He was different, out there in the slowing rain. Less pompous. More energetic. He even looked different, in the near-dark that was cut through by a strip of evening light widening a bright gap between sky and ground over to the west.

'You know we call you King Midas' son,' Brigid said.

'I heard you whispering it, but I didn't think you meant me. At least,' he corrected himself, 'I thought you did mean me, but I couldn't understand why, or what it meant.'

'You didn't seem like a real person,' Brigid said. 'You seemed like the outline of a person, done by someone who didn't know any actual real people.'

'A boy, made out of gold. A statue created by mistake,' Kick clarified.

'I see.' He sounded hurt. 'And yet I am as real as anyone.'

'You are now. Nearly, anyway,' Brigid assured him.

'Only nearly?'

'Still a tiny hint of gold . . .'

'I cannot help that.' He said it stiffly.

'She's teasing,' Kick said.

Brigid, slightly ahead by now, ducked under a mass of laurel leaves and, turning, batted them back towards Fritzi so that the weight of water resting on them flew at him, drops landing on his face and chest. He laughed, and pushed the branch back at her. Except that the leaves had shed their covering of rain and simply made a swishing sound as they moved.

'You know,' he said then, 'at times, I do feel like a statue. Everyone looking and looking at me, saying what I am and how I am made . . .' He sounded plaintive.

'Is this going to be a long chat about you?' Brigid asked. It was the kind of thing Maureen would say, Kick thought, but Brigid said it kindly.

'No. I do not mean . . .'

'Oh, it's fine,' she said, 'go on. Get it off your chest, whatever it is.'

'Just that,' he said. 'Everywhere, always, I am looked at. Considered. Observed.'

'I think I know what that might be like . . .' Brigid said thoughtfully. 'I know why they look at me. But you – what is it that everyone looks for? Your wonderful good looks?'

Kick laughed. Fritzi too.

'No, although I am told they are indeed wonderful.'

'Do not fish,' Brigid said. 'You will get nothing.'

'It is not my looks. It's not even really me,' he continued. 'It's what I might do. What I might be used for.'

'Like a small pot,' Brigid said. 'One that might be a vase, or a place to keep pins, or bits of hair ribbon.'

'Perhaps.' He looked confused.

Kick laughed again. She was willing to bet no one had ever teased Fritzi the way Brigid teased him now. 'You don't have sisters, do you?' she asked.

'I do, two, but they are younger and I have been more with my brothers. Three, all older than me.'

'Six of you? You are nearly up to Kennedy standards.'

'When I marry, I should like many children. Five, at least. I would like them to be close in age and good friends with one another. Not like we were.'

'I think you have to encourage children to be friends,' Kick said. 'You have to make them. And then they are.'

They had walked a good distance from the house by now, and came out of the clump of laurels. Ahead of them was lawn, but boggier and more pitted than the smooth green expanse by the tennis court and pool.

'Who is Doris?' he asked then.

'I thought you knew her,' Brigid said. 'You seemed to, at the tennis.'

'I've met her, but I don't know her.'

'She's a friend of my sister. They were at school together ever so long ago. I think Doris might be Honor's favourite person in the world.'

'I see.'

'Why? Is it because you danced with her and are now in love with her?'

'No. More because she remembers.'

'I don't understand.'

'Well, she was there, that night, with all the men of the SS command, who were invited by my grandfather to celebrate his grandsons joining the Luftwaffe.'

'I don't think I really know what that is,' Brigid said.

'It is the air force, like your RAF.'

'I see. Go on.'

'And your Doris was there too. I remember her so clearly.'

'People do tend to. Men, especially.' Brigid said it wistfully, Kick thought.

'I think everyone was in love with her,' Fritzi said. 'Certainly I was.' Beside her in the wet gloom, Kick felt Brigid stiffen. 'But there she was, and now she is here, and I don't know why.'

'Must there be a why? She lives in Germany, in Berlin, you know, and I suppose must go to parties there, same as anyone would, and now she is here, to stay with Honor. It doesn't seem so very mysterious to me. I mean, you were in Germany, at that party, and now you are here. Is it not the same?'

'You are right. I was, and now I am. And so is she. And perhaps there is nothing strange at all.' He looked more cheerful.

'You *are* jumpy,' Brigid said.

'I feel I am watched, always. Here I'm watched because I am German; in Germany I am watched because of my family, my grandfather.'

'Even now? After joining that old Luftwaffe?'

'Oh yes. Maybe especially now. We joined because my father said we must. He said it was a useful bargain to strike. But I think maybe he was mistaken. He said it would show loyalty, and that was important. But it doesn't seem like that will be enough after all.'

'But *are* you loyal?' Brigid asked. 'If you are only showing loyalty, not meaning it, that might be more dangerous again . . .'

'It depends to what. My father is loyal to the family.'

They slowed down and turned, all of them, to look back at the house. It stood, large and square, behind them. The windows on the ground floor showed light, fuzzy and muted, through closed curtains, while those of the top floors were in darkness.

'How lonely it looks from here,' Brigid said.

'You're thinking about the ghosts, aren't you?' That was Kick.

'A little,' Brigid admitted. 'Imagine dying in a fire.'

'Imagine dying at all,' Kick said. Fritzi lit a cigarette, then took it from his mouth and offered it to Brigid, who shook her head. He offered it to Kick. 'Mother would kill me. But why not?' She took the cigarette and, leaning back against the trunk of a tree, took a deep drag, blowing smoke out into the charcoal air.

'You don't seem like it's your first cigarette,' Brigid said, amused. She put her back to the tree trunk also, leaning into it and drawing her white cardigan tight around her.

'Oh, the boys are always making me smoke, ever since I was a kid,' Kick said. 'They reckon it's important that I know how to do it, in case a young man I like ever offers me.' She breathed out again. 'They said I would be ridiculous if I began to cough and splutter and that I should learn to do it properly. Shall we keep walking?'

'Where are we going, anyway?' Brigid said. 'There's nothing in the stables. No horses. Yet. My sister wanted to fill every stall, but Chips has said to wait. He hasn't decided if they will hunt here, or merely shoot.'

'It will make a difference to the horses they buy,' Fritzi said thoughtfully. 'An interesting choice.'

'Is it?' Brigid said vaguely. 'Let's go there anyway.' She shivered. 'See how wet my shoes are.' She held up a foot. Even in the dim light, her white canvas shoes were dark with mud and rain.

'You must take my jacket,' Fritzi said.

'I suppose I must,' she agreed.

He draped the jacket around her, then said in friendly tones, 'But what of you, Kick?' It was the first time he'd called her that.

'I'm alright,' Kick said.

They walked to the stables, which weren't empty after all. A heavy carthorse stood patiently in the first stall, in a deep bed of straw. He ambled up to the half door to look at them. 'What a beauty you are,' Brigid said, putting her arms around the horse's neck. 'I love carthorses. I think they are my very favourite. Don't you, Fritzi?'

'It depends,' he said cautiously. 'For pulling a cart, yes.' Brigid made a face. 'But for hunting, no, I prefer a hunter. For racing, a racehorse. For showjumping—'

'Yes, we get it,' Brigid said impatiently. 'A showjumper. For dressage, a dressage horse. How little imagination you have! But for a friend – give me a carthorse every time. One just like this fellow, who is the dearest chap I ever met.' The horse was nosing gently at her. 'See, he's looking for something. An apple. A carrot. If only I had a handful of sugar. If I'd known he was here, I would have brought some.'

'I will bring some to him tomorrow,' Fritzi promised solemnly.

'And that will have to do. I say, I wonder who's room that is?' She gestured to a light in a room above the stalls at the far end of the yard. There was no window covering so that it shone, hard and yellow in the dusk.

'Like a ship's lantern,' said Fritzi.

'I didn't think there was anyone here. Come on, we'd better get back. They will be looking for us. I know a quicker way.' They walked back faster, talking less, coming around the other side of the house and through the gardens at the back. The dressing gong went just as they passed the pool house. 'Go in that door, Fritzi, and you can go straight up the stairs to your room. We'll be quicker through the side door.'

'You like him a little more?' Kick asked when they were alone.

'He is more human, less golden. That's all.'

'And perhaps that will be enough.'

'Enough for what? Don't be cryptic, Kick.' When Kick didn't answer, 'He seems *quite* afraid, doesn't he?' she continued. 'Poor chap.'

'Sometimes that's all it takes,' Kick said wisely.

'What is?'

'Sympathy. Pity. A little seam of lead where there has been only gold.'

'Honestly, you are absurd. Now come, we will be late.'

'You go. I'm going to stay here a few minutes longer. I'm quicker to dress than you are anyway.'

Alone, Kick found a low stone wall and sat on it. The moss was wet and quickly soaked through the cotton of her dress so that, where she had been cold, now she was shivering. But she couldn't make herself go in just yet. Not when there was so much to think about.

She yawned. More than anything, she would have liked to go to the kitchen, eat a bowl of soup with bread, and tumble into bed. Not to face the cross-currents of insult and inquiry that the dining room would bring. But there was no way to escape it. Even if she could have given her excuses to her host, her mother would never have allowed it.

She yawned again, and stretched her arms up high into the air. The sound of water was everywhere; dripping, trickling, rushing. It animated her. Made her feel as though she too could bend and swerve and flow the way it did, gathering itself, dispersing, gathering again, connected with everything around it, drawing strength and giving strength.

That, she thought, was how she would like to live her life. With or without Billy. And, after all, better to know now rather than later. Could Brigid be right? she wondered. Was it the very ways that she was different that made him like her, if he did like her? And if so, how far might that stretch? Far enough to cover her Americanism? Her father's film and talk of failure? Her Catholicism?

It would want to be a very keen interest in her differences to take in all that, she thought. Very keen indeed.

Maybe he'll ring tomorrow, she had thought when he'd left the night of the film. Ring up and say something casual about 'that frightful row last night' and then it would all be over. But he hadn't. She knew from Debo, who wrote to her, that he was now staying at Blenheim, and that Irene was there. *Please do not tell me anymore*, she wrote back, *for if it's not to be then I want to forget about it as fast as I can . . .*

But she didn't forget. Couldn't.

How strange it was, she thought then, when you considered how alike people were – same arms and legs and eyes that were blue or brown or green but really all the same sorts of sizes and shapes – how, amongst them all, there was one whose voice you heard more clearly, one whose eyes met yours and seemed to leave something inside you. And how that glance told you more than words could, in a way that you heard more clearly than words.

She squared her shoulders. The clean night air whispered of love but she would not allow herself to listen. She couldn't because if she did, she would hear something, even though there might be nothing there for her to hear.

Chapter Thirty-Nine

Maureen

Maureen was surprised that Duff came to her room. She hadn't expected him. But as soon as she saw his face, she understood. He was there because his anger was such that he couldn't not be. She dismissed the maid and, once the girl was gone, turned to Duff. She ran through the idea of disarming him, of trying to, by apologising, but nothing she saw in his face told her that he would allow that. And so she went the other way.

'What brings you here?' she asked, almost idly, turning from him back to the dressing table. Leaning close to the looking-glass, she began to paint her mouth red with lipstick.

'Damn you, Maureen,' he said. His voice was low.

'You'd better shut the window if you're going to quarrel with me,' she said. 'You don't want the entire house to hear.' He crossed to the sash window and pulled it down violently. It landed with a snap and rattled in its frame. 'Or maybe you do,' she added. 'Honestly, there is hardly time to have a proper row. The dinner bell is about to go.'

'Stop,' he demanded.

'Stop what?' She looked up at the mirror, meeting his eyes in it with an expression of bland innocence.

'Stop it, Maureen.' He almost shouted. His hands, she saw, shook. He pushed them into the pockets of his jacket, either to hide them, or keep them occupied. 'What did you mean by it?' he demanded.

'Mean by what?'

'By your vile interference? Your insults and jeers at the tennis. Your mocking of my mother. And leading me to tell that story about McMahon.'

'Everyone knows your mother is odd. And as for the tennis, I was only saying what was obvious. Frankly, I was embarrassed for you. You could hardly hit the ball. You were slow to everything and missed even easy shots. I thought you would welcome someone saying aloud what everyone must be thinking.'

'Did you? Did you really think that?' He stared at her through the mirror with such intensity that she wondered it didn't shatter. Unable to meet his eyes more, she turned and got up. 'And McMahon? You encouraged me to tell that story. Prompted me.'

'You should have realised what you were doing,' she said nastily. 'How is it my fault if you're too drunk to weigh your words?'

'You did it on purpose. But why?'

'You and *Madam Ambassador* were getting altogether far too fond.'

'You are joking! For that, for nothing, you did *this* . . .?'

'Hardly nothing.'

'Nothing. How can you think it?'

'And why should you care now what I think? Why care, or even notice?' She moved past him towards the wardrobe but he grabbed her arm as she went by, holding it just above the wrist. She watched as the white skin around the bones turned red. 'You're hurting me.'

'You hurt me too,' he said. 'And what's more, you know it. Your words are never idle, Maureen. You know exactly what you do.'

'Well, and what of it?' She let her own anger boil up to meet his. 'I must have some defence.'

'Except it is not defence, it is offence.'

'It is defence!' she spat. 'How else am I to counter the insults you deal me?'

'What insults?' He was shaking visibly. He kept his voice low but that shook too. 'I try so hard to make you happy. To keep up with you. You exhaust me, Maureen. You exhaust everyone.' How often she had heard that, she thought. All her life – how exhausting she was, how much she demanded, how she was too much. 'And so I drink,' he continued. 'Yes, I drink, far more than I should, and more and more I see that the drinking has consequences. There are times when I am slow, and confused, when I make mistakes. Like today when I didn't notice how you set me up. And yet I find I cannot stop myself.'

'You do not try to keep up with me. You don't even notice me. All you talk about is Churchill and politics. It's all you think about, care about.'

'What else am I to do? No one understands, no one sees the seriousness. Do you have any idea what war will mean?'

'How do you know it's war? Everyone has been saying that

for a year now, and still there is no actual war. What makes *you* right, rather than Chips or Ambassador Kennedy? Or Chamberlain – who, after all, is our prime minister, and not Churchill, for all that you and he behave otherwise.'

'They're wrong.' He released her hand and went to sit on the side of the bed. Maureen rubbed her wrist, tracing the pattern of his fingers, pressed deep and picked out in red and white. 'It will certainly be war. If not in six months, then in a year. And when it is, we'll be ready, despite the efforts of men like Chamberlain, and Chips, and the American downstairs, with his film projector and cowardice.'

'Probably in his room now, not downstairs,' Maureen corrected him. She spoke automatically, busy thinking about what her husband had just said. She didn't think the ambassador was a coward, not exactly. It was something else with him. She was about to say this, but she was too slow.

'Must you always contradict?' Duff said wearily. Then, 'I will leave tomorrow. My visit here has been a failure. The ambassador and I can't find common ground. Certainly not after this afternoon.' He sighed. 'If I go soon I can take a few days and go to Clandeboye. I can bring Sheridan and see the girls. One of us, at least, should be with them from time to time. If I must fail at state business, at least let me not fail them.'

'But Nanny is there.'

'They aren't puppies, Maureen, to be raised entirely by servants. Besides, I have business in London first.'

'What business?'

'With Churchill.' He said it almost triumphantly, knowing, she thought, how it would infuriate her.

She moved to stop him – 'Wait!' – but it was too late. He was gone. The door closed quietly behind him. Maureen went to run after him, then stopped herself. What was she to do? Chase her husband down the corridors of a house that was not hers? Where any door might fly open and a curious face look out: '*Is everything alright, Maureen?*' She imagined the sly look on Elizabeth's face. On Chips'.

The dinner gong went. Could it really only have been ten minutes that he was in her room? Ten minutes to pull down the certainty of everything she thought she understood about their marriage?

She needed time, but there was none. Now they must both go downstairs and sit through the evening, and behave as though nothing had happened. She twitched at her dress, lining it up better with her hips and waist. It was too long: she must change her shoes to a pair with higher heels. She went to pick up the new pair and found that her hands, too, were shaking. Her heart hammered at her chest, whether because of the quarrel, or what Duff had just told her, she didn't know. She sat on the side of the bed, where he had sat, and tried to think but nothing would come clear. All she knew was that he had swept away what she had believed, and she didn't know what to put in its place.

She had always believed that he was the one who was aloof and out of reach; only slightly, but enough that she must stretch for him and work to keep him alert and unsure of what she would do next. She had believed her role was to entice, his to be enticed. And now he had changed all that. Recast it by what he said. And she didn't know where she was any longer.

She went to the window and opened it again, leaning out over the sill into the evening air. It had stopped raining, although the sound of water was everywhere. Beyond the garden, she could hear the river, louder now, swollen with a thousand tiny rivulets that rushed towards it, as well as the rain that had fallen all afternoon upon it.

A movement in the gloom made her look down. Someone sat on a low wall beneath her window. Maureen couldn't see who it was. As she watched, the figure stretched arms up into the air and leaned backwards, with back arched and head dropped down behind. A woman. Not Honor – too slim – but as for who it was, she couldn't tell. There was something contented, even expectant, about the movement that made her think it could not be Elizabeth; must be one of the young girls. Envy ran through her with a bitter rush. Envy for a time when it was possible to sit on walls and look out into the evening and feel certain that it was full of good and exciting things. That out there in the dark, waiting, were the wonderful things that would happen. That all one needed to do was be there to receive them. She sighed. Was it age or marriage, she wondered – the closing off of all that joyful certainty? She wished there was someone to ask, but Honor was no good for that sort of thing; her sisters Aileen and Oonagh would seize on what would seem to them weakness, and ask was something *wrong* with her. Maybe Doris, she thought. There was something different about her, since Germany.

The gong went again.

Chapter Forty

Honor

Because of Doris, last night's seating had been rearranged so that, Honor saw with relief, she was no longer beside the ambassador. Now, Doris was. It did make the lack of men all the more glaring, but better that than another night of Joe Kennedy's questions. Doris, she saw, took her seat beside him with a smile, and said, 'How nice this is.' The ambassador drew his chair eagerly towards her.

'They say that more rain fell today than in the last two months together,' Chips said. 'The river is quite dangerous now. No one must go near it.'

'No one will go near it, Chips,' Maureen said. 'Honestly, what unnecessary warnings you do give: "*Do not stand with your feet in the fire*," she mocked. '"*Do not put your arm into the lion's mouth. Do not eat the rat poison.*" Unless of course your party is so very boring that we will be rushing to the river, either to drown ourselves and escape, or simply for some excitement.'

'Maureen!' Honor shook her head. Even for her, this was a bit much.

Maureen looked back at her. The silvery-green sequins of her evening dress clustered and clumped at the shoulder like barnacles. Honor imagined them living on top of one another, fighting for space, and felt her stomach squirm for a moment. Her face was pale, powdered thick, but underneath the make-up, two hot spots of red burned high up on each cheekbone. Had she been drinking? Or was it Chips, with his paper-twists of white powder? But no, Honor thought. There hadn't been time for either. It had been late when they had gone up to dress, after an afternoon that had stretched, long and sleepy, after the outburst. She recalled with a tight smile the diligent heaping of banal impressions, one on top of the other; talk of plays watched, films seen, books read and the eager way they had all participated in putting distance between Duff's remarks, Doris' interjection and Rose's response. Once that had died down, once they were all in small and separate groups, reading or talking quietly, she had heard only the sound of rain on the windows, so soporific that the hours had drifted by like clouds that herald nothing.

'Where did you get to?' she asked Brigid. A distraction. 'You were gone so long I thought we'd have to send someone after you. But then Andrews rang the bell and there you were suddenly, like magic.' She smiled at her sister.

'We went to the stables,' Brigid said. 'And found the dearest piebald. Quite the sweetest fellow.'

'There are no horses in the stables,' Chips said.

'There's one,' Brigid said. 'Not for riding. This chap pulls a farm cart or some such by the looks of him.'

'But a piebald,' Chips said, face scrunched.

'I'd forgotten how superstitious you are,' Doris said, amused. 'Chips hates black cats, magpies, piebalds – anything black and white,' she explained to the table. 'I've seen him veer away from a guinea pig in the nursery at Elveden.'

'I remember that guinea pig,' Brigid said. 'Mrs Twigs. She was Patsy's. Not the most rewarding of pets . . .'

'That's enough,' Chips said irritably. 'Doris exaggerates, of course,' he said to the ambassador, who looked confused by the turn the conversation had taken.

Honor looked at Doris and shook her head, although she didn't bother to hide her smile. How much more manageable Chips seemed, she thought, when Doris was there to tease him, to mock his relentless pressing and scheming. How much less oppressive. Suddenly, she felt she could breathe again. As though Doris had pushed back the overflow of Chips that had invaded Honor's life, and made space for her again. 'What shall we do tomorrow?' she asked.

'I rather thought we might visit a place of interest nearby,' Chips said. 'The ruins of a Roman bathhouse. Mrs Kennedy, what do you say?'

'Yes, indeed. We would greatly enjoy that.'

'Well, that's settled then,' Chips said, looking around. Honor noticed that no one else agreed. Indeed, Duff and Elizabeth both dropped their gazes to their plates and carefully avoided eye contact with Chips that might be interpreted as assent.

'Why is there a light in the rooms above the stables?' Brigid asked idly. 'I thought they were empty.'

'That's where Fritzi's man, Albert, is,' said Chips. 'Apparently he finds the servants' rooms too noisy, so he asked to be moved. And as dear Fritzi says he isn't exactly a servant, it was agreed.'

'I hope it has been no trouble?' Fritzi asked. 'I did not know . . .'

'No, dear boy, no trouble at all.' Chips waved his hands expansively. Waved away even the possibility of trouble. 'For you, there is no trouble.'

Honor saw Fritzi glance at Brigid and grin, and Brigid's answering grin. What it meant, she did not know, except that they were somehow in sympathy with one another. Chips saw it too.

Later, in the drawing room, Elizabeth came and squeezed in beside Honor. 'It's not a sofa, Elizabeth, just an armchair. There isn't room,' Honor protested.

'There's space for teeny me,' Elizabeth said. 'If you will just sit like a lady with your knees politely together and not like your mother, who sits like a man.' She giggled. Then, 'Isn't Fritzi popular,' she said slyly.

'What do you mean?'

'Surely you have noticed how sought after he is?'

'By who?'

'Everyone. Chips, *obviously*.' She winked. 'But the ambassador as well. And Duff. Both of them are always asking him to walk with them, sit beside them, asking what he thinks about this and that. Now that Doris is here, she does exactly the same. Even Brigid seems happy for his company.'

'They do seem to be getting along better.'

'But why?' Elizabeth asked, opening her eyes wider than ever. 'Why?'

'I don't know. Because they like him?'

Elizabeth waved the idea away. 'Don't be silly. He's hardly the most fascinating company, is he? Hardly a wit.'

'Well, then, because he is a prince?'

'I thought of that. And it almost holds water – with Chips certainly, it could – but no. It's not enough. He has something. Something they want. I feel it. I just don't know what it could be . . .'

'Well, do tell me if you find out,' Honor said, deliberately sarcastic, and went back to her book.

'I certainly will,' Elizabeth said with dignity. 'It is the least I can do when you have been so kind as to invite me and lend me your clothes.'

Honor felt bad. Was she become so surly that even Elizabeth – careless, reckless Elizabeth – put her to shame?

Chapter Forty-One

Doris

The girls' trick, their ghost story and its aftermath, had changed something, Doris could feel it. Something had shifted in the air between all of them. The ambassador and Rose had withdrawn. They were far too polished to make it obvious – indeed, were as polite as ever – but the willingness they had shown to be drawn into this group was gone. Both avoided Duff now, who allowed them to, making no effort to regain the ground he'd lost, while Chips flitted almost awkwardly between the two. He was like a bird building a nest, Doris thought, moving swiftly back and forth with a twig or piece of grass in its beak.

With Doris, however, they were a little more warm. After dinner, Rose patted the seat beside her and, when Doris had sat down, asked her a great many questions about Dorset, almost none of which Doris could answer because they were so precise: did the temperature differ from London, and how? How many men worked in her father's quarries? When the men joined them, Rose got up to offer her place to her husband, saying she must ring for water: 'It's the only drink they don't bring,' she complained.

'I hope you aren't going to ask me about Dorset's micro-climate,' Doris said with a laugh, leaning back. 'Your wife knows far more about it than I do.'

'I won't,' he assured her. 'I don't imagine you came here to talk about that.'

'We're back to that, are we?'

'Only if you wish to be,' he said urbanely, settling his back against the sofa and swirling the ice cubes in his whiskey glass.

'Well, perhaps you're right . . . You know,' she dropped her voice, 'I was asked to come here.'

'I thought you might have been. Who by?'

'That I can't tell you.'

'Well then, why?'

'I can't tell you that either – or not much. I can tell you that you were one of the reasons.'

'I thought that too.' How complacent he sounded. What was it his daughter called him, affectionately? *The most popular girl at the dance.* The man everyone needed.

'I came because they asked me. But I came for my own reasons too. You have just been appointed as chairman of the Evian Commission, haven't you?'

'Vice chairman, but how did you know? The news is barely announced.'

'Never mind that.' She put a hand on his arm. 'So now you are the man who decides which refugees will find new homes outside Germany, and which will not.'

'I am part of a committee. . .' he said evasively.

'All the same. Vice chairman . . .' She smiled. 'I hoped I could talk to you about it?'

'What do you have in mind?' he asked cautiously.

'Can I tell you about someone I met? A girl, and her family?'

'In Berlin?'

'Yes.'

'No.'

'No?'

'No. I can't listen to individual stories.'

'Why not?'

'It doesn't serve me.'

'Must everything serve you?'

'Well, yes. Otherwise I cannot do my job. Which is to serve America. If I get snarled up in sad stories and desperate tales – there are so many – I won't be able to see what my way is.'

'But surely your way would be lighted by those stories?'

'You would think so.' He said it pleasantly. 'But no. They only cloud matters.'

'You know, I used to think I couldn't listen to individual stories,' she said. 'And for the very same reason. But now I realise they are the only things to listen to.'

'No,' he repeated.

'You know your daughter called you the most popular girl at the dance?'

He laughed. 'So I believe.'

'Well, you should know what very often happens to that popular girl.'

'Which is?'

'In the end, everyone walks away from her.'

'I see.'

'I wonder do you?'

In all, it was an evening of strained conversation, with too many currents eddying between people so that every remark, even the most bland, seemed to offend someone or be designed to highlight something hidden. It was barely midnight when the party broke up, even Elizabeth saying, 'I think I'll go up.'

'Good idea,' Chips had said with relief.

The house quietened down quickly so that it was barely an hour later before Doris left her room and moved quietly along the hallway, down to the side door and out into a clear night that still sang with drips and the trickling of water.

The next morning had the meek beauty of a child who has behaved very badly and tries to charm its way to forgiveness. It was so early that the edges of the day were still fuzzy, and the light was pale gold, without the yellow heat of the day before. The poor battered plants were once more upright, rather than the sodden heaps of green they had been. Able to see clearly, Doris was struck by the tranquil beauty of the place. The tilled fields and evenly paced landscape. No dramatic plunging and rising, no mountains, no moors. It would have been a good place for a school, if managed better. She remembered Miss Potts'; the friendlessness of it, the paltry comforts and kindnesses. Schools were always neglected, she thought. Places of thin blankets, watery gruel, ice on the surface of the wash basin on winter mornings. She must remember to tell Duff that, if he was still talking to her. It wasn't Catholics; it was everyone. Parents sent their children to school and asked almost nothing of their care. Her own father – comfortable Dorset merchant that he was – had been horrified by the spartan dormitories, the worn trestle tables in the refectory. Had wanted to take her straight home, certain there had been 'a mistake' and this wasn't – couldn't be – a place where the gentry sent their children. Doris had understood, and had insisted on staying. It was, she said, 'exactly' what she needed.

And it had been. She had met Honor, and because of her, with her, Doris had left the pleasant comfort of her upbringing and moved into this absurd, intoxicating world of people who spoke in code intended to confuse and deceive. Once there, she found she was as good – better – at it than any of them. And so she had chosen to work where they only played. To take the skills of dissembling and disarming they had taught her, and use them in a way that was deadly serious.

She crossed the garden quickly now, drawing her coat close about her. Not that it would provide much real protection – it was bright red, 'the colour of tomato sauce', Honor had said – but at least with the collar up she could shield her face. Not that anyone would be watching. It was too early. Or so she hoped. She reached the side door. The one she had come through the night before, an hour after going to her room, when the house had seemed quiet and in darkness.

The door was locked. Drat. She tried the handle again, in case, but no, it was definitely locked. Someone must have come after she had slipped out. The front door was certainly locked too. There was bound to be a way in through the kitchens, she thought. She stepped back out of the porch, thinking that if she made her way by hugging the side of the house, there was less chance she would be seen from any of the bedrooms. Just then, above her, the sound of a window being pulled open. She looked up, before realising that, really, she should have ducked back into the shelter of the porch.

'Doris?' It was Honor. What luck. She recalled Honor saying how badly she slept, and hoped she hadn't been awake too much of the night.

'Darling,' she hissed up. 'Come and let me in, will you? The door's locked.'

'Of course.' Honor, bless her, asked no more questions, simply ducked back into her room and closed her window. Alas for Doris, it scraped noisily. Loudly enough for whoever was in the bedroom next to Honor's to hear. A face appeared, peering out, then that window too was raised.

'Well!' It was Chips, eyes still heavy with sleep, but already a look of delight was dawning. 'Locked out, are we?' he whispered, but loudly and not as though he cared who he woke. 'It can't be much after five. You are an early riser. Or perhaps a *late* retirer . . .' He smirked down at her. 'Shall I come and let you in?'

'Please don't trouble yourself,' Doris said, sighing. 'I will be in in a moment.' Just then Honor reached the side door, and Doris heard the sound of the bolt being drawn back, then the key turned.

'What are you doing out here?' she whispered once she had got the door open.

'Nothing much. Come on, back to bed. We can talk in the morning.'

'It is the morning.'

'Later in the morning,' Doris said firmly. 'I must get a few hours' sleep.'

By the time she got up and bathed and dressed, a few hours later, the promise of the dawn had been more than fulfilled with a day that sparkled and enticed, begging her to step out into it.

Downstairs, breakfast was laid in the morning room. Silver dishes covered with silver domes were heaped on the sideboard, the long table set with many places, most occupied.

'Doris.' Chips, of course, looked up immediately she came in. 'I'm surprised to see you.'

'Surprised and no doubt delighted,' she said, crossing to the sideboard.

'Surprised that you have not already breakfasted,' Chips explained patiently, 'when you were up and about so early. What were you doing, out in the garden at that hour?' His eyes gleamed at her and she felt the force of his curiosity like a dog or horse, nudging at her, demanding something.

'An early walk,' she said, shrugging slightly. She looked around for the coffee pot.

'Must have been early indeed, if it happened before Andrews made a tour of the house and locked all the doors,' Chips said, eyes open wide and innocent. 'Usually, he does that shortly after everyone has gone to bed. Certainly while it's still dark. And yet there you are, locked out in the bright light of early morning.'

'Perhaps your house is not as well run as you like to think,' Doris replied. 'Perhaps Andrews goes to bed earlier than you know, and cheats by doing his rounds in the morning.' She saw the footman who stood beside the sideboard, ready to lift the dome on any dish, stiffen.

'Perhaps,' Chips said with sly delight. 'Perhaps. Or perhaps it was Fritzi's man who took the responsibility. He was up and about at the same early hour. I watched him walking in the direction of the stables. Did you meet him, on your early walk?' He opened his eyes very wide and looked at Doris, waiting for an answer.

'No,' she said, turning towards the toast dish and uncovering it before the footman could reach it. 'I did not. I saw no one at all.' She took two slices of toast, then a heap of mushrooms. 'But then, I wasn't looking. Not peering around and watching. Not like you, Chips.'

'I wasn't *peering*,' he said with dignity. 'Or *watching*. I heard a noise and just happened to look out the window, that's all. I saw you fumbling with the locked door, and then I looked the other way and I saw Albert making his way towards the stables, and I thought, *I wonder did those two meet?* That's all.'

'How did you get in?' Rose asked. She took a tiny bite of toast-and-marmalade, then laid the slice down.

'Honor came down and opened the door,' Doris said cheerfully. 'And really, none of it was nearly as exciting as Chips has made it out. An early walk, on such a beautiful day. One of the servants must have noticed the door I left on the latch, and very properly locked it. But Chips does love a mystery. If he can't find them, he invents them. Even so, I don't know why he thinks five on a summer's morning is so very early.'

'No,' Rose agreed, 'I am often up at that time.'

'But in that coat . . .' Chips pursued.

'First thing that came to hand,' Doris countered. 'Now, please don't spend any more of your valuable time on me. I know you have an excursion to plan.' She smiled sweetly at Chips and, taking her plate, retired to the far end of the table. 'Duff,' she muttered, 'if you have forgiven me, give me some of your newspaper, for the love of God, that I may hide in it.' Duff's lips twitched. He handed her a section from the middle of *The Times* and they both bent their heads low over the print.

'I have ordered the cars for eleven,' Chips said. 'That means we will reach the outskirts of Colchester shortly after midday.

We can take lunch with us. Honor has had a bad night and won't be joining us.'

'And I alas am unable,' Doris said. 'There are things I must do here.'

'As am I.' Duff looked up. 'I must make a phonecall. Chips, may I borrow the library for an hour?'

'Yes, of course, but really, it's too bad! I had thought we would be a larger party. I don't imagine for one moment that Elizabeth will be down in time.'

'Probably for the best,' Rose said with a chilly smile. She couldn't fathom Elizabeth at all, Doris had noticed. Indifferent to Elizabeth's charm – which was grown patchy, but still considerable when she marshalled it – all Rose saw was the immense fecklessness and indulgence. The drinking, the smoking, the foolish remarks that were never, really, as foolish as they seemed. But this was lost on the Kennedy parents, who observed her with mistrust.

'Brigid and Kathleen, you will both come with us?'

'Yes, but may we swim first?'

'And Fritzi?'

'Happily. I believe these ruins are particularly fine.' Doris watched as Brigid rolled her eyes. Watched too as Fritzi saw her doing it and, instead of being offended, grinned at her. She smiled to herself. And looked up to find Chips watching her, one eyebrow raised. She shook her head slightly and bent over her newspaper again.

After breakfast, Doris made her way to the gardens and caught up with Brigid as she crossed the lawn to the pool. The grass was already dry after yesterday's rain.

'Are we not the luckiest people in England, to have a pool during such a summer?' Brigid asked her.

'It more than makes up for the next ten years when it will be barely used,' Doris agreed.

'Will you swim now?'

'No. Later.'

'Tired?' Brigid asked mischievously.

'So, you were listening.'

'Impossible not to.'

'I never feel,' Doris said, as though she were changing the subject, 'that being a guest in someone's house means one owes them an account of every minute of one's day.'

'Or one's night,' Brigid agreed solemnly.

Doris laughed. She slowed her steps and the girl slowed with her. 'Very good. But what of you? I was about to say how very different you are, in the space of just little more than a year, but then I look at you, and I see that you aren't.' She smiled. 'Under the new hairstyle and the London dresses, you're the same as ever, I think.'

'I should hope so!' Brigid said. 'I wouldn't wish to change.'

'And yet you are very much a young lady.'

'If you say so.' She smoothed her hair as she said it, brushing a strand back from her face where it had blown loose, and tucked it in. Beyond her, the windows of the pool house reflected light onto the water that had its own light.

'It is nothing to do with what I say. Chips, of course, has noticed too.'

'He has.'

'And thinks to cut you in on his schemes?'

'He does. Oh, Doris,' Brigid started to laugh, 'you cannot imagine the chats we have! He likes to spend no end of time, he and I, in which he proposes young men he thinks are suitable, and asks for my opinion. And pretends to listen when I give it.

Why, in the last month alone we have talked of Billy Cavendish, of David Ormsby-Gore. And each time, he turns over all their virtues and all their failings, exactly as though he were breeding horses – I swear I heard him say the Mannings were "too long in the back; too tall".'

'And you, what do you do?'

'Nothing much. I let him talk, and I agree. But in the end, I will make up my own mind, you know.'

'And what of Fritzi, who beneath the affectionate nickname is actually Prince Friedrich; what faults and virtues does he have, in Chips' eyes?' Doris asked, looking sideways at Brigid.

'No faults at all, only virtues. The most beautiful and eligible of young men. According to Chips, that is,' she added hastily.

'He is certainly beautiful. Perhaps . . .?'

'Impossible!' Brigid shook her head. 'I may say little, but that doesn't mean I don't think. I will not let Chips choose for me, when he doesn't know how to choose for himself.'

'What do you mean?'

'How can I possibly adopt the plan of a man who cannot see that his own marriage is gone disastrously wrong?' She stopped walking, stood still on the wet grass. 'Who can't acknowledge the truth of that, or his own part in it? *You Guinnesses are so stubborn,* he says – *not you, Brigid, but your sisters, even your wonderful mother.* He pretends he means it fondly. *Honor is not unhappy. She is set in ways that no longer suit her, but she is too stubborn to see that. If she would only listen, I could, I'm sure, tell her half-a-dozen things she could try* . . . Imagine, I think he tried to tell me that all is not well between them . . . well, in the bedroom.' She blushed.

'No! Even for Chips . . .'

'Yes. In fact I'm certain of it. Only I would not let him.'

'I should think not,' Doris said. Then, 'I didn't know you saw so much.'

'How can I not see? Anyone who is in the same house as them, the same room as them, must see. And feel. Sometimes I think unhappiness is something to be touched,' she said. 'A blanket, woven in the air from all the sad thoughts, dropping around the shoulders of whoever is in company with those poor souls that think them. And Belgrave Square, for all its magnificence and Chips' pride in it, is a sad place really. Every room seems thick with things that cannot be said, or hopes that cannot be filled.' She made a shrugging motion with her shoulders, as though to push the thought away.

'Poor Honor,' Doris said.

They began walking again, and reached the swimming pool. Brigid made no move to change, just dropped her towel on the little wrought-iron table. Behind them, a bird sang urgently into the still morning. Perhaps it knew the gathering heat would soon defeat it, Doris thought.

'Yes. But I do not know what to do for her. I have tried, you know.' Brigid looked earnestly at her. 'I really have. Patsy too. But we do not know what to say and she will not talk to us; behaves as though we're still in the schoolroom and too young to be told. I'm glad you're back.'

'I'm glad too.'

Kick came into sight, running towards them from the house, already changed into her bathing suit, a white towelling robe draped over it. 'Sometimes I look at Honor and I think – that's what Chips wants for me,' Brigid blurted out, just before Kick came into earshot. 'A husband who hardly knows me and hardly considers me. A marriage just like his. And then sometimes I think he would be happy to replace my sister with me, should she really leave him. And that's why he doesn't push harder for Fritzi or Billy Cavendish.'

Doris was too shocked to respond. She stood and said nothing, and then it was too late.

'I'll race you,' Kick called, reaching them and throwing off her robe. From the far end, she executed a perfect dive and swam the length of the pool underwater, surfacing to call, 'Come on, Biddy! Hurry up!' In all that sparkling water, she was, Doris thought, as though made of water too; just as quick and shining and supple. She sat and watched the girls swim and splash, remembering the elastic bounce of youth and how quickly misery could be swapped for joy. She saw Fritzi arrive and tell them it was time to leave, that Chips was impatient. He waved to her, and asked how she did, but he didn't blush, or linger, or try to find an excuse to sit with her. Doris smiled to herself.

She had known he would be here, of course she had, but not *how* he would be here; the friendship with Brigid and Kick that made him an actual person, out of uniform and suddenly real. How naive he seemed when no longer yoked to the ugly Nazi pageantry of cross and badge. Last night, when the three of them had come back from their walk, cheeks pink, brimming with mischief and something else – something that had overtaken them out there in the evening air – she had known instantly that her plans must change.

She had learned – long learned – to have many plans, all mutable, so that she might always be in motion towards a goal that shifted frequently, as circumstances shifted. Always the same goal, but aimed at by different routes. She had learned to abandon one plan and follow another, even while she looked to do nothing much at all. To make use of circumstances as she

Emily Hourican

found them and to keep her net wide open. And so, after the
tennis tournament in which they had played so well side by
side, when Albert had tried to kiss her, rain streaming down his
face, she had let him. Later, when she twigged that there was,
or might be, some glimmer of friendship between Brigid and
Fritzi, she had been glad to have another plan already part
begun that she might switch her efforts to.

She had seen immediately that this – Brigid and Fritzi – was
a scheme of Chips', which made her suspicious that it could be
any good. And yet, she had also seen an affection in the way
Brigid and Fritzi looked at one another, that might be nothing
and might be something if only they were left alone. How funny
that the person most likely to destroy Chips' plans was Chips
himself.

Either way, she decided, she would do nothing. She would
not build upon that early admiration for her that Fritzi had
shown in Berlin. She would be cool and distant and avoid any
kind of intimate conversation. It was exactly what she'd been
told not to do – make her own plans. How lucky there was
Albert! A plan begun without any great foresight. Rather, she
thought with a smile, like coming across a safety pin and picking
it up and putting it in a pocket, in case, only to find sometime
later that a tear required it. How pleased one felt then, to put
a hand in and discover that casually collected thing. Except it
wasn't casual, not exactly, but rather the knowledge born of
experience – anything might prove useful; turn nothing away.
Let things found by chance be gathered by design. She didn't
yet know what she expected, or even hoped, of Albert. Only
that he was more than he said, and at such a time, that was
enough. Perhaps he was simply a crook and had a bad past to
hide. Perhaps he was in love with the wrong person, or had

once been close to a dubious politician. But perhaps it was more? If he was here with Fritzi then it might well be more. Whatever it was, Doris intended to find out.

She sighed, and stretched in the morning sun and yawned.

She was tired, she knew it. Tired from having to be so constantly in motion, always planning and watching; tired too from the need to be charming and seductive, to flatter men and find out what they knew without ever asking. Well, it wouldn't be for much longer.

Chapter Forty-Two

Honor

Honor waited until she heard the cars depart before getting up. She had listened to the voices – Chips', as always, loudest – in the corridor outside her room and later in the hallway below, and tried to decipher who was going and who staying. She heard Rose Kennedy's quiet tones and assumed if Rose was going the ambassador was too. Brigid and Kick were clearly of the party – Brigid barged in, hair still wet, to ask if she might borrow a sunhat, her own was lost – and Maureen, just as clearly, was not. Elizabeth, she felt she need not even ask. Duff? She hoped, if Maureen wasn't going, that he was. The idea of a day alone with the two of them, if they were anything like the mood of the evening before, was too much.

And Doris? There, she felt as certain as she had of Elizabeth; Doris would not be going. She dressed quickly, unwilling to wait for her maid; unwilling to waste a minute of a day that stretched before her with such glorious freedom. It would be hours before they returned. She had heard Chips talk of a picnic.

She checked her reflection in the long looking-glass. How drained she looked. Dark shadows under her eyes that did not – as they did with Doris – make her look fragile or interesting. Honor just looked exhausted. Defeated. She sucked in her stomach and stood sideways. She was getting stout.

She looked out the window. At the far end, beside the pool house, she made out a figure in a broad-brimmed hat sitting at the little table. It was a woman, but the hat was angled in such a way that Honor couldn't see her face. The woman poured herself a cup of coffee from a silver pot that caught the sun and sent it winking cheerily on. The way she lifted the coffee cup to her lips and drank told Honor it wasn't Maureen or Elizabeth.

Quickly, she finished pinning back her hair and pulled on a pair of sunglasses. The idea of a morning, even an hour, alone with Doris in the swirling shade of the old elm beside the pool house was delightful. It was the certain knowledge that Chips was away, could not come upon them or send for her or intrude. Knowing she would not hear the sound of his voice, catch sight of him in his pale flannels crossing a path or catch a breath of his cologne on the breeze, was as galvanising as the sound of the huntsman's horn used to be in the days when she got up early on winter mornings. She felt a busy stirring of excitement.

'Tell Andrews I will take breakfast outside,' she said to her maid when she came with tea. 'Ask him to bring a fresh pot of coffee. And you may take the morning off. Miss Ponsonby can look after herself, if she gets up.'

Doris, she thought as she drew close, still looked tired. But she turned her face to Honor and gave her a dazzling smile. 'Come and sit this side,' she said, moving her chair up. 'The shade is better.'

'More coffee is on the way,' Honor said, sitting down.

'And there I was, wondering if there was any way this day could be more perfect.'

'I thought you might need another cup,' Honor said.

'Did you?' Doris opened her eyes wide. 'Why on earth?'

'Don't tease, darling. Now tell, what were you *doing*, out in the early morning with the dew still wet on the ground?'

'I could tell you what I told Chips, and Brigid, and Rose, and all the others who have asked,' Doris said slyly. 'An early-morning walk, on a beautiful day.'

'But you won't,' Honor said, settling back in her chair. She took one of the freshly baked biscuits Andrews had brought with the coffee.

'If you must know, I was coming back.'

'Yes, that much was rather obvious. From where?'

'The stables.'

'The piebald . . .?' Honor asked, bemused. Then, 'Oh. No. Albert?'

'Yes.' Doris looked straight at her. She was refusing, Honor saw, to be abashed in any way. 'Albert.'

'But why?'

'Only you would ask that,' Doris said, amused. 'There are a thousand women I could tell that to, and they would simply smirk and say "*Yes, I see* . . ."' She laughed. 'I tell you, and you blurt out "*But why?*". However, you are correct. There is a why.'

'Which is?'

'I wonder how much to tell you.' She glanced away, across

the lawns, towards the river which could be heard, swollen and greedy, running over the new ground it had claimed.

'Everything. Tell me everything.'

'Not everything, darling. It isn't possible. But I will tell you some. What I may. Are you sure we will not be interrupted?'

'Perfectly certain. Nearly everyone is gone, thank goodness. Elizabeth will not surface for hours. Maureen and Duff seem to have their own matters to attend to . . .'

'Yes, I rather thought that last night . . . Well, alright then. The truth is, darling, much as I love you, I am not here entirely to see you. Yet again, all unknowing, Chips has done me a service.' She grinned. 'You know a little of why I am in Berlin?' She lowered her voice and looked around, a quick, nervous glance that was, Honor thought, quite unlike her.

'I know what you have told me, which is very little, and what I have understood, which is a little more.'

'I am a reporter.'

'I have seen your articles in the *Express*. Approving accounts of race meetings and sporting events.'

'Exactly. I go about. I meet people. I have the very gayest of times. And I watch. I listen. I remember.'

'You were always good at that.'

'And when the time comes, I repeat what I have seen and heard and observed to people who have more pieces of the puzzle than I. Who know what to do with the information I gather.'

'How glamorous you are.'

'I'm not. I am often scared and maybe useless. Certainly I am very low in any chain of importance. I have little faith in what I do, and less all the time – perhaps what I pass on has no value at all? – but it is the best I can do, and I suppose that is something.'

'Maybe glamorous is not the right word. Brave, then. It sounds dangerous.'

'It is. But not as dangerous as what others do.' She paused, and silence fell between them. A swallow dipped to the surface of the pool, angling its wings sharply, then turned and soared. 'Recently it has become more clear that there are some Germans who no longer support the Nazis. They believe Hitler to be a danger and would be happy to see him gone, if there were a way for that to happen that would be fairly painless. There are enough of them, but they aren't united. Mostly they mistrust one another. They each have their own reasons, their own gripes and demands, their own views of what should replace him. But we believe—'

'Who is "we"?'

'Better you don't know that. Actually,' Doris laughed, 'I hardly know myself. There are many.'

'Go on.'

'We believe that if all of these different strands could be woven together and persuaded to adopt one plan of action, they could put aside their differences and turn their discontent into action. If they have a purpose, they will make a plan. And so we try, discreetly, to help the making of that one plan.'

'Which is?'

'That's where it gets complicated. In order to have one plan, apparently we need to consider many different plans. One is Fritzi.'

'Him?'

'I know. It does seem . . . Well, you know him; so you know what it seems. But after all, he has the name, he has the background. He is known, but not too well known. He offers the reassurance of familiarity, along with the promise of something new. There is a chance that he might be the very person behind whom others can unite.'

'Funny,' Honor said slowly, 'it is almost the very same thing Chips used to say to him. How he had the personality to be the natural successor to his grandfather, and restore the House of Hohenzollern . . . But what about his father, who is still alive?'

'Hopelessly compromised,' Doris said cheerfully. 'Far too much friending and falling-out with Hitler. No one knows what he's about anymore, nor trusts him. There are the brothers, of course, and at least one of them is interesting too, but my charge is Fritzi.'

'Does he know?'

'Not a thing,' Doris said.

'Why?'

'No point, until it is decided.'

'So Chips flatters Fritzi that he could be the kaiser. His father forces him to join the Luftwaffe. The ambassador encourages him to be vocal in his support for Hitler, so he can write to President Roosevelt and tell him that even Germany's princes support the Reich. And all the while you conspire to see will he do as the figurehead of a coup. And the boy himself knows nothing?'

'In a nutshell.'

'No wonder he's on edge, even if he doesn't know the half of it. Funny, Elizabeth said something yesterday . . . Asked me had I noticed how very popular Fritzi was . . .'

'Did she now? That girl is far less empty-headed than she lets on.'

'No one could possibly be as empty-headed as she lets on! But what has this to do with Albert?'

'Albert is a bit of a detour . . .'

'How so?'

'Well, I'm here for Fritzi. But once I saw that Albert was not really a servant—'

'How do you know?'

'Oh, I think we all know . . .'

Honor remembered Maureen: *Quite a different creature . . .*

'He's an unknown quantity,' Doris continued. 'He's been here, in England, with Fritzi, since he arrived two years ago, and we want to know why. Whose man is he really? Everyone thinks he was sent by Fritzi's grandfather, to keep an eye and report back to the old man. But now, well, I wonder if the Reich don't believe Fritzi's protestations of loyalty. Even though he swore an oath.'

'Yes, I've seen him clicking his heels, for all the world like a wooden marionette, when he meets von Ribbentrop.' Honor tapped her own heels together, sharply, but the effect, in her white plimsoles, was feeble.

'He joined – and his brothers – because his father wished it. Hitler was just one of Wilhelm's many schemes to restore the family; he's like a dog with many buried bones. But that particular bone may choke him. Hitler is nothing like the usual cavalcade of madmen with whom he has made common cause. Albert is certainly watching Fritzi. But who is he watching for? Is he watching to confirm that Fritzi is what he says he is – loyal to the Reich – or is he watching in case he is the exact opposite? And if so, on whose behalf does he watch? He might even be at the same game I am, only for a different group of well-wishers; there are so many now—'

'It's like the bit at the end of a steeplechase when the entire field converges just before the finish line, all straining to be first?' Honor said.

'Exactly. But either way, I want to know.'

'Hence your visit to him last night?'

'Indeed.'

Honor made a face. 'I see it now. But how can you, Doris?'

'How indeed? I wonder myself. Necessity does strange things.'

They were silent then, as they had been silent together so many times, as the day grew and swelled around them, an orchestra where all the seats are filled.

'I say, Doris, you don't think it's a bit suspicious that Albert made such a pass, so very quickly?'

'You've obviously never been in a taxi with Oonagh's husband, Dom,' Doris said with a laugh.

Honor laughed too, but mechanically. 'I don't mean to suggest for an instant that you aren't irresistible, darling, but really – what if Albert is watching you, just as you are watching him?'

'I hadn't thought of that,' Doris admitted. 'Trust you to see something I didn't.' She nudged Honor's shoulder gently with her own. 'I don't think you're right, but it would be reckless not to consider it.'

'So what will you do?'

'Spend more time with him.'

'You know Chips will find out?'

'Which is why you must be careful to be shocked and disapproving, just as you usually would be.'

'I *am* shocked and disapproving.' Honor leaned back and rested her head against the top of the chair, tilting her chin so that she looked straight up into blue sky. 'It is as though we were in a play, on a stage,' she said after a moment. 'In the audience are all sorts of people, all watching for their own ends. We cannot see them, and they cannot see each other, but still they watch.' She shivered, even though the sun was high and hot. 'I don't know how much I like it.'

'Not at all, I should think. But you mustn't let it affect you. Try to forget I told you any of this. It was simply the most marvellous coincidence that Chips should be so keen himself on Fritzi; should bring him here, with you, with the Americans, all neatly tied up together with a bow.' She burst out laughing. 'He does me good turn after good turn, your husband, and it kills him to know it.'

'Later, when you have gone and I am particularly low,' Honor said, 'I will try to remember that.'

'By all means,' Doris said. 'Although what I really hope is that there is some way for you not to feel so low.' She reached over and took one of Honor's hands and held it. 'I think we must try to find a way out of this for you.'

'You mean divorce?'

'I do.'

'I can't see the point,' Honor said, shrugging. 'All that fuss and upheaval, and for what? What would I even do, if I were no longer to be Mrs Channon?'

'I don't know,' Doris said, 'but I am certain you would quickly find out. And – whatever it is – it would be better than staying married.'

'I am used to being married. If there was someone else . . . Someone to be free for, then I might . . .'

'There is yourself.' Doris was almost stern.

'It's not enough,' Honor said sadly. 'I find I cannot stir myself on my own behalf. Especially when I think how much my mother would hate it.'

'I daresay she would hate it more if she knew how unhappy you are.'

'I daresay she would not.' Honor laughed, a little.

'Well, if not yourself, Brigid.'

'Brigid?'

'Chips wants to see her make the exact same type of marriage that you made. A man older, more worldly. A dazzling match, but one she will be happy in? I don't see it.'

'I think Brigid is a good deal sharper than I ever was.'

'Perhaps. But she's also very young.' Doris poured another cup of coffee and added cream, stirring so that it swirled through. 'Now tell me, have you been gardening without gloves?'

Honor looked down at her hands. Her nails were unpolished, split and the cuticles ragged where she had bitten them. Recently, she had been too nervous to allow the maid anywhere near them, unable to sit still for the time it took to buff and polish. She recalled the figure that had looked back at her from the looking-glass that morning. Large, untidy, sprawling. Unhappy. 'We can't all be beautiful,' she said.

'You are a handsome woman, Honor. On a good day, splendid. But there aren't so many good days just now, are there?'

'It is a long time since I have bothered very much. Chips likes to see me dressed up. He always notices what jewels I wear. But beyond that, he never looks at me. Why should I make any effort for a man who doesn't look at me?'

'What if it wasn't for him at all, but for yourself?'

'I could be tidier,' Honor agreed, putting a hand to her hair, which had already escaped its pins and was starting to straggle. She smoothed the front of her dress. 'Perhaps I should ask Elizabeth for some of my clothes back?'

Chapter Forty-Three

Maureen

Once the house was empty, Maureen tracked Duff to the study where he had retired with the newspaper and a transistor radio. She arrived, Pugsy in her arms, in time to hear the pips for the midday news, followed by '*Lord Runciman has arrived in Czechoslovakia*' in the crisp tones of the announcer. '*He has been sent by Prime Minister Chamberlain to mediate in the looming Sudetenland crisis . . .*' Cigarette smoke swirled around his head and the room was unbearably close. The curtains had been pulled back, but badly; crooked – she wondered had Duff done it himself? – so that the room was dingy in contrast with the brightness outside even though the garden doors were open.

'May I come in?' she asked, standing in the doorway.

'I cannot stop you.' Hardly a good start, she thought. He

barely looked up as she entered. She had dressed with great care, a grey gingham dress that tied loosely at the neck. She knew he liked it but he said nothing now.

'You haven't told Chips you are leaving?' she began. She knew that if he had, she would certainly have received a visit from Chips before he departed for his Roman ruins, lamenting that the balance of men to women was now a disaster, and insisting she do something to make Duff stay.

'Not yet.' Perhaps he had changed his mind, she thought. 'I'm waiting on a telephone call.'

'From who?' For a terrible second, she wondered was it Marjorie. And what she would do if it was.

'Churchill. He is to ring me this morning. There may be reasons why I need to stay a little longer.'

'You'd stay for him, but not for me?'

'Yes.'

'I see.' She let silence fall between them. Then, when it was clear he would not break it, as if he might even get up and walk away, to keep him she asked, 'What does Churchill want?'

He closed the garden doors. 'There is a man on his way to London from Berlin, von Kleist-Schmenzin—'

'Such a mouthful, these German names,' Maureen complained.

He ignored her interruption. 'He's an emissary, one of a growing number of Germans who want rid of Hitler.'

'Why is he coming here?'

'He's looking for support. He thinks there's enough resistance in Germany, if it can be mobilised and focused. He comes to talk to Chamberlain, who will not listen, and to Churchill—'

'Who has no power.'

'Who will listen.' Again, he ignored her. 'And so it may be

that I am to stay, even though I have failed with Ambassador Kennedy—'

'Not failed,' Maureen tried.

'Failed. But there may be new benefit to being here. A new plan to put into action.'

'What new plan?'

'Just a new possibility,' he said evasively. 'Something else to be considered. A chance that Chips has provided; all unknowing, of course.' His lips twitched.

'The ambassador again?'

'No, not the ambassador.'

Maureen started to laugh then.

'What's so funny?'

'You are.' She sat bolt upright. 'This is. All of it. All this intrigue at a country party . . . I almost suspect Chips of starting it all, because he's so afraid we shall find Kelvedon dull. And so, instead, he has devised a Boy's Own adventure, to keep you and the ambassador happy. He should just lay on some grouse shooting. It would be so much easier.'

'I assure you, it is deadly serious.'

'You say that, because you need to believe it.'

'And why do I need to believe it?'

'Because . . .' she spoke slowly, knowing how he would hate it, unable to stop herself, 'if it's true, then you are important, and correct in your judgement. But if it isn't, well, you and Churchill are just two men who have backed the wrong horse, trying to redraw the race so that you will be right.'

'How like you to see it in those terms.' He said it so coldly. As though she were someone he barely knew. Someone he didn't much like.

'I came to ask you not to go.' She had to force herself to say the words. No matter how much she wanted something, any appeal was hard for Maureen.

'Well, it looks as though you may have got your wish without having to ask anything.' He bowed stiffly in her direction. 'Congratulations.'

'But . . .'

'You know,' he said then, in a way that was almost conversational, so that she leaned forward eagerly, 'I almost welcome it.'

'Welcome what?'

'War.' He opened the double doors to the garden again so that she caught the grateful smell of wet grass.

'How is that possible?'

'An end to the talking, the trying and striving and scheming to prevent what in all probability cannot be prevented. For all that Kennedy thinks we're eager for war, determined to rush towards it, that's not true. We too are trying to avoid it. Only not at any cost. But it's like putting our hands up to stop a train or a tractor, some heavy engine that has begun to lumber downhill. It cannot be stopped, only slowed. And so – a new phase, of action.'

'But you won't fight. You said at lunch with the Devonshires that you would not.'

'No. *You* said I would not. I said nothing.'

'But you are under-secretary of state . . .'

'And when war breaks out, I will resign and enlist.'

'Duff! You must not! Why?' It had never occurred to her that he would join up. Through all that talk of war, she had always been a little indifferent. Even watching that terrible film the ambassador had put on, she had felt remote. Pity, of course, for the young men around her – poor Billy and Andrew, that fool

Hugo – but it had been a pity without urgency. She had felt safe in the knowledge that her father was too old, Sheridan a baby, and Duff secure in his government post. How, she thought suddenly, had she not realised that he would join? Of course he would.

'Why?' she said again, but without the same emphasis this time. It was a word to say, that was all. She knew why. He had told her – told them all – over and over. Only she had not listened. But now, instead of talking boldly of duty, honour, he said something quite different.

'I am in a mess,' he said, coming towards her. 'Even I can see it. For all that your barbs are vicious, Maureen, they're not wrong.' He raised his hands to his head for a moment and pressed his fingers into his temples. 'That ghastly blunder yesterday. I know you began it but you're right, I should have noticed and stopped it immediately . . . Perhaps war will be a chance for me to begin anew. A chance to make you proud of me. To make Sheridan proud. Caroline and Perdita too.'

'I *am* proud of you,' she said.

But he didn't stay to hear her. He stepped out through the open doors onto the paved patio and into the blazing day. For a moment he was framed within the window, the sun behind him so that he was a dark silhouette. Then he set off across the garden.

Chapter Forty-Four

Doris

'IF you want your clothes back, here comes Elizabeth now.' Doris flicked her eyes towards the house, from where Elizabeth could be seen, wearing Honor's cream silk pyjamas, picking her way across the lawn in a pair of silver heels.

'She will leave holes,' Honor said in irritation. 'And Andrews will be furious because he is about to serve lunch and she'll be looking for breakfast.'

'Poor Honor,' Doris said lightly. 'Such a bore for you.'

Honor laughed, reluctantly. 'I know you think my concerns are ridiculous,' she said, 'but they are my concerns.'

'Not ridiculous, just unworthy.'

Elizabeth reached them and dragged over a chair to the little table. 'Maureen and Duff are quarrelling most magnificently.'

She took a cigarette case from the pocket of her pyjamas. 'I heard them as I went by. I lingered awhile. Just to make sure.'

'Make sure of what?' Doris asked, curious. Elizabeth hadn't bathed, she thought. There was a musty smell from her. She edged her chair away.

'That they really were fighting properly.' She lit the cigarette and inhaled deeply, exhaling with a sigh. 'Not just rowing idly, the way they like to.'

'And?'

'They were,' she said in satisfaction.

'You're pleased, aren't you?' Honor said.

'Rather. Isn't it lovely when the men are away?' She stretched her legs out into the sun. 'And the Americans. And the young people. Honor, do you think we might have drinks out here?'

'Elizabeth, it is scarcely noon.'

'That is the downside, of course,' Elizabeth said. 'Without Chips, one is left to your tender mercies. And they aren't so very tender. Who cares if it's "scarcely noon". Don't be so middle-class,' she complained.

'Oh, very well. Kill yourself with drink if you must. What's it to me?'

'Precisely. Now, watch Duff follow the tray. Once he sees Andrews and the cocktails, he'll be out like a shot.'

But Duff didn't appear. Andrews, ever a mind-reader, came and deposited a jug with slices of orange and a ruby-coloured mixture with the bitter, herby smell of Campari, to which Elizabeth helped herself. Doris and Honor both declined. Elizabeth had a second glass, and still no Duff. 'It must be a worse row even than I supposed,' she said happily.

'Why so pleased?' Doris said.

'You'd be pleased too if, your whole life, Maureen was always in front of you – better, richer, happier. Like a hare going around a greyhound track that you can never catch, no matter how fast you run. And always – always! – flaunting it so that you knew her happiness grew on yours, fed off yours, grew stronger as yours grew weaker.'

'But why so personal? That's just Maureen, surely?'

'All those Guinnesses,' Elizabeth insisted. 'Not you, Honor, but the others. You might think it's not, but it *is* personal. Even my wedding – especially my wedding – poor bit of a thing that it was—'

'Hardly!' Honor said. 'Quite the social event.'

'It was alright, until Oonagh thoroughly eclipsed it by having her own, barely a week later, in the same church—' Her voice took on a whining tone.

It was a tale – pitiful, irrational – they had heard before. 'Everyone gets married at St Margaret's,' Honor tried to say.

'—and the most lavish wedding of the season. But even that I didn't mind, until Maureen took such pains to point it out to me – all the ways in which Oonagh's wedding was better than mine. At least Oonagh's marriage to Philip came a cropper too,' she said.

'Don't be cruel, darling, it doesn't suit you,' Honor said. 'I know it is not how you really are.'

'And it's not really the wedding, is it?' Doris asked after a minute in which she had watched Elizabeth smoke furiously, finish one cigarette and start another with an angry snap of her lighter.

'Of course not.' Elizabeth shrugged. 'I can't even pretend to myself that it is. Maureen married the man she loved, and so did I. And now, eight years later, she has three children and the man she loves is still in awe of her, and what do I have? Nothing.

Nothing at all. No children. No money. Pelly and I don't talk. We barely lasted four years. The constant rows about money did for us.'

'Not just money, from what I heard,' Doris said.

'Money,' Elizabeth reiterated firmly. 'Imagine the misery of trying to scratch a living? Never, ever more than half above water, liable to drown at any time. Knowing that every time my parents saw me, they knew I would ask for a loan. Or if I didn't ask, that they would feel compelled to offer, and I would say yes, because I couldn't afford to say no. Endless hopeless jobs in nightclubs, in hotels, in a dress shop.' She shuddered.

'Hardly Maureen's fault,' Honor said loyally.

'Maybe not, but it became intolerable. To be constantly comparing myself and my poor scraps with her abundance.' She shook her head, then picked a shred of tobacco from her top lip. 'So yes, when I hear Maureen and Duff fight, there is a part of me that is simply thrilled.'

It was, Doris reflected, awful. And yet, the awfulness was really in how much Elizabeth must mean it. It was one of the few serious things she'd ever heard from her.

'I say,' Elizabeth said then, eyes gleaming suddenly, 'what's this I hear about you being out all night, Doris? And being caught sneaking in at dawn . . .?'

'You should really turn your talent for intrigue to better use, Elizabeth. You're barely up, haven't seen a soul as far as I can tell, and already you know everything.'

'One picks things up,' Elizabeth said vaguely. Then, 'I think I'll walk down to the village. Another afternoon hanging around here, waiting to see what exertions that Kennedy girl forces us into, I cannot bear!'

'You'd better change,' Doris said. 'You do know you're still wearing your pyjamas?'

'My pyjamas,' Honor corrected automatically.

'Yes, I'm aware,' Elizabeth said with dignity. 'I am not a complete fool, you know.'

'Not a fool at all, Elizabeth, that's my point,' Doris said. 'Why don't you come with me to Berlin? I'm sure you could be useful.'

'As you are useful?' She gave her a shrewd look.

'Yes.'

'I think not. But thank you for asking. And for thinking I might be of some use. Most people see me as rather ridiculous.'

'You're not that.'

'No. But I do feel rather obliged to behave that way.'

'Why?'

'People expect it of me.' She left then, taking off the silver shoes and walking barefoot back to the house.

'I suppose she will raid my wardrobe now, and Molly will be unable to stop her. You know, you are different, Doris. I can see it, but I don't know what it is, exactly.' Honor looked consideringly at her. 'It isn't the way you look. Or even the way you behave, so much. It is a feeling . . . Oh, I explain so badly . . . But I feel that you are less yielding, like clay that has hardened overnight.'

'Something of that is probably true,' Doris said.

'There are things you haven't told me, aren't there?'

'Yes. I couldn't even if I wanted to.'

'You are not allowed?'

'No. Or rather, yes, but it's not that. I don't know how to put them into words.'

'Try.' Honor took her hand in both hers. Her hands were dry and cool.

'Very well. I will try. I don't have the habit of saying things anymore.'

'Take all the time you need. We have hours.'

Doris sat in silence, trying to find a place to begin. She cast back through memories that were only half in place, because she had never allowed herself to fully absorb them, trying, now, to single them out, to squash the instinct she had learned to deny them. Because, she realised, if she didn't speak them to someone, they would swamp her. There was too much that she had pushed away.

'At first, it was such fun,' she began. 'The daring, the intrigue. Boring too, often, of course, but always with the feeling that something might happen, and knowing that what I was doing was, in its way, useful. And I knew no one, except the people I was sent to know. Mostly men, mostly officers. My mother's family are all here now, thank goodness. But then, I made new friends that I didn't intend. The family in the flat beside mine; a mother, father and daughter. Hannah. She played the violin. Terribly.' A tiny smile.

Honor smiled back. 'Go on.'

And Doris told her. About Hannah, her violin. Beatrice, her plea for help. Doris' failure.

'I couldn't ask for the help they needed, even though I knew the very people who could have helped them. Because to do that would have been to risk everything I did there. Everything I had been sent to do. That's when I realised the terrible truth of the position I was in, and I hated it. In order to help many, I couldn't help the few who were in front of me. I did nothing. Except listen. I listened every day to Hannah, scraping away, trying so very hard.' She gave a weak and shaky smile. 'The sound of that violin to me was as though she were the greatest soloist in the world. Because it meant that she was still there. Until she wasn't.'

'But you did try to help,' Honor said.

'Yes, but too late. They were gone before I could do anything. Just as I had decided that I didn't care anymore, that I would help them whatever it took, they were gone.'

'Do you know where?' Honor asked when it seemed that Doris could say nothing more.

'No. I never found out. They left everything behind. Their furniture, Hannah's violin. I took it from the back of the lorry and I have it still. After that, nothing was quite the same.'

'But you stayed?'

'Of course. To do what I went there to do. That can't change.'

'But you are changed?'

'I think I must be.'

Doris waited for Honor to tell her to be careful. She didn't. 'How lonely you must be,' she said.

Chapter Forty-Five

Brigid

'**I** knew this outing was a mistake,' Brigid muttered to Kick after they had wandered around for an hour or so, peering at a series of tumbled-down walls that meandered in and out of each other in a way that looked purposeful, if one could be bothered to decipher the purpose. There was a wind up there on the downs. She wished she'd brought a cardigan.

'It's kind of interesting, no?'

'No.'

Kick looked at the place in front of her where a series of stone steps had been cut into the ground. 'This looks like it was a swimming pool. It's very like the one at Kelvedon. Same size, same shape. I wonder did a lot of Roman versions of us play around in it?'

'Who cares if they did?' Brigid wandered off. The day, she

thought, had been deathly. The way Kick's mother enthused about the ruins – apparently they were part of an old bathhouse or something – made her want to scream. Rose asked a million questions and put forward a million theories: 'This must be where they . . .' Even Chips began to flag. As for the ambassador, he took a quick and cursory look, pronounced it 'very interesting', then went to sit in the motorcar with the newspaper and a writing pad, saying he must work. Brigid could see him now, chewing the end of his fountain pen.

Standing there in the brisk force of the wind, she realised how tightly Kelvedon was squashed into its sheltered hollow. Like being in a closed fist, she thought, wrapped tight and hot inside something that yielded to a push but did not willingly open. She stretched her arms out on either side, leaning into the wind that seemed as though it would bear her up. She revelled in the space, the expanse of land around her that travelled on in rolls of springy turf, to the horizon. Was it really only a few days since they arrived? It felt as though they had all been cooped up in that house for far longer, boiling and suffocating together.

'You look like you're about to float away,' Fritzi said, coming to stand beside her.

'Don't you feel like you could just let go, and the wind would hold you up?'

'It wouldn't.'

She sighed. 'I know it wouldn't, I said don't you *feel* like it would. Go on, lean back, into it. Put your arms out and let it take over.' He did as she said, cautiously – 'Arms further out!' she instructed – then smiled.

'I see what you mean. Like the old feather beds in my grandfather's *schloss*. They were stuffed so full, it was like flying. I used to imagine I was on the back of an enormous goose, soaring above the Swabian mountains.'

Brigid burst out laughing.

'What's so funny?'

'You. On a giant goose.'

He smiled at her. 'I imagined that I could see everything below, not just the *schloss* with all its turrets and flags flying, but the villages with their little houses, the fields, the farmers, their beasts. Women churning butter, brewing beer, even sewing tiny pieces of fabric together to make quilts.'

'You know, that's the first thing I've heard you say that isn't entirely practical,' Brigid said thoughtfully. 'Just as I had given up believing there was anything romantic to you at all.'

'It's not that I am unromantic,' he protested. 'It is that this is not a time for romance.'

'I don't know,' Brigid said lazily. 'Others seem to think it is. Kick, and maybe Billy.' She looked sideways at Fritzi, but he didn't seem interested in whatever she was hinting at. 'The threat of war, of change, talk of young men enlisting. I mean, I know it's horrid, but surely there is something a little romantic about it?'

'Not for me,' he said. 'For me, it is only alarming.'

'Why? You start these things, and then you don't finish them.' Severely. 'What exactly is so alarming for you? More than for others? Most young men are silly about war.'

'I feel I am a tethered goat – made to stand and be seen that I may bring the lions prowling around me,' he said bitterly. 'And they in turn may be seen and be shot. Or seen and approached, I am not even sure which.'

'Who are the lions?' Brigid asked, trying to follow his thoughts, which – just like the giant goose – were so unlike his usual practicalities.

'I don't know that either. Only, I know that my family are part of it, and that they think less of me than they do of themselves.'

'They throw you out, like bait, to see who will be drawn?'

'Exactly.'

She felt suddenly sorry for him. His English was no longer faultless. If anything, he struggled to express himself, and where he struggled, there was the hint, now, of an accent. Instead of the polished young man, he seemed confused. Unhappy. Human.

'You could say no,' she said.

'I couldn't.'

'Of course you could,' she insisted, impatient.

'But I don't know what to say no to, because no one has asked me anything.'

'You really don't know?'

'No, and maybe there is nothing to know. Maybe I have made it all up. But I don't think so. And sometimes I think even your uncle, Chips, knows more than I do. And I do know that I despise what my family has become – we are lapdogs, a pekinese with a bow around its neck, that Hitler may pet and tease and show off. My father thinks that we play the Nazis at a clever game, but we don't. They play us.'

'So many plays and plots.' She rolled her eyes. 'First lions and now dogs . . . You know how silly this all sounds?'

'Only for someone who has always lived in England. In Germany, everyone has been scared and suspicious for a long time.'

'I'll tell you what I think,' she said, suddenly brusque. 'I think not only is this a lot of nonsense, it's a lot of dangerous nonsense. It's just the kind of thing that starts almost like a game – and indeed you sound to me like you are showing off – but ends up being far too serious when the wrong person decides to take it seriously.'

'You are surprising,' he said then. 'I thought you were just like English girls. Tennis. Horses. Always hearty. Secretly embarrassed by opera—'

'Not so secretly,' she said.

'—fonder of dogs than people. A person made in a mould that has already turned out thousands of others.'

'Well, I didn't have a very good impression of you either,' she said with a laugh.

'I know that. *King Midas' son*.' He laughed and Brigid did too.

'What are you both laughing at?' Kick came upon them. She had a bottle of lemonade which she offered first to Brigid, who accepted and took a long swig, then Fritzi, who refused with a shake of his head.

'Nothing here, that's for sure,' Brigid said. 'Surely we must be finished exploring by now?'

'You obviously don't know my mother,' Kick said wryly. 'Not while there is a stone unturned, a question unasked.'

'I almost feel sorry for Chips,' Brigid said gloomily. 'Though not as sorry as I feel for myself.'

'He does seem to have run out of answers,' Fritzi agreed. 'I've seen him looking quite desperately at the guidebook twice now.'

'That's my mother for you,' Kick said.

It was, Brigid thought, exasperated, but also fond, even admiring. She could hear Rose now '. . . imagine the hub of activity this must have been? A place for everyone to meet and tell their news.'

Despite herself, Brigid found that she was imagining – a girl like herself, with the same dreams and worries, with a store of sad and happy memories, little songs that she sang, a pet name her mother called her. A girl who worried that her hair was too coarse and her eyes less pretty than her sister's. Who had come here with a basket and the hope of meeting someone in particular. Whose heart thumped hard just like Brigid's did. And that girl, who was just as real for a second as she herself was, had grown and changed and lived and died and been remembered and then forgotten.

The thought made Brigid dizzy because of what it meant. If that girl had been real, then she too, just as real, would one day be nothing.

'Are you alright?' Kick asked. 'You look awfully odd.'

'I'm hungry.'

The picnic was as dreadful as picnics usually were, Brigid decided. No spot was comfortable once you actually sat there. The plaid blanket was hairy, and scratched at her bare legs so that she had to sit on her sunhat, which crushed it. The food, so pretty-looking packed into the big wicker basket in porcelain containers with pewter lids, then laid out on the patterned china plates, was altogether less appealing when you had to fight for it with wasps and ants. The ambassador took his sandwiches back to the car with him. His wife sat on a rock with Chips and made the best of it in a way that was elegant and determined and disappointed and was, Brigid thought, the way she did almost everything.

She and Kick and Fritzi ate a great deal and drank lemonade from a stone bottle that was still cold, but the many different foods – chicken, tongue, a potato salad – made her feel sick. She was still chilly.

'Take my jacket,' Fritzi said, seeing her shiver. He placed it around her shoulders.

'Thank you.' She found now that being warmer made her feel sleepy. She stretched out on the lumpy ground and shut her eyes. Lying flat, the wind was less noticeable, and she had just begun to drift off to the sound of Kick and Fritzi chatting beside her when Chips bustled up.

'Time to get on,' he said. 'Will you pack up the picnic? We've been gone quite long enough.'

What, she wondered, did he imagine might have happened in their absence?

It was surprisingly hard to pack the basket back as it had been when they opened it. Only Fritzi seemed able to get the hang of it: 'The preserve jar goes into the tea mug, see? And the plates stack – dinner plate, side plate, saucer – one on top of the other, before you buckle them back in again.' He wouldn't allow Brigid to tumble the dishes and cutlery in any old how, saying, 'But it won't close if you do that.'

'Who cares? The servants can put it right when we get back to the house.'

But he wouldn't, insisting on everything in its rightful place, until Brigid handed him his jacket back in fury and went to sit in the maroon-coloured Rolls Royce with Kick, saying, 'No room, you'll have to ride in the other car,' when he tried to join them.

'But there are more people in the other car . . .' he said, momentarily confused.

'No room,' she said again and shut the door.

'My mother won't allow the windows down. He'll be like a dog, desperate for air,' Kick said. She rolled her window right down. 'But I think you're being pretty hard on him.'

'Did you see how he fussed over the butter tin? As though it had *diamonds* or something in it.'

'He's meticulous, that's all.'

'Fussy.' Her early sympathy for him was gone, she found. Probably he had just made all that stuff up, about being surrounded and watched. 'What shall we do when we get back? There'll be heaps of time before dinner.'

'I'll teach you to dance the Big Apple. It's harder than it looks and you need a lot of people to do it right, because you have to make a big circle, but I can show you the steps. You and Fritzi can dance together.'

'If he can dance,' Brigid said. 'I hate a man who can't dance.'

'We'll ask him.'

Chapter Forty-Six

Honor

'Darling.' Chips said the word with impatience. 'I must have a word.'

He had tracked her to the small drawing room. Honor had chosen it because it was out of the way and might, she hoped, be overlooked. It was only half finished, Chips had said – meaning that there were only half the number of curios and objects and cushions that he would usually favour. Through the windows she could see down to the pool, empty now, a flat rectangle of blue in the sea of green grass. In any case, it wasn't out of the way enough because here was Chips, sounding peevish. 'Elizabeth was seen cycling to the village on one of the maid's bicycles. Wobbling dangerously all over the road,' he said.

'Yes, she said the front wheel wasn't straight.'

'Once in the village, she shoved the bicycle against a wall and made straight for the pub. Walked in and ordered a Tom Collins.'

'Oh dear. How naughty she is. Were they very upset?'

'Yes, very. She refused to sit in the ladies' lounge—'

'One can hardly blame her. I doubt any but sheepdogs have been in there in years.'

'Maybe, but Thompson said some of the regulars were quite up in arms. Wanted her removed from the pub and, when Thompson said he could hardly do that, left themselves. Now I shall have to go down there and buy them all a drink, or they'll tell everyone they meet that we are a group of London degenerates.'

'And then, come election time, no one will vote for you,' Honor said wryly.

'It's not that. Well, a little, but really, she is too bad. Why can't she stay put?'

'She says she's bored.'

'Well, she shouldn't have come.'

'Certainly. But now she has, perhaps we could have a party? Invite the Blounts, their house party, a few of the neighbours.'

'I'll think about it. But you must talk to her.'

'There she is now. I'll tell her.' Honor went and rapped on the window and, when Elizabeth turned towards the sound, beckoned her over, unlatching the door and holding it open for her. 'Darling, you really mustn't be upsetting the poor regulars in Mr Thompson's pub,' she said when Elizabeth was in.

'They were sweet,' Elizabeth said vaguely, perching on the edge of the sofa. 'Kept insisting I'd be more comfortable in the ladies' lounge. Dreadful pokey place. I think the landlord keeps pigeons in there. There seemed to be a great deal of birdseed.

In any case, I assured them I'd much rather the bar, and we all had a perfectly jolly chat.'

'No you didn't, they didn't want you there at all,' said Chips.

'Not want little me? The idea.'

'Well, they didn't,' he insisted. 'And really, you shouldn't be skulking around the village like that.'

'I never skulk. And I wasn't the only Kelvedoner there.'

'You're not going to try and tell me anyone went with you?'

'No, but I saw Albert. That fellow who goes about with Fritzi. If it's skulking you want, he was definitely doing it.'

'You must be mistaken. Why would he be in the village? There's only one shop, and nothing at all Fritzi might need.' Chips sat forward, animated by the idea that Fritzi might require something, and that he might be the one to provide it. 'Perhaps he's out of pomade,' he mused. 'I shall offer him mine . . .'

'I don't know *why*,' Elizabeth said. 'I didn't talk to him. Only saw him.'

'You do talk nonsense, Elizabeth. And now I must go and reassure Andrews about the maid's bicycle. I shall have to have the wheel straightened. It really is too bad.'

'It was buckled when I got it,' Elizabeth said.

'That's not the point, though, is it? Now that you've used it, I shall have to make good, no matter what condition it was in when you took it.'

'How seriously you take everything,' Elizabeth said idly. 'Who cares about a buckled bicycle wheel?'

'The maid will care, very much,' Chips snapped. 'And really, so should you. You are *careless*.'

He left, and Elizabeth stretched a hand out towards Pugsy, who lay curled up on the other side of the sofa. She touched the dog's ears and Pugsy leapt up and yelped in alarm. He bared his teeth, tiny and white, and Elizabeth laughed. 'His mistress' dog alright.'

'Did you really see Albert?' Honor asked.

'Oh yes. Talking to a chap in a small navy car. I know it was him because when he saw me, he looked shocked and pretended he hadn't. I can always tell.' Yes, Honor thought, probably that was true. 'And then he shuffled around so his back was to me and his head almost inside the window of the car, so no one could have known it was him.'

'Did you speak to him?'

'No. Too busy trying to stop that maddening bicycle from wobbling me off. It was like being on a jolly naughty pony.'

'Well, maybe don't say you saw him to anyone else? Fritzi mightn't like it.'

'You have my word,' Elizabeth said. 'And now, if we are finished, I'm going to change. I don't suppose you have any more clothes I can borrow.' She looked beadily at Honor. 'I've worn everything I brought.'

'Everything of mine you brought,' Honor corrected her mechanically.

'Yes,' Elizabeth said impatiently. 'Obviously.'

Honor sat for a while, mulling over what Elizabeth had said, then went looking for Doris. She found her at last in the stables, scratching the nose of the heavy piebald. 'Isn't he a darling?' she said, putting her arms around the horse's neck and leaning her face into its cheek.

'You'll be covered in hair,' Honor said.

'Who cares for that.' Doris closed her eyes and breathed deeply. 'Don't horses smell heavenly?'

'They do,' Honor agreed. 'They smell . . . I don't know, *kind*?'

'That's it exactly,' Doris said, standing up straight. 'Clever you, Honor.'

'Can we go somewhere else? I need to talk to you.' Honor looked around the empty stable yard. 'Poor fellow, must be very lonely here.'

'Who, the horse, or Albert?' Doris asked.

'Sshh! He'll hear you,' Honor said. She tugged at Doris' sleeve. When they were a distance from the stables, deep in the laurel bushes that had their own smell, clean and medicinal, she twitched at Doris' sleeve and made her stand even closer.

'Are you going to kiss me?' Doris asked with a laugh.

'Don't be silly. It's about Albert. Elizabeth saw him in the village today.'

'So she did go? She didn't walk there in those silver shoes?'

'No. Took the maid's bicycle.'

'Goodness, how naughty.'

'Yes, but that's not the point. She saw Albert.'

'Perhaps it's his day off.'

'Doris, it's a Friday. It certainly is not his day off. Anyway, Elizabeth said that he was talking to a chap in a navy car, and when he saw her, he was shocked and moved himself around to avoid being seen by her, only it was too late.'

'Is she certain it was him?'

'Yes, she says; positive. She says it was the way he pretended he hadn't seen her. She says she can always tell.'

'Yes, I imagine she can. Poor Elizabeth. Well, there may be an entirely innocent explanation.'

'There may indeed. But also there may not. And I thought you should know.'

'Yes, I see. I mean, it still doesn't answer any of my questions, only confirms that I'm right to ask them. I'd better make a telephone call. May I? From somewhere rather quieter than the library?'

'I'll ask Andrews to bring the telephone to my room.'

Back in Honor's room, once the telephone had been brought, Doris said, 'I'll have to ask you to leave me alone. I'm sorry. It's frightfully rude.'

'That's perfectly alright, darling.' Then, when she reached the door, 'Doris, you will be careful, won't you? Remember, if you know and suspect things about Albert, he may know and suspect things about you.'

'How clever you always are, dearest Honor. But please, do not by even a whisper suggest such a thing. Will you wait outside the door, in case your husband tries to come in?'

'It is highly unlikely that he will,' Honor said.

'Yes, but wouldn't it be just like him to come now?' Doris laughed. 'When he is least wanted.'

'I'll stand guard.'

Chapter Forty-Seven

Brigid

Back at Kelvedon the house was quiet but with something fractious about it, Brigid thought, as though they had arrived a split second after raised voices and slammed doors, so that there was silence, yes, but the air was disturbed; bunched and agitated. As if all the talk of war and bad things that had fluttered overhead for so long now that she almost couldn't remember a time when it wasn't there, had landed, like a flock of starlings. Only there were more of them, many more, than anyone expected.

She shook the feeling off. It was still just talk. Probably, she thought, the talk would go on and on, and then one day it would stop, like a toothache, and almost you wouldn't notice it had stopped until weeks or months had gone by and you were able to look back and go '. . . funny, no one says those sad, grim things anymore . . .'

She smoothed out her sunhat – Honor's sunhat – distracting herself with trying to unroll the creases she had made. But it didn't work, the feeling persisted. When the sound of Paul crying from the nursery upstairs started, it wasn't, Brigid thought, a *new* sound, but rather an old sound, paused, then taken up again.

'Andrews, where is Mrs Channon?' Chips asked, coming into the hall.

'Down at the stables, sir.'

'The stables? Why?'

'She and Miss Coates have taken sugar to the horse, sir.'

'That beast is a nuisance. Shouldn't even be there. Very well. I am going to the nursery.'

He was, Brigid reflected, at his most appealing when with his son. His gentle concern for Paul made him more human than at any other time. She'd seen the way Honor looked at Paul, the reluctance with which she took his hand, the formal way she spoke to him. As though he were a stranger, and not a terribly interesting one at that. It bothered Brigid. She knew it bothered their mother too, although Lady Iveagh had never spoken of it.

'Fritzi, can you dance?' Kick asked then. The prince was hovering in the hallway, clearly hoping they would include him in their plans.

'I can.'

'I mean proper dancing, not the shuffling-slowly-round sort that old couples do?'

'I can dance.'

'Then you may come with us.'

They went to the unfinished room at the end of the corridor past Elizabeth's bedroom, the one they had said was haunted, because it had no furniture in it and no one would be disturbed by the music. They brought Kick's gramophone and a stack of records.

Fritzi was right – he could dance. Kick was right too. The Big Apple was harder than it looked, especially the light side-to-side shuffling steps, but they tried again and again – 'From the top!' Kick kept calling; she'd seen it in a movie once, she explained – and by the time the gong went, 'I'd say you're pretty well perfect,' Kick declared.

'I think we need to practise more,' Fritzi said.

'You would,' Brigid said. But she smiled at him. 'Come on, we'd better change.' On the way to her room, she passed the nursery. Paul had stopped crying but was shouting now. She heard, 'I won't, Papa, I won't I tell you! And if you try to make me I'll thump you . . .' Brigid hurried past.

In her bedroom, Minnie was laying out her evening clothes. 'I missed you,' Brigid said, hugging her.

'By which you mean you were bored?' Minnie said.

'Hopelessly. The most dreary day, you cannot imagine. What's been happening here?'

'Elizabeth Ponsonby took a bicycle down to the village that belongs to one of the housemaids, and she bent the wheel and the maid – Clara – is furious, but Mr Channon has promised to replace the bicycle.'

'How much more fun you have than me.' Minnie tugged at her hair. 'Ow. I know, you think I'm being absurd. Maybe I am. It just seemed like nothing went right today. Or it did and I didn't enjoy it as much as I thought, I'm not sure which,' she said thoughtfully. Why must liking people be a painful thing? she wondered. Surely it should be the exact opposite? And in a way it was – there was such fun in finding Fritzi amusing, and in watching for the way he looked at her and spoke to her. But there was bother too. She realised that she minded his being worried and scared. She could see he was, and it made her feel bad for him. And that was uncomfortable. Besides being too much what Chips wanted. She would put a stop to it, she decided. If she could. 'So what did Elizabeth *do* in the village?' she asked.

'Tried to have a drink in the public house bar.'

'Oh dear. Were the men *very* upset?'

'Very.' Minnie's mouth twitched. 'And she saw Albert, the prince's man.'

'Goodness, what was he doing?'

'She didn't find out. Only saw him, and then he pretended not to see her. He was talking to a man in a blue car.'

'You really do know everything.' Brigid said. 'Is it his half-day?'

'It's a Friday, Lady Brigid.'

'Biddy. Right, so not his half-day.'

'Not that he waits for days off.'

'Really? Do tell.'

'He comes and goes as he pleases. I've never met a gentleman's gentleman like him.'

'Seems he's an old family friend.' Brigid began to fidget with a silver bangle, spinning it on its edge and watching it fall, then picking it up and spinning it again. 'Not exactly a servant.'

'All the same,' Minnie put a hand over Brigid's, to stop her fidgeting, 'the way he carries on is odd.'

'Maybe he has a girl in the village?'

'How could he have a girl in the village, when he's only been here a few days, same as you?'

'Some men are fast movers.' It was the sort of thing Maureen said, Elizabeth said. Brigid didn't know what they meant exactly, but judging from the tightening of Minnie's lips and the way she dug the bristles into Brigid's head, it wasn't suitable.

'That's enough of that, Lady Brigid. I'll tell you what, though.' She leaned in. 'He's an odd fish, make no mistake.'

'Was Chips very cross about the bicycle?' Brigid lost interest in Albert.

'Very. Came right down to the kitchen to apologise. Poor Clara was mortified.'

Chapter Forty-Eight

Honor

It was unusual for Chips to be openly angry, Honor thought. He never shouted, rarely even raised his voice. He could be irritable, peevish, critical, but had very little temper. He was a schemer and a plotter, but not a ranter. For that, at least, she was grateful. But it made his rare outburst all the more surprising.

'When is the last time you saw Paul?' he demanded, coming into her bedroom without knocking.

Honor was in bed. Not a nap, exactly, she had told herself. Just a rest before the ordeal of dinner. Something that might help subdue the growing agitation brought on by so many nights spent awake and needlessly watchful. She had lain down for an hour, and fallen into a deep, dreamless sleep so that, now, she struggled to catch up to where Chips was.

'Yesterday.' She sat up. Was it, she wondered? 'I was about to pay a visit to the nursey now.' She wasn't. Or hadn't been. But now she supposed she'd better.

'I've just come from there.'

'And? What of it? Is all well?'

'All is not well. Our son is becoming bumptious and even a touch impossible. He was very rude. I nearly smacked him.'

'Perhaps you should have.' She didn't really mean it – she remembered, far too well, being smacked as a child. The humiliation that was almost stronger than the rage. The way the nursery-maid would snap, 'What have you to cry about when I hardly touched you and it couldn't have hurt a bit?' How impossible it had been to explain, or even understand, that it wasn't pain that brought tears, but shame. That someone could reach out a rough hand and lay it upon you because they were bigger and stronger and wanted to, and there was nothing you could do to stop them – that was what the tears had been for. So no, she didn't mean it, but really, Chips was so righteous, so full of bristling indignation. And she was so tired. Her head ached dully. Anyway, what was it to her if he had nearly smacked Paul? It wasn't her who had.

'How can you say such a thing?' Chips was clutching the post at the end of the bed so hard that his knuckles were white, contrasting with the meaty red of the rest of his hand. 'He should not be smacked. I have always said it, and you have always agreed. He is a darling, but recently I have seen a change in him. He is more wilful and inclined to tantrums.'

'It's the age,' Honor said vaguely. And perhaps it was, she thought.

'I don't believe it is. I think it's more than that. A question of character. And I cannot help think that if you saw more of him, spent more time with him, showed him more affection, he would be more tractable.'

'So it is my fault that you nearly smacked our son?'

'That's not what I said, but Honor, you must see . . .'

'Why must I? Because you wish it?'

'Because it's true. You never take the least trouble with him, and it's beginning to affect his character.'

'Do go away, Chips. You are here to berate me over something that is none of my concern, and I wish you wouldn't.'

'*None of your concern?* How can you possibly say so?'

'Because it's true. Now, go away so I may get up. It's time to dress for dinner.'

'That you are an indifferent wife I can accept, but an indifferent mother I cannot.' He moved to the window and pulled viciously at the cord that looped the curtains back. 'I—' He broke off, leaning forward. 'Good Lord!'

'What is it?'

'Diana, and Mosley.'

'What of them?'

'They are outside, getting out of a rather fine motorcar.'

'Here?'

'Yes, here. Did you invite them?'

'Certainly not. I can't abide her. Are you sure you didn't?'

'Perfectly sure. How would I, with the ambassador here? Really, this is damned awkward.'

Honor went to the window and stood beside Chips. Sure enough, below them Diana, dressed in a navy silk dress, stood beside Mosley, thin and dapper in a grey suit. She watched as Diana cast a look around at the house and grounds, then leaned in to say something to Mosley that made him laugh. Just as Honor was about to draw back, Diana turned slightly and looked up to the window. Seeing Honor, she waved at her.

'If it's only awkward, we'll be doing well,' Honor said, drawing back. 'What a cauldron you have assembled, Chips. I do hope it doesn't all catch fire.'

'I didn't assemble it,' he said. 'What can Diana be thinking? I do hope they don't intend to stay to dinner.'

Chapter Forty-Nine

Honor

*T*hat you are an indifferent wife I can accept, but an
indifferent mother I cannot. Was it true? Honor
wondered when Chips had left, bustling down to greet
Diana, furious and excited all at once. Was she an indifferent
mother? She supposed she was. Once admitted, the thought was
less terrible than she would have expected it to be. The realisation made her sad. But something else too. Something she didn't
quite understand yet.

She was on her way downstairs, past Rose Kennedy's door,
when it opened and Rose appeared. Honor felt awkward. She
should say something genial. But what?

'I do hope you're having a nice time,' was all she could come
up with.

'Thank you.' Rose inclined her head graciously. She didn't say she was, Honor noted. 'May I ask you something?'

'Of course.' Honor hoped it would be something quick – where might she get a darning needle or hair pins, perhaps – but Rose stepped back and held the bedroom door wide so that Honor found no way not to walk inside. Rose closed the door behind them.

'Will you sit?' she asked. Quite as if it wasn't Honor's house, Honor thought. She perched at the edge of an armchair. Rose took the dressing-table stool, which meant Honor could see her elegant, bony face reflected three ways. 'I wanted to ask you if I have understood something correctly,' she said, fixing Honor with unblinking eyes. 'Am I right to believe that Billy Cavendish's parents would very much rather that my daughter and their son did not continue to be particularly friendly?'

Good Lord, Honor thought. *Really?* 'I'm sure it's nothing to do with Kick—' she began.

'Kathleen.'

'—Kathleen. Nothing to do with her personally.'

'Indeed not. How could it possibly be?' Rose said sharply.

'Of course. Only I imagine they don't much want Billy to form a friendship with someone who isn't, well, you know . . .'

'English?'

'Exactly.' That would have to do.

'Thank you. That's what I hoped you'd say. I can be easy in my mind now. It means we are as one on this, they and us. Usually, you know, it goes the other way.' She smiled thinly. 'The reluctance is very often all on our side.'

'I'm sure the Devonshires must know just what you mean,' Honor said, stifling a laugh. Really, Rose understood nothing about this country. She couldn't wait to tell Maureen. She looked around the room then, wondering if she might now leave. Rose's things were so neat as to be almost invisible. A hairbrush, a lipstick, a jar of cold cream and a can of hairspray were lined up on the dressing table. Other than that, there was no evidence of her at all. No shoes, no clothes, not even a scarf. Everything must be stowed away in the wardrobe.

Beside the bed stood a gold crucifix as tall as a lamp. Pinned to it, the figure of a man, face contorted in agony. At its base, two fat golden cherubs sat on either side of a little basin filled with water. Holy water, she assumed. It certainly hadn't been in the room – anywhere in the house – before. Honor, fascinated and appalled, blurted out, 'Your own?'

'Yes, I bring it with me when I travel.'

'Such a comfort . . .' Honor tried, but couldn't continue. 'You must be very virtuous,' she finished vaguely.

'I'm always astonished at the way people think Catholics are virtuous.' Rose sounded amused. Which was unlike her.

'Well, aren't they? Aren't you?'

'Not at all. If anything, that's the point,' Rose said. 'We aren't. And we don't expect to be. Or expect others to be. Not at all. You see' – she held up a thin hand. How didactic she was, Honor thought; she never could seem to understand that she wasn't talking to one of her nine children – 'what we understand is *trying*, and trying again, even when you don't at all wish to.'

'So you think one should always try again?'

'Oh yes.' Rose opened her ice-blue eyes very wide. 'I most certainly do. Especially at the important things. Like motherhood. And marriage.' She smiled a neat smile and folded her hands in a way that Honor suspected was meant to be inviting. Of confidences. Of burdens.

'You've been most tremendously helpful,' Honor said briskly. 'Now, I must get on.' And Rose had, Honor thought, as she made her escape. Most tremendously helpful indeed. If *trying* was what Rose Kennedy did – if Honor's marriage might resemble Rose's – well then, she wanted no part of it. A future in which Chips did exactly as he wished – after all, everyone knew about the ambassador and his 'friends', including that German actress Marlene Dietrich; 'Trust him to pick a Hun,' Maureen had said, 'even in his choice of mistress he can't be loyal' – while she, Honor, stayed at home and had baby after baby so that he could present a large and handsome family to the world . . . She shook her shoulders back. No. That was all.

Chapter Fifty

Kick

Teaching Brigid and Fritzi the Big Apple had been fun, Kick thought. At least as much for what it told her about them, and the way they were together, as for the teaching. She wondered could Brigid see it – that she liked Fritzi best when he admitted he didn't know something or was unsure of himself; was irritated by the veneer of bland self-confidence he assumed so much of the time. It was the ways in which he was uncertain that she warmed to, not the perfection of King Midas' son. If Chips could harness that, Kick thought, he may well succeed. But she wouldn't be the one to tell him. If it really was to be war with Germany, she thought shrewdly, and if Fritzi chose to stay in England – as he swore he would – then he would tumble abruptly, from royalty to undesirable. She wondered what that might do to

Brigid's feelings for him; whether he would be an enemy, or a pitiful friend?

She arrived downstairs at the same time as her mother who looked, Kick thought, rather strained. For the first time, she wondered how long this stay was to be. What did 'a few days' mean, when they were days spent at Kelvedon? The drawing room was almost full, everyone except Chips was down, and Kick made her way to where Doris sat beside an open window.

'How were the ruins?' Doris asked.

Kick began to tell her when Chips came in, with Diana and Mosley. 'We have visitors,' he said smoothly, urging them forward into the room. Kick looked for Debo with them, but they were alone.

'How nice to see you,' Honor said, moving to greet Diana, who remained standing in the doorway, smiling at them all, headlamp eyes fixed on a point above their heads.

'Isn't it,' Diana agreed loudly. 'We felt sure you had no idea how close we were, or you would certainly have telephoned.' Beside her, Mosley's moustache twitched over his lip.

'Certainly,' Chips assured them. 'Do come and say hullo to –' he cast about the room, then '– Maureen,' and he led them to the opposite side of the room to where Kick's father stood.

'That's unexpected,' Doris said to Honor, who came to where they sat. She too looked tired. The visit was starting to try all their nerves.

'Very,' Honor muttered. 'Unexpected and unwelcome.' At that, Diana turned and looked at her, even though she couldn't possibly have heard.

'Come and say hullo,' Honor begged.

'Don't ask me,' Doris murmured, 'I simply can't. Not Diana. Not even for you.'

'Isn't she beautiful?' Kick said, watching Diana smile at something Chips said. It was a perfect smile. A delicate curving of the mouth upwards, and one that conveyed nothing of mirth.

'I suppose so. If the cold white of marble is your thing. I prefer something with more life,' Doris said. 'More heart.'

'Oh, she has plenty of *heart*,' Honor said. 'Only Mosley gets all of it.' They both laughed at that, and Kick looked from one to the other, trying to understand what they meant.

Doris saw her confusion. 'Don't listen to us,' she said. 'We are frightfully cynical. Go and say hullo if you wish.' So Kick did.

'Darling Kathleen – Kick – how lovely to see you again.' Diana leaned a little on the last word and held out a hand for Kick's, to draw her closer and the two of them a little apart from the goup. Maureen, Kick saw, watched them go with an arched eyebrow. 'My dearest Debo told me she spent a simply delightful day here with you recently. And Billy too.'

'Did she really say that?' Kick asked, overcome suddenly with a need to hear that it was OK. That the day hadn't, after all, been the wrecking of everything. She had heard so little from Debo since, and nothing from Billy. Was he still at Blenheim? With Irene? All the questions and regrets Kick had been squashing rushed back up at her. Maybe Diana could reassure her.

'She did,' Diana said. 'And I'm certain if I had asked her, she would have said Billy had a delightful day too.'

'Pa showed such a mortifying film . . .' Kick blurted out. She hung her head. 'And now I'm afraid Billy won't want to speak to me again.'

'Nonsense. Of course he will. Young men in love don't think about such things.'

'Do you really think . . .?'

'I do. I'm certain of it.' Diana patted her arm.

Did she mean it? Kick wondered. And if she did, how could she possibly know? Yet she spoke with such certainty. None of Brigid's hesitancy – her vague reassurances: *I'm sure it will all come right* . . . 'In any case, was it so very bad?' Diana continued.

'It seemed like it was. All those men – boys really, no older than Jack, some of them – blown up and shot, dying there on screen.' She shuddered.

'But after all, his intention was good. To keep England out of a terrible war.'

'Yes, but no one sees it like that. Not Billy or any of them.'

'I do. I see exactly what he meant.'

'You do?' Kick looked gratefully at her.

'Oh yes.' Diana squeezed her hand. 'How I should like to tell him so.'

'Come with me, then you can tell him.'

But it wasn't that easy. The ambassador moved smoothly away as Kick and Diana approached him, apparently deep in conversation with Duff. And when they went to him again, a few moments later, it was Elizabeth – to whom he had barely spoken, Kick thought – who claimed his attention. In fact, he proved astonishingly skilful in his evasions, managing to be always elsewhere, always on the move and just out of reach. If he heard Kick's requests – 'Pa, can I—' – he ignored them. Even Mosley, moving with elegant determination as though choreographed, was no match for Kennedy's determination not to be met.

It was like having a pair of panthers in a room of deer, Kick thought eventually, with a laugh that she tried to hide. Everywhere Diana and Mosley moved caused a ripple through the group as her father and mother, Duff too, made sure to move as well, always in the opposite direction, always newly out of reach. It seemed they worked together, her parents, Duff, even Elizabeth and Maureen; an unexpected alliance.

'We must get on,' Mosley said at last, with barely concealed irritation. 'We're expected for dinner.'

'See you very soon, darling,' Diana said loudly to Kick, leaning in to embrace her on both cheeks. 'You must come to Eaton Square again when we're all back in London.'

Kick looked up and found Doris watching her with an unusually serious expression.

Chapter Fifty-One

Honor

When Honor came back after seeing Diana and Mosley off, Chips' mood had switched to a curious, un-focused gaiety. At first she thought it was simply relief – the same relief she felt – at dispatching their unexpected guests, but soon she realised he had been at his powders – his 'dynamite'. She saw all the signs. He proposed cocktails outside, on the terrace. 'There won't be much more of this weather,' he said. 'I believe it breaks tomorrow. We may as well enjoy the last of it.' It was true, Honor thought. There was a dampness in the air, an underlying coolness that was nothing like the sudden explosion of the storm – was it really only two days ago? – but instead a reminder of a bill past due: the usual disappointments of an English summer.

'I can bring my gramophone,' Kick said excitedly. 'It winds up.'

'As long as you don't play it too loudly,' her mother said.

Outside, the birds, perhaps stirred to competition by the sounds of Duke Ellington's 'Prelude to a Kiss', sang their own evening songs louder, more aggressively. Albert was brushing leaves from the tiles around the pool into neat piles. There was a feeling of tidying up, of setting things back into place that had been disrupted by their coming. But it wasn't his job to sweep up, and Honor felt irritated by what felt like presumption. Why couldn't he leave the gardeners to do that? Why was he suddenly diligent? Was it to distract from the fact he'd been skulking around the village all day?

Fritzi and Brigid danced a few steps, cheered on by Chips who called 'Exquisite!' from over by a small table that had been set up, where he was mixing drinks.

'If only Billy were here to dance with you, Kick,' Brigid said. There was a sharp little pause, and then she blurted out, 'I say, sorry!' which only made everything worse.

'I always said we needed more men,' Elizabeth drawled. 'The poor prince will be worn out.'

'Fritzi is equal to anything,' Chips said, and for a minute Honor was grateful that he had turned the conversation from Billy; she could see the way Rose was looking at her daughter, and how carefully Kick avoided her mother's gaze. But only for a minute.

'I've always said it, dear boy,' Chips continued, 'and your grandfather has too. You are the very person to succeed him, and to restore the position of the family. Not your father, not any longer' – he shook his head sadly – 'and not your brothers. You, Fritzi.' He stirred the cocktail jug with a long glass stick that had a silver pineapple in place of a handle. He held it up like a baton, for silence.

'We have discussed it many times, your grandfather and I.' He twinkled at them all. 'There could be no one better suited than you to be emperor. Play your cards right, my boy, continue as you are – be careful, be discreet, say nothing bad about the Nazis, but watch them—'

'Channon, this is not the time or place for this conversation.' Duff stood up so abruptly, spoke so loudly, that everyone turned to stare at him, even, Honor saw, Albert, who was now gathering various discarded items from the chairs by the pool – towels, an inflatable ball, a shirt that had been draped over the back of a chair.

'Oh, nonsense,' Chips said, waving him away. His eyes were like saucers, big and black. 'We are among friends. Anyway, I have long said it. You remember, Fritzi, when we first had this conversation, a year ago? And you were not at all against the idea then?'

'Yes, but so much has changed since . . .' the prince began.

'Not so very much,' Chips said. 'Not so much at all. When one considers the thousand years the Hohenzollern family have ruled.' He looked gayly around at them all. 'Why, this last decade is a blink of an eye.' His powders always gave him a rolling, roiling confidence beyond even what he usually had. There was a sheen of sweat across his top lip that he dabbed at with a handkerchief. 'We have talked about it, a great deal, your grandfather and I. How you, of all your brothers, are the most possessed of the personality, the *temperament* shall we say, for the job.'

'Hardly a *job*,' Elizabeth muttered.

'You have the élan, the brio—' Chips had his arms spread wide now.

'Is he just going to keep saying made-up foreign words?' Elizabeth asked no one in particular.

'—the *comme-il-faut*—'

Elizabeth giggled loudly. She was clearly a little high too.

'Channon,' Duff spoke louder. 'Hush! It is not the time.' He dropped his voice, almost to a whisper. 'It is not the time,' he repeated.

'Emperor Friedrich,' Chips said, bowing low at the waist.

Poor Fritzi started and took a step back.

Duff laughed out loud. It was a laugh without any real mirth, and unusual enough for everyone to turn and stare. 'You are joking,' he said.

'Why should I be joking?'

'Emperor of what?' Duff demanded. 'There is no room for emperors where there is already a dictator.'

'Not *emperors*, just one emperor,' Chips said.

'One teeny-weeny-tiny little emperor,' Elizabeth mocked.

'Can you not be quiet?' Chips suddenly rounded on her. 'Why are you even here?'

Elizabeth's round eyes grew rounder again, like a baby encountering pain – confused as much as hurt by this thing it doesn't understand. And, just like a baby, her eyes slowly filled with water, their blue submerged and diluted, like the bottom tiles of the swimming pool, Honor thought.

'Chips!' she said. 'There is no need to be cruel. Elizabeth, I beg you not to listen to him.'

'I think we should go indoors.' That was Duff.

But the drawing room was no better. 'You are born to this,' Chips declared.

Fritzi by now looked as though he too might cry.

'Stop hounding him, Chips,' Brigid said, indignant.

Chips ignored her. 'And when your grandfather dies – and after all, even the kaiser cannot live forever – there will be a wave of Hohenzollern sentiment that you must be poised to take advantage of—' He was flapping his arms now, like some kind of great bird. Honor imagined him taking off, borne aloft on the wave of excitement that had overtaken him, disappearing out the double doors that stood open behind him and up into the saturating sky.

'Do not say such things!' Fritzi suddenly spoke more sharply than Honor had ever heard him, instantly backed up by Duff.

'Do not,' he agreed loudly. He crossed to the doors behind Chips, shut them firmly and drew the curtains across. 'Maureen, perhaps you would play something for us?' He looked at his wife, then at the piano and, to Honor's astonishment, Maureen – who was not musical and could barely play at all – looked back at him and nodded. No caustic reply, no display of searing wit. Just a nod. She went and sat down and opened the instrument. She played one of Bach's Preludes, badly, and too fast, but loudly and for long enough – she played it twice, starting at the beginning the very moment she reached the end – that they had a chance to settle themselves, for the agitation in the air to dissipate.

Honor watched them move about the room and form smaller groups. Kick, Brigid and Fritzi gathered by the door as though looking for an escape. Doris and Elizabeth went to stand with Duff in a way that seemed almost protective. The ambassador and Mrs Kennedy sat close together, at a remove, and Honor realised that the visit, from that perspective, had been a failure. They had not been folded in, in the way Chips had hoped. Or the way Duff had hoped. The early promise – the charm of Kelvedon, of the lazy days and good weather, Rose's inclination to be intrigued by Duff – had all come to nothing.

Was it the Catholic outburst? she wondered. Kick's obvious attraction to Billy that was just as obviously disapproved of by her parents – and his, she thought, remembering Moucher's look of horror when Kick had airily said, *We saw His Holiness?* Chips' clumsy and unwanted championing of Fritzi's cause?

Maybe all those things, and enough time spent together to realise that, after all, they didn't understand each other nearly as well as hoped. They would make their excuses and leave early, she realised. As early as the next day even. The ambassador would find a reason why he must return to London, would insist his wife and daughter came with him. Chips would be disappointed. He would feel his failure all the more keenly after this evening.

But perhaps it was time for them all to go, she thought, looking at Brigid and Fritzi, laughing together at something in a magazine. Whatever might or might not be happening there, she would slow it down, she decided. Not encourage it.

Maureen finished at the piano and gave a mocking bow, to scattered applause. She came and sat beside Honor. 'I had no idea you played so well,' Honor said politely.

'I don't and you know it,' Maureen said, lighting a cigarette. 'But it was that or juggle.'

Honor was still puzzling out what exactly she meant, when Duff came over and put his hand on Maureen's shoulder. 'Thank you,' he said. Maureen leaned her cheek sideways so it rested against his hand.

'No need to thank me,' she said, looking up at him. Maureen, who insisted on being thanked for the smallest kindness. And to Honor's astonishment, she turned her head and kissed the back of his hand where her cheek had been. Her eyes were strangely bright, and Honor, if she hadn't known better, might have said she was crying.

*

Later, in her bedroom, where Doris was brushing her hair, a tap at the door. Brigid. 'Can I come in, or are you telling secrets?' she asked, putting her head round.

'Come on.'

'What a horrid evening.' Brigid sat on the bed, tucking her feet under her and leaning back against the end-board. She wore striped flannel pyjamas and had a mug of something hot so that steam rose around her face, making it glow pinkish. She looked, Honor thought, about twelve.

'Horrid,' Honor agreed. 'What are you drinking?'

'Cocoa. Minnie insisted on making it for me. I said I didn't want it, and then, when she brought it, I realised it was exactly what I wanted.'

'Clever Minnie.'

'So,' Brigid asked, looking first at one then the other, 'what was that all about? Chips was like a madman. Poor Fritzi. It was like watching a hare chased by hounds. Every way he turned, Chips was there before him, shouting about emperors.' She laughed a little.

'You mind that he should be hounded?' Honor asked.

'I felt sorry for him, that's all.'

It was, Honor thought, looking at her sister, the truth. Mostly the truth, anyway. 'I doubt it was anything much,' she said. 'Just Chips being, well, himself.'

'Rather *more* than himself, I thought,' Brigid said. 'Like one of Cook's concentrated sauces. Boiled right down and all the more intense for it. What was he complaining about before dinner, anyway?' she asked then. 'In here? I heard him as I passed by.'

'He thinks it's my fault that Paul is throwing tantrums and cheeking the tutor.'

'And the nanny,' Brigid added. 'He cheeks her too. I've heard him. Adorable child,' she hastened to say, 'but terribly bold.'

'Yes, I suppose so. And now Chips.'

'Oh dear.'

'Yes. Chips has decided it's because I'm not with him enough. Although I don't at all see what I could do, when Chips is the only person Paul pays attention to. I don't see how my being more with him would make any difference.' She looked at them both, desperate for agreement.

'I think perhaps children are like puppies,' Brigid said. 'Look at Pugsy, who is only ever with Maureen; how disagreeable and snappy he is. I feel sure that if he were with, say, Kick, he would be quite different. Outdoorsy and jolly.'

'How clever you are, Biddy.' Doris gave her a quick smile.

'You may be right,' Honor said sadly. 'But even if you are, it won't change anything.'

'Will it really not?' Doris asked her gently.

'No. I can't let it. I have made up my mind that I must go.'

'Go where?' Brigid said.

'Anywhere. Anywhere that Chips is not.'

'I see.'

'And if that means leaving Paul also, then it is wise not to get too fond of him.'

Neither Doris nor Brigid said anything. Brigid stared at her mug of cocoa, now empty, as though afraid to look up and meet Honor's eyes. Doris was silent too, but she held Honor's gaze in the looking-glass and after a moment said, 'Shall I see if Molly will bring you up cocoa too?'

'That would be nice,' Honor said. 'Biddy, you should go to your room. Doris, will you stay a while?'

'I must get back to my room too,' Doris said.

She spoke evasively, so that Honor, as soon as Brigid had gone, asked, 'Surely you aren't going to the stables? It isn't safe.'

'It's safe enough. Anyway, it's what we decided. In the telephone call. I need to, Honor. Will you be sure to let me back in?'

'Of course. I was unlikely to sleep anyway, and even less likely now. But I can't like this, Doris. You are shooting completely in the dark.'

'I am, rather,' Doris agreed. 'I don't much like it either. But perhaps tonight I will learn more . . . In any case, it's what we decided,' she repeated. 'What they decided.'

Chapter Fifty-Two

Doris

At breakfast the ambassador announced, with a great show of regret, that he '. . . must leave. Urgent business requires me in London,' he said, eyes gleaming behind his glasses.

'I'm sorry to hear it,' Doris said. Honor had been right, she thought.

'You'll stay for lunch?' Chips asked hopefully.

'I'm afraid I can't.' The flat 'a' was more pronounced than usual. He sounded, she thought, thoroughly American.

'But Mrs Ambassador and Kathleen will stay a little longer? A few more days?'

'We must all go.' Kennedy was firm in the face of Chips' pleas, and finally, Chips had to settle for a promise of a night in London soon: 'Theatre and a late supper,' he said, already starting to plan.

The weather had broken without fanfare and the day was grey and drizzly. Doris retreated to the library after breakfast, hoping to see no one until Honor came down. She sat in the corner with the best light and started a piece about the failure of Lord Runciman's mission to Czechoslovakia, but didn't get on well with it. She thought of Albert, late at night, his face half-visible in the light of a thin candle. The stable block had no electricity yet. She thought of all her carefully artless questions – what did he think of England? Did he miss Germany? – and the blandness of his answers that suggested a dull mind. Or deliberate dissembling. Which was it? How he had asked his own questions – equally artless – and the studied dullness of her answers.

She almost laughed: two people, so very careful in their carelessness. It had been a relief when dawn had arrived. It was a relief now when Kick came in.

'Am I interrupting?' the girl said, standing half in, half out of the doorway.

'Not if you make up your mind to come in or go out,' Doris said with a smile.

'Well, I'll come in then,' Kick said. 'If that's OK?'

'Are you pleased to be going back to London?'

'Yes.' Kick sat on the arm of a chair, swinging her bare legs. She wore a green summer dress and a white cardigan. Her legs were brown and freckled and strong. 'It's been an interesting visit, that's for sure.'

'*Interesting*? That bad?' Doris asked with a smile.

'I learned some things,' Kick said. 'And no, they weren't terribly nice.'

'What things?'

'That my father will always do what suits him, even when he knows it will be hard on us. But I suppose I knew that already.

And that being Catholic here is different to what it is back in America.'

'How?'

'There are the ones, like Diana and Mosley, who behave as though being Catholic is like a game, kind of silly really. And then there are the ones like Billy's parents, who behave as if it's a secret society and not a very nice one. As though there is something dark and a little bit . . . unsavoury about us. I just don't know why it's such a big deal here. But it's pretty rough weather, being despised for something that isn't anything you've done, but only what you *are*.'

'It is,' Doris agreed. 'Hard, but not at all unusual.'

'You know, I said that very same thing, almost anyway, to Brigid, and she looked embarrassed, said *No one could despise you, darling*, and changed the subject,' Kick said, swinging her legs harder.

Doris laughed. 'That sounds like Biddy alright. Don't be cross; she doesn't mean anything except that she doesn't know what to say, because she can't really imagine what you're talking about. With the Guinnesses, it goes the other way, you know. They are admired, not always for what they do, but for what they are. Do you want to tell me more?'

'Somehow, I feel that I do,' Kick said. 'You were the only one to stick up for us, when all that awful mess happened, with Duff . . .' She moved her legs around and allowed herself to fall into the armchair. 'I wish you'd been there when Billy's parents visited. Maybe *Moucher*' – she said the name with heavy inflection – 'wouldn't have looked at me as though I were something strange and unpleasant. A train running late. How is it you know what to say?'

'I know this story. I've heard it before. I've watched it and listened to it. And been part of it.'

'You?' Kick asked, astonished. 'But *everyone* is in love with you.' She sounded wistful.

Doris smiled. 'Not a bit of it, they aren't, although some might pretend or even believe it for a little while. But yes, me.'

'How? Why? You're not Catholic. Are you?' she asked hopefully.

'No. Jewish.'

'I see.' By the long pause that followed Doris thought that, yes, she did see.

'And so I know all about the prejudices of this lot.' She gave an unhappy smile. 'Only I refuse to take them to heart.'

'Hard not to.'

'Not hard at all,' Doris insisted. 'I no more listen to their views than I wear the same clothes, eat the same food, go to the same half-dozen places as they do. Easiest thing in the world.' She laughed. 'Imagine if everyone thought like Chips? Like Billy's mother, charming though she is? Like his pleasant but impossible father? Even like your own mother? Think your own things, Kick. Whatever they are, make them your own.'

The girl looked struck. 'I see what you mean . . .' she began.

'Which reminds me,' Doris said, 'Diana and Mosley?'

'What about them?'

'I didn't realise you knew them. Or certainly not so well.'

'I don't. I mean, I've been to dinner, once, with Debo. But when they arrived yesterday and Diana was so very friendly, well, I wasn't expecting it.' Doris looked at her a moment. Kick was flushed. 'Honestly, without Debo there, I didn't know *what* to say to her.'

Doris laughed. 'You know,' she said, 'I always forget with Diana, and even Mosley, that underneath all that charm, really they are no different to the rough men I see on every street corner in Berlin; who shout and break things and shove people, protected behind the Nazi armbands they wear. It takes me a while to remember that, when I meet them again. But I think you are cleverer than I am. Certainly clever enough to see beyond the charm. And to understand that when someone wants something, how careful they are to appear terribly friendly.'

'Terribly friendly, and really quite frightening,' Kick admitted.

'More frightening than you know.' Doris took up a piece of embroidery that lay on the table beside her and, turning it over, examined the knots and stitches that made up the hidden side. 'Look how different they are,' she said, showing Kick first one side and then the other.

'I guess I see what you mean,' Kick said.

'If one dislikes prejudice – as I see you do – it's terribly important to dislike it in all guises,' Doris said. 'Otherwise one is a hypocrite.'

'I'm not that,' Kick said stoutly.

'No, I was certain you were not.'

'Mosley is like Pa. He wants to avoid a war . . .' Almost, it was a question.

'I have seen things that are no different to war,' Doris said. 'As cruel and ugly and stupid. Only as it is, there is no force to oppose them. In a war, there would be two sides. There would be a fight. Right now, there is only one side and the things happen without a fight. Without resistance.'

They sat in silence then and Doris picked at a loose thread, a piece of yellow silk that had come unravelled. She tied a careful knot in it.

'I think if Diana asks me again, I will say no. To dinner,' Kick said.

'I think the ambassador might thank you if you did.'

'Wasn't he brilliant?' Kick said with a laugh.

'I've never seen anyone evade so successfully.' Then, after a while, 'Was anyone else at the dinner?'

'Unity.' Doris made a face. 'Debo, of course. A man called David.'

'David Envers?'

'Yes, that was it. He barely said a thing.'

'I see. Did he—' and then she broke off. 'Never mind.' There was no point asking more. No point asking what she most wanted to know – did Envers talk about her? Ask after her? The answer belonged in a past she dared not dwell on.

'Would you rather I didn't say anything, even to Pa?' Kick said then, getting up and stretching her arms high above her head.

'I would. The Jewish side of my family is a secret, for now. I've had some long talks with your father about Germany and what's happening there. I hoped to persuade him to take a different view although I'm not sure I've succeeded.'

'Hard to, when Pa has made up his mind about something,' Kick said sympathetically. 'They think he's a coward. Billy and Andrew and Hugo. I've heard them say it. But it's not that. He really, truly believes war is terrible and must always be avoided, whatever the cost.'

'Whereas your young men, like all young men, believe shame is worse than war?'

'I guess they do.' She looked gloomy. 'What do you believe?'

'Does it matter?' Doris said. 'Does it ever matter what women think about war? Does it much matter what anyone thinks at this stage?' From overhead came a thump, then the sound of a door slamming. 'The house awakes,' she said. 'We'd better get on.'

'Will you go back to Berlin?'

'I will. For a while anyway. Now, go and pack. I heard your father say they have ordered the motorcar for twelve.' She twisted her wrist to look at the tiny gold watch. 'That gives you half an hour.'

Outside the library, the house was full of comings and goings. A second door slammed and there was the sound of running feet on the back stairs. Doris decided she'd go outside. But she was too late.

'Doris, might I have a word?' Chips bustled up. He was clearly bursting with news of some kind.

'If you must.'

He gave her a beady stare. 'Fritzi's man, Albert, has disappeared.'

'People don't disappear.'

'He can't be found. He didn't wake Fritzi this morning – the dear boy almost missed breakfast; I had to send my chap to shave him – and no one has been able to find him. He is certainly not in the house or anywhere in the grounds.'

'I see.'

'I wondered whether you might know anything?'

'Anything about what?'

'About Albert.'

'Why would I know anything about Albert?'

'So you don't?'

'I don't.' It was as though she had taken a wrapped present away from a child, she thought, seeing how disappointed he was. 'I'm sure he will turn up.'

'Fritzi is insisting we search the river banks. He says it is impossible that Albert should be gone anywhere for so long unless there is mischief involved.'

'And will you?'

'I suppose I must. It's very awkward. I had just made up my mind to go to London. I have had a phonecall. My new car is ready.' He beamed at her. 'A Rolls, in deepest emerald green. *Nero* green, I call it.' His face softened. 'It is the loveliest and most expensive car in the world, and now that I know it is arrived, I must see it.'

Doris ducked her face so that he wouldn't see her laughing. 'You'll excuse me. I'm going to find Honor.'

'She is still in her room,' Chips said. 'And not at all in good form.' He sounded cross again. 'The ambassador is looking for you,' he said then. 'I wonder why?' He looked beadily at her.

'No idea.' Perhaps she would go to her own bedroom, Doris thought. At least there, no one would bother her. In the upstairs hallway she bumped into Duff.

'This house is starting to be like *Mrs Tittlemouse*,' Doris said with a laugh. 'Unexpected appearances at every turn.'

Duff ignored her reference. 'I believe we're a man down,' he said abruptly.

'Albert?'

'Yes.'

'Fritzi is apparently distraught. And uncomprehending. Insisting Chips have the river searched . . .'

'Is he indeed? And you, what do you think?'

'I?' She opened her eyes every wide. 'I do not think anything.'

'Do you not?' He stared at her and Doris did her best to return his gaze. 'Well, I'll tell you what I think. I think Chips shouting about Fritzi's destiny – how he must watch the Nazis and bide his time; how there will be a wave of useful sentiment when his grandfather dies – I think those were stupid things to say, and dangerous.'

'Indeed. You said as much.'

'I was right.'

'So, which one proved dangerous, the Nazis or the grand-father?'

'I don't know. But something has made the fellow bolt. And the bolting troubles me. I don't suppose you know anything?' He watched Doris, who stayed silent. 'Nothing you can say . . . Well, I must go and persuade Maureen to get up.'

'You leave today as well?'

'God, yes. Nothing to stay for now.'

'Fritzi?'

'No longer of importance. Things have changed.'

'Things change fast.'

'They do.' He shrugged. 'It's a time of change. Surely you will leave too? Even your plans must be put out.'

'I don't have plans,' she said. 'Although I do think a little shopping in London . . .'

He looked at her for a moment and then – a gesture so unex-pected she nearly twitched – reached a hand out and squeezed hers. 'Good for you,' he said. 'Now, I must find my wife.'

In her room Doris poured a glass of water and took it to the chair beside the window. Outside, the garden was empty, shades of grey folding into dull green in a way that was blurred and fuzzy and terribly English. Even the flowers were subdued, heads languishing as though they couldn't, on such a day, be bothered. The sun appeared in fits and starts as a bright dot, layered with mist as though veiled for church. She would miss this, when she went back to Berlin as she must. Just this – this quiet, soft, damp greyness that was so very much home.

Was Duff right? she wondered. Had Albert run off? Taken his tales of disloyalty to whoever it was he spied for – the kaiser? The Nazis? Even her own side? It was certainly possible. And if so, what did that mean? But she couldn't work it out, because it meant something different each time, depending on where – to whom – he had gone. She didn't know what she needed to know, to decide. And so she must simply carry on with her own plans although these were half at least in darkness.

Duff didn't know about the phonecall she'd made yesterday. Not that he would have been surprised, she realised. Had that conversation, she wondered, short and discreet though it had been, had anything to do with Albert's disappearance? Did it mean that he had not gone, but been taken away? People were, she knew. It was never talked about, but it happened.

No one ever said anything much – certainly, no one said the word torture. They said 'questioned', or 'interrogated'. The impression – wilfully given – was of a crisp verbal exchange. But Doris had heard stories. Of the Gestapo who came, not at night but by day, loud and large, breaking doors, bundling men and women into the backs of lorries. But stories about their own side too. These were only ever whispers, hints – never confirmed. They might have been nothing. But there were enough of them that they might have been something.

Had what she had said – sparse reports of Honor's suspicions, what Elizabeth had seen – set such a thing in motion? She couldn't ask – they wouldn't tell her: '*The less you know . . .*' Only then did it occur to wonder why, exactly, the less she knew . . . What exactly was it they feared? That she would talk? Surely they knew she would not. That she might be made to talk? She put the thought from her.

In any case, there was nothing to suggest that Albert's going was anything to do with her. And if it was – what then? She searched her mind like a person methodically looking for a letter or document that might be in a desk, going through each drawer carefully and quickly. What she looked for was regret at the part she might have played. She could find nothing. Not even any real sense of Albert. He was a pair of brown eyes, a voice in the dark, short answers to simple questions, the glowing end of a cigarette in the half-light of early morning. No, it wasn't his face she saw when she went looking, but Hannah's. Always Hannah's.

'Can I have a minute?' It was the ambassador.

'Of course. Come in.'

He came in, but left the door open behind him. 'The story you wanted to tell me . . .'

'What story?'

'A girl, her family? I wouldn't listen. But now . . .'

'You'll listen?'

'Yes. Be brief, but I'll listen.' And she told him. Hannah's name, everything she could remember about the family. 'I never heard another word,' she finished. 'If I could only know what happened to them . . .'

'Let me see. I promise nothing, you understand.' Then, already half out of the room, 'Thank you for taking such trouble with my daughter. She's at an age where she is very impressed by beautiful women. I'd rather she listened to you than Diana Mosley.'

Chapter Fifty-Three

Doris

Honor was next. 'Doris, darling, you will leave with us?' she asked. 'Everyone is going. The visit is quite spoiled. Chips is determined to take delivery of his new motorcar and leaves after lunch. Elizabeth, as soon as she heard he was going, announced that she was too bored for words and would go too. Even Brigid has remembered a party she promised to attend with Lady Iveagh.'

'What about Albert? Is Chips really searching the river?'

'I rather thought you might know . . .'

'Not a thing.' Then in response to Honor's silence, 'Truly, nothing. I left at dawn and he was perfectly alright then.'

'Well, it seems there are enough of his things missing – his shaving brush and razor, cufflinks Fritzi had given him – that it seems likely he has gone, rather than that an accident has befallen him. So Fritzi says he will go back to Cambridge, and that perhaps Albert will arrive there. Keeps saying, *He is not a servant, he is free to come and go*, but not at all as though he believes it.'

'And you don't think we should wait and see . . .?'

'See what? He's not a *friend*, Doris. Just a sort of companion. Whatever Fritzi may say. Whatever you might say.'

'*I?* I say nothing.'

'Perhaps he is the type who needs to let off steam from time to time,' Honor said. 'The way young men do . . . Honestly, darling, I don't care at all about Albert.' She came closer. 'But I fear this means something bad for you. You don't know what he knows about you, or suspects of you, and who he might say it to. That's also why I want to go to London. So you can meet whoever it is you meet, and tell them. But you shouldn't go back to Berlin, Doris. I'm certain about that.'

'We'll see,' Doris said. 'If I must, I must. And anyway, I must go and collect the rest of my things. And Hannah's violin. I cannot leave that.' Then, 'Last night . . . have you really made up your mind? About leaving Chips?'

'I have, although I won't do it straight away.' Honor was silent for a minute. She looked out at the misty grey garden. 'You'd never think that only yesterday we were huddled in the shade, complaining at how hot it was. How quickly and thoroughly yesterday is scrubbed away.'

'What changed your mind?'

'Who, actually; not what. Rose.'

'Rose?'

'Yes, by being all dutiful and patiently wifely . . .' She laughed. 'Nothing could have shown me what I do not want more clearly than that. But also Maureen. Looking at her last night, with

Duff. The way she played the piano because he asked her, when Maureen hates to do anything she doesn't do well and won't ever do anything anyone asks, unless she makes them beg. And yet she got up and did it without any fuss at all. They argue so viciously that it's terrifying. And yet, when they make up . . . There is something rather splendid about it. I think I should have a chance to know what that's like.'

From downstairs they heard the sound of Chips talking to Andrews: '. . . I will go up after lunch, you may follow with the luggage later.' He was excited, his voice loud and busy. Doris leaned a little closer in to Honor and said, '*Nero green*,' in a whisper. Which made them both laugh so hard it was another minute before Honor said, 'I suppose I'd better start to pack.'

Crossing to her room, Doris met Maureen. She was humming under her breath, the Bach concerto she had played the night before.

'You look pleased,' Doris said.

'Oh, I am,' Maureen assured her. 'What a jolly few days it has been.'

'Has it? I'm not sure anyone else agrees.'

'Duff does.' She smiled lazily. 'Now, anyway. And I don't need anyone else to agree.'

Chips came along the hallway towards them. 'There is something missing from the drawing room,' he said irritably as he bustled past. 'A glass stork. Murano. Rather valuable. Andrews has just told me. He thinks it was the maid, but I am certain Elizabeth has taken it. I shall have to confront her, otherwise Andrews will certainly sack that girl.' He was moving on when Maureen, having stared at his back for a long moment, called after him.

'You might as well know, I broke that stork. So you needn't go confronting or sacking anyone.'

'You?' Chips stopped and turned. 'Why didn't you say anything?'

'I'm saying it now, am I not? Frightfully silly little thing anyway, with those long blue legs. Just waiting to be broken.' And she carried on down the hallway, still humming Bach.

Doris shut the door behind her. She hadn't touched a thing but already her room looked different. Withdrawn. She began piling clothes neatly into her case. It didn't take her long.

She looked out the window. The Kennedys' motorcar – long and low – had been brought around and Rose and Kick stood beside it. Kick wore the same jersey and skirt she'd had on that morning, but Rose had changed into a pink linen suit. Duff lounged in the doorway, smoking. As Doris watched, he dropped his cigarette onto the gravel, ground it out with the toe of his shoe and crossed to the Kennedys. He shook hands solemnly with both, saying something to Rose that made her smile. Behind him, one of the footmen bent and picked up his cigarette butt.

Fritzi stood to the left of the front door, alone. Undecided. He started to make a move towards the Kennedys but stopped when he saw Duff reach them. He hovered, his indecision plain to Doris watching from the window. The ambassador and Chips came out then, and together they walked past him. Chips' hands were moving excitably and Doris was certain that, should she pull up the window, she would hear the words '. . . *new Rolls* . . .'

Fritzi made as though to follow them but again he stopped. Stayed where he was, ignored by the group around the motorcar. What was it Duff had said? *Things have changed* . . .

Brigid came around the side of the house then with a basket of cut flowers. She looked at the Kennedys but went to Fritzi and took hold of his arm, giving it a little shake. She said something to him that made him laugh. He took the basket from her and brought it towards the front door while she went to say goodbye to the Kennedys. He moved more easily now. With relief, Doris thought. The relief of someone who has been given something to do.

One Year Later

1939

Chapter Fifty-Four

London, September
Kick

Kick had begged every way she knew how. She had pleaded how much she wanted to stay; how useful she would be – all the things she could do for her father once Rose was gone; how she could keep Rosemary company, because Rosie, it seemed, was to stay. But the ambassador was adamant. She was to go home, sail on the *Washington* with her mother and siblings. Jack was here to escort them home.

'Why does Rosie get to stay?' Kick demanded.

'Rosemary is settled here. It wouldn't be good to move her,' was the evasive answer.

'I am settled here too,' she protested.

'You are more adaptable,' her mother said crisply. She didn't say *It doesn't matter where Rosemary goes* but Kick felt it.

'But why can't we both stay? We can be company for one another,' Kick begged. 'I can't go now. Think how bad it will look, when Brigid and Debo are learning to drive ambulances and make themselves useful, for us all to run, as though we are afraid.'

'It doesn't matter. You're not English, Kathleen, may I remind you. You are American. What happens here, now, is none of your business. England is at war, America is not. It doesn't matter what people here think of you. It's time for you to go home.'

'But Pa is American too, and is not going home,' she said.

'I will be,' her father said shortly. 'Now that it's war, there's nothing for me to stay for.'

Still Kick couldn't reckon with the word 'war'. She had heard it for so long, out there, part of every conversation, but no more substantial than the weather. *Will it rain and must I bring a coat? Will it be war and must I go back to America?* Each as insubstantial as the other. Because sometimes it didn't rain, even when you had a coat. And so many times, it hadn't been war, even when they were told for sure it would be.

But now it was.

And suddenly all the new rules were overthrown. The way her parents had learned to listen to her and consult her about what she did was finished. Now, she was no more than Pat or Eunice, to be sent where they decided. The views she heard when out with friends that she had passed along to her father, these mattered no longer. The rush to enlist, to learn bandage-folding and basic nursing duties, the ambassador didn't care to hear about them. And when Kick complained that she felt left out, all he said was, 'It's not our war.'

*

'At least you tried,' Brigid said later, when they sat in Kick's bedroom, with the gramophone playing softly; Glenn Miller, 'Wishing (Will Make It So)'. She lit a cigarette, breathed in deeply and coughed.

'Smoking?' Kick asked.

'Trying. It seems the thing, no? Now that I have a *job*.' She wore the slightly baggy green dress and burgundy cardigan of the Women's Voluntary Service with as much pride as she had ever worn Schiaparelli, Kick saw.

'Don't,' Kick begged. 'It's so unfair.'

'Well, it's foul,' Brigid said, dropping the cigarette onto a saucer. 'I cannot make any headway with it.'

'Not the smoking, silly, the job. I'm so very jealous.'

'Jolly hard work,' Brigid insisted cheerfully. 'Yesterday we lugged old saucepans and ladles about for hours, great piles of them, all to be melted down. Mamma was frantic that we didn't have more to give. Silver isn't much use, they say. Then Papa pointed out that we've already had all the iron railings taken up around Grosvenor Place and Elveden, and even the great iron knocker from the front door, and perhaps that would do for now.'

'Here too,' Kick said, looking out the window. 'It's like an obstacle course out there.' The railings outside Prince's Gate and all around Hyde Park had been torn up and out so that only deep holes remained. It looked, she thought, as though some angry, careless creature had lost something, and dug all over in a frantic effort to find it. Without railings, the streets and green spaces seemed to bleed into each other. Trenches had been dug across the entrance to the park, deep scars of brown in the soft green; graves, open and waiting. And the very same people who, only a year ago, had scolded Teddy and Bobby for trampling the grass or knocking a flower had watched without comment, except to say, 'They won't be driving any tanks through here,' with quiet satisfaction.

'Somehow, one doesn't think war will be so *practical*,' Brigid said thoughtfully. 'Everyone talks of sacrifice and duty, but in the end it's miles and miles of bandages to roll and jumpers to knit and pots of tea to make and pour.'

'How I wish I could stay, and roll and knit and pour with you,' Kick said. She lay back on her bed, arms behind her head. 'How sickening it is to leave now. To run away.' She looked sideways at Brigid. 'I guess our friends think I'm the worst sort of coward?'

'No one thinks that, darling,' Brigid said vaguely. 'We know you'd stay and help if you could.'

'I still hope to persuade Pa. The *Washington* doesn't sail for a week yet.' She sat up, suddenly energetic. 'Why, anything can happen in a week.'

'Anything,' Brigid agreed. Then, 'What of Billy?'

'Joined his regiment weeks ago. The Coldstream Guards.' Kick knew she sounded proud and tried to be nonchalant. 'Andrew too. And Chatsworth is to be a boarding school for girls.'

'I see,' Brigid said slyly. 'And what does your mother have to say about all that?'

'Doesn't know. Or not much.' Rose may not have known, Kick thought, but that didn't mean she didn't have a sense. Or something. She had asked Kick to stop seeing Billy, to give up all thought of him, and Kick had said she would. It was the first time she had deliberately lied to her mother. Because of that, she no longer found any comfort when they prayed together, and maybe her mother sensed it, because bit by bit, they began to pray alone. 'Have you said your prayers, Kathleen?' Rose would ask, but she no longer suggested Kick come to her bedroom and say them with her. It was the opening of a gap that could only get wider. Kick knew it. But she didn't know how to stop it.

'Did you really leave the south of France in your tennis clothes?' Brigid asked.

'We did.' Kick laughed. 'There I was, about to win a set, and the message came from Mother that Hitler was invading Poland, and me and Eunice were to leave at once – that very minute! – and our things would follow.'

'How exciting,' Brigid spoke enthusiastically.

'It was. I suppose. But you know, it was . . . well, it was sad too. Mother said something about who knew when we would be back on French soil, and what it would look like by then, and suddenly I sort of thought a great deal more about what war might actually mean . . .'

'Yes,' Brigid said. 'In all the talk of what must be done, one rather forgets all the things one *can't*, any longer, do.'

'You know Jack and Joe were in Germany just two weeks ago? How strange it seems now . . .' Kick trailed off, then reached over to stub out Brigid's cigarette, which was still smoking in the saucer. 'They saw Unity. Jack thought she was about the strangest person he's met. Said she was the most fervent Nazi he ever encountered, and quite in love with Hitler.'

'Poor Unity.' Brigid got up and walked to the window. She pulled herself up onto the rather high window seat, and sat with her legs tucked under her, looking out to the street below. 'What does Debo say?' She opened the window a crack. The air smelt cold and fresh, of apples and wood fires, in contrast with the heat of the bedroom and its clinging hint of perfume.

'That only Unity could take a bullet to the brain and survive.

That she will outlive them all. You know Debo.' Kick shrugged a little. 'And underneath she is terribly sad and sorry and rather mortified, only she won't ever say it. Even insists that it's a good thing Unity pulled the trigger herself, because of how she's a terrible shot, and if someone else had done it – and they most surely would – they wouldn't have missed and she'd be dead by now.'

'Which is exactly what everyone else wishes had happened,' Brigid said bluntly, turning back towards Kick. 'Then they would be able to commiserate decently with Lord and Lady Redesdale, and forget all about it. This way, no one knows what to say and it's terribly awkward. Chips is simply furious. Says it's *So like Unity, who always was impossible.*'

Kick laughed. 'How like Chips.' Then shuddered. 'Can you imagine? She is in hospital in Munich, and they say the bullet cannot be got out. That to remove it would be more dangerous than to leave it where it is.'

'*The iron has entered her soul,*' Brigid quoted. 'Except that, being Unity, it's her brain, not her soul . . . Chips is helping to get her out, although she cannot be moved yet. Says Hitler is being frightfully decent and visiting her.'

Kick made a face. 'How is Chips?'

'He'll be here any minute so you can see for yourself. You'll notice a change.' Brigid laughed. 'All of a sudden he's terribly patriotic, but also still insisting that Hitler is badly advised and will soon come to his senses.'

'And Honor?'

'Worried that she hasn't heard from Doris and pestering Andrews to see if there has been any post or any phonecalls. It seems there is a girl called Hannah arriving tomorrow. Someone Doris knows from Berlin. Doris arranged it. Actually, I think your father has something to do with it, only I don't know what . . . Anyway, Doris made the plans, and the hope is that the girl's parents will follow later. But now Honor has heard that Hannah travels alone – Michaels is to meet her at Euston station – not with Doris, and she can't get Doris on the telephone, and she's fretting. There is never anyone in when she telephones to the flat in Berlin, and now so many days have gone by without hearing that she is in rather a state . . .'

Teddy tapped at the door and put his head around to say, 'Mother says you're to come down.' He was wearing a hat with paper stuck along the sides to make it round, like the Home Guard.

'Alright. And don't let Mother see you wearing that hat.' And to Brigid, 'She thinks we are all far too English.' Then, 'Come out with us tonight? Jack is here. He sails home with us on the *Washington* next week and tonight he's taking me to the Café de Paris.'

'Who else will be there?'

'Billy has leave.'

'I rather thought he might,' Brigid said slyly.

'He's dining with his parents, but says he'll meet us later. He and Jack get on real well, you know,' with one of her brightest smiles. 'Jack's thesis for Harvard is *England's Foreign Policy Since 1931*. Billy is helping him a whole lot.' And she sang along with Glenn Miller's band, about *wishing long enough then wishing will make it so* . . .

'I told him Jack thought as he did, not like Pa,' she continued then, 'when we were at Kelvedon, but I don't think he believed me. Not until he met Jack. That changed everything.' She spoke with satisfaction. 'They met at the Mountbattens when we went to lunch there, and had such a long talk. And the very next day, just as I had given up thinking he ever would, Billy asked me out. Only to the pictures, but still . . .'

'Do you not think that when you go back to America all this will fade?' Brigid asked as she climbed down, gesturing around the room and out towards the street outside.

'How do you mean?'

'Well, you know. When you're not here anymore, it – we – will all start to dwindle and recede and seem like a funny little dream you had? Everything in America is so much bigger and shinier and louder. Even your fridge.' Brigid laughed.

'Never,' Kick declared. 'Mother thinks my real life is back in America, but I know it's not. It's right here. Now, come on.'

That evening, she and Jack made their way to the Café de Paris through streets that were completely, carefully dark. Blackouts had begun. They walked, even though it was more than half an hour, because Jack said he wanted to. 'Can't you feel how eerie it is?' he said excitedly, as they made their slow way through Hyde Park, stepping around the slashed ground, then along Piccadilly, where the occasional car with black paint over its headlamps moved slowly past them, as though feeling its way into the night.

'Don't,' Kick said.

'Don't what?'

'Don't forget it's real, that's what. I know it's easy to. To get all caught up like Teddy is in make-believe, because we will be going away. But don't forget that after we are gone, our friends will all still be here.'

'I'm not seven, Kick.' He put his arm around her. Around them, Kick could hear the tap-tapping of umbrellas and canes as people felt their way along from darkened lamppost to darkened lamppost. Jack seemed to know his way by instinct, leading them surely in and out of barriers and blockages. 'I don't forget that. And I know it's just terrible.' He gave her shoulders a squeeze. 'But how much more terrible would it be if there was no war? If they didn't fight? If they just rolled over again and again?'

'You've been talking to Billy again. Don't let Pa hear you.'

The lighted sign had been switched off above the Café de Paris and the curtains drawn tight across the inside so that they nearly walked right past it. Only at the last minute did Kick say, 'Oh, we're here.' And then, for a moment, she wondered did she even want to go in. How dark it looked; how lonely, this place that had always streamed light and laughter.

But once inside and down the double staircase that circled the dancefloor and bar like a pair of friendly arms sleeved in red velvet, it was as gay as ever. Every table was full, the bar was thick with people and the dancefloor filled with couples. Jack found them a table and they sat close together. Kick nodded and waved to anyone she knew, and Jack pointed out any girls he thought especially pretty. There was no sign of Billy yet.

'Why is Pa in trouble?' she asked after a while. 'I see the papers say pretty terrible things about him. Is it because he's sending us all home?'

'Partly that. And partly because he said that democracies and dictatorships have to learn to live together in the same world, whether anyone likes it or not. And that this isn't a cause for war.'

'It's no more than he said in the garden at Kelvedon last summer.'

'But now he has said it publicly, and everyone is angry. The English are angry, Roosevelt is angry. I guess he'll be recalled soon enough, only it suits Roosevelt to leave him where he is for now. Pa in disgrace is a fine thing for Roosevelt.'

'How so?'

'There'll be no bid for the presidency now.'

'The what?'

'The presidency. Come on, Kick, surely you knew that's what his plan was?' He looked amused.

'I hadn't an idea in the world.'

They danced, then Jack went to dance with a girl Kick knew while she sat and watched. 'Perhaps he's not coming,' she said when Jack came back.

'He'll come,' Jack said. He didn't need to ask who.

'I don't know why he likes me,' she said then.

'I do.' Jack took her hand and squeezed it. 'I've met enough English girls by now to see exactly why. They might be pretty – some are very beautiful, like that blonde girl over there – but they're dull. You're so different to them, you're like a swan among ducklings.'

'I thought I might be the exact opposite,' Kick said. 'A duckling, invisible among swans.'

'Never.'

'How nice you are, Jack.'

'And how right. Look.' He nudged her. Sure enough, there was Billy, tall and thin and elegant in his green-grey uniform, coming down the stairs. He had seen them and made straight for their table, despite the hands and voices that reached to detain him.

'I say, frightfully sorry. Dinner took longer than expected.' He asked Kick to dance, and she said yes, and saw Jack make his way over to the blonde girl.

On the dancefloor, pushed close together by the couples around them, Billy apologised again. 'I had to have rather a long talk with my parents,' he explained.

'About the boarding school?' Kick asked.

'The what—? Oh, no. About you, if you must know.'

'Why me?' Her heart began to thump, like it had forgotten how to beat properly. She wondered could he feel it through the scratchy khaki of his jacket.

'I said I was coming on to meet you, and they had rather a lot of questions. Why, and what did I mean by it; that sort of thing. They weren't terribly thrilled with that rot you wrote for the Catholic Women's League about the new pope,' – he grinned – '*the pale and wan figure who lifts his hand in the sign of the Cross.* I rather thought my poor father might choke when he read that. Especially given that it was Cardinal Pacelli, who was turning into Pope . . .'

'Pius XII,' Kick supplied.

'Yes, him. And everyone knows he's an old friend.'

'An acquaintance. And now pope, so . . . Anyway, I did think about it,' Kick admitted. 'But then I thought, I can't be more like what they want me to be, because I don't even know what that is. I can just be myself.' She stumbled as a couple, moving faster than the rather melancholy tempo of the song the West Indian orchestra were playing, bumped her. 'Which may not be at all what they like, but it's the best I can do.'

'In any case, I told them it didn't matter.' He spoke as though she hadn't. 'That I was jolly well going to keep seeing you.'

'Oh, Billy, did you really?' Kick knew her father would leave – either because Roosevelt recalled him, or because he couldn't bear his post any longer – and that her mother would be pleased. That Prince's Gate would be packed up. And maybe she would have to sail on the *Washington* next week, because they would make her. But she also knew – knew as surely as she knew how to find C on a piano, or the right way to throw a football – that she would come back.

America, no matter how hard she called it to mind, had little reality for her now. In her memory, it was pale and candy-coloured and shallow. It was all surface and reflection, it didn't have the deeper layers that England did. That way of getting inside her – the way that everything, from the smell of soot and sodden wool in London, to the sound of trees, the wind through old walls in the countryside – sat deeper within her than anything else ever had. It was Billy, of course it was. But it wasn't just Billy. It was a recognition, a rightness, to here and herself here, that she couldn't give up.

She'd go – she'd have to – to America, land of soda fountains and pool parties and college football games. But she'd be back. That was the important thing. *Somehow I will come back*, she told herself. *I don't know how, but I will. This is where I'm going to grow old and die, I swear it.*

'Tell me exactly what you said to them,' she said to Billy, turning her face up to his so that he could kiss her if he wanted to.

Chapter Fifty-Five

Brigid

On the other side of Green Park, that lay so dark it was like a blob of black ink, Brigid sat in the armchair beside her bed and tried to read. But mostly she listened to the silence. Her mother was at a Women's Institute meeting, planning the evacuation of children from London. Her father was at the House. It was where he always was, these days. Without them, there was no life to Grosvenor Place. The usual discreet clatter of servants was no more. So many had left already, busy with the greater urgency of factory production lines. It was like being on a ship, she thought. An abandoned one.

She went again to check the bedroom that had been prepared for Hannah on Doris' instructions. To make sure it had everything a twelve-year-old girl would need. She checked the clothes hanging in the cupboard, a neat row of dresses, jerseys and skirts. Then the books she had gathered from her own bedroom and brought here. She knew Hannah spoke German, but perhaps she would learn English and be able to read them: *Swallows and Amazons, Just William, The Velveteen Rabbit.* On top of the low white-painted bookcase was a violin. Hannah played; Brigid knew because Doris had told them. And so they had borrowed a violin for her. *Do not buy one,* Doris had written, *because I have Hannah's to bring with me when I come.* That had been in the last letter from Doris. Since then, there had been no word. That was when Honor had begun to worry. The silence, she said, was unlike Doris. The empty flat in Berlin where the telephone rang and rang and was not answered. The fact that Hannah travelled alone. That too was unlike Doris. Brigid didn't know what to say to reassure her, except, *She will telephone when she can. She will write when she can. Maybe Hannah will know, when she comes.* It wasn't much.

Everything in the bedroom was in order: neat and pretty and clean. There was nothing more for Brigid to do there. She went back to her bedroom, wondering should she go to the Café de Paris after all. But there was no one to take her and she didn't want to walk the pitch-dark streets alone.

She picked up the last letter Fritzi had sent her – he wrote often these days, from Cambridge. *I go by Count von Lingen these days,* in his elegant scrawl. *Although I don't suppose it is much of a disguise.* Was he making a *joke?* she wondered. *My grandfather says I should come back to Germany, that I will be rounded up if I stay here. But I won't go back, Brigid, I cannot . . .* He didn't say why he wouldn't go back, and she was trying to puzzle it out when Minnie came in with an armful of clean dresses in the mossy green of the Women's Voluntary Service. Minnie had joined too, so that now, when they did things, they did them together, both the same in the green; 'both equal, only you are far better at *everything* than I am,' as Brigid had said.

'Imagine who I saw today?' Minnie said, setting the dresses down.

'Who?' Brigid reached a hand out for one and began to fold it.

'Albert. Who was Prince Friedrich's man at Kelvedon, and then he disappeared.'

'What? Where?'

'On Victoria Street, just as I was turning the corner onto Abingdon Street. There he was. I hailed him, by his name, and he ignored me. So I hailed again, and he turned and looked at me as though he didn't know me and then turned back to his companion and said something in a low voice and they both laughed.' She flushed at the memory, but carried on defiantly. 'I said, "Well, look at you, large as life after disappearing in a puff of smoke. You know we looked for you, the whole household, for days, and even had the police in? Not that they were terribly interested, what with you being German." He looked a bit shook at that, and said, "I think you must have me confused with someone else," and the thing is, Lady Brigid—'

'Biddy,'

'— Biddy.' She grinned. 'He sounded as English as ever you or I. Then I did wonder was it him. But it was. I'm certain of it.'

'Who was his companion?'

'I don't know, but he was English too.'

'Are you sure?'

'Certain.'

'What then?'

'Nothing. He walked off, quick as ever he could. Almost, he ran.'

What could it mean? Brigid had no idea, but knew she must tell Doris quickly. Because somehow, Albert being spotted in London when he had vanished so mysteriously, and now speaking like an Englishman, might mean something bad for her. Even if Albert's strange reappearance now was nothing more than coincidence, it was a reminder of all the ways in which what Doris did – whatever it was that she did, exactly – was dangerous. And now Brigid, as much as Honor, wanted to see Doris safely out of Berlin. But she couldn't think how to write such a letter – what could one say? What, even, was the post like between England and Germany now? She must go to Belgrave Square, she decided, to tell Honor.

'Will you walk with me?' she asked Minnie. 'It's so very dark . . .'

Honor, Andrews informed them, was out. 'Mr Channon is in his study, however.'

'Darling, how lovely,' Chips said, greeting her and nodding politely to Minnie. Out of uniform, Brigid had noticed, even people like Chips couldn't always tell who was a servant anymore. 'You are just in time,' he continued, handing her a drink. He immediately began complaining that trenches had been dug across the lawns at Kelvedon, on the say-so of the estate manager. 'How dared he? And when I complained he only said, "We are at war, sir," all self-righteously. I know very well we are at war. I was in the House when Chamberlain announced it: *This is a sad day for all of us, and to none is it sadder than to me.*' He had the line by heart, Brigid noted. Almost, she felt sorry for him, trying to turn desperately in midstream, like a great ship that must be wrangled about, towed laboriously into a different path by tiny tug boats.

'Why sadder for him?' she asked. 'Chamberlain will not be the one fighting,' she continued tartly, and saw Minnie's lip twitch. 'But I'm not here to talk about trenches . . . It's about Alfred.'

'Who?'

'Fritzi's man. You remember. Alfred, who disappeared at Kelvedon—'

'Went off, not *disappeared*,' Chips corrected her. 'You make it sound so sinister . . .'

'Well, but perhaps it is. Minnie has seen him . . .' And she told Chips, although she had not planned to, because there was no one else to tell. 'What do you think it means?' she asked, when she had finished.

'I think it means that we had better telephone to Doris immediately.'

'You think it is bad?'

'I don't know what it is. But the timing of his disappearance . . . Perhaps we should have been more suspicious.'

'Honor has been trying to reach Doris, but she told me her telephone never answers anymore.'

'I see.' He looked beadily at her. 'Well, there are some other calls I can make.'

'I thought you didn't care for Doris,' she blurted out.

'I don't. But that's hardly the point now, is it? I will make some phone calls. You'd better wait in the drawing room. I'll come and find you when I'm finished.'

'Thank you, Chips.'

Minnie said she must get back, so Brigid went upstairs alone. The fire had not been lit and there was a smell of cold ash and soot in the room. She was about to ring the bell and order Andrews to light it. But she didn't. Like the silent house at Grosvenor Place, the unlit fire meant something. It meant, she thought, that there were more important things now. That the comforts and convenience of families like theirs were no longer of much concern.

She strained to hear Chips' footsteps, an opening or closing door; any sound that would say he was on his way up to her with news. But there was only silence. She looked out. A few doors down she saw a sliver of light from between blackout curtains. Even as she watched, it disappeared, drapes shaken into tighter folds by an invisible hand. She heard the rumble of a lorry, heavy over uneven flagstones, and in the distance the plaintive wail of an air raid siren. These had started days ago, within minutes of Chamberlain's announcement, and none so far had signalled a real attack. One day soon they would.

Chapter Fifty-Six

Honor

The car moved slowly through the dark and empty streets, headlights painted over in streaky black so that the light they cast was no more than a bicycle lamp. A fog had gathered, surprisingly dense for the time of year. That slowed them further. Honor asked Michaels to let her out at the far end of the square, saying she would walk the rest of the way. The air raid siren started as she approached Number Five, mournful in the foggy night, and she wondered whether to continue on to the shelter around the corner. It was almost certainly another drill, but the shelter would be a way to avoid Chips for several more hours, until the all-clear was sounded. The idea was appealing. If only she had brought a book, to read by lantern light. But she hadn't, and the reality of the shelter was less appealing. All those people. All that determined gaiety.

Andrews opened the door. 'Miss Brigid is upstairs.'

'I'll go up. Would you bring something on a tray? For both of us.'

Brigid's head appeared, startled, over the balcony then and she called down, 'Is it really you? Come quick, Honor, for something has happened. It's Doris.'

Honor took the last few stairs two at a time. 'Tell me.' A story about Minnie, and that man Albert who had been Fritzi's fellow at Kelvedon. A chance meeting. An English voice.

'What does it mean?' Brigid asked when she had finished tumbling words out one after another. 'I cannot work it out.'

'Possibly nothing,' Honor said, sorting Brigid's words quickly and deftly in her mind. 'If Albert was English all along, watching Fritzi for our side, our purposes – whatever those may be – then I don't think any bad will come to Doris from it . . .'

'But if he's not?'

'If he's not . . .' She paused, still trying to understand. 'If he's German and now pretends to be English, then he is working for someone else. It can't be Fritzi's grandfather or he would not still be here. And so, if he is German, he was watching Fritzi for the Gestapo. But in watching Fritzi, he will have learned things about Doris. Dangerous things. Things that mean she needs to leave Germany immediately.'

'How can we find out?'

'We can't. But we need to warn Doris either way.'

How little attention they'd paid to Albert's disappearance, really, Honor thought then with dismay. Chips, with his urgent desire to see his new car. The ambassador, mind already on other matters. Even Honor herself, frantic to get away from Chips, back to London where she could disappear deeper into her own life and leave him behind. They had allowed themselves to believe it didn't matter – a servant, running off – but it had. Clearly it had. They had ignored the timing of it, the implications of that, and allowed themselves to assume all was well.

Only Doris had realised, and she'd said nothing. Or not much. Simply shouldered the knowledge and gone back to do whatever it was that she did, now with one extra piece of instability in the map she flew by. They hadn't stopped that.

'What does it mean?' Brigid asked again.

'I don't know,' Honor said, distraught. 'But not knowing isn't good enough. We must tell Doris, in case she understands better than we do. But I cannot get hold of her. I have tried. I have written and telephoned – to her flat, to that restaurant, Horcher's, that she goes to – and I cannot get her.'

'Chips is trying now. He says there are people he can ask . . .'

'People,' Honor repeated. 'What people?'

'Does it matter, if they answer?'

Honor heard the sound of a door slamming downstairs, then Chips' footsteps, urgent on the stairs. They both went to meet him. 'Anything?' Honor called out as he came up. Her voice was thin in the quiet, heavy house.

'I may have found Doris. It's possible she's in France. On her way home.'

Honor sat down suddenly, on the top step. Her legs felt cotton-woolish, as though she had been ill. 'But when will you know?' she asked.

'We are not the only people trying to find someone,' he said, but he said it gently. 'In truth, it feels like all of Europe is on the move. They will telephone me when they can.'

He sat beside her on the step and tried to take her hand. Honor pulled it away but she stayed beside him. They would hear the telephone better from there. Brigid squeezed in on the other side and for once Honor was glad for the broad sweep of that foolishly grand staircase, that it could fit them all. Brigid put an arm through hers and they drew close. Andrews hadn't lit the hall lights and so below them was only gloom. The house was silent and the square outside too. It was as though all the city waited in that moment with them, on the edge, above the dark.

Afterword

Britain declared war on Germany on 3 September 1939, two days after Germany invaded Poland. That was the end of a long period in the UK of trying to avoid war by appeasing Hitler.

Indeed, Chamberlain's words, in that radio address, talking about the ultimatum issued to Germany to withdraw troops from Poland, were: 'I have to tell you now that no such undertaking has been received, and that consequently this country is at war with Germany. You can imagine what a bitter blow it is to me that all my long struggle to win peace has failed.'

Throughout the late 1930s, while Chamberlain was indeed trying to 'win peace', there were many, like Churchill, and Basil Blackwood, Marquess of Dufferin and Ava – 'Duff' in this book – who were certain that Hitler couldn't and shouldn't be appeased, and that war was inevitable.

Joseph P. Kennedy, ambassador to the Court of King James from 1938 to 1940, father of John F. Kennedy and eight other children, including Kick, was very much of Chamberlain's view: prevent war, whatever it took.

That radical difference of opinion and policy is the backdrop to this story of Kennedys and Guinnesses. After writing *The Other Guinness Girl*, which is largely the story of Honor and Chips, I discovered mentions in Chips' diaries of the Kennedys – and of balls and parties the two families had both attended – and a particular detail that made me laugh. Brigid Guinness, Honor's youngest sister, and Kick Kennedy were almost exactly the same age. At Brigid's coming-out dinner, she sat beside Billy Cavendish, who later married Kick; while at Kick's coming-out dinner, she sat beside Prince Friedrich, 'Fritzi', who later married Brigid.

That was enough to send me off thinking about all the ways in which their lives must have intersected. The story is mostly invented, but drawing together bits and pieces of real life, in a way that I believe fits plausibly with the rest of these characters' real lives.

There is a curious pocket of silence in Chips' diaries, from 7 August to 1 September 1938. He writes nothing, and when he resumes, it is to say that Honor has been 'nervous and unhappy and a little mad'. It's unusual for him; he was generally pretty diligent at recording his doings. I wondered what had happened during those three weeks. Perhaps things he felt it would be unwise to write about? A house party, to which he has invited various players in the escalating European conflict . . .? I've filled in the blank with my own imaginings, but with, I hope, proper regard for the known truths.

Kick Kennedy did leave England in 1939, but she came back a year later, and joined the war effort in London. Her parents were certainly unhappy at the idea of her marrying Billy Cavendish, heir to the Duke of Devonshire – almost as unhappy as his parents were – but marry they did, in May 1944. Billy was killed four months later, in September, while trying to take a town in Belgium from the German Waffen-SS. Kick died four years after him, in 1948, in a plane crash.

The marriage of Brigid and Fritzi was a wish dear to Chips Channon's heart. He writes about it as something to be aimed for as early as 1936, when Brigid was only sixteen – at the same time as he speculates that Fritzi could leapfrog his father to succeed his grandfather as kaiser (August 1936: *Prince Fritzi came to see me . . . I told him that I hope, and even thought, that he might become Emperor. He must be tactful, he must perfect his English . . . he must be manly . . . he agreed with all that I said.*)

Fritzi and Brigid met many times before the war, but it was only when Brigid went to nurse him after an accident involving a tractor, shortly after Fritzi was arrested, interned and then released, that they got engaged.

I was intrigued by the idea that this was when they fell in love – when he was weak and she was looking after him.

They married after the war, in 1945, and had five children. Fritzi died in 1966. He had been missing for two weeks before his body was discovered in the Rhine. The exact circumstances of his death – suicide or accident – were impossible to determine.

Chips' own marriage, to Honor Guinness, was unravelling fast at the time this book is set. He writes very openly, first about the lack of 'marital relations' between them, and then about an affair Honor has had, in a way that is really quite eye-poppingly horrible:

Entry for 20th August 1937: *I then knew that H was Palffy's mistress, although she has only seen him three times . . . It is a plot, probably to get money out of Honor . . . Very calmly I accused her of having an affair with that obvious ruffian . . . She sat down and admitted the truth. My marriage has crashed in ruins at my feet . . . Men never find H attractive, certainly not men of his type. He wants her money, and I am not going to let him.*

In fact, Honor did meet someone – Frantisek Václav Svejdar, whom she married after her divorce from Chips in 1945 (a divorce in which she gave up custody of their son, Paul). Frankie was a Czech pilot who came to England and joined the RAF after the fall of Czechoslovakia. He and Honor married in 1946 and lived for a long time in Ireland. People who knew them then tell me that they were very happy together, and adored one another. That Frankie was jolly and funny and easy-going, far less handsome than Chips, but a truly kind and nice man. I'm happy to think that all this lies in Honor's near future at the end of this book.

Doris is an entirely invented character. She first appeared in *The Other Guinness Girl*, and I just liked her far too much to let her go. I found it hard to leave her fate so unresolved at the end of this book – I want her to be safe, on her way back to England, or even to America – but the truth is that I couldn't believe it would be as easy as that. So many people got 'lost' in the weeks after war was declared – sent this way and that among the great movement of people, all desperate to get to a place of safety; all trying frantically to decide where that was. Many eventually made their way to where they wanted to be, but not all.

This is a work of fiction, but within that, I have tried to be faithful to the facts. And so I have kept the end deliberately hazy, as a reflection of that time.

The detail about Chips' cigarette lighter – a gift from Göring whom Channon describes as 'the most lovable, he is large, flabby, mischievous (probably sexually vicious, for I saw in his grey eyes the look I know well), intelligent, eunuch-y' – is correct, although my twist about Doris nicking it clearly is not. Ambassador Kennedy did indeed gather Kick's British friends, young men such as Hugh Fraser and Billy Cavendish, and show them film footage of soldiers killed and injured in the First World War, exactly as I have it here, only he did that in London. His intent apparently was to persuade them that war must be avoided, but all it did was infuriate them and make them more resolved than ever to fight. The mention of Ewald von Kleist-Schmenzin is also accurate – he was an active opponent of Nazism from the start, and in August 1938 he was sent secretly to London to plead with British authorities to abandon the policy of appeasement and join an anti-Nazi coup. Chamberlain dismissed his mission as unimportant, but Churchill was sympathetic.

Unity Mitford did indeed shoot herself in the head when Britain declared war. She survived, and was hospitalised in Munich, where Hitler frequently visited her. He also paid her bills and arranged for her return home. She lived almost ten more years but never fully recovered and was apparently 'incontinent and childish', according to the neurosurgeon who attended her.

Basil Blackwood – 'Duff' – resigned his parliamentary position when war was declared, and enlisted. He went to Burma, and wrote very touching letters home to Maureen and the children from there: 'I love you very much you silly old thing . . . I hope we and the children will be very happy after the war and in the meantime . . . be good as gold and very faithful'. He was killed only days later, in March 1945.

Billy's father, William Cavendish, took over Duff's role as under-secretary of state for India and Burma in 1940 when he resigned. There is some suspicion (as per Paula Byrne's book, *Kick*) that Maureen was William's mistress for a time – which would tie the two men even more closely together – but I have left that out of this story as I couldn't corroborate it.

The plot around Prince Friedrich is invented, but it is inspired by the many plots involving German princes around this time. There were a host of these, that came to various levels of fruition. May were motivated by self-interest.

When Kaiser Wilhelm II (Fritzi's grandfather) abdicated in 1919, he left a considerable power vacuum, and a great many disgruntled nobility, including four 'kings' of Germany – Prussia, Bavaria, Saxony and Württemberg – and also six grand dukes, five dukes and seven princes, who along with all of their heirs, successors and families lost their titles and domains.

In the scrum to recoup some of this, many joined the Nazis. Hitler was quick to spot an opportunity, and frequently appealed to these former princes by expressing sympathy for a restoration of their lost inheritances. The Berlin Federal Archives list 270 princely members of the Nazi Party in the years 1928–42.

However, there were some who saw opportunity – and duty – in other ways, and lent themselves to plots against Hitler. The best-known was probably the Oster Conspiracy of 1938, which planned to overthrow Hitler and the Nazi regime and restore the monarchy under Prince Wilhelm of Prussia, grandson of Wilhelm II and eldest brother of Prince Fritzi.

There was also Prince Friedrich zu Solms-Baruth III, jailed and tortured in 1944 for his part in Operation Valkyrie, another failed plot to kill Hitler, and various others. Even now, every few years, letters or documents come to light, often in private collections, giving details of other princes who were the focus of all sorts of plots, small and large.

In writing those parts of the book, I liked the idea that, really, nothing about the plot actually exists. It's a series of whispered conversations, a number of 'what if's' that even the principal character knows nothing about, and that is abandoned summarily when overtaken by events. Once war was really inevitable, the plots to get rid of Hitler and put Prince X or Y in his place dwindled. In the book, that's exactly what happens. Fritzi is of supreme interest one day, immaterial the next. All without him knowing anything.

Joe Kennedy was a complex man. He seems to have been public-spirited but also selfish; courageous but without much in the way of clear moral values; striving to be a realist but highly pessimistic. His ambassadorship was a cautionary tale: a dazzling start, and an ignominious end. He failed to follow the shift in public opinion, in England or America, and found himself thoroughly out of step with public sentiment when that swung behind the idea of standing up to Hitler's gross ambitions.

He has been accused of being anti-Semitic, and there is evidence for that. He certainly saw Jewish conspiracy in efforts to persuade the US to enter war with Germany. But as vice-chairman of the Evian Commission from July 1938, he was also in negotiations to get some Jewish children out of Germany. According to biographer David Nasaw, in his book *The Patriarch*, Kennedy showed genuine concern for the refugees, and was deeply frustrated by how slow any action was. At the Evian

Conference on refugees, Kennedy, representing the US, urged countries to find a solution (with very limited effect; only the Dominican Republic was willing to accept more refugees at that time).

Kennedy did little to persuade the US to relax its restrictions, but he did help arrange for 190 Jewish children to be brought into Boy Scout camps in England.

By 1938, about 150,000 German Jews – one in four – had already fled. Many more wished to leave – like Hannah's parents in this book – but couldn't find anywhere willing to take them in. By the time war began, Britain had admitted some 70,000 European Jews, but about 500,000 more had been denied.

That too is why I didn't feel I could close this story with a happy ending; because that wasn't the case for so many people.

Acknowledgements

It is a bit ironic that the more books I write, the shorter my acknowledgements become. This shouldn't be – if anything, the more I write, the more people I have to thank. And the more thanks I have to offer to the same people; those who have worked with me so many times now.

Chief amongst these is my editor, Ciara Doorley. This is our eighth book together. In that time, Ciara has always been brilliant at encouraging me, talking ideas through and giving the kind of feedback that makes the books better. Ciara, you are a joy to work with. Thank you!

And ditto the rest of Hachette Ireland, especially the wonderful Breda Purdue and Joanna Smyth.

My agent, Ivan Mulcahy. For the super-smart advice, the clever industry analysis and the hilarious chats.

My sister Bridget, who I mostly now spare the work-in-progress read, but whose opinion still matters to me more than anyone. When you told me that my last novel, *The Other Guinness Girl*, had kept you up reading 'til late at night, I was on a high for days.

My brother Francis, who runs Bridget a close second as a reader. You telling me how much you liked Doris made me realise I had to take her story a bit further.

All my amazing friends. You know who you are. I am not exaggerating when I say your company is vital to me. Your funny, witty, kind gorgeousness is the ballast of good times and the consolation of bad.

My writer friends, including but definitely not limited to, Eliza Pakenham, Annemarie Casey, Martina Devlin, Andrea Mara, Lia Hynes, Sophie White. No one gets it like you guys do.

My wonderful husband, David (who would probably appreciate the odd supermarket shop or bit of cooking, but is stuck with getting more book dedications instead), and our three amazing children, Malachy, Davy and B. You guys are the literal best.

The readers. Those of you who read and enjoy these books, and especially the ones who get in touch to tell me so. Thanks for joining me in this alternate reality of glamour and privilege, where the troubles and heartaches are real too. And especially the many who have taken the time to tell me their own Guinness stories – tales of their encounters with Aileen, Honor, Maureen or Oonagh; or indeed time working in the Guinness breweries. It's fascinating for me to hear these, and everything helps build my pictures of these people.

Finally, my father, Liam. For absolutely everything, all the time. But also, most recently, this – found in a letter he wrote to me when I was in Irish college sometime in the late 1980s (it's dated simply 'Friday evening') – 'Your last letters were disjointed and atrociously presented. Please in future write vividly about interesting things.'

He was joking (I think) about the first, but not at all about the second. Possibly the best piece of writing advice ever: 'write vividly about interesting things'.

Thank you.

Bibliography

The following books were invaluable resources in writing *An Invitation to the Kennedys*:

Kick by Paula Byrne was where I first learned about the short, brilliant life of Kick Kennedy.

The Kennedys Amidst the Gathering Storm by Will Swift, and *The Patriarch* by David Nasaw. These were also vital reads that gave me a different view of Joe Kennedy.

Simon Heffer (ed.), *Henry 'Chips' Channon: The Diaries, 1918–38*

Marion Crawford, *The Little Princesses*

Nancy Schoenberger, *Dangerous Muse: The Life of Lady Caroline Blackwood*

Joe Joyce, *The Guinnesses*

Frederic Mullally, *The Silver Salver: The Story of the Guinness Family*

Michele Guinness, *The Guinness Spirit*
D.J. Taylor, *Bright Young People*
Claud Cockburn, *The Devil's Decade*
Paul Howard, *I Read the News Today, Oh Boy*
Jonathan Guinness and Catherine Guinness, *The House of Mitford*

For the details of daily life and the mood of the times, I always hark back to my favourite novels of the 1930s, particularly those by Patrick Hamilton, Stella Gibbons, Virginia Woolf, Aldous Huxley, George Orwell, Evelyn Waugh, Daphne du Maurier, Agatha Christie, Eve Garnett and Noel Streatfeild.

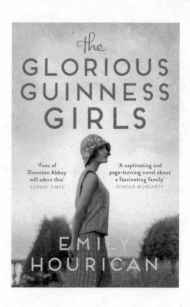

The Glorious Guinness Girls are the toast of London and Dublin society. Darlings of the press, Aileen, Maureen and Oonagh lead charmed existences that are the envy of many.

But Fliss knows better. Sent to live with them as a child, she grows up as part of the family and only she knows of the complex lives beneath the glamorous surface.

Then, at a party one summer's evening, something happens which sends shockwaves through the entire household. In the aftermath, as the Guinness sisters move on, Fliss is forced to examine her place in their world and decide if where she finds herself is where she truly belongs.

Set amid the turmoil of the Irish Civil War and the brittle glamour of 1920s London, *The Glorious Guinness Girls* is inspired by one of the most fascinating family dynasties in the world – an unforgettable novel of reckless youth, family loyalty and destiny.

Available in print, audio and ebook

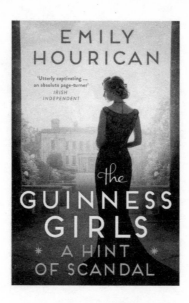

As Aileen, Maureen and Oonagh – the three privileged Guinness sisters, darlings of 1930s society – settle into becoming wives and mothers, they quickly discover that their gilded upbringing has not prepared them for the realities of married life.

At Dublin's Luttrellstown Castle, practical Aileen has already run out of things to say to her husband. Outspoken Maureen is very much in love but feels isolated at the crumbling Clandeboye estate in Northern Ireland. And, as romantic Oonagh's dreams of happiness in London are crushed by her husband's lies, she seeks comfort in her friends – but can they be trusted?

As the sisters deal with desire and betrayal amidst vicious society gossip, their close friends, the Mitfords, find themselves under the media glare – and the Guinness women are forced to examine their place in this quickly-changing world.

Inspired by true-life events, *The Guinness Girls: A Hint of Scandal* is a dazzling, page-turning novel about Ireland and Britain in the grip of change, and a story of how three women who wanted for nothing were about to learn that they couldn't have everything.

Available in print, audio and ebook

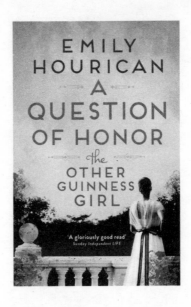

Surrounded by wealth, glamour and excitement Lady Honor Guiness is a reluctant wallflower. But that all changes when she marries Henry 'Chips' Channon, a charming and ambitious American. On his arm, she finds herself at the heart of 1930s London's most elite social circles, mingling with aristocrats, politicians and royalty. But it's not too long before Chips begins to prioritise his aspirations over all else, and Honor begins to wonder who exactly she has married.

By her side is her best friend Doris, a young woman eager to establish her place in society. A social butterfly who keeps the details of her family background to herself, Doris is hopeful her beauty and charm will win her a suitable husband, but she has no interest in a romantic attachment. Until she is introduced to 'the most devastating man in London'.

Inspired by true-life events, *The Other Guinness Girl: A Question of Honor* is an elegant, captivating story of two young women navigating friendship, loneliness, love and desire as they try to find their places in a society where the rules seem to change every moment.

Available in print, audio and ebook